M000210717

A FORBIDDEN PLEASURE

"Where I come from," Mattie said, "it's considered... uncivilized...to act upon our desires. Instead, we keep them leashed, hidden away."

Sakote pushed up on one elbow and frowned down at her. "And this is civilized?"

She nodded. It truly *was* silly when you said it aloud.

He broke off the stem of a foxtail, rolling it thoughtfully between his fingers. "So if you have a desire to eat?"

"You pretend you're not hungry at all."

His scowl deepened. He brushed the furry tip of the weed lightly under her nose. "What if you have an itch that needs to be scratched?"

She twitched beneath his teasing touch. "You keep a stiff upper lip."

He tossed the stem aside and let the tip of his finger take over, caressing her mouth with infinite patience, making his tortuous way down her throat, between her breasts, and lower. "And if you wish to feel pleasure?" he murmured.

"You...deny it."

His soft chuckle was as rich and delicious as cream. "I think I do not wish to be civilized."

She smiled on a sigh. "Nor do I," she whispered.

This work is a work of fiction. Names, places, characters and incidents are the product of the author's imagination or are used fictitiously. Any resemblance to actual events, locales or persons, living or dead, is coincidental.

NATIVE GOLD

Copyright © 2013 by Glynnis Campbell

Cover design by Tanya Straley & Richard Campbell
Formatting by Author E.M.S.

Glynnis Campbell – Publisher
P.O. Box 341144
Arleta, California 91331

ISBN-10: 1634800001
ISBN-13: 978-1-63480-000-6
Contact: glynnis@glynnis.net

Published in the United States of America

NATIVE GOLD

CALIFORNIA LEGENDS BOOK 1

DEDICATION

For the good people of Paradise
from the Gold Nugget Queen of 1975

Other Books by Glynnis Campbell

THE WARRIOR MAIDS OF RIVENLOCH
The Shipwreck (novella)
Lady Danger
Captive Heart
Knight's Prize

THE KNIGHTS OF DE WARE
The Handfasting (novella)
My Champion
My Warrior
My Hero

MEDIEVAL OUTLAWS
Danger's Kiss
Passion's Exile

THE SCOTTISH LASSES
The Outcast (novella)
MacFarland's Lass
MacAdam's Lass

THE CALIFORNIA LEGENDS
Native Gold
Native Wolf

ACKNOWLEDGMENTS

Thanks to
Evangeline Lilly and Nathaniel Arcand,
Khris Pierson and the four Campbell brothers,
Ma Joan for introducing me to Dame Shirley,
Pa Campbell for sharing the joys of research,
Mom for driving me to obscure museums
and overgrown cemeteries,
Geraldine Allen, one of the last Koyongk'awi,
for her inspiration,
Anthony Salzarullo, Koyongk'awi of the heart,
for his generosity of spirit,
Sue Epperson, for sharing her treasures,
Sonia Johnson of the Colman Memorial Museum,
Betty Davis of the Butte County Pioneer Memorial Museum,
the helpful docents of the Gold Nugget Museum,
Huell Howser, for loving California like I do,
and Rich, for showing me the waterfall

PROLOGUE

"Ladies and gentlemen, if you please!" Ambrose Hardwicke clapped his hands, earning the attention of the American nobility packed into his glittering ballroom.

Mattie creased the rose satin of her too-tight gown with her nail-bitten fingers. This was her moment.

It wasn't the first time her uncle had paraded her before the cream of New York society. Ambrose never forgot his duties to his five charges—the four daughters who were his by blood, and seventeen-year-old Mathilda, who'd been thrust upon him as an orphan two years ago. Chief among those duties was seeing that his girls married well.

To marry well, Ambrose said, one had to possess Quality. Something Mattie apparently lacked. Something Ambrose worked hard to instill in her.

His four daughters, blessed with their mother's beauty and poise, would grace the arm of any man he chose for them.

Mathilda, however, didn't have their porcelain skin, pale gold tresses, or angelic features.

Some of her flaws were a matter of birth. Some of them she owed to her affection for the sun and her aversion to bonnets. Her complexion bordered on tawny. Her brown hair was streaked with lighter strands of a most contrary color, which were in startling contrast to her bright green eyes. And to everyone's horror, she had a sprinkling of tiny freckles across her nose that no amount of powder could hide.

But worse than her appearance, according to Uncle Ambrose, was her temperament. She didn't have her cousins' gentle manner. She tended to speak before she was spoken to. And often, what came out of her mouth wasn't suited to polite society.

So Ambrose had decided that wayward Mattie must be marketed by merit of what he regarded as her only gift—her talent for painting.

"If I may have your attention!" he bellowed.

Mattie chewed at her lower lip. Aunt Emily smiled tightly, sending her a chiding glare. Proper ladies didn't fidget. None of her cousins, currently lined up in graceful ascending height beside their mother, ever moved a muscle that wasn't absolutely essential. Even now, the sisters seemed to float above the hubbub of the evening unperturbed, like thistledown atop a swirling eddy.

Not Mattie. She was wound as tight as a clock spring.

It didn't matter that Uncle Ambrose hosted these galas at least twice a season and that they always included a viewing of Mathilda's latest work.

Tonight was different. Tonight she'd show the audience a masterpiece. Tonight she'd bare her soul.

This painting was the best she'd ever done. The image had emerged upon the canvas in a rush of passion, like a fevered outpouring from her heart. It seemed like she'd painted it with her own blood and tears.

A thrill of improper excitement coursed through her as

she thought about what sat upon the easel beneath the velvet drape. This was no muted, delicate watercolor of the countryside. This painting would take their breath away. It would open their eyes, the way her eyes had been opened by the artists of the Pre-Raphaelite Brotherhood—Millais, Rossetti, and Hunt—whose work she'd seen in London last year.

Just thinking of how those young artists had brazenly challenged the Royal Academy made her heart race.

They followed no rules but those of nature. Gone were the stifling standards of Sir Joshua Reynolds. Dead were the outdated concepts of the Renaissance.

Art was no longer slave to man, but expression to truth—a truth Mattie was about to reveal to the guests, who were silent now except for soft murmurs and the rustle of silk skirts.

"My niece informs me," Ambrose announced, smoothing one waxed tip of his gray mustache, "that she has abandoned landscapes this time in favor of a portrait."

A few polite ahs and approving nods were sent her way.

"She has chosen to paint, from recollection, her dearly departed parents—my brother, Lawrence, and his wife, Mary."

There were a few sympathetic whispers as he grasped the corner of the drape. Mattie held her breath. Then, in a dramatic sweep of velvet, he revealed the painting.

The crowd gasped, awestruck.

Mattie knew intimately every brush stroke, every shadow, each strand of hair and droplet of water, but the painting amazed even her. Had she truly done it herself? Or had the spirit of the Pre-Raphaelites possessed her soul, guiding her hand?

Her mother and father, lost at sea, she'd depicted in vibrant oils as a Siren and a sailor.

On the left, the nude female figure half-reclined upon stark black rock, her scaly fish tail barely visible beneath the swirling emerald depths of the sea, her pale bosom slashed by strands of her dark, wet hair. Her lips were parted as if in melancholy song, and her face appeared to glow with ethereal light.

Below her, the sailor, his shirt torn from his shoulders, his bronze hair drenched, his face tormented by wondrous obsession and fatigue, sank in the waters at her feet, one hand reaching up towards her in supplication.

Just looking at the painting, Mattie could feel their tragedy. Yet the scene spoke of hope as well. From the skies above the doomed pair, the somber clouds broke to reveal a single shimmering bolt of sunlight, a guiding beacon to heaven and happiness beyond.

So enrapt was she, reliving the emotion of the painting—sorrow, frustration, promise—that at first Mattie failed to hear the whispers. When they finally registered, she couldn't have been more astonished.

"Good God!"

"What kind of daughter—"

"—not even a stitch of clothing!"

"Lawrence would turn in his grave if—"

"How could she—"

"Indecent, I tell you!"

The spell of the painting broken, Mattie turned a bewildered face to the crowd. Some of them stood with open mouths, as if she'd just unveiled a three-headed calf. Uncle Ambrose's face turned ruddy, and he shook with outrage. And in the corner of the room, her perfectly composed cousin Diana fell over in a dead faint.

A full hour had passed since the debacle in the ballroom. Yet Mattie still waited, picking at the arm of the worn leather chair facing her uncle's deserted desk in the library. Clearly he intended to let her stew until all the guests departed before he came, as he'd promised, "to deal with her." She wondered if he made his petitioners fidget in this chair before they begged him for a morsel of his considerable funds.

She chewed at her lip. She didn't understand why everyone had reacted so badly to her work. Surely Diana's swooning had less to do with what she'd seen on the canvas than with the tightness of her stays—which was a perfect example of what the Pre-Raphaelites fought against. Restraint was a thing of the past. Constriction of one's artistic expression made no more sense than the wasp-waisted devices of torture women endured in the name of fashion.

Yes, she thought, scooting the chair back with a harsh scrape. That was it. She'd explain it all to her uncle when he came to speak to her. *If* he ever came.

She rubbed a damp palm over the arm of the chair, then pushed herself up again and began pacing. Had the Brothers faced such scorn when they first presented their paintings to the public? She supposed she'd have to inure herself to criticism if she wanted to ascend to their prominence in the art world. For above all—as her parents had told her from the time she was old enough to hold a paintbrush—she must never fight her nature. She must be true to herself.

It was no easy task when one was shuffled from one household to another, as she'd been since her father's...accident. Only Uncle Ambrose had even made the attempt to tame Lawrence's "wild child." The other relatives seemed to consider Mattie a curse to be passed from kin to kin, a wicked girl as foolhardy as her father. They whispered that it was her father's flagrant disregard for convention that had killed him, that Mattie was surely destined for the same fate.

But Mattie knew the truth. She wasn't wicked, only...different. So her parents had said.

If her fingers found much more delight wrapped around an artist's pencil than stuck in a sewing thimble or lilting across piano keys or any of the half-dozen or so activities appropriate to a lady's station, it wasn't because she was wayward. She was only using her God-given talent.

Just because she'd rather spend her afternoons sketching the sailors at the docks than sipping tea in some old biddy's parlor didn't mean she was depraved.

Just because her portraits of family members were painstakingly accurate, down to each wrinkle and scar, rather than obsequiously flattering, didn't mean she was vulgar.

And whose business was it if her sketchbook, her *private* sketchbook, contained a bare male torso here and there?

Besides, it wasn't nonconformity that had killed her father. Yes, he'd lived a dangerous, exciting life, traveling and writing papers about exotic places—the jungles of India, the sands of Egypt, the wilds of Africa.

But his love of adventure hadn't killed him. He'd died of a broken heart. When his wife succumbed to fever on their excursion to the West Indies, he'd cast himself from the ship into the waters of the Caribbean, deciding there was nothing left to live for.

No one spoke of his brief letter of sad farewell. Instead, Lawrence Hardwicke was tactfully proclaimed "lost at sea."

In the five years since then, Mattie, too, had floated like a ship adrift, finding temporary harbor with various kin whose expectations she could never quite fulfill.

But she was almost eighteen now. Soon she'd no longer worry about their expectations. She'd embark upon her own life, just as her parents had done, put her ship in order and let the winds take her where they willed.

The mantel clock chimed. Mattie shivered. Another quarter hour had passed, and the fire, reduced to red-limned coals, needed tending. But she didn't dare touch it. Everything in the library belonged exclusively to her uncle. He'd made that abundantly clear when she'd arrived two years ago and helped herself to a precious volume of Renaissance art. He'd rapped her knuckles with a ruler and lectured her about personal property in booming tones that were probably heard in Yonkers.

But she'd never forgotten the lesson. No one touched what belonged to Ambrose Hardwicke.

Mattie sighed, her anxiety dulled to restless boredom. She leaned forward toward the mahogany desk and straightened the blotter. Then, on a devilish impulse, she set it askew again. She flounced back into the chair and began drumming her fingers atop the glossy, lemon-oiled surface of the desk— forward and backward, forward and backward. The day's newspaper was scattered across the blotter, and she inclined her head to peer at the headlines.

Casting caution aside, she shuffled the paper together and reversed it so she could read it. There was nothing of much interest to her, mostly politics, financial enterprises, and the usual stories of murder and mayhem. Then, on the fourth page, a small advertisement caught her eye. She rested her finger on the column and traced the words.

"Man of a Decent Age and Not Unhandsome desires God-fearing, Respectable Woman to head West for purposes of Matrimony. Will pay for Transport by Steamer and provide Sustenance in the form of a Modest Home, Full Provender, and whatever niceties a Woman of Dignity may require and my profession as a Physician and Gold Miner may afford, in exchange for Maintenance of that Household, including Purchasing of Supplies, Preparing of Meals, Laundering of Clothing, and other customary wifely duties. All interested parties send Correspondence to Paradise Bar, California. Yours faithfully, Doctor James Harrison."

Mattie smiled. How strange those Californians were,

advertising for a wife. "A God-fearing, Respectable Woman" indeed. What Respectable Woman would head west to marry a man she'd never met? Her cousins were Respectable Women, and they'd sooner walk into the path of a runaway carriage than allow themselves to be dragged aboard a steamer bound for California.

Mattie's musings were interrupted by the click of the library door behind her. She swiftly pushed the newspaper back across the desk and, for once, wisely waited for Ambrose to speak first.

"I've had to call the physician for Diana." He didn't boom this time, but somehow his low growl seemed far more deadly than the verbal cannonballs he usually fired.

Wary of his volatile temper, she kept her back straight and her eyes focused on the desk before her, and then gently cleared her throat. "Is she all right?"

"No, she is *not* all right." Mattie could almost hear the grinding of his teeth. "She's had a shock."

She swallowed guiltily. "Actually, I believe it may have been the tightness of her stays rather than—"

"What!"

She grimaced. There it was. The cannon.

His boot heels clacked heavily on the floor as he marched up behind her, and she prepared to listen to a thunderous tirade. But it never came. Instead, he hissed at her like one of the coals smoldering in the fireplace.

"Is this what comes of my generosity? How I'm rewarded for taking in my brother's child? First with that lascivious painting, and now with vulgar speech?"

He seized the arm of her chair and wrenched it around towards him, startling a squeak from her. She shrank as his beefy hands clasped both arms of the chair, trapping her between them.

"Tell me, girl, and I won't hear any lies." His jaw was

clenched, and his mustache quivered. "Who did you connive into it, eh? Who sat as a model for your filthy painting? Which servant am I going to have to dismiss?"

Surprise widened her eyes. A model? Dear Lord, did he honestly believe that any of his servants had the time to sit for...

"Who was it?" He rattled the chair, and she glimpsed murder in his purpling face. Good heavens, he was serious.

She gasped. "No one!" She didn't dare tell him the truth—that she'd styled the figure after herself, painting in her room before a looking glass, bare to the waist. "I did it...from my imagination."

He narrowed his eyes, obviously unconvinced. Then he stepped briskly from her, muttering, "I should never have let Lawrence's brat sully my household."

Mattie's throat tightened. She'd grown accustomed to her uncle's bluster. Most of it was as harmless as a spring storm blowing through. But she'd never heard him say such a hurtful thing. The pain of it made her eyes water.

He growled and leaned something against the desk—her painting. It was draped again. She supposed he considered it too vile to expose.

"Blazes, girl," he grumbled. "Can't you do anything right? Now you've let the fire die." He crossed to the hearth and jabbed briskly at the coals with a heavy iron poker, adding two more logs.

Mattie's head swam as she bit back tears. Nothing she did ever pleased him. She supposed she should be used to scorn by now, but it always hurt.

"I've tried to civilize you," he muttered, his back to her as he prodded the flames. "God knows I've tried to bring you up to Hardwicke standards. I've given you every opportunity to make something of yourself. I've fed you and clothed you like one of my own. I've introduced you to the best of society. Damn it all!"

15

She flinched. No matter how angry Ambrose Hardicke was, she'd never heard him swear, never.

"I've let you consort with my own innocent daughters, even when it was against my better judgment."

A hard lump clogged her throat like a half-swallowed lemon drop. How could he say such things to her?

"And this!" he said, gesturing toward the painting with the poker. "This is how I'm repaid. With this...this revolting monstrosity of a painting that's an affront to the memory of my dear brother and a public humiliation to the Hardwicke name."

Mattie sat, too stunned to answer, too paralyzed with pain to defend herself. Was that what he thought of her masterpiece? That it was a monstrosity? Was that what *everyone* thought?

The flames snapped and flared behind him, and for a moment Ambrose looked like the Devil himself silhouetted against the inferno. Then he set the poker into its stand and thoughtfully stroked the end of his mustache.

"Henceforward, Mathilda, while you live beneath my roof, you will no longer indulge in such licentious avocations. I've had the servants remove the paints and canvases from your room, along with your sketchbooks."

His words sucked the very breath from her lungs. Not her art. It was all she had. He couldn't take that away from her.

"As for this abomination..." He snatched up the painting.

She sprang to her feet and grabbed his sleeve. "No!" Surely he didn't mean to take her masterpiece as well. As a desperate afterthought, she added, "Please."

He extracted his arm. "It's for the best," he said sternly.

"No." Panic seized her by the throat, leaving her voice a feeble whisper. Lord, she hated to beg. "Not my...please-Uncle-don't-take-my—"

"I won't have filth like this infecting the Hardwicke house."

16

"But it's…" She tried to modulate her voice to a reasonable tone. "It's mine." Lord, what did he intend to do with it? Pack it away in the attic? Give it to the servants? Sell it?

His eyes flattened like storm clouds as he turned away from her. And suddenly she knew what he intended.

"No!" she screamed.

She dove for his coattails, trying to stop him, and skidded on the hem of her skirt. The satin ripped, and her knee banged on the polished oak floor as she caught the back of his coat. He grunted, nearly losing his footing himself.

"Please!" she shrieked.

He half-turned toward her, his eyes rolling in fear as if a madwoman pursued him.

She reluctantly loosened her grip on his coat. It wouldn't do to frighten the man. Swallowing hard and licking her lips, she willed her heart to stop racing, willed her voice to return to a sane pitch.

"I'll do anything you say, Uncle Ambrose. I'll stop painting. I'll be good. I promise. Just please…" She was truly begging now, on her knees, no less, clutching at his clothing like a waif in the streets pleading for a crumb. But she didn't care. She was desperate.

"Unhand me, Mathilda."

She stared into his narrowed eyes. Could she change his mind? Would he listen to her? Reluctantly, she let go of his coat and gave him a watery, hopeful smile.

She saw his jaw tighten once, then release. His eyes softened, and he breathed a long sigh. He reached down to cup her chin affectionately in one hand, as he often did with his own daughters. For one brief moment, she glimpsed forgiveness.

Then he murmured, "It's for the best, girl."

Before she could digest his words, he slipped off the velvet drape and cast her painting, her best work, her masterpiece, into the heart of the fire.

"No!" Despair ripped through her throat, as if her spirit was torn from her body. "No!"

Sparks leaped up and collided with the canvas like falling stars. Black smoke curled towards the flue. Orange fire licked at the edges of the painting, moving inward voraciously.

Mattie screamed as the flames seemed to sear her soul. It was like watching her child burn.

She scrambled forward on hands and knees, hampered by the tangle of her voluminous skirts.

Liquefied in the heat, the oils began to smoke and bubble, lending eerie life to the sea she'd painted.

Her eyes tearing and her throat clogged with sobs, she fought her way across the slippery floor.

A sudden burst of flame shot through the middle of the painting, startling them both, snapping at the figure of her father like a ravenous shark.

"No!" She knocked Ambrose out of the way and lunged toward the hearth, where a hellish darkness slowly fell over the painting's ethereal light.

Throwing caution aside, Mattie thrust her hand into the flames, desperate to salvage her masterpiece, desperate to spare her parents a fiery doom.

She didn't feel the pain of the burn till much later, after the physician had applied a butter salve, wrapped her hand in a linen bandage, and she was tucked into her bed. Even then, it was nothing compared to the agony of her heart.

It was gone—her finest work. Just like her parents—as if they'd never been.

And she might as well have been tossed onto the fire alongside her painting, because she wasn't wanted either.

Her uncle had minced no words when it came to telling her what an affront she was to the Ambrose Hardwicke household. And now she'd exhausted *all* the Hardwicke households.

She had no one to turn to. She didn't belong anywhere.

In the darkness, her eyes filled with hot tears, and she clenched her jaw against the trembling urge to sob.

Though she'd tell no one—not even God—in these deep, hopeless hours of the night, when her heart ached and she felt as unloved as a runt pup, she sometimes wished death would come for her. If she died, she might follow her parents, wherever they'd gone. Then she might finally belong.

A ragged sob escaped her then, and she stifled it with her bandaged fist. Why did no one approve of her? Her parents had never criticized her or made her feel unwanted. They'd loved her the way she was.

She closed her eyes, and a tear trickled out to wander down her cheek, lost.

What would become of her now? She couldn't stay here, not knowing how her uncle felt. But who would take in a streaky-haired, tawny-skinned waif who painted monstrosities?

She sniffled and turned her head on the pillow to watch the gold moon sink slowly beyond the lace curtain. Was there nowhere out there in the vast world where she could be true to herself? Somewhere she could start over? Somewhere she'd be accepted despite her differences?

With blurring eyes, she watched the moon lower in the west, past the stone wall, between the distant treetops, and beyond, toward plains and mountains and forests and rugged land.

And then it came to her.

California.

The Golden West.

Land of opportunity.

Her breath stilled.

No. She couldn't. She was only a girl—too young, too unworldly for the wilderness. The notion was absurd. Only fallen women and fools went to California.

19

She flounced onto her side, away from the west, away from the empty promise that called to her beyond the window, and shut her eyes tightly against the ridiculous notion.

But she was her father's daughter. The curious possibility wouldn't leave her alone. While she tossed and turned and tried to sleep, it tugged inexorably at her conscience. The adventure beckoned to her as irresistibly as the song of the Siren in her painting. And by the chiming of the next hour, she'd plotted her course.

Wide awake now, her heart pumping, she reached hopefully beneath her feather pillow. The servants had missed the pencil and sketchbook she kept hidden there. She brought them toward the window, where the moonlight gleamed on the sill. Opening the book to a blank page, she tapped the pencil thoughtfully on her bottom lip. Then she smiled.

Despite the impediment of her bandages, the self-portrait was finished before the hall clock chimed the hour. Mattie penciled a quick title across the top and composed a brief message to go with it. In the morning, before the light of day could show her the folly of her actions, she'd send a servant to post it. Then it would be too late for regrets.

With a sigh that was half trepidation and half relief, she scribbled her new signature for the first time at the bottom of the page.

Mrs. James Harrison.

CHAPTER 1

SPRING 1851
NEAR PARADISE BAR, CALIFORNIA

Dr. James Harrison, Doc Jim to those who knew him, ran shaky fingers through his dull, thinning hair and squinted down at the drawing again.

"PROSPECTIVE" BRIDE, it said.

The woman's face wasn't unattractive, if the penciled drawing could be believed. She had the right number of eyes, and her features were even, except for that crooked smile. Her dress was as drab as Missouri dirt, but the cinched waist showed a bit of female curve. On the whole, she looked too frail for the gold fields, but the fact she'd drawn herself hefting a gold pan and a pickaxe said a lot about her determination, and the title said something about her sense of humor. If that gleam in her eye lasted past the grueling journey from New York to California, he supposed she'd do fine.

He burped, stuffed the rumpled drawing back into his coat pocket, and kicked the empty flask of whiskey at his feet.

He was finally liquored up enough to face the walk back to

camp. But lately it took more and more of his hard-won gold dust to get that way. And it also seemed like none of those sons-of-bitches he called friends ever cut him any slack. Damn it! Didn't they know a man needed a drink once in a while when he spent day after day up to his arse in a freezing cold creek?

He staggered forward, stubbing the toe of his boot on a rust-red rock. He kicked it again just for spite and cursed as the sharp pain penetrated his drunken stupor. Lord, he hated California.

"Golden promise!" he crowed to the cedars, shaking an upraised finger like a seller of patent medicine. "Untold wealth!" He cackled ruefully.

The only wealth he'd found in this God-forsaken place was doing the same thing he'd done back in St. Louis, where he'd had a *real* house—doctoring. But now there wasn't enough of that to keep him in beans, let alone liquor. And to rub salt in his wounds, his kid brother Henry, who had a hankering for Lady Luck and a talent for five card draw, had struck it rich in San Francisco. Why, for pride's sake, Doc Jim had had to out-and-out fib to Henry about the riches of his claim.

He shook his head, then shoved his rumpled hat down over his disheveled hair and cursed again. He supposed he'd have to spend another dollar on Tom Cooligan's barbering if he was to meet his wife-to-be this week. Hell, the woman wasn't even here yet, and already she'd cost him close to two hundred dollars, what with the advertisement, the trip by steamer, and posting that fancy letter Tom had written up for him.

"She better be worth it," he told the trees, adjusting his trousers with a decisive wrench of his belt. "She just damn better."

But no one answered him. He was alone in this neck of the woods. It seemed like he was *always* alone these days, usually at the bottom of a bottle. Which was why he'd resorted to consoling himself with the local Indian squaws, who were always by the creek, digging up bulbs for their dinner, and who didn't put up too much of a fight as long as he had a gun in his hand. It was also why those flea-bitten codgers at Paradise Bar had talked him into getting himself a wife. They thought maybe he'd settle down and straighten up once he had a woman to look after him.

He frowned down at the pine needle-lined trail, wondering if any of the boys back at camp had a stash of liquor. There was still a good half-hour of sunlight left, and damn if he wasn't out of whiskey. He sighed, pitched his pick and shovel atop his shoulder, and staggered forward.

He was still trudging through the woods, almost home, when the brush just ahead of him gave a rustle.

Squirrel? Jay? Skunk? No. Something bigger, by the way the manzanita leaves shivered. The whiskey suddenly froze up in his veins, and his heart lurched ahead of his brain. Might be a bear. Or a mountain lion.

He dropped the pick and shovel and reached under the flap of his coat with a quaking hand to pull out his Deringer pistol, a puny thing that looked like it was made for shooting mice.

The manzanita rattled again, its leaves shaking like silver coins. He raised the loaded gun, his two hands nearly swallowing the pitifully small thing, and aimed it at the bush.

A figure slowly emerged then, and when he saw it was only one of the local Indian girls, the air rushed out of him in an explosion of relief.

His relief quickly turned to anger. "Damn it all! What are you tryin' to do, sneakin' up on a man like that? I almost shot you, you stupid Digger!"

He lowered his bunched shoulders, then hawked up the nasty taste of spent fear and spit it out on the ground. He thought it might be the same squaw he'd had his way with this morning, but it was hard to tell. They all looked the same to him, with their coppery skin and the black stripes they painted on their chins.

Like all the Diggers this time of year, her feet were bare, except for a circle of white shells around her ankle, and she wore a reed skirt that just covered her knees. Her eyes were as black as coal, and her hair fell over her shoulders like two glossy horsetails, not quite hiding the fact that she was naked on top.

Too bad she'd scared the daylights out of him. Otherwise, he might have felt like availing himself of her charms again.

"What do you want?" he growled, gesturing her forward with the gun.

She took a step forward and cautiously lifted one trembling arm. To his amazement, in her hand was the one thing he found more appetizing than her budding breasts.

A bottle of whiskey.

"Well, now," he said with a surprised grin, "what do you know?" He licked his lips. "Is that for me, little darlin'?"

She lowered her eyes and offered him the bottle.

He put away his gun. "Well, ain't that nice." He rubbed his palms together before reaching out to take the whiskey from her. Maybe he'd made a mistake, writing back East for a wife. These Digger girls knew how to show a man the proper respect. And they were grateful for his attentions.

He unstopped the bottle and took a whiff. It was the genuine article, by god. He lifted it in a salute to the squaw and slugged back a healthy couple of swallows. The rotgut burned his throat, but it was hard to find good whiskey in these parts. The important thing was, it took the edge off his fruitless day of prospecting.

Before he could thank the girl, she'd scurried off into the brush.

The sun was at the top of the sky when Sakote emerged from his swim in the bracing creek and climbed up the broad, flat rock overhanging the water. He shook his long black hair, scattering bright droplets everywhere, and scooped up his breechcloth, tying it around his hips. Then he stretched out atop the great gray boulder like a deerhide curing, his limbs spread wide. The rock was warm, and drops of water trickled off of him like tiny lizards skittering across his bare skin. He let out a long breath, squinting against the powerful light of the sun, and thought about the vision he'd had last night—the same one he'd had several nights in a row.

In the dream, a snowy white she-eagle with green eyes circled above the village, her wings shining golden in the setting sun. As she spiraled down, Sakote saw that she grasped two speckled eggs in her talons. When she swooped toward him, he didn't cower, but stood with arms upraised in welcome. She flapped her wings to hover just above him and gently released the eggs into his open palms. Then she dropped down and snagged him by his deerskin cloak, flying up into the sky with him until the village was only a tiny speck hidden among the trees. Still he felt no fear, even when the eagle turned north and he knew in his heart that he would see his people no more.

The Konkow elders couldn't tell him what the vision meant, but they agreed it had strong magic and power. Sakote suspected it was a sign that his destiny wasn't, as the tribe expected, to be the next headman of the Konkow, but something else...some*where* else.

This troubled him. He and his people had lived in these foothills since the beginning. He couldn't imagine living anywhere else. Every year, more strangers came, bringing sickness and greed and violence. Now, more than ever, the Konkow needed a powerful warrior like Sakote to protect them. How could he think of leaving?

He closed his eyes and listened to the world—the world he knew and loved. Over the loud rushing of the creek, wasps and dragonflies buzzed on the air. The fish he'd speared earlier lay quiet beside him within layers of grass. From the far bank, a squirrel clucked angrily, reminding him of his little sister, Towani.

The corner of his lip drifted up in a smile. Towani had come home late again last night. Each day she spent more and more time in the valley with her miner friend, Noa. Sakote didn't understand what the miner saw in his scrawny little sister. Maybe the flower season, *yo-meni,* had made Noa crazy. But one day soon, he was sure they would marry. Then Towani wouldn't come home at all.

Yo-meni was a good time—a time of plenty for the Konkow. The animals made their young, and the plants grew heavy with seed so that the tribe wouldn't go hungry when the snows came.

A breeze blew across his skin, fluttering his breechcloth, teasing him with its cool breath. Soon the sun would drink all the water from his body, and he'd be as warm as the rock. He took in a lungful of air. The scent of bay leaves and manzanita was strong, but he detected something else, something familiar—the unmistakable tang of little boy sweat.

The child had been quiet. His bare feet made little noise across the rocks. But his odor gave him away. He'd gone too many days without a bath. He reeked of...

An abrupt hard blow to Sakote's belly knocked the wind from him, folding him in half, and suddenly Hintsuli was straddling his stomach. The little boy's dark eyes shone like obsidian, and his white teeth flashed like shells as his face lit up with victory.

"I have captured the great *pano,* the grizzly bear!" Hintsuli crowed, pounding his small brown fists against Sakote's chest.

Sakote caught his little brother's skinny wrists and grinned. "Is that so? Or has the *pano* captured you?"

Hintsuli squealed.

"Hmm," Sakote said, turning the boy this way and that to examine him. "You're too small for this *pano*. I think I'll throw you to the fish instead."

"No!" Hintsuli screamed in delight. "No!"

"Oh, yes," he decided, hauling Hintsuli up by his wrists and dangling him over the swirling water. "Brother Trout will be grateful for this little grub."

As Hintsuli dropped through the air, he cried out one final protest that ended in a gurgle when the creek closed over his head. Then he popped up again as quickly as an oak gall, his shiny black hair hanging in strings over his giggling face.

Sakote laughed. "You're so filthy, even the fish spit you out!"

A sudden rustling from behind him, high on the hillside, intruded upon their moment of play. Sakote whipped his head around, instantly alert, his eyes flicking momentarily toward his fishing spear.

Atop the ridge stood a man as dark as a Konkow, his arms crossed over his chest as he surveyed the scene before him, slowly shaking his head. His teeth bloomed white against his swarthy face.

Hintsuli waved a skinny brown arm in greeting. "Noa!"

Sakote relaxed his stance and grinned. He'd known Noa would come sooner or later. He watched the man scale recklessly down the hill toward them, one hand holding the hat to his head, one arm swinging in counterbalance.

If ever there was a man Sakote could call brother with pride, it was Noa. He'd arrived four leaf-falls ago, before the great herd of miners, from a place he called Hawaii. Unlike most of the white men since, he'd always looked upon the Konkow with respect. He'd shared their deer and learned their customs. In exchange, he'd taught Sakote English and everything else he knew about the world of the *willa*—the white man.

Noa's boots crunched on the pebbles at the bottom of the hill. Silence was the one Konkow trait he'd never mastered. Sakote smiled as Noa jumped up beside him on the boulder, a bunch of withered blue lupines drooping from his hand. Sakote knew who the blossoms were for.

"What brings you here?" Sakote asked, switching over to the language he knew as well as his own now. He slicked the hair off of his forehead and bit back a grin as he slyly nodded toward the clump of blossoms in Noa's fist. "Are those for me?"

Noa frowned awkwardly down at the blooms, as if he had no idea how they'd gotten there.

In the water, Hintsuli giggled. Then the little boy's attention was quickly diverted to a grandfather trout gliding along the silt of the creekbed, and he dove straight down, all slippery bottom and scrambling legs.

Sakote chuckled and clapped Noa on the shoulder. "My friend, I fear there's no hope for you. Every day for two moons my sister goes to you in the valley. Today you bring her flowers. Maybe in another two moons you'll bring her a deer." He leaned toward Noa and rapped the buttons of his blue miner's shirt. "She'll be an old woman by the time you sleep in her *hubo*."

Noa turned as red as manzanita bark. "Sakote!"

Sakote flinched at the use of his name. He'd never grow accustomed to the way the settlers threw sacred names about as casually as rocks.

"You know that isn't the way I do things," Noa said. "It just...it wouldn't be right." He absently whacked the flowers against his dusty thigh and grimaced. "Towani is...she's special. And young. And pretty. Pretty as the bloom of an aloalo."

Sakote felt laughter creep into his eyes. He had no idea

what an aloalo was, but it was funny to see his friend so befuddled by his little tadpole of a sister.

"You should take my sister from the village," Sakote said, shaking his head. "She's no use to us. She's ruined the weaving of three baskets this past moon with her lovesickness. She burns the trout. She spills the acorn meal. And every morning, she rises before dawn to walk to the valley. Maybe that," he added, thumping Noa on the chest again, "is why she didn't return to the village last night until everyone was already asleep." He winked. It was a good gesture, one he'd learned from Noa.

But Noa didn't return his smile. Instead, he blinked in confusion. Then he drew back in disbelief. "You think she came to *me?* That she spent the…"

He backed up a step, and Sakote had to make a grab for his arm before he stepped right off the boulder. Noa sniffed and pulled his arm away. Sakote had obviously offended him.

"I've known you for four years," Noa said. "You've been like a brother to me, Sakote, and I've always treated Towani with respect. I would never…" He lowered his voice and straightened proudly. "I would never take her like that without the benefit of a proper Christian marriage."

If Noa hadn't looked at him so solemnly, Sakote would have burst into laughter. For the Konkow, there was no such thing as a proper marriage. If a man felt affection for a woman, he simply moved into her *hubo,* her home. If she didn't cast him out, then they were wed. But Sakote understood Noa's customs and his concern. He nodded and slung a companionable arm across his friend's shoulders.

"I know, my brother, I know," he told Noa gently. "But you know her heart already belongs to you."

Relief softened the lines in Noa's forehead. Sakote knew it would be a good marriage. Noa and Towani would live in the place the miners called the Valley of the Squaw Men, where she'd find companions among the other native women who'd married settlers.

"Wait." The happiness dimmed in Noa's eyes. "What did you say about Towani?"

"That her heart belongs—"

"No, no, no." He looked faintly alarmed now. "About last night."

"That she didn't return until..." Sakote frowned. "My sister wasn't with you last night?"

Noa shook his head almost imperceptibly.

"Then where..?"

"*I* know where she was," Hintsuli volunteered, squinting up from his perch on a small boulder in the midst of the stream. His interest in the trout had obviously waned some time ago, and he could understand enough of their words to know they were talking about Towani.

Sakote nodded for him to continue.

"She went to the *willa* camp."

Noa stiffened beside him.

"What?" Sakote asked. "Why?"

Hintsuli shrugged. "She said she was taking medicine to the white healer."

Sakote's scowl deepened. Medicine? What medicine? And who was this white healer? Going to the *willa* camp was forbidden. It was too dangerous for the Konkows to mix with the white miners. Towani knew better.

But he could see that Noa's thoughts were traveling a different path. Noa worried that someone else—this white healer perhaps—might be vying for Towani's heart.

Sakote clasped Noa's forearm. "Don't worry. I'll sort things out." He *would* sort things out, even if he had to deal with Towani the way the whites handled disobedient children, by taking a willow switch to her backside. "You go home. I'll talk to my sister."

"No talk! No talk! No talk!" Hintsuli chanted cheerfully in English, tromping up the bank of the creek, his wet, bare feet making mud boots of the fine silt. "She's in the time of *yupuh*. She's gone to the women's hut."

"What?" Sakote glared sharply at his little brother. How did Hintsuli know about *yupuh?* Had he peered into the women's hut? "Wicked boy! It's forbidden to look—"

"I didn't look!" Hintsuli jutted out his smug chin. "She told me to tell you she was in the time of *yupuh*."

Sakote tightened his jaw. A shadow had fallen across the beautiful day. His sister was up to something—sneaking off to the miner's camp and telling Hintsuli to lie for her—and he had to find out what it was.

"I promise, brother," Sakote swore to Noa, "I'll find the truth."

Noa nodded brusquely, but his step was heavy as he began the long journey home, and Sakote's heart ached for his friend. He squeezed his hands into fists. He wanted to shake his foolish sister, shake her till her teeth clattered like a *shokote* rattle and she came to her senses.

CHAPTER 2

When Sakote returned to the village, he resisted the urge to barge into the women's hut and yank his sister out. Instead, he let his blood cool in the lengthening shade, filled his belly with trout, and waited patiently for her to emerge.

But she didn't. Not when the women returned from digging bulbs beside the creek. Not when the sweet smoke of roasted fish drifted into the canyon. Not when the young men finished gambling beside the dying embers of the fire. The hunting-bow moon moved far to the west, the tribe retired for the night, and still she didn't come out.

Sakote spit onto the gray coals of the cooking fire, making them sizzle. He glared toward the women's hut. Did she think she could hide in there forever? Towani had always been willful, but how dared she defy him—the man who was to become the next headman of the Konkow? And how could she break Noa's heart with such deception?

He poked at the charred remains of the fire with a dogwood branch and scanned the cluster of *hubos*—the bark-covered houses that made up the village. No smoke curled from the tops of the conical roofs. The Konkow slept.

Sakote had seen his people through another day, brought food to his mother's fire, told a tale of Oleili, Coyote, to the children, and listened to the wisdom of the elders. He should be content. Yet it was never contentment he felt when the sun went to sleep behind the hills. It was always relief. Which was why his sister's defiance troubled him.

Their world was changing. The elders didn't see it, partly because they didn't travel as far or see as much as Sakote did, and partly because they didn't want to. They didn't see how the white men arrived as thick as grasshoppers in the flower season. How they planted sticks in the ground as if they could possess the land. How they fought with fists and drank whiskey till they couldn't walk. How some of them looked upon the Konkow with hateful eyes and Coyote's sly grin.

Noa was different. He understood the Konkow ways. He would provide meat and shelter for Towani, and he'd carry her in his heart. They'd make babies together to grow and thrive among the other children of the valley. Noa would care for Towani. He'd protect her. And Sakote would have one less Konkow to worry about.

But if Towani mingled with the white men from the mining camp...

One brave cricket attempted to sing, his chirrup slow and hesitant across the cool night. Sakote pulled the deerskin up over his shoulder and dropped the dogwood branch onto the coals. He sighed, and it felt as if his spirit left him with his breath.

How could he protect Towani? How could he protect the village and his people? There were too many white men, and he feared what his vision foretold—that he wouldn't be around to keep them safe.

The chirping cricket abruptly ceased his song, and Sakote

froze, pricking up his ears. Furtive but heavy footfalls approached, crunching the mulch of the forest. It was a man, by the sound. Sakote slipped his knife from its sheath, testing the edge with the pad of his thumb, and stared quietly toward the source of the commotion.

The footsteps slowed as a figure broke through the shadowy cedars into the village clearing. When Sakote saw who it was, he put away his knife and waited.

Noa hunkered down beside him. "We have to talk, Sakote," he whispered. "Something's happened. Something bad, very bad." He rubbed his fingers nervously across his mouth.

Sakote's heart thudded. He despised the English language at the moment, with its subtleties and endless ways to stretch out the telling of a story.

"A friend of mine brought news from the mining camp," Noa said under his breath, "about that white healer Towani went to see. Doc Jim was his name, Dr. James Harrison. It seems he...well, he up and died last night."

Sakote's heart turned to ice.

"No one knows what he died of," Noa continued, "since he was the only doctor for miles around. There weren't any marks on him or anything. He just dropped dead in his cabin."

Sakote stared hard into Noa's eyes, black as pitch in the darkness, and he feared he knew what was behind the white healer's death. Towani's "medicine."

Noa bit his lip. "Most of the miners suspect it was too much liquor. It seems he had an unnatural hankering for whiskey." He dropped his head down, his hat shielding his eyes. "But if someone were to look too closely into the man's liquor bottle...or if there were, I don't know, a couple of long black hairs on his coat or a...a footprint by his cabin where there shouldn't be..."

Sakote's blood, frozen in fear, now began to heat with rage. How could his sister have done such a thing? How could she have killed a white man? How could she have endangered their people in this way? He clenched his fists and thrust out his jaw. His nostrils flared with a breath deep enough to feed a loud bellow of outrage. But he remained silent, instead channeling his fury into the icy glare he shot toward the women's hut. Noa seized his arm, trying to stop him as he lurched forward, but Sakote wrenched from his grasp.

Noa cussed under his breath and followed Sakote as he stalked off.

It was forbidden for a man to enter the women's hut. The Great Spirit, Wonomi, would be vexed. But at the moment, Sakote didn't care. He'd waited long enough. He ducked down and crept through the low crawlway.

Little light penetrated the hut, and it took Sakote a moment to see that there was only one person sleeping inside. He edged forward, and when Towani stirred, he made a grab for her. She had time for one short squeak of surprise before he clapped his hand over her mouth and hauled her up with an arm wrapped around her waist. She struggled like a trapped cougar kitten, snarling, twisting her head, and clawing at his arms.

"Quiet!" he hissed.

When she heard his familiar voice, she ceased fighting, but she still held her body stiff, wary of him.

He lugged her out of the hut, eliciting a curse of irritated disbelief from Noa, and then carried her off into the woods with Noa at his heels.

When they reached a starlit break in the trees, far from the ears of the village, Sakote set his sister abruptly onto her feet.

"Speak!" he commanded, crossing his arms over his chest.

Towani flinched momentarily, but then lifted her proud chin and stared off into the night. "I have nothing to say."

Her voice cracked, and it was hard to speak roughly to her

when she looked so pale and sleepy in the moonlight. But he had to do it. He had to know the truth.

"You've killed a white man," he bit out, "and you have nothing to say?"

She glanced at him, clearly startled that he'd found out.

"What did you give him?" he demanded. "What did you put in his whiskey?"

She looked nervously at Noa, and Sakote grabbed her by the shoulders.

"Answer me."

Her eyes glistened wetly. "Buckeye."

Sakote's chest felt as if it would cave in. Somehow he'd hoped he was mistaken. Somehow, impossibly, he'd hoped that Towani knew nothing about the white man's death, that she was innocent, that she was still his wide-eyed little sister whose worst flaw was a stubborn streak. But it was not to be. In one word she'd condemned herself. In one word she'd become a murderer.

"Why?" Sakote choked, unable to rectify the innocent trembling of his sister's chin with the murderous truth of her actions. "Why, Towani?"

Hearing him use her name made tears fill her eyes and spill over onto her cheek. Beside them, Noa grimaced and fidgeted uncomfortably. But she didn't answer.

"Do you know what you've done?" Sakote freed one hand from her to rake his hair back in frustration. "Do you understand what you've done, my sister?"

"He was only a stupid *willa*," she muttered, though she dropped her eyes in shame to speak the insult.

Fury rose in him like a creek in the storm. "And who are you, that you would kill *anyone* needlessly and without sorrow? Not Konkow. Not my sister." He jerked her shoulder. "Who are you then? A *hudesi*?"

She gasped. The *hudesi* were people so depraved and evil

that they couldn't enter the spirit world after they died, but became ghosts, forever wandering the earth.

"Why did you do it?" Sakote demanded, digging desperate, fearful fingers into her shoulder.

"Stop it!" Noa protested, shoving at Sakote's back.

"Why, Towani?" Sakote insisted.

"You leave her alone, Sakote," Noa warned, "or I swear I'll—"

"Why!"

Towani burst into sobs, jolting Sakote from his rage. He released her like a hot cooking stone, and she buried her face in her hands. Noa went to her, enfolding her in his arms.

"I'm not evil," Towani mewed in English, instantly filling Sakote with self-loathing.

Noa soothed her. "Of course you're not," he said, combing her hair with gentle fingers and flashing Sakote such a glare of accusation that he felt like a *hudesi* himself.

"The *willa* was a...a bad man," she sobbed.

Sakote pressed his lips into a straight line and stared at the moon, which seemed to grin at him in mockery. Towani didn't understand. Not only had she done a terrible thing, but she'd put all the Konkow in danger. She might feel justified in what she had done, but the white man's ways were different, and they often destroyed what they didn't understand.

"Many of the *willa* are bad men," Sakote said. "But you can't kill them just because—"

"I had to kill him," Towani said quietly. The faraway look on her tear-stained face sent a chill along his backbone. "My spirit wouldn't rest. It wouldn't be still...until I took vengeance."

Sakote frowned. What was she talking about?

"I couldn't tell you, my brother," she said. "You would have slain him like a warrior, and the *willa* would have hunted you down. But a woman..." A teary smile faltered on the corners of her lips as she stared up at the stars. "She can be clever, like Coyote." She shook her head at him. "They won't find out. I left no signs. No one saw me. It is done. *Akina.*"

Sakote's thoughts spun like leaves caught in a whirlpool. "No, it's *not* done. You speak of vengeance. For what? How do you even know this man?"

Sakote saw Towani's throat bob as she swallowed hard. "That is between The Great Spirit and me."

"The hell it is!" Sakote barked, borrowing Noa's expression. "You poison a white man. You put our people in danger. And now you hide the truth from me, your own brother!" He raised a fist of anger, though they both knew he'd never struck anyone in his life, not even another man. "Tell me why."

Towani's eyes grew bright with fear, but she said, "No."

"Towani," he growled.

"I won't. I won't ever tell you." Her chin began to quiver again. "I won't tell anyone!" she cried. *"Akina!"*

"Towani!" he roared.

Sakote wasn't prepared for the great shove Noa gave him, one that sent him sprawling on his backside in pine needles. Shock displaced his rage, and he looked up, bewildered, into Noa's snarling face.

"You know what you are, Sakote?" Noa spat. "You're a fool! A big, dumb, ugly, blind fool!"

With those parting words, Noa yanked the deerskin from Sakote's shoulders and wrapped it tenderly around Towani. Then, with one backward glance of condemnation, he guided Towani through the forest on the path toward the valley, toward his home.

Sakote collapsed onto his back with a defeated sigh and lay upon the scratchy leaves, staring up at the stars. Somewhere on a distant hill, a coyote yipped and howled. Nearby, a deer mouse rifled through the mulch. An owl floated on silent wings across the sky, like a lazy arrow shot from the bow of the moon.

As Sakote's blood calmed, his profound confusion cleared, and his eyes finally opened to the horrifying truth, a truth that left his chest heavy with pain. Only one thing could make a woman seek such vengeance on a man. Only one thing could compel her to such secret violence.

His heart felt sick. It couldn't be, he despaired. Not Towani. Not his little sister who used to tag along in his footsteps, who could charm the *cheeztahtah*, the robin, from her nest, who'd been initiated into the women's dance only three leaf-falls ago.

And yet he knew it as well as he knew the stars. The *willa* bastard had raped his sister.

His blood stilled. How could this have happened to her—his sweet, gentle sister? How could he have *let* it happen?

For a long while, he stared up at the stark sky, allowing cold grief to wash over him like a stream scrubbing the roughness from a pebble. But anger still burned silently in his belly, a forgotten coal he yearned to stir to life. Towani had been right. His was a warrior's rage. He hungered for a warrior's revenge, thirsted for the blood of his enemy. He longed to bind the *willa* to a tree, to shoot him full of arrows until the white man's voice grew hoarse with screaming and the last of his coward's blood stained the earth.

But Towani had stolen his vengeance. And in doing so secretly, she'd protected the tribe. His little sister had been wiser than he in this. How well she knew his heart.

As he gazed up at the icy chips of stars journeying across the black night, they doubled and blurred in his vision. The world of the Konkow was changing, and like the stars, there was nothing he could do to alter its path. The best he could hope for was to keep his people safe.

Already he was failing.

CHAPTER 3

"Farm?" Mattie repeated, wrinkling her freckled nose as she beat the dust of the final trail to Paradise Bar from her skirts. "Are you saying my husband-to-be, *Doctor* James Harrison, has become a farmer?"

She supposed she shouldn't be astonished. After all, her long journey west by steamer and bungo, mule and riverboat, had been nothing but a series of surprises.

Mr. Ezekiel Jenkins' cornflower blue eyes pierced hers with an odd sort of bemused fascination, as if she were some creature the skinny old prospector had never seen before.

His companion, a giant of a man called Swede, with a chest that strained his suspenders and a face so rosy it looked as if he scrubbed it a dozen times a day, irritably cuffed the smaller man, nearly knocking him down.

"'Bought the farm'?" he asked Zeke, shaking his head in disgust. "Ma'am, what my friend here means to say is the doc, well, he..." He raised the hand holding his felt hat to scratch at the blondest hair Mattie had ever seen. "That is, he..." He

40

stared at her for a long while, hesitant to speak. "Well, shucks, ma'am, I'm afraid your husband-to-be...well, he kicked the bucket yesterday."

Mattie glanced blankly from one man to the other. She had no idea what they were saying, between their fanciful talk of farms and buckets and their outright butchering of the English language. But she was already imagining the wonderful portrait she'd make of the two prospectors, here among the ramshackle lean-tos that must serve as storage sheds for the residents of Paradise Bar.

Zeke was as wrinkled, salty, and lean as a stick of jerky. Long gray waves of thinning hair hung over his protruding ears and draped his bony shoulders. His nose had a slight bend in it, as if he'd stuck it once where it didn't belong and found the wrong end of a fist. His lips all but disappeared into a beard that looked like a fracas between a kitten and a dozen spools of multi-colored thread. The map of wrinkles etched in his sun-weathered face told of hardship and laughter, bitterness and hope. But his eyes—they'd be the focus of the portrait she'd do of him one day. Twinkling with wisdom one moment, snapping vexedly the next, those eyes had witnessed the good part of a century.

Swede's face was bare, save for a faint peach fuzz of blond whiskers. The black hat jammed over his head a moment ago only accentuated his sunburned ears and the startlingly bright, bone-straight hair that stuck out around them like straw. Though he spoke in all seriousness at the moment, the crow's feet at the corners of his indigo eyes and the waves across his high forehead reflected a life of mischief and glee, and his wide mouth seemed made for laughter. He had shoulders as broad as an ox, and ham-like hands that she suspected could tenderly milk a cow as well as throw a mean punch.

"Aw, she don't get it, Swede," Zeke decided, scratching at his scraggly beard.

"Well, shit! I mean, shoot!" Swede quickly corrected. "Beggin' your pardon, ma'am."

Mattie bit back a smile. These two were far more interesting than the proper, simpering gentlemen of New York. Oh yes, she thought, she was going to like it here. It was colorful, just as her voyage to California had been.

Her portfolio was bulging with sketches she'd made of the journey. There was a rendering of the ship she'd boarded in New York, its twin stacks exhaling clouds of steam, passengers crowded along its whitewashed railings, their faces bright with promise as they gazed across the white-capped sea.

And there were sketches made days later of several of the passengers: a nervous young minister clinging to his Bible like a tot to a favorite blanket; four beardless prospectors in flannel shirts and heavy boots as new as their faces; an old sour-faced woman in cropped hair and men's trousers with a pickaxe slung over her capable shoulder; a sparkle-eyed Irishman with a missing tooth and more patches in his coat than coat.

She'd sketched their lodging at the mouth of the Chagres River in Panama—a thatched hut where gentlemen stretched out beside beggars and Mattie learned that if a young woman was weary enough, she could indeed fall asleep in a room crowded with strange men.

And there was a wonderful depiction of bare-chested natives paddling a bungo along the jungle trail from Gorgona to Panama, where moss dangled from the trunks of lush trees and dipped into the murky waters of the river.

Despite the grousing of discontented travelers at every leg of the voyage, Mattie found adventure in the adversity. For once she felt free of society's dictates.

While others hung over the railing of the steamer, moaning about the roiling of the ship, Mattie stood brazenly on the foredeck, relishing the icy wind and salt spray upon her cheeks.

While they complained about the meager rations along the Chagres—beans and pork with hard bread and molasses—Mattie lured the monkeys out of the forest by tossing them bits of food.

While the male passengers looked upon the Panama natives with disdain, and the few females aboard avoided looking at them at all, Mattie spent hours studying their fascinating gestures and language and physiques. Several sketches of the squat, nut-brown, raven-eyed guides were scattered throughout drawings of spectacular birds and ramshackle huts and stocky palms dripping with rain.

Even the civilized jungle of San Francisco enchanted her with its chaotic tangle of abandoned ships and more chaotic array of humanity—men from China and Africa and Mexico, some vying for a spot on the next transportation to the gold country, some finding their fortunes second-hand, hawking laundry service, gold pans, or room and board to the prospectors.

But for Mattie, a different treasure awaited, a treasure she'd already begun to sample. She could start a new life here. In California, where gambling men lost fortunes and paupers grew rich, where women wore pantaloons and cursed and drank whiskey, she could start over. And this time, she'd find out just who Mathilda Hardwicke was.

Not Hardwicke, she corrected. Harrison. It still rattled her to think about the rash decision she'd made in choosing a husband, sight unseen, for better or worse. But it was too late to do anything about it now.

"I told you we should have skedaddled while the gittin' was good," Zeke muttered, spitting out a thin stream of chewing tobacco that almost didn't clear his beard. "Everyone else had the good sense to go work their claims today."

"Damn it, Zeke!" Swede said, whacking his hat on his meaty thigh.

Zeke narrowed one warning eye at him.

"Beggin' your pardon, ma'am," Swede apologized again, and then turned back to Zeke. "*Someone* had to stay behind and tell her."

"Tell me what?" Mattie asked politely, though her patience with the two men was beginning to wear thin.

Despite her good spirits, she'd come a long way, and she looked forward to settling in, especially after the harrowing ride up the ridge. It was a wonder there was any blood left in her knuckles, since her nasty-tempered mule had delighted in braying loudly at the most unfortunate moments. More than once, she was sure the beast planned to buck her off the narrow trail and send her tumbling down the treacherous gorge.

But she'd arrived, safe and sound. She'd made it to California, to the land of gold, despite all odds. She'd escaped the cholera, which had claimed a number of sea-faring Argonauts like herself. She'd managed to subsist well enough on the spare rations on the voyage, though by the looseness of her dress, she was probably closer to the size of her lissome cousins than she'd ever been. She'd survived the conniving of a murderous mule. And though the voyage had cost far more than she'd expected, she'd had enough coin left over to launder her dirty clothing in Sacramento before her arrival, so she could greet her husband-to-be looking like a proper lady.

But where was he? True, she was surrounded by about all her senses could take in at the moment, what with the lovely clearing, redolent of pine, and its darling creek running past all those quaint little storehouses. But she was eager to see Paradise Bar proper, and she was anxious to meet her husband-to-be, to see his farm or wherever it was he'd had the altercation with the bucket.

"Maybe we should just show her, Swede," Zeke said.

"Shit...shoot, you old fool." Swede tugged his hat back down over his ears and kicked awkwardly at the dirt. "You can't just..."

They cut their quibbling short when they heard someone coming through the trees. Mattie squinted in the direction of the noise, against the orange light of the setting sun. She could make out the silhouettes of a pack of men, pickaxes slung across their shoulders, hats slanted atop their heads. They kicked up little clouds of rust-colored dust as they came, their noisy arrival punctuated by barks of laughter and the clank of gold pans.

Mattie straightened and nervously chewed at her bottom lip. *He* must be with them, she thought—her new husband. Her eyes flickered over the band of prospectors, searching for the face she'd drawn in her mind a hundred times.

The lead man stopped abruptly when he saw her, and all the others bungled into him, tainting the air with clattering tools and cussing. Then they grew quiet, keeping their distance, but spreading across the path so everyone could get a good look at her. A few of them had the presence of mind to doff their hats.

They were the sorriest bunch of souls Mattie had ever laid eyes on. Their clothes were filthy. Most of them were soaking wet from the thighs down, and their march through the dust had made a muddy, brick-colored mess of their pants and knee-high boots. Their wrinkled shirts bore dark sweat stains along the collars and deep under the arms, and their hats were as lumpy as the crust of an overstuffed pie. Those who could grow beards had done so, it seemed, with nary a scissor or comb to keep them the least bit presentable.

"Well, don't just stand there like a bunch of no-counts," Swede scolded. "Where's your manners?"

Mattie froze to the spot, though she wanted to turn and

run. She'd just as soon not move an inch closer to the growing mob. If they looked that foul, God only knew what they smelled like.

But her father had raised no shrinking violet, to faint away at the slightest insult to her sensibilities. After all, Lawrence Hardwicke had rubbed elbows with pirates and ruffians and all manner of savages. If he could do it, so could she.

Summoning up a brave smile and holding her breath, she stepped forward to greet her new neighbors, feeling as out of place as a mouse in the parlor. "How do you do?"

They only stared at her, silent, awestruck, as if she'd just stepped off of a cloud into their midst. There were about two dozen in all, mostly young men, a few old enough to be grandfathers, a couple of olive-skinned lads, a man as black as a crow, and one who looked suspiciously female.

"Well, dang it," Swede said, crossing powerful forearms across his belly. "Ain't anyone gonna say hello? Where's Frenchy?"

"At your service." A handsome, stubble-chinned man with a feather in his hat stepped forward like an elegant fop asking her to dance. He took her gloved hand in his callused one, roguishly winked one of his brandy-brown eyes, and bent over it with the suggestion of a kiss. "Allow me to apologize for these mannerless pigs," he said, his voice thick with a French accent. "I am Lucien Lafayette, *ma cherie*, known as Frenchy to *mes amis*. Welcome...to our little slice...of Paradise." He seemed surprised and pleased with his awful rhyme, and Mattie had to smile.

"Thank you," she murmured.

Frenchy lifted one brow in challenge to the rest, and they edged forward to make her acquaintance.

She met young Billy and Bobby Cooper, whose hands shook as they tipped their hats, Jasper Colton, who looked as dangerous as a gunslinger, and Red Boone, who sported a fiery beard. She met two Welshmen who gave her a Gaelic greeting she couldn't decipher. Four strapping lads introduced themselves as the Campbells. Amos, the black man, contented himself with a polite, but cautious nod. And Granny, the only other woman in the camp, showed her with a stern glare that there'd be no feminine camaraderie between the two of them.

She met them all and remembered about a quarter of their names. None of them were Dr. James Harrison. She was about to inquire yet again as to her husband's whereabouts when out of one of the less dilapidated shacks stepped a nattily-dressed man.

Dr. Harrison. It had to be. He was somewhat shorter than she expected, but he was well-groomed, as a physician should be, with a neat brown mustache and close-trimmed hair. His black coat was only slightly dusty, and the derby perched on his head gave him a jaunty air. She could see by the wrinkles about his eyes that he was a cheery man, a kindly man, and she breathed a silent sigh of relief.

He raised his brows in greeting and tugged down his vest before stepping off of the makeshift porch.

"Ah, ye must be Miss Mathilda Hardwicke then." The man's brogue was as thick as Irish mist. "I'm Tom Cooligan, mum, pleased ta meet ye."

Mattie hoped her disappointment didn't show. So far, Tom was the only man who even slightly resembled the husband she'd sketched for herself.

'Tis sorry I am ye've come so late," he said, his eyes taking on a melancholy cast, "but I hope ye'll be likin' my work."

She frowned. What did he mean?

He caught her by the crook of the arm and led her back toward the shack, chattering away. The rest of the town, apparently unwilling to be left out of the excitement, trailed after them.

"Ye see, we've a shortage o' real tradesmen here in the camp, so I've become the local barber."

Ah, he must have given the groom a fresh shave and haircut in her honor.

"Though, sad ta say," Tom continued, "my barberin' talents are seldom called upon by this sorry lot."

"Uh, Tom…" Swede interjected.

"Well, all right," Tom allowed. "Swede here comes once a week, on Tuesday, ta have his shave, but the rest of 'em—"

"Tom!" Swede blurted out.

The Irishman waved him away and opened the door of the little shed.

"Ye know, mum," he confided, "we don't usually go ta so much trouble, but what with ye comin' an' all, an' tomorra bein' Sunday…"

He swung the door wide and ushered her in.

"Anyway, I hope ye like what I've done with him."

Mattie looked up and froze in her tracks.

She could honestly say she liked almost everything about her husband-to-be. He looked remarkably like the drawing she'd made. He was good-sized, not too plump, not too spare. He had a thin, but freshly cut crop of chestnut hair and a tastefully scissored mustache. His face, though weathered a bit from exposure to the elements, was not overly ruddy, and his hands were suitable to his profession, pale and slender. He was attired in a black, embroidered silk waistcoat with a fairly clean white shirt, along with creased pants, a well-tailored cloth coat, and boots so shiny she could almost see her reflection in them.

He was perfect. Tom had done an admirable job. In fact, the only thing she didn't like about Dr. James Harrison was the fact that he was as dead as a doornail.

CHAPTER 4

Stupefied, Mattie blinked at the Irishman, who seemed poised for some compliment from her. But she couldn't speak, couldn't think, couldn't breathe. Dawning reality slowly squeezed the hope from her like a cider press crushing juice from apples.

Of all the things that could have gone wrong, this one she hadn't considered. She'd tossed on Atlantic seas wild enough to tear a hole in a vessel as easy as a thumb in pie. She'd watched men die in a matter of hours from jungle cholera. She'd rowed beside ravenous crocodiles, slapped at disease-bearing mosquitoes, and suffered a belligerent mule that could have sent her sliding down a mountain to her death. Yet she'd bucked up, faced it all bravely, and survived. To what end?

Her reward was gone. Mattie the Argonaut had fought her way past peril and misfortune, only to have her Golden Fleece vanish into thin air.

"Is she gonna faint?" Zeke asked, narrowing his eyes for a closer look.

That snapped Mattie out of her paralysis. No, she wouldn't faint. After all, she was her father's daughter. But a sudden rush of panic so engulfed her that her legs turned to custard, and she felt an overwhelming need to sit down.

"Oh, lass, didn't ye know?" the Irishman asked gently. Then he cuffed the tall Swede. "Didn't ye tell her, ye big lummox?"

Swede glared at the smaller man, then guided Mattie by the elbow back outside through the crowded doorway, towards a three-legged stool tottering on the lean-to's makeshift porch.

"Give her some air, boys," he said, motioning the others back. He sat her down and fanned her face with his big black hat. "You gonna be all right, ma'am?"

She nodded and closed her eyes, envisioning the newspaper advertisement she'd answered a lifetime ago, curling and burning, till there was nothing left but ash.

Dear God—what had she done? She had no money. She knew no trade. And now, she was no man's wife. She was a stranger here—to the people, to the land, to prospecting. She'd gambled everything on her new life, never imagining that in one fell swoop, one fatal twist of fate, it could be lost.

"She looks kinda peaked to me," Zeke said, spewing a stream of tobacco juice onto the planks at the edge of the porch.

"Aw, hell," Swede said, then amended, "heck."

Frenchy snapped his fingers smartly. "Someone fetch her something to drink, no?"

All the prospectors moved to lend assistance, but it was the sour-faced old woman who grubbed around in her pack and found a half-empty brown bottle first. She uncorked it and gave the lip a vigorous scrubbing with her dirty sleeve. "Take a slug o' this, honey. It'll make you right as rain."

Mattie eyed the dirty vessel with its mysterious contents.

Then her gaze flickered over the faces of the residents of Paradise Bar. They stared at her with a mixture of emotions—some scornful, some challenging, a few awestruck, but most concerned. They were as ragtag a band as Robin Hood's merry men and as filthy as barnyard pigs. But in this untamed country of rushing rivers and plunging gorges, where a person had to eke out a living from the raw elements of the earth, they were all she had. She couldn't afford to offend them.

She steeled herself to take the bottle. It couldn't be that bad. The spirits she could smell even at this distance would kill anything harmful. And she'd nursed brandy before, which was strong, but not unpleasant. With a brief smile of thanks, she grabbed the bottle. Upending it, she downed a fortifying gulp.

And almost spit it right back out in a most unladylike fashion. Instead, she choked it down, and the liquid seared a fiery path down her throat, stealing her breath. Her eyes teared up, and her face flushed hot.

Strong didn't describe the brew. A far cry from the smooth cognac she'd sipped in ladies' parlors, it seemed a closer cousin to the noxious potions concocted in chemist shops.

But she was unwilling to disappoint the scruffy miners that gathered about her with hopeful stares.

"Thank you," she gasped when she was finally able to draw breath, handing the bottle back with perhaps more enthusiasm than was polite.

One of the Campbell boys shuffled shyly forward, his hands stuffed into the waistband of his trousers. "Is there anything else we can get you, ma'am?"

She glanced up at the lad. Yes, she thought childishly. There was something he could get her. He could get her a ticket home. Or he could find her another husband, only one far more refined than any of the filthy wretches she'd met thus far. And while he was at it, he may as well bring her parents back to life. A lump closed her raw throat, and the earnest expression in the boy's amber eyes almost made her dissolve into tears.

"No," she answered instead, "thank you."

"I brung your bag, ma'am," another Campbell boy said, lifting her satchel onto the planks.

She gave him a brief, grateful smile.

Tom came from inside the lean-to, stepping onto the porch and circling the rim of his doffed derby with nervous fingers. "I'm terrible sorry, lass, fer springin' it on ye like that. I was led ta believe ye knew." He cast Swede a pointed glare. "If ye'd like, we can keep the doc in state fer…well, fer a day or two at most, considerin' the warm weather…"

"No!" Mattie blurted out, then amended, "That is, I'd prefer he found his peace as soon as possible." The last thing she wanted was to closet herself with a dead man she didn't even know. "If you don't mind," she added diplomatically.

"Not at all," Tom assured her. "We'll see him buried first thing tomorra. 'Tis often better ta do these things quickly," he said with a wink, perching his derby atop his black curls, "leave yer past behind ye."

Leave her past. That's what she'd done. But now her future lay just as empty. She looked at the carpetbag at her feet. Everything she owned was inside it. That was her life now. Her pampered world of ladies' teas and downy quilts and carriage rides was gone. And there was nothing in that bag to sustain her in this uncivilized and unforgiving land.

Aunt Emily had warned Mattie about her foolhardy dreams, told her she spent too much time with her head in the clouds. Here was proof. She'd journeyed west on the scrap of such a dream, on a promise scrawled on a piece of notepaper that was no more substantial now than the wind. Only this time, it wasn't just a frown or a harsh word she'd earned for her impetuousness. This time she'd lost everything.

"You ain't gonna cry, are you?" the old woman asked, her face puckered in disgust.

That was precisely what Mattie wanted to do. But now, of course, she wouldn't, not for the world. There *was* one thing she hadn't lost after all—her pride.

"Don't you worry none," Swede said, giving her an awkward pat on the shoulder. "Me and the boys decided, what with you being just the one day shy of becomin' the doc's wife, why, there wasn't no reason you couldn't just go right ahead and take over his claim and all."

Mattie looked at them uncertainly. Some looked less content than others about that decision, and, honestly, Mattie didn't have the vaguest idea what she would do with a gold claim. But it was something, some small piece of earth in this vast wilderness.

"And of course, you can have the cabin," Swede said.

"And all o' the doctor's personal effects," added Tom.

At least that news was encouraging. She'd have a roof over her head and sustenance for the time being, thanks to the miners' kindness. She scanned the faces of the prospectors once more, and this time, she saw them through eyes that lifted the tarnishing veil of dust from their cheeks and looked into their hearts. They were good people, most of them, despite their coarseness. They were decent men she owed a debt of gratitude.

"Thank you," she said, smiling wide then, her first genuine smile since she'd arrived. "Thank you very much."

Some of the miners returned her smile, some continued to scowl, and some stood with their jaws lax, as if they'd never set eyes on a woman before. Feeling suddenly magnanimous, Mattie decided she'd invite them all to the doctor's residence tomorrow, once she was settled in, for a luncheon after church services and the funeral. It would have to be simple fare, of course. Cooking had been left to the servants, so there was very little that Mattie knew how to make. But it was the least she could do to thank them for their generosity.

"Well, are we gonna jaw all night," Zeke snorted, "or is one of you gonna cart the lady's belongings to her *cabaña*?"

Several eager lads volunteered, but Swede stared them down, swallowing up the handle of her carpetbag in his oversized paw.

Mattie stood and politely tipped her head. "It was so nice meeting you all. I look forward to seeing you at church tomorrow."

That brought a peculiar silence over the group, but before she had a chance to wonder why, Swede jumped down from the porch and headed down the dusty path, where Mattie was obliged to follow at a clip.

She hoped it wasn't too far. Already, the sun dipped below the horizon, and though at present it cast wondrous coral light across the scattered clouds, soon the sky would darken, rendering the thick woods shadowy and foreboding.

"I'm awful sorry about your husband, ma'am," Swede mumbled as she half-skipped to keep up with him. "But just so's you know, there's any number of fellas right here in Paradise Bar who'd be happy as all get-out to have such a pretty young thing for a wife."

"Ah. Thank you." Mattie wondered if Swede counted himself among those eager to wed her.

"Some of the miners, they've been here a long while. It gets pretty lonesome, and exceptin' for Granny, we ain't had a lady come through camp since last fall."

Mattie would have asked about their autumn visitor, but Swede abruptly turned up the path toward one of those ramshackle lean-tos tucked underneath a big pine and plopped her bag down onto the porch.

"Here it is, ma'am, your new homestead."

There had to be some mistake. This shack was no bigger than the sheds they'd just come from along the...

"It's a fair piece from the rest of the camp. Doc liked his peace and quiet. But I don't want you to worry none. If you're ever in trouble, you just give a holler, and any of the boys in earshot, they'll come a-runnin'."

The walls were scarcely parallel, and the pitched roof, which appeared to be made of shingles cut from the outermost bark of several varieties of trees, sagged on one side.

"There's supplies that come from Marysville once every couple of weeks and mail and such, but if you want somethin' special, you got to wait for a man to come from Sacramento."

Dear Lord, she realized, those storage sheds were the men's houses, which meant the dusty path she'd just trod was...the main street of Paradise Bar.

"There's water aplenty down at the crick," Swede told her, pointing down the hill, "and a whole forest of firewood." His fair cheeks blushed faintly as he added, "Me and the boys, we saw to it you had enough vittles and tinder to last the week anyways. There's some salt pork and beans, a bit of jerky, a couple pounds of flour and such."

"Th-thank you," Mattie managed, trying desperately to sound grateful.

Swede leaned in close to her and confided, "There's also a rifle in there, ma'am. Now, have you ever fired one before?"

Mattie shook her head.

"Well, you're gonna need to learn. What with the bears and drunks and Injuns around, you never know when you're gonna need to chase away one varmint or the other."

Mattie could only stare helplessly up at him.

"Tell you what." He rubbed his meaty palm over his chin. "Me and the boys'll learn you to shoot tomorrow. How's that?"

On the edge of hysteria, Mattie wondered if that would be before or after the luncheon she planned to serve the residents of Paradise Bar in her luxurious new abode.

She smiled politely instead and nodded, stepping up onto the porch, which was little more than pine planks nailed together and half-sunk into the mud.

"All right, then. You take care. I'll be back at the camp if you need anything."

As she watched Swede lumber away, trepidation closed in on her like the advancing night. Bears and drunks and Injuns, he'd said. What had she gotten herself into? But as dark fell around her, Mattie could vividly imagine even more formidable foes, like solitude, hunger, and plain ignorance.

Hovering on panic, Mattie watched until Swede's blond head vanished between two firs, and then braved the front door.

The canvas-covered wood frame hung crookedly from three leather hinges, and she had to lift the thing to even swing it open. When she did, the sweet-acrid smell of burnt pine assaulted her. The interior of the tiny room relied upon the filtered light coming through one window of stretched white cotton, which was scarcely serviceable after sundown, but Mattie wondered if it wasn't just as well. She wasn't certain she was ready to see the hovel's contents by the stark light of day.

Nonetheless, she dragged her bag across the doorsill and onto the knotty planks that made up the house's floor, took a deep breath, and scanned the room.

A pot-bellied stove crouched in one corner, and a tiny bottle of matches perched atop a nearby narrow shelf that looked like a stick of kindling nailed to the wall. The walls were half-covered with ragged scraps of red calico, and where they were devoid of cloth, the rough-hewn wood boards butted against each other with about as much charm as an old geezer's gap-toothed grin.

Shelves of varying size and quality were tacked to the walls, crowded with sundry items: a metal plate, a comb, a coffee pot, spools of twine and thread, a half-full flour sack, tins of peaches, a hand mirror, a tiny scale, several blue and brown glass vials with medicinal labels, a slab of salt pork, a frying pan, a sack of beans, a can of coffee, an iron kettle, cream-colored candles crammed into a half-dozen assorted bottles, a set of bone-handled eating utensils propped in a tin cup, and a sticky jar marked MOLASSES that was crawling with tiny black ants.

A rifle roosted between two wooden hooks, from which hung a ribbed washboard. Twill dishcloths were draped over a thick rope slung across one corner, and below them stood a pair of well-worn boots. A low cot near the stove featured thin ticking and a brown wool blanket, and a weathered black bag at the foot announced the doctor's profession. Mining tools—a pickaxe, a pan, and a shovel—leaned against the wall, next to a stack of split firewood. A chair with legs made out of whole oak limbs tottered on three of them, and a traveling trunk covered with green oilcloth completed the room's furnishings.

The decor looked like the work of a child, and all of it lodged within a space scarcely half the size of her bedroom in Aunt Emily's house.

The way Mattie saw it, she had three choices.

She could laugh. She could cry. Or she could make do.

Since the first two would offer her little comfort against the encroaching night, she opted to attempt the third.

First she'd build a fire. The miners had left her plenty of wood, and she found the bottle nearly full of matches. Rolling back her sleeves, she decided to take a peek inside the pot-bellied stove. She lit a stumpy candle and crouched down, creaking open the cast-iron door. Two tiny shining eyes stared out at her. She screamed and scrambled back, tripping and landing with a plop on her skirts. A sooty, striped rodent scampered out and scurried across the floor, just inches from her toes, its furry tail held straight up. Mattie drew her legs back with a gasp and watched as the little beast disappeared out a hollow knothole in the wall.

She sheepishly got to her feet and braved the stove again. There were no more animals holed up inside, but ash lay at the bottom like a thick blanket. She blew sharply to clear it.

And was instantly sorry. Ashes shot out of the stove like smoke from a cannon, instantly coating her face, stinging her eyes, and extinguishing the candle. She coughed and blinked rapidly as tears streamed down her cheeks.

The sudden darkness might have frightened her if she hadn't been so vexed. But she was furious—with this hovel of a house, with Dr. James Harrison for dying on her, and mostly with her own ignorance. Was she so helpless that she couldn't even light a stove?

Mattie refused to believe that. She may have been coddled the better part of her life, but she was the daughter of Lawrence Hardwicke, and she could conquer anything.

Feeling her way to the matches, she relit the candle and set it atop the stove. By the flickering light, she approached the woodpile, wary of more furry residents. She chose a few chunks of firewood and stuffed them into the belly of the stove. Then she tucked splinters and small odds and ends from the pile around the larger split logs, arranging them as she would flowers. She lit a match from the candle and held it to the biggest log. The match burned, but the wood remained uninspired. The flame bit her, and she dropped the match with a yelp, popping her affronted finger into her mouth.

Three matches later, the thing still wouldn't light. Exasperated, she flung open her satchel and dug out a piece of drawing paper she'd purchased in New York. It was foolish, she knew, and wasteful, but she was determined to get the stove lit if it took all night and her entire stack of precious paper. Fortunately, the next match devoured the first piece greedily and even sampled the kindling as a second course. But its interest soon waned, and only by sheer desperation and begging and blowing upon the foundering embers did Mattie encourage the fire to revive.

It didn't last long. A kettle of water would never have boiled over the meager heat, and she doubted the little animal she'd found inside could have even warmed his toes by the flame. But she'd done it. She'd started a fire by herself. And for some reason, that was important. It meant she could survive here. She might not know how to shoot a rifle or pan for gold or even cook herself a proper meal yet. But she could learn. She had to.

Mattie shook out the bedroll as the fire died down, and thankfully, no small mammals issued forth. She changed out of her traveling clothes, laying them out across the cloth-covered table, unpinned her hair, and slipped on her white cotton nightrail. The blanket seemed clean, if not terribly warm, and even though the cot was a poor substitute for the downy mattress she was used to, it was comfortable enough to entice her to skip supper in favor of a long and deep slumber.

While she slept, she dreamed.

She was drawing. In the forest, by the light of the full moon, she sketched a shadowy figure, a man. Her hand recreated his contours with strong, angular strokes. She peered into the wood, trying to get a better glimpse at what she was drawing, but her subject kept vanishing, and the image on the paper remained unclear. She felt she must finish the drawing—was obsessed with it—and yet she was unable to do so.

The next thing Mattie knew, she was waking to the sound of urgent knocking upon her door. The buttery hue of the room told her morning had arrived.

"One moment," she called out, her voice scratchy from sleep.

Having packed no wrapper, she swept the woolen blanket about her.

The rapid knocking resumed.

"Just a moment," she repeated, raking her hair back from her face in some semblance of civility.

The knocking continued relentlessly.

"Good heavens," Mattie muttered under her breath, shuffling toward the door.

She wrenched the door open, letting in a blinding stream of light, and peered out in time to see a red and black bird flit from the house to the side of a nearby pine. But no one was on the porch. Puzzled by the disappearance of her guest, she watched the little red-crested bird. For a moment it hopped along, clinging vertically to the trunk. Then it reared back its head and began pecking furiously at the bark.

Mattie chuckled. There was her knocking visitor.

It wasn't alone in the tree. Above the bird, circling mischievously, scampered a fat gray squirrel. He twitched his tail, teasing the bird, then retreated into the needles of the pine.

Mattie stepped onto the cold planking of the porch in her bare feet and took a deep breath. The air was just beginning to warm, perfumed with the scent of wildflowers and evergreens. The first insects buzzed in patches of sunlight, and dew glistened on the shaded grasses. The sky was clear and as bright blue as the lupines she'd spotted along the mule trail. It was a glorious morning.

Impetuously, Mattie tossed off the blanket and walked out into a pool of sunshine. After all, for all intents and purposes, she was alone. The grassy dirt was soft beneath her feet, and the sensation of the sun filtering through her thin nightrail felt sinfully good. She closed her eyes, and the sun washed her vision orange. A delicate breeze rustled the pines all around her and played with tendrils of her hair, tickling her cheek. She smiled and lifted her arms above her head, luxuriating in a huge, self-indulgent yawn of which society would never approve.

Then she began to twirl, humming happily the tune she'd learned on the Sacramento riverboat, "Sweet Betsy from Pike," whirling till her gown floated like a great white camellia about her.

A sudden violent rattling of the brush nearby stopped Mattie in her tracks. She gasped and wrapped her arms protectively about her. Something, some large wild animal, set the bushes aquiver as it made its escape. Her heart in her mouth, she staggered back toward the cabin, silently cursing herself for forgetting that she now lived in the wilderness.

Panicked, she scanned the cabin's interior for a defense of some sort. Her eyes alit at once on the rifle.

It smelled of sweet oil, but the black steel felt cold, heavy, and forbidding in her hands. She didn't like holding it, but she didn't want to become some bear's breakfast either. The beast might have run off, but it might be back, and by the looks of the thin cotton lining the window and the flimsy canvas frame door, getting inside the cabin would be the work of but one raking paw.

Her heart slammed against her ribs, and her hands shook as she gingerly shifted the weapon in her arms, holding it as far away from her as possible.

She didn't want the animal cornering her in the house. The bed was too low to hide under, and there was only the one window. So she decided she'd stand guard on the porch.

Warily she crept out the door, her eyes alert to any sudden movement from the meadow or the thick forest surrounding the cabin. She could hear her own pulse rushing through her ears.

At first, every tiny sound made her jump—the robins fluttering in the trees, a bee making its morning rounds, a squirrel dropping a picked-over pine cone. Every flicker of a leaf in the morning sunlight, every turn of a sparrow's wing, startled her. Her sweaty palms slicked her grip on the rifle, and she had to wipe them several times on her nightrail. Her toes curled anxiously on the pine boards. Time passed with agonizing sloth, and the gun grew heavier by the minute in her aching arms.

Several long minutes later, fatigue finally made her relax her guard. Whatever the danger was, it seemed to be gone for good. Nothing but creatures of the small, harmless sort encroached on her parcel of land. A blue jay squawked from the low branch of a tall pine, mercilessly teasing one of those peculiar striped rodents that zigged and zagged over the roots of the tree. A pair of white butterflies made a tumbling flight toward a patch of wild sweetpeas. High against the rich blue sky, a bald black condor with outstretched wings coasted in patient circles.

This land truly was a paradise. The air smelled sweet and clean, of fir and young grass, bay and wild mustard, and the landscape was alive with color. Dewfall painted the earth brick red, and every shade of green from light apple to deep moss colored the vegetation. The iridescent wings of the jay echoed the sky's azure hue, and a full palette of yellows and whites, purples and oranges, dotted the clearing on the petals of wildflowers strewn across the emerald carpet.

Somewhere in the back of her mind, she remembered that she had to get dressed, that she had to prepare for church, that she had to—dear Lord—bury her husband-to-be. But the land beckoned her with its loveliness, and all she could think about was sketching. The world blossomed before her. She had to capture it, quickly, before the moment vanished.

Swinging the rifle one last precautionary time along the perimeter of her clearing, she turned a deaf ear to the call of responsibility and propriety. And for one foolish instant, she forgot about Mother Nature's dangerous face.

CHAPTER 5

Sakote had almost finished the arrowhead. Translucent flakes of obsidian made a small pile between his doubled knees, and when the stone knife chipped away a few more, the sharp point would be complete.

The women of the village were up, making small cooking fires for acorn mush and chatting softly. Their talk didn't disturb him. It was part of the Konkow music, as much a part of the morning as the song of the *cheeztahtah*—the robin, or the hum of the honeybees.

One slender flake dropped to the ground as Sakote studied the point to discover the best place to make the final cut. He set the blade gingerly to the edge.

"Aaaah!" Hintsuli flung himself out of the brush with a panicked cry, making Sakote slip with the knife. The arrowhead split into two useless pieces, the work of the morning instantly destroyed. But Sakote, too concerned to be angry, dropped his tools and sprang to his feet, catching Hintsuli against his thighs.

"What's wrong, little brother?"

The small boy's chest heaved from his running. He panted like a bear run to ground, and he trembled in Sakote's arms.

"The *kokoni!* The *kokoni* of the white man! I saw it! I saw it!"

"What?" Sakote said, frowning. "Where? Where did you see this *kokoni?*"

The women behind him had grown silent, and he knew their ears were pricked up like those of a vigilant doe.

Hintsuli dropped his head guiltily. Sakote tipped it back up by the chin and raised a brow in question.

"At the white healer's *hubo,*" Hintsuli murmured.

"What?" Sakote hissed. He cast a dark look over his shoulder, and the women returned to their labors. "What were you doing at the *willa* camp?" he whispered.

"I wanted to see if the dead man left any...toys." He used the white man's word.

Sakote compressed his lips. Ever since Noa had given Hintsuli that painted wood spinning toy, the boy had been obsessed with the playthings of the white man.

"I told you not to go there. I told you it was dangerous," he scolded. "Maybe you'll listen next time."

He knew Hintsuli hadn't seen a ghost. Sakote had chanted the words of protection to keep the white healer's *kokoni* away. It was probably only Hintsuli's guilty imagination that made him believe he'd seen the spirit of the dead man.

But Hintsuli wasn't satisfied.

"You don't believe me," the boy said with a glower. "Come see for yourself then. He is terrible—all white, like ashes. His robe is white deerskin, so thin you can see the trees through it. His hair is the color of fallen leaves and longer than grandfather's. And he moans." Hintsuli's face became grim. "It is the song of the dead."

Sakote wondered at this. Something *had* frightened Hintsuli. He could feel the boy's heart hammering like a woodpecker as he held him against his leg.

"You've seen this with your own eyes?" Sakote asked.

The boy nodded.

"And you're sure it wasn't a white deer or—"

"It was the *kokoni* of the white man," he insisted, adding, "and he was dancing the dance of the dead."

Sakote scowled. What could Hintsuli have seen? He stared at the boy a long while, and then sighed. He'd have to save his carving for another day. Clearly, Hintsuli would give him no rest until he solved the mystery of the white man's *kokoni*.

Sakote ignored the dubious glances cast his way by the women, who might doubt his wisdom, but wouldn't dare to challenge the son of a headman. He shrugged on his deerskin cloak, retrieved the stone knife and broken point, and, as a measure of caution, slung his bow and a quiver of arrows over his shoulder. If Hintsuli *had* seen something, Sakote was certain it was mortal, and therefore vulnerable to the weapons of man.

"Come," he said. "Show me this *kokoni* of yours."

Sakote slipped carefully, slowly, silently through the stand of pines until he could just glimpse the healer's house between the sprays of green needles. Hintsuli, obediently quiet, tugged at the back of Sakote's breechcloth. Sakote nodded once. There *was* a figure standing before the cabin. For a moment, his eyes tricked him, and his heart tripped as he thought maybe Hintsuli was right, that it was the healer's ghost. Then he frowned at his own foolishness.

He had to get closer to get a better look. Indicating with a movement of his palm for Hintsuli to stay there, he crept through the manzanitas until he could get a better angle on the dwelling.

Hintsuli was right about one thing. Sakote *could* see the trees through the thin white wisp of a garment. But that wasn't all he could see. His breath caught in his chest as a light breeze caught the fabric, pressing it close against a body that was not only mortal, but unmistakably female.

Her skin was as pale as acorn milk, and the long curls spilling over her shoulders gleamed in the sun like a field of yellow grass. She had a delicate appearance that reminded him of a slender flower blowing in the wind. Where her garment clung to her, he could see the outline of her gently flaring hips, the peaks of her breasts, and the intriguing spot where her legs were joined, and the thought of all those womanly curves, barely concealed, fired his blood. She turned toward him then, and he saw her face was radiant with some secret joy. Gazing at her, Sakote felt that joy enter his own spirit. For a long moment, he couldn't breathe, but stood entranced by the white woman's magic, drinking in her power, feeling his heart beat strong, as if for the first time.

Then a sudden rattle came from a clump of manzanita close to where he'd left Hintsuli. The woman heard it, too, and whipped around, her eyes wide. She clutched a white man's long rifle before her, and it was pointed near the place where Hintsuli was hiding.

Sakote didn't even think. In one smooth movement, he nocked an arrow to his bow and aimed for the woman's heart.

A good warrior would have shot instantly. He should have. But something in the woman's magic, something about the way her hands trembled on the weapon, made him hesitate.

The gun wavered before her for an interminable time, but she finally lowered it. Another rustle of the brush revealed the source of the noise—a mother quail with her brood of chicks. The woman pressed her palm to her breast.

She laughed in relief, her voice as playful as a babbling creek. "Are you my big hulking beast then?" she said as the quail scurried in a straight line across the grass. "And you're so proud of your children that you've brought them marching by my house? Well, a good morning to you," she said, bowing her head, "even if you did scare the devil out of me."

Sakote frowned. Who was this woman who spoke with the animals?

"You stay there," she told the quail, "while I fetch my sketchbook."

Sketchbook. That word was strange to Sakote's ears. Sketchbook. Maybe it was another weapon. He should get Hintsuli out of danger. The woman twirled and disappeared into her house. Only then was he able to thaw himself from his shooting stance. As swiftly as he could, he shouldered his bow, returned for his little brother, and set off through the wood for his village.

"I told you it was a *kokoni*," Hintsuli boasted when they were out of hearing.

"It's not a *kokoni*." Sakote spoke the truth. The lady was no evil spirit. She was far more dangerous than a *kokoni*. She was white, and she was a woman. "It's Coh-ah-nuya," he lied.

Hintsuli's eyes grew as round as river pebbles. Coh-ah-nuya was a horrible old woman who ate children for supper. She was imaginary, of course, but useful for the disciplining of young boys. And Sakote would rather frighten his little brother with a lie than risk encountering the white woman again.

"Coh-ah-nuya," Hintsuli repeated with hushed reverence.

"Don't go near that *hubo* again," Sakote warned, stomping carelessly off through the leaf fall.

He didn't know why, but now that the danger was past, he felt irritable, as if the wind drove thistles against his naked back. There was something about that woman, some secret power she possessed, that disturbed him. He should have pierced her heart with an arrow the moment she took aim at Hintsuli, he thought with self-disgust. She could have ended his life with a single bullet. His little brother relied on him for protection, and Sakote had frozen like a startled deer. Something had stopped him, some force he couldn't name, and he swore he'd break his bow before he let anyone make him feel that helpless again.

The gun exploded, nearly deafening Mattie and knocking her shoulder out of its socket, despite the steadying grip Swede had demonstrated. Everyone peered forward through the puff of smoke.

"Didn't even hit the tree," Granny at last proclaimed.

Zeke punctuated her statement with a spit of tobacco.

"Gor', 'tis only the lass's first time," Tom said, hooking his thumbs in his suspenders.

"The first time *I* ever shot a gun, it near blew up in my hand," one of the Campbell boys assured her.

And then everyone else joined in with so many words of advice and encouragement that Mattie could scarcely sort them out.

She couldn't help but smile, despite the ringing in her ears and the ache in her shoulder. The miners of Paradise Bar had cleaned up "real nice," in Swede's words. Today their faces were scrubbed, if not shaved, and most of them looked as if they'd actually run a comb through their hair. If their clothes still had a reddish cast to them from the dust that seemed to permeate everything, it wasn't their fault. There wasn't a decent laundry to be found north of Marysville.

The church service had been the strangest she'd ever attended. Tom Cooligan, who was as near they had to a minister, presided over the informal gathering—miners seated on several three-legged stools and rough-hewn wood chairs pulled up under the outdoor altar of a cedar. There were only a half dozen Bibles between the lot of them, and the men crowded around the books as if seeing them for the first time.

Which Mattie suspected was true. Halfway through the sermon—an extemporaneous outpouring about the sufferings of humanity, centering largely on the sufferings of the Irish in particular and liberally laced with that country's wit and love for truth-stretching—Mattie realized that this was not an ordinary Sunday exercise. A good quarter of the miners were missing—gone to work their claims. Those who remained looked anything but comfortable. The men who sported cravats tugged at them. Some shifted on their perches, as if eager to be done. A few drifted off to sleep. Mattie saw a bottle of spirits being passed down the back row. And those who studied the Scripture most intently exchanged nervous looks with Mr. Cooligan, like stage actors waiting for cues.

Bless their hearts, Mattie realized, they'd done this for *her*. They probably never congregated for worship, not a bunch of straggling men, far from the influence of home and family. They'd honored her by sprucing up and dusting off their Good Books so her husband-to-be could be buried with grace.

The funeral was thankfully brief. As the makeshift plank coffin was lowered to its final resting place, Frenchy delivered an eloquent eulogy. The Campbell lads put their backs and shovels to covering the grave, and Swede gently led her toward a huge oilcloth-covered table of split logs, where the rest of the miners began laying out a feast of sorts.

Mattie was half-starved. She hadn't eaten any supper, and this morning, she'd been so busy defending her home and sketching woodland creatures that she'd only stuffed a morsel of jerky into her mouth for breakfast.

Now they treated her like a queen. Tom brought her a kerchief for a napkin, and Frenchy poured her a tin cup of coffee, which was as black as coal tar and just about as tasty. Amos served as cook, presiding over his outdoor kitchen— which consisted of pots and pans roosting on rocks of varying heights around a bed of coals—with all the panache of a medieval alchemist. He served up slices of smoky ham and, of course, a cauldron of beans that had probably been cooking for days. He fried up a pan of potatoes and onions, throwing in a tin of oysters for good measure. And for dessert, he set four knobby-crusted dried apple pies to baking over the embers.

After Mattie was served, the men wolfed down slabs of ham and bowls of beans as if they were the last in all the world, which couldn't be further from the truth. They made quick work of the pies and slugged down the bitter black coffee, chewing up what they couldn't drink.

Following the banquet, Billy and Bobby Cooper, blushing furiously, their hats in their hands, provided entertainment with their rendition of "Clementine." Their mournful harmony resembled the cry of a coyote Mattie had heard coming up the canyon, but she applauded enthusiastically at the conclusion of the song.

Tom Cooligan followed, playing a merry tune on a tiny tin whistle, and Amos took a break from his cooking to sing a slave song his father had taught him.

The men adamantly refused Mattie's help in cleaning up, which she would have been glad to do, seeing that they mostly just wiped down the plates with dirty kerchiefs and stacked them up for the next meal.

After that, the thread of piety began to unravel. A few men wandered off to play cards on a blanket spread over a patch of ground. A couple set up a table for monte. Some grabbed up their picks, pans, and shovels, and lit out to work their claims. Others resigned themselves to an afternoon in the shade with a jug of fermented cider for companion.

Even Tom, who'd preached the word of God all morning, couldn't resist the lure of commerce. He set up a desk of sorts, covered with a square of blue chintz, where, for a spoonful of gold dust, he would scribe letters for those who couldn't write. Mattie noted with some surprise that it was his hand that had penned Dr. Harrison's return letter to her.

Two Mexican brothers slumped against a tree on a brightly colored woven blanket, their hats pulled down over their eyes, and dozed. Amos left with a nod of his head to go visit a friend in the valley. Frenchy eyed the monte table, but chose instead to keep Mattie company.

And now she was learning to shoot a gun. Swede had reloaded the rifle and had his big arms wrapped rather familiarly around her, nearly swallowing her up as he guided her aim toward the row of empty tin cans perched on the branch of the live oak.

"That's it, ma'am. Slow and steady. Just squeeze it nice and..."

The report came earlier than she expected, and her elbow was thrown back again, this time banging hard into Swede's belly. He grunted, staggering back a pace, and she turned in horror to apologize. But the rifle was pointed at him now, and he stepped judiciously backward, throwing up his arms. She wheeled toward the others in turn, who did likewise.

"Perhaps," Frenchy suggested, licking his lips nervously, "*Mademoiselle* would care to lower her weapon, eh?"

Mattie did so at once. "I'm sorry. I didn't..."

The Campbell boys sprang to her rescue.

"Why, that's all right, ma'am."

"Don't you worry none."

"Why, the first time *I* ever—"

"She hit the tree!"

Mattie spun around to look. The cans still stood in their jaunty little line, taunting her.

"See there?" the youngest Campbell said. "Right below the burl. That's your bullet hole, ma'am."

Mattie grinned, despite the fact she'd missed her target by

nearly a yard. There it was indeed. A bullet hole. Proof that she could fire a rifle and hit...something.

"My aim isn't very good," she admitted.

"Ah, but your form," Frenchy said with a wink, "she is perfect."

"Now, ma'am," Swede told her, "you gotta hold on to that pistol like a runaway mare."

Mattie nodded solemnly. She'd never ridden a runaway mare. She'd never even sat astride a horse. She *had* ridden a mule on her recent journey, but it ran about as fast as molasses in winter.

"I'll try," she promised. This time she'd be ready for the noise. She squeezed her eyes shut.

Swede, in a show of staunch bravery, resumed his position as instructor. He helped her steady the rifle toward the target.

"She cain't shoot straight with her eyes closed," Granny muttered.

Mattie reluctantly opened her eyes and sited along the barrel toward the first tin on the left.

"Real gentle now," Swede whispered. "Slow...slow..."

The tin on the far right jumped off the branch almost before she heard the bang from the gun. Then a wild whoop went up from the men around her.

"Yippee!"

"She done it!"

"Shit-howdy! I mean, shoot!"

"Ma'am, you blowed a hole clean through that one!"

Mattie's grin went as wide as her bullet had. The Campbells hooted and hollered and tossed their hats in the air. Swede clapped her hard on the back, and then blushed at his own roughness. Granny applauded. Even Zeke's narrowed eyes twinkled at her as he nodded his approval.

"The bears and the wildcats and the Indians," Frenchy said, "they had better watch out for you, no?"

Mattie smiled. With her present skills, if she aimed at an Indian's heart, she'd be lucky to shoot the feather off his headdress. But she'd improve. There was plenty of time to practice. In another fifty or so attempts, she'd be as handy with a gun as a mountain man.

By the end of daylight, she was weary and out of ammunition. The Campbells escorted her safely home, where she fell onto her cot in exhaustion. Her arm quivered like a baby bird, and her shoulder felt like it had been kicked by a mule about a hundred times. Lord knew how it would feel tomorrow.

She wearily punched her pillow flat and smirked. Some mountain man she was.

CHAPTER 6

Mattie hadn't used a broom since the time she'd picked up the maid's when she was twelve years old, only to have it slapped out of her hand by her Aunt Margaret. But she soon found there was no trick to it, and despite the tenderness of her shoulder, by late morning, every cobweb, ash, and ball of lint had been swept from the tiny room and out the door.

Encouraged by the improvement, she decided to make use of the scraps of dirty calico drooping on nails stuck into the walls. She ripped them down, wet them in the bucket of water she'd hauled up from the creek, and set about wiping down the shelves, table, chairs, even the stove, which blackened the fabric beyond redemption.

Of course, she thought, tossing the rags into the inky water and flopping down on the bed, now something would have to be done about the enormous cracks in the walls. Apparently, wallpaper was out of the question. More fabric was in order, she supposed, something in a cheery yellow, something flowery. She'd have to send for some chintz from Marysville the next time the express man came. By then, with any luck, she'd have harvested enough gold from the good doctor's claim to pay for improvements.

The following month she'd purchase a new down mattress and coverlet. Then she'd order new oilcloth for the table, curtain fabric, and a pane of real glass for the window.

If she planned carefully, setting aside the profit she didn't need for food and a new frock now and then, by the end of the year she might have, if not a mansion, at least a well-furnished cottage of which she could be proud.

She let her gaze drift to the tools propped in the corner—the pickaxe, shovel, and miner's pan. Tomorrow she'd make her first attempt at gold panning. Thank God there was gold in California, or she might find herself destitute indeed. There was no occupation for a decent lady with limited domestic talent, unless she resigned herself to becoming wife to one of the callus-handed miners of Paradise Bar.

It shamed her to realize she wasn't honestly ready to settle down, despite the fact that marriage had brought her here in the first place. Now she considered Dr. Harrison's passing a blessing in disguise. She might have found herself shackled to a man who gambled every afternoon and drank himself senseless every night. In fact, if the collection of empty bottles behind the house and the half-drained flask of spirits Mattie found tucked among the calomel pills and quinine powder in his black bag were any indication, the doctor had imbibed to excess.

No, Mattie would take her chances first with the Harrison claim, a fertile plot of streamside land with treasure ripe for the picking.

Today, however, she'd put her house in order and learn to cook.

Now that the cabin was free of dust, she felt safer starting a fire for her midday meal. She tucked a couple of chunky logs inside the stove and used Amos's trick for romancing the flame, cramming handfuls of dry pine needles between the pieces of wood. The fire caught on the first match, and ten minutes later, still burning, it chewed slowly away at the undersides of the logs.

A victorious thrill coursed through her until she realized she had to fetch another bucket of water for the beans and coffee. Peering in anxiously at the blaze and adding one more log for good measure, Mattie prayed it wouldn't extinguish itself. She dumped the dirty water next to a pine sapling off the porch and scurried off to refresh her supply.

Thankfully, the fire was still burning when she returned. She distributed the water between the pots for coffee and beans, saving out a little to mix with the flour and the sourdough starter Amos had given her to make biscuits. A half hour later, her first home-cooked meal bubbled and baked atop the stove.

Dusting the flour from her hands, Mattie decided to do a bit of drawing while the beans simmered. A pair of baby blue jays had recently hatched in a nearby nest lodged in the low crook of a sugar pine, and she wanted to capture the fuzzy-headed, greedy-beaked creatures in her sketchbook.

She clamped a pair of pencils between her teeth and, sliding the finished drawings from her portfolio onto the table, tucked the sketchbook under her arm. There was just enough time before the biscuits baked to make a decent drawing.

Of course, once she'd sketched the nest, complete with intertwined twigs, bits of eggshell, and scrawny chicks with gaping maws, Mattie spied a wild tiger lily hidden among the grass, begging to be rendered, its black spots stark against the bright orange hue of its petals. Mattie couldn't resist. And after that, she spied a tiny lizard sunning itself on a rock in its mottled gray armor, flexing its elbows and winking its sleepy eyes. She'd wandered far from the cabin, putting the finishing touches on a study of lichen lace on rough oak, when she remembered the biscuits.

PROUD MOTHER.

Hintsuli's heart fluttered as he held the thin white hide between his trembling fingers, staring at the...what did his friend Noa call them? ..."letters" at the bottom.

He should not be here in Coh-ah-nuya's cabin. Sakote had warned him away. The child-eater might return and want to add him to her supper.

But Hintsuli was transfixed by the quail on the strange hide, the quail that he could see, by the pale sunlight leaching through the cloth window, were real, but somehow not real. He ran his thumb over the feathers. He could feel nothing. The quail lived on the piece of hide. They looked like they might scurry off at any moment, but something kept them there. Magic. Coh-ah-nuya's magic. The quail spirits were trapped on the hide. Coh-ah-nuya had trapped them.

The bitter smoke of Coh-ah-nuya's supper was beginning to fill the cabin when Hintsuli heard a noise from outside. His heart bounded against his ribs. Coh-ah-nuya returned! He must run! If she caught him...it was too terrible to think about.

He glanced at the magic hide. Sakote had told him it was wrong to take the things of the white man. But he couldn't leave the quail behind.

Clutching it to his belly, he slipped out the gap in the window's cloth covering and lit lightly on the grass outside.

Wonomi, The Great Spirit, was with him, for the woman didn't see him, even when he crept past the entrance of her *hubo*.

When he reached the forest, he ran. And he kept running until his chest ached.

He stopped not far from his village, but he wouldn't go there yet. Sakote had told him yesterday to stay away from the white man's camp, from Coh-ah-nuya, and he had disobeyed. If Sakote found out... Hintsuli let out a great sigh, imagining his brother's fierce frown.

Hintsuli wasn't to blame. He couldn't resist adventure. Even his sister said he was cursed with the curiosity of the raccoon.

He flopped down on a mossy mound and gazed up at the pine boughs overhead, woven together like a Konkow basket. Hintsuli wasn't afraid of the white man. The *willa* were interesting. They had food that came in little cans and knives made of shiny metal. Their faces were full of hair, like the bear, and their skin was sometimes pale like moonlight and sometimes as red as sunset. They didn't gather acorns or seeds or grasshoppers, but were given gifts of food by men who arrived every new moon on *lyktakymsy*—riding-dogs— which Noa called "horses." They didn't hunt for fish in the streams, but instead searched for little yellow rocks that made them whoop with joy. And they had...toys.

Noa had given him the white man's spinning toy. It had power. Hintsuli would sit in one place while the sun walked across the sky, spinning and spinning it. He could keep it spinning by itself for as long as it took Sakote to eat a bowl of acorn mush. It was a magic toy, and Hintsuli wanted another one of the white man's playthings.

He rested his head against the lichen-covered oak trunk and looked at the quail on the hide again. This was surely a magic toy. Maybe he could learn its secret. If he discovered how to release the quail spirits, maybe he could use the magic hide himself. He glowered hard at the flat gray birds. If he set them free, if he made the hide empty, he could fill it again with whatever he wanted. He could trap bad spirits there. His eyes widened. He could trap Coh-ah-nuya there! How proud Sakote would be then. The tribe would sing victory songs for him, and the Konkow people would tell his story for many leaf-falls to come.

For a long time he sat in the speckled sunlight, concentrating, frowning at the hide, pleading silently with Wonomi, but the quail stuck fast.

With a sigh, he carefully folded the hide and tucked it into his breechcloth. He must return to the village now, before Sakote began to worry. Perhaps it wasn't the right time. Perhaps the hide's magic wouldn't work now. He would carry it with him until the time was right, until Wonomi granted him the power to use it.

By the time Mattie dashed in the door, the cottage was filled with noxious gray smoke and the biscuits were burned to charcoal. Upon closer inspection, she found the coffee a thick black tar that clung to the sides of the pot, and the handful of beans, still hard as pebbles, had swollen to proportions fit for an army.

"Damn!" she shouted for the first time in her life, waving the blanket from her bed to shoo the smoke out the door.

When the haze diminished, she sank dismally onto the stool in the middle of the room, which tipped back and forth on its mismatched legs—just for spite, she was sure. The day was getting on. There wasn't time to cook another supper. Reluctantly, for she knew they were hard to come by, she took a tin of peaches down from the shelf and made a meal of the sweet fruit. At this rate, she thought, in another month she'd be able to fit *two* of her into the rich satin ball gowns she'd left in New York.

It took Mattie the better part of an hour and the last of her strength to scrub the burnt residue from her pots. By then, so little daylight remained that she had to light several candles to see.

She'd tossed her new sketches atop the old on the table, and she took a moment to study them now. The baby blue jays made her smile with their fuzzy, wrinkled necks and ugly, straining beaks. The lichen had been difficult to depict, with its curious texture and convoluted form, but she'd managed to recreate the contrast of the tiger lily's spots without the use of color, which pleased her.

Shuffling through the old sketches, she could see improvement. These newer illustrations possessed more detail, more life. The pencil strokes were surer, well-defined, bold. The animals looked as if they might leap off the...

Mattie frowned and perused the drawings again. Something was missing.

PROUD MOTHER—her sketch of the quail. It should be on top. She leafed through the pages. Nothing. One by one, she sorted through them again. There were drawings of monkeys and Panama natives, New York harbor and the Sacramento dock, renderings of old men and young squirrels, dozens of tiny studies of branches and hands and blossoms. But nowhere could she locate her family of quail. She glanced quickly around the room. Where had she left the drawing? It wasn't as if there were many places for it to hide.

She overturned pots, searched under bedding, lifted the sack of flour, emptied her carpetbag, and even peered into the chipmunk's escape hole, wondering if he'd decided to steal the drawing for his own parlor. But it was nowhere to be found.

"Damn," she muttered again, vaguely wondering if she was picking up the language of the miners.

Her stomach growled an ode to failure, and with a vexed puff of air, she blew out the last light, unlaced her shoes in the dark, and burrowed into her bed to hide from her disappointment.

"Where's my sister?" Sakote's harsh demand and the fist he snagged in the rough fabric of Noa's shirt clashed with the serene evening air of the Konkow village. "What have you done with her?"

Sakote's nerves were already stretched taut. His little brother had worried him, disappearing all day, and he'd given the boy a stern scolding. Now Noa had shown up without Towani.

The last smoke of the cooking fire rose like a wisp of spider's thread against the violet sky, and the stars shimmered silently. But Sakote felt far from peaceful.

"She's fine," Noa insisted. "She's in my cabin. She's got womenfolk all around her and every man in the valley ready to put a slug into the first fool who lays a hand on any of them. She's safer there than here, and we both know it."

Sakote caught the inside of his cheek between his teeth and stared hard at Noa. At long last, he sighed and nodded, letting him go. "She's shared her body with you then?"

Noa's eyes widened, and he grabbed Sakote by the front of his deerskin cloak, hauling him forward until they stood nose to nose. "That's none of your concern. Damn, Sakote!"

Sakote reared his head back and looked haughtily down his nose. "It *is* my concern. She's my sister."

Noa glared at him a long while. Finally he released Sakote, shaking his head. "No."

"No?" Sakote frowned.

"No." Noa crossed his arms over his chest.

"This is not good," Sakote told him. "For your spirits to join, you must join your bodies. Until she goes to your bed," he said, lowering his voice to whisper what they both knew, "my sister's spirit is still joined with that *hudesi,* the one who raped her. His *kokoni*—"

"Don't chatter at me with all your *kokoni* nonsense. Towani isn't ready. She needs time to...to recover. You don't just grab a woman and go at her like that." He snapped his fingers, a trick Sakote had never quite been able to master.

Sometimes Sakote didn't understand Noa. If Towani wanted Noa, and Noa wanted Towani, it seemed foolish for them to sleep apart. He sighed again.

"Anyway," Noa said with a sniff, "that's not why I came. I think we've got big trouble. Amos came to visit me yesterday. They have a new resident in Paradise Bar. A woman."

Sakote stiffened. The image of a sheer white gown and long tawny hair danced through his thoughts.

"But not just any woman," Noa continued. "That doctor? The *hudesi* you're talking about? This lady was going to be his missus."

Sakote's breath caught. Missus? The white woman with the gun was supposed to marry *him*—his sister's defiler? What kind of woman would share her body with such a monster?

"She got to Paradise Bar," Noa continued, "and there was her husband-to-be, laid out in his Sunday best, dead as last year's claim." He scratched the back of his neck. "Towani is upset. She says she's got to take the woman in, going on about it being her fault that the woman is alone. But I don't have room for an extra boarder, and I don't think the lady would be keen on the idea anyway, what with—"

"The tribe will take her in." Sakote said it without thought and accepted it without question. The Konkow always took in the defenseless families of warriors they'd slain. In his village lived members of the tribe who'd been born of their enemy, the Yana. They'd been adopted so long ago that few remembered they hadn't always been Konkow. If the white healer had left behind a wife, it must be so with her as well.

"Take her in?" Noa shook his head. "I don't know. White women don't take too kindly to being told what to do and where to go."

"The way is clear," Sakote insisted. "The Konkow must care for her. It's what my people have always done." Yet even as he said the words, doubt crept in to taunt him. What would the miners think about his bringing a white woman amongst his tribe?

"But like I tried to tell Towani," Noa said, "there are plenty of white folks who'd be happy to take her off your hands. Every miner I know would give the shirt off his back just to have a woman to wash it. And just because Amos says she isn't a miner, but a real lady from back East who wouldn't know pepper from gunpowder and probably never touched a broom in her life doesn't mean she can't learn."

Sakote wondered if that was true. Was the woman that ignorant? Perhaps her speaking with the quail wasn't a sign of magic after all, but of simple-mindedness. If she didn't know how to pan for gold, she wouldn't last a week in the camp, where the white man lived not on Wonomi's gifts, but on what spoons full of yellow dust could buy. She needed a man to care for her, or she would die. But surely the odds of her finding a new husband were good. Not only was there a shortage of females in the mining camp, but the white woman was young and beautiful, the kind of wife any man would be proud to...

He frowned at the disturbing direction of his thoughts, then came to a decision. "Tell my sister that I'll watch over the white woman for the passing of one moon. If no *willa* offers to take her, then she will have a home with the tribe. *Akina*, it is so."

"That's real generous of you," Noa said. Both of them knew it wouldn't come to that, but Noa seemed thankful to have good news to relay to Towani.

Sakote knew he was doing the right thing. If the woman died, Towani would be stained not only by the doctor's death, but by that of the white woman and the generations of offspring they might have had. Only if the woman lived could Towani's spirit be redeemed. As long as Sakote kept an eye on the white woman, the doctor's *kokoni* would not haunt the Konkow. And by the next moon, the woman would certainly find a husband among her own people.

But before Sakote risked spying upon the white woman, he had to know one thing.

"Tell me, my brother," he said, bending close and speaking softly, fearing the word might possess some mystical power. "What is a...sketchbook?"

CHAPTER 7

A good night's sleep gave Mattie the determination to face another day. With the sunshine pouring across her sill like buttermilk and the sparrows and robins beckoning in sweet counterpoint, it was all she could do not to leap from her bed and rush outdoors. She dressed in her oldest chemise, hastily brushed and tied back her hair, and tugged on the oversized pair of knee-high boots the doctor had left behind. With the pan, the pickaxe, a stick of jerky, and a little canvas bag for gold, she set off for the Harrison claim.

At first it was great fun. The claim consisted of a piece of staked creekbed about forty feet long and fifteen feet across, situated in a sunny spot along the sparkling water. Her neighbors were already hard at work when she arrived, but they gave her a nod and a friendly "good morning." The air was clear, the sky cloudless, and the water gurgled and swirled happily along banks lined with reeds and tree roots and mosses. Insects stitched at the air, and birds sang a busy symphony over the percussive barks of chipmunks. The odor of pinesap mingled with bay, and the breeze brought a delicate perfume of mixed wildflowers across the stream.

Mattie dawdled at the task of panning, observing her fellow miners a long while before she began to chip gingerly at the streambed herself. She carefully scooped up a modest amount of gravel, circled the pan gently so as not to splash her skirts, and allowed the water to lap just at the toes of her boots. Which she soon discovered was completely ineffective.

No, if she wanted gold, she'd have to roll up her sleeves, hike up her skirts, and wade into the thick of things.

Before long, Mattie stood knee-deep in the midst of the stream, her drenched skirt splayed atop the water's surface like a spent blossom. Tendrils of her hair had come loose from their ribbon and curled down over her forehead. Her legs shivered with cold while her cheek blushed from the bold kiss of the sun. The swirl of the gravel in the gold pan was hypnotic, and Mattie soon found a comfortable rhythm of movement.

But as time wore on, her feet grew numb, her face began to tingle with heat, and the pan became heavy. Her eyes were exhausted from hunting for the elusive yellow rock that she learned, to her utter humiliation, looked nothing like the shiny flakes she'd so enthusiastically displayed for her fellow miners, the metal the old-timers called "fool's gold." To her dismay, despite panning all day, she didn't find a single speck worth anything.

Mattie trudged back toward her cabin as the sun set, trying to ignore the fact that her wet skirts and her spirits grew heavier with each step. There was no cause for concern, she reasoned, fighting to keep despondency at bay. After all, it was only her first try. Things would improve tomorrow. She'd get an earlier start. Tomorrow she'd "find the color." Surely there was gold to be had or the residents of Paradise Bar would go home, wouldn't they?

So intent was she on keeping her chin up that she never

noticed the pair of jet-black eyes watching her every move as she climbed the wooded rise toward Paradise Bar.

Sakote heard the woman slogging through the wood long before he saw her. He grimaced. She'd never be able to hunt her own rabbits if she always made such noise. From the sharp smell of burnt food he had detected while circling her empty cabin earlier, she didn't have much skill in cooking either. He hoped Noa was right, that some miner would take her to wife and provide for her, for she appeared to him to be as useless a woman as he'd ever seen.

Until she emerged from the trees. Then Sakote felt the scorn drain from him like water from a fishing seine.

By The Great Spirit, she was beautiful. Even weighed down by the heavy miner's pick and in her long brown dress coated with red mud, she walked with her head held high. Her hair had come loose from its tie, leaving wisps as feathery as eagle down around her face. Her cheek was streaked with dirt, but she looked as proud and noble as a Konkow warrior.

His breath caught in the trap of his ribs, and his skin burned as if the sun still blazed at the top of the sky, searing him with mysterious fire.

Perhaps he was wrong about the white woman, he thought, as she neared the cluster of cedars concealing him. Perhaps there was more to her than he'd first imagined. She possessed some inner strength, some core of rock-hard will that might allow her to survive after all. The best hunters were not always those with the keenest eye or the strongest arm, but those with the most fortitude.

Then the woman stumbled directly before him, only a spear's length away, knocking the pick from her shoulder, and he went as still as stone. This close, he saw her mask of confidence slip and glimpsed a trembling in her pointed chin as she stooped to retrieve the tool. Unbidden, his heart leaped out to her, and he nearly followed its path in an irresistible impulse to help her with her burden. He stopped himself in time, but not before he felt the full effect of her vulnerability in the softening of her eyes.

Suddenly, Sakote feared he might not take another breath or another step. The woman's eyes...they were the same startling green as those of the white eagle that had come to him in his dream. The sight froze him like the snows of *komeni* froze the earth. What could it mean?

It must be magic, he thought. The woman must possess some enchantment. Sakote had never felt such...stirrings.

There could be no other explanation for it. After all, she was useless. She couldn't hunt. She couldn't cook. And from the sorrow in her face, she'd found no *oda*, no gold. Her skin was too delicate for the sun's light, and her body seemed too frail to even bear children. She was nothing but a burden. And yet...

He had this strange overpowering desire to care for her. He wanted to hunt for her, to bring her deer meat and acorn bread and rabbit fur blankets, to do something for her that would return the shimmer of joy to her eyes. It was foolishness, he knew, but as he followed her in silence, it felt as real as the earth beneath his feet.

All Mattie wanted to do, traipsing home after her grueling day of fruitless gold panning, was collapse in a pathetic heap, tell her growling belly to be quiet, and cry herself to sleep.

What was she going to do? How would she live? She couldn't even blame her bad fortune on lack of skill. Jasper and Red, up to their thighs downstream from her, had been only too delighted to tell her that Doc Jim hadn't found a nugget in weeks on his claim.

If that were so, if there was no gold left, how would she survive here? She scarcely had two pennies to rub together. She couldn't even afford the trip home.

Not that she wanted to go home. Not that she even *had* a

home. No, she was stuck in this God-forsaken hellhole until...

That finally made her smile, if only halfheartedly. God had most certainly not forsaken Paradise Bar. It was the most beautiful place she'd ever been.

She stopped and peered up at the pine tops swaying majestically in the last golden rays of the sun, and beyond them, the apricot-pink rosettes of cloud scudding across the wide sky. A red-tailed hawk winged up from one of the lofty spires and soared over the dense stand of trees, its high-pitched cry the only sound against the soft soughing of the breeze.

No, Mattie thought, this truly was Paradise, and God would find her a difficult Eve to cast out. She would dig in her heels and find something, anything, to earn her own way here—take in laundry, raise chickens, even learn to cook—anything short of giving up and relying on some hapless man to take her in.

Unfortunately, the young miner standing on her porch as she emerged from the wood didn't appear to concur. She watched him in silence as, unaware of her presence, he shifted restlessly from one foot to the other before the closed door, clutching a wad of wildflowers. He was one of the Cooper boys, either Billy or Bobby—she couldn't remember which. He finally cleared his throat and knocked softly on the door frame.

"I'm here," Mattie called from behind him, startling the poor boy so badly that he dropped the blossoms, scattering them across the pine planks.

"Oh! Oh...hello, m-ma'am," he stuttered. "I was, uh, well, I was in the, in the neighborhood and, uh..." His eyes trailed slowly down her dress, not so much in appreciation as in surprise.

"I've been panning," she explained.

One side of his mouth rose in an uneasy smile. "Find anything?"

"Only some muscles I'd forgotten I had," she said sheepishly, swinging the pick down from her shoulder.

He frowned, not quite understanding.

"Won't you come in?" she asked, frankly hoping he wouldn't.

But misfortune seemed her lot.

"I'd be much obliged, ma'am," he replied, glancing bleakly down at the flowers and deciding it was perhaps better to salvage his dignity and let them lie.

She resisted the urge to sigh and instead graciously invited him in.

The hairs along Sakote's neck bristled like a wolf's mane as he spied on the couple from the trees.

What was that boy doing at the white woman's house?

Sakote watched while they held a brief conversation on her porch and then entered the cabin and closed the door.

Of course, Sakote knew what the boy was doing, even though he pretended he didn't. He'd brought flowers for the woman. In the world of the *willa*, that meant one thing. He was courting her.

Sakote didn't know why, but this angered him. The boy was just that, a boy. He couldn't have lived more than fifteen leaf-falls. He'd probably never even hunted a deer or speared a fish. He couldn't provide properly for the white woman. She should have laughed at him and thrown him off of her doorstep.

But she hadn't. The clumsy boy had dropped his gift to her, littered her porch with the blossoms, and still she invited him into her home. It was...irresponsible.

Did she think a beardless, butter-fingered boy would make a suitable husband?

He spit derisively. She obviously didn't understand what made a good mate. This *willa* boy was so thin, he'd starve before the first frost of *se-meni.* He possessed neither the strength of the bear nor the cunning of the coyote. In fact, Sakote wondered scornfully if he was even of an age to father offspring.

The woman needed a man, someone to fill her drying racks with salmon and deer, a man who could build her a *hubo* to withstand the winds of *ko-meni,* a man who would keep her fat with child, a man like...

Sakote kicked at the dirt and glared at the cabin before he could finish the thought. Trickster Coyote must be playing with him to make him think such a foolish thing. No matter how the woman intrigued him, no matter how his heart leaped at the sight of her, they were from two different worlds. He was Konkow, and she was *willa.* He was the son of a headman, and she was the woman of a defiler. Better that she find a husband—any husband, even a bad one—among her own people.

Sakote knocked the back of his fist once against the trunk of an oak, and then turned to go. He had to get back home before he began thinking about silly things like picking bunches of blue flowers for the white woman.

The silence stretched awkwardly as the door closed behind Mattie and her guest. She stacked her tools in the corner and washed her hands in the bucket of water by the stove.

"Well..." Billy or Bobby, she wondered. "Can I offer you..." She perused her meager stores and forlornly settled on the last two gaily painted tins. "Peaches?"

His eyes lit up. "Oh, yes, ma'am."

She was afraid of that. Now she would be just one tin closer to starvation. She dried her hands, pulled up the stool for him, and, summoning up a brave smile, served them each a bowl of the precious fruit.

He polished off the lot of it with a happy grin.

"More?" she reluctantly asked from her perch at the edge of the bed.

"Oh, no, ma'am. My mama told me...well..." He blushed all the way to his ears. "It just ain't right to make a pig of myself."

Mattie didn't know what to say to that. She speared one of the sweet slices and chewed it slowly, pretending it was a three-course meal.

"Well, ma'am, what I...what I came for was to, well, to let you know that..." His gaze caught on something behind her, and he gladly changed the subject. "Hey, are those yours?"

She followed his stare to the mattress, where her sketches were scattered across the coverlet. She frowned. Hadn't she put them away?

"Uh, yes...yes, they're mine."

"Could I take a gander at them?"

"Mm-hmm." She was sure she'd tucked them back into her portfolio. But then she'd been in such a hurry to get to her claim this morning.

"These are...well, ma'am, these are just about the best pitchers I ever saw."

"They're only sketches," she said with a shrug.

"Well, they're damn good...I mean..." He blushed furiously. "Pardon me, ma'am."

Something about the drawings bothered her. She was almost positive she'd replaced them this morning. She recalled thinking that perhaps the wind had carried off her quail picture and that she didn't want to lose any more.

"They're awful good," he amended. "Why, I'll bet some of the boys'd be real happy to have their pitcher done so they could send it home."

Mattie was only half-listening. She was tired and baffled by the scattered sketches.

"Please, you'll have to forgive me, Billy…"

"I'm Bobby."

"Bobby. I'm really rather exhausted and—"

"Say no more, ma'am," he said, straightening. "I just wanted to stop by and let you know that if you need anything, why, I'd be plum happy to…you know…help or…do just…" His voice trailed off along with his nerve.

"I understand," she assured him. "Thank you."

"Thank *you*, ma'am, uh, for the peaches."

She was happier than was courteous to watch him depart. He couldn't be more than fourteen, bless his heart, barely out from under his mother's wing. The last thing she needed was a lovesick boy courting her.

Fetching a stick of jerky from the can, she sat on the bed to munch it and put her sketches back in order. To her astonishment, another drawing was missing, the one of the monkey in the tree along the Chagres River.

What was going on? Could Bobby have sneaked in her house and taken it before she arrived?

No, he'd been surprised by her drawings. He'd even said…what was it he'd said? That some of the boys might like to have their "pitchers" done.

She stopped chewing and swallowed the unwieldy lump of jerky. Was it possible? Would the miners pay to have their portraits drawn? Could she make a living with her pencil?

A pleasant thrill of hope coursed up her spine. Perhaps she wouldn't have to stand thigh-deep in the stream another day, swirling pans of dull sediment. Perhaps she wouldn't have to wash miners' shirts till her hands grew red and raw. Maybe she wouldn't need to bake pies all day long or scrub dishes all night. Maybe she could use her God-given talent to eke out some kind of existence here.

Of course, first she'd have to thwart the thief. If her art was going to be her livelihood, she couldn't give it away. Tomorrow she'd set a trap for the culprit. With any luck, she'd catch the villain red-handed.

By the time Mattie slipped between the bedlinens, she didn't care that her stomach still growled for food, that she'd hung her dress up filthy, or that the empty tin of peaches would be crawling with black ants by morning. She dreamed of the bright future before her and the sketches—her sketches—that would soon travel by mule and wagon and ship to destinations all over the world.

UMBRELLA.

It was a tree, Hintsuli guessed, but he'd never seen such a tree. Its huge leaves sprang up like a headdress of condor feathers, so long they drooped back toward the earth. Rain dripped in fat drops from the underside of the leaves. The trunk looked like it was painted in a Konkow basket design. But the tree wasn't as interesting as what was clinging to it, protected from the rain by the great leaves. Hintsuli was not sure what the creature was. It appeared to be a tiny, dark baby with a round face and big eyes. But it had a tail, and its arms and legs were long and thin. Hintsuli didn't know what it was, but now it belonged to him.

He held the skin out before him, so the animal seemed to dance in the flicker of the dying fire. He'd stolen the second hide this morning after Coh-ah-nuya had gone. All afternoon, he'd spoken to Wonomi, praying for a vision, pleading with The Great Spirit to reveal to him the magic of Coh-ah-nuya's hide. But still he couldn't free the animals.

He must go back to her *hubo* again tomorrow. It wasn't that difficult. He'd crept as easily as a mouse into the cabin twice already. Coh-ah-nuya, like the other *willa*, went to hunt for gold when the sun was up. As long as he was cautious, there was no danger.

Next time, he would take *all* the hides. Maybe they were powerless by themselves. Or maybe the charm was in the strange little sticks he'd seen beside the hides. He would take them, too. He must find the source of Coh-ah-nuya's power.

CHAPTER 8

Mattie realized, after having made a huge show of leaving her cabin at sunrise, slinging the pick over her shoulder and stomping across the clearing, whistling "O Susanna," that she'd only thought her plans through halfway. She shifted on her haunches in the clump of manzanita and wondered just what she'd do if she did spy the thief hanging about her cabin.

She'd left her rifle inside, which was probably just as well. How could she point a gun at someone who admired her work enough to steal it? Still, she thought as a pair of pesky gnats circled frantically in front of her face, she ought not to have left the weapon for the thief's use.

She wrinkled her nose as one of the gnats alit, attempted to slap it away, then froze in mid-swat as a movement from the edge of the wood caught her eye.

It was a little girl...or maybe a little boy. She wasn't sure. The poor thing was naked except for a small, fawn-colored square that hung fore and aft over the parts that would tell which gender the child was. Long, tangled hair as black as pitch hung past a pair of shiny dark eyes and over bony shoulders. The child's skin was the color of strong English tea, and by the gangly quality of the limbs, Mattie guessed the little urchin to be about six years of age.

A thrill of excitement shot through her as she watched the child steal with imperceptible noise across the clearing toward her cabin. She must be seeing her first Indian! Already she imagined the sketches she'd make—the little squaw or brave dancing before a fire in a feather headdress, riding bareback on a pony, standing proudly beside a teepee. She'd seen such drawings in the published journals of mountain men who had traveled West twenty years before, but none of them seemed to capture the vitality she saw now in the subject before her, that spirit the Pre-Raphaelite artists celebrated.

The child bypassed the front door of her cabin and crept instead over the windowsill, lifting the fabric flap and sliding in headfirst. Mattie smiled in triumph and waved away the bothersome gnats. She had her thief now.

Mustering up all the patience she could manage, she left her tools in the bushes and took one stealthy step after another toward the cabin till she stood on the pine planking of the front porch. She heard the telltale rustling of paper inside.

She'd have to move fast. By the looks of the wiry child, scampering out the window would be the work of an instant. Bucking up for the encounter, Mattie counted slowly and silently to three. Then she burst headlong into the cabin.

The boy—it *had* to be a boy—yelped and sprang up from the bed like a spooked kitten, straight up. Sketches and pencils scattered everywhere. Even before he came down, he was eyeing the window.

But Mattie was prepared. She slammed the door shut behind her and moved to block his path. She was ready for his flight to the sill. And she was ready for him to try to wrestle past her to the door. But she wasn't ready for his heart-rending scream of terror.

For an instant, she wondered if a bear had followed her into the cabin. Surely *she* couldn't instill such fear in the boy. But his eyes widened, and he continued to shriek, scrambling from one end of the bed to the other like a caged lion.

She wanted to catch him, but she didn't want to scare him. Using the universal placating gesture to calm the boy, she faced her palms toward him.

"It's all right. I won't hurt you," she said in her gentlest voice.

His gaze still bolted in panic around the room, and he continued to whimper, but at least he stopped flailing himself across the bed.

"That's it," she encouraged. "It's all right. I won't hurt you. I just want to..."

She took a tiny step closer, and he bounded from the bed toward the window, fast, but not fast enough to avoid the arm she hooked toward him.

"Wait!" she cried, hanging onto his waist as he dragged himself toward escape.

He almost made it to the sill, till Mattie managed to get both arms around his squirming torso.

He turned in her grasp then and fought like a wildcat, clawing and kicking and baring snowy teeth. His fist caught her tender shoulder, and she grunted in irritation, but she wouldn't let go. His heels drummed at her shins, and he gave her several sharp jabs in the ribs with his elbows, but she held fast. Then his pointy little fangs sank into her forearm. She yelped in pain and tossed him back onto the bed, holding his arms fast and sitting on him to keep him there.

Catching her breath, she glanced at her injured arm. The skin wasn't broken, but a double crescent of red throbbed where he'd bitten her. The boy still fought her with all the fury of a storm, but she had the advantage now. She watched through tendrils of her disheveled hair as his struggles weakened.

"I'm *not* going to hurt you," she reiterated, though she was sure he couldn't understand a word. "It's all right."

For a long while they stared at each other. He truly was a beautiful child, she decided, when his claws were sheathed. His skin was flawless and of such a rich color that it looked as if it radiated sunlight. His eyes, set deep within his face, above wide cheekbones and beneath slashing brows, were so dark as to be impenetrable. His pearly teeth hid now behind lips pressed tightly into a grim line. She wondered how long she'd have to sit on the pitiful child before that murderous look vanished from his gaze.

"You're a strong little boy, aren't you?" she asked, drawing an even fiercer frown from him. "I wonder what your tribe calls you. Spitting Wildcat? Charging Bear?" She glowered back at him. "Scowling Wolf?"

His small chest still rose and fell with rapid breaths, and she could see the quick beat of his heart in the hollow of his stomach. The poor lad couldn't understand a word she spoke. How could she assuage his fear?

"My name is Mattie. Mattie. Mattie."

The boy only stared at her.

"Actually Mathilda Hardwicke, but you may call me Mattie."

The boy's mouth parted just enough to murmur, "Coh-ah-nuya."

"Is that your name? Coh-ah—"

The boy winced as if she intended to strike him.

"I promise I won't hurt you." She tucked her lower lip thoughtfully under her teeth and considered the boy. Her Aunt Emily had taught her that when a lady was at a loss for words in conversation, she should find some common interest. But what could a properly schooled lady from the city possibly have in common with a little savage boy?

Of course.

He liked her drawings. Enough to steal them.

She smiled at him.

"You're my first benefactor, you know, although I must say the commission arrangements leave a bit to be desired."

The boy's arms relaxed infinitesimally beneath her grasp.

"Do you like my sketches?" She nodded to the drawing that lay beside his head.

He warily turned to peek at it.

"That's a steamship. I traveled aboard her to get here." She glanced toward another. "And that's the mule that carried my bag across Panama."

He shifted to look at the second drawing, and his fists unfurled.

"This one," she said, daring to release one of his wrists to hold the picture up for his inspection, "is a tiger lily I found in the meadow."

While he studied it, she let go of his other arm and picked up the rough sketch of an acorn.

"*Utim,*" he said at once.

"*Utim?*" Her heart fluttered.

"*Utim.*"

They were communicating. It was a heady feeling.

"*Utim!*" she cried, beaming.

Inspired, Mattie rifled through the scattered drawings until she found one of a chubby little boy clutching a tiny wooden sailboat to his chest.

The Indian boy took the page in both hands and studied the picture with all the solemnity of a jeweler inspecting a diamond through his loupe.

"Do you like it?"

"Toy," the boy whispered as clear as day.

Mattie gasped. How did he know that word?

"Toy," he repeated louder. Then he pierced her with his ebony gaze. "Toy?"

"Yes," she replied, unnerved. "Yes, it's a toy."

Unadulterated hunger instantly suffused the boy's face. He wanted that toy, more than he wanted anything, more than he feared her.

"Don't you have any toys?"

He was too transfixed by the sketch to listen to her. Slowly, cautiously, she shifted her weight off of him and took one of his small, warm hands in hers.

"Would you like to play with a toy?"

He glanced briefly at his hand trapped inside hers and set aside the drawing.

"Toy?" she asked, coming to her feet.

He scooted off the bed, his fear completely replaced by eagerness now.

Unfortunately, Mattie couldn't think of a single thing in the cabin she could call a toy. She cursed herself for her short-sightedness. It was as rude as inviting someone to tea when your cupboards were bare.

"Hmm." She tapped her chin and looked around the room.

"Hmm." He imitated her gestures, as if they were part of some mystical rite.

She bit back a grin. How adorable the little warrior was. She could hardly wait to draw...

Draw. The pencils. Of course.

She bent toward him. "Would you like to draw a picture?"

He cocked his head at her, one brow raised in inquiry.

"Come. I'll show you how."

With his help, she gathered up the drawings and pencils, and then pulled out two sheets of fresh paper from her portfolio. Settling him upon the stool, she placed the paper on the table before him and wrapped his fingers around a pencil.

"What shall we draw, hmm? Shall we start with something simple?" Standing behind him, she smelled the faint odor of smoke in his hair. "How about *utim*?"

"*Utim*."

She guided his pencil carefully around the curve of an acorn cap and along the smooth sides of the shell, shading the length of one side to give it the illusion of depth. When it was done, the boy dropped the pencil and excitedly picked up the page, examining it so closely his breath fluttered the paper. He turned it over and peered at the back side as well, as if he thought the object might actually have dimension.

She chuckled. His innocence was delightful. She wondered what his name was.

"My name is Mattie," she said, laying a palm across her bosom. "Mattie. What is your name?" She touched her fingertips to his chest.

He ignored her. He was far more interested in drawing than polite conversation. And, truth to tell, she could understand perfectly.

"Would you like to try another?"

The boy went through five sheets of paper over the next several hours, filling them front and back, corner to corner, before his little stomach began complaining.

A particularly loud growl made Mattie giggle, and the boy giggled back, the sound of his laughter like water bubbling over rocks. He quickly leafed through his drawings until he found the one of a small black bear she'd seen across the canyon on her way to Paradise Bar.

"*Pano*," he told her, then pointed to his stomach.

"*Pano*," she repeated with a grin. Then she growled and playfully tickled his belly. "Very hungry *pano*. We need to feed you, don't we?"

Mattie perused her shelves. There was still ample jerky,

but that was about all. The beans would take hours to cook, there was nothing she could do with the flour, and she doubted the child would be too enthused about a pot of coffee. Then her glance alit on the last tin of peaches, and she smiled.

"I'll bet you've never tasted the likes of these," she sang as she opened the can and dumped the last of the precious fruit onto a dish for him.

His eyes grew round with pleasure as he sampled the sweet peaches, and he cleaned his plate before Mattie could even set out the jerky. Her own stomach grumbled in complaint, but she was too preoccupied with indulging her guest to pay it any mind.

Watching him eat, she wondered again at his beauty. From paintings, she'd expected that Indians were squat and ugly, with weathered faces and lined mouths that turned down at the corners. This boy was far from unattractive. Why, with a good barbering and the proper clothes...

He looked up, rather nervously, she thought, which she supposed was natural. She'd been staring at him, after all, and rather openly. She politely lowered her eyes, and then, with an inspired grin, turned to rummage through her carpetbag for her comb.

"Would you like me to comb your hair?" she asked while he worked on his last piece of jerky.

He stared blankly at her. She ran the comb through the ends of her own hair to demonstrate, but he seemed unimpressed. She supposed even Indian boys couldn't get very excited about grooming.

"Here," she said, gently combing the very ends of his hair.

He gave a small sigh of defeat. Apparently, he knew the process then. He suffered in silence, only wincing once when she tugged at a particularly stubborn knot.

His hair was coarse and thick, straight as a horse's tail, and where she smoothed the tangles from it, it hung like a glossy gossamer veil past his shoulders. He sat patiently through her ministrations, and when she finished, she was sure that, aside from the uneven ends, his lush mane would have been the envy of any woman in New York.

"Now," she said, tucking the comb away, and drawing the boy to his feet, "what about the rest of you?" She cocked an eye at his wiry body. "I wonder..."

The doctor had left a few articles of clothing behind in his travel trunk. Removing the oilcloth-covered board that proclaimed it a dining table, Mattie opened the trunk and hauled forth a faded red calico shirt. She held it up to the child.

"Well, it's several sizes too large, but if we fold up the sleeves..."

She helped him slip his arms into the shirt and buttoned it all the way up. Then she rolled the sleeves back till they hung just above his wrists. It looked more like a dress than a shirt, but the vivid color contrasted beautifully with his black hair, and at least it would keep him warm. She only wished she had shoes to give him.

"My, don't you look handsome," she exclaimed, while he fingered the cloth in wonder.

But his interest in her ablutions waned quickly. By the envious glances he stole at his drawings, he obviously wanted to go back to the "toys."

"Shall we take them outside?" she asked, scooping up the pencils and several sheets of clean paper.

It surprised her to see how late the day had grown. Only an hour or so of sketching light remained. The sun cast long shadows from the swaying pines, and pie wedges of shade shifted across the flower-dotted meadow. Sparrows and finches flitted by too quickly to draw, making their last rounds through the branches. But Mattie had learned, if she sat still long enough, subjects would come to her. The boy sat beside her on the edge of the plank porch, pencil poised, mimicking her quiet vigil.

Sure enough, within a few minutes, a delicate buff-colored doe lifted her velvet muzzle at the far end of the clearing. Mattie touched the boy's arm.

"Look," she whispered.

As the deer picked her cautious way across the grass, nibbling at the tender shoots, Mattie discovered the twins behind her, a perfectly matched pair of spotted fawns tottering on pencil-thin legs.

"*Tem-diyoki*," the boy whispered.

"*Tem—*"

"*Diyoki*," he breathed.

Moving as imperceptibly as possible, Mattie brought pencil to paper and wrote the word, TEM-DIYOKI. Then she began to draw, scarcely looking at the page, only watching the doe grazing with her two babies.

The boy did likewise, and when Mattie hazarded a glance at his paper, she saw that, though his work was rough and done with an untrained hand, he added details he couldn't possibly see at this distance. The doe had long, curling eyelashes and the hint of a smile at the corners of her dark lips. The fawns' spotted fur stood up a little on their back, and he drew the black hooves with a clear split up the middle.

Mattie smiled. This was his world. He knew it far better than she. She could illustrate what she saw, but he sketched what he knew.

All at once, the doe's head lifted in alarm, her ears forward. She stood frozen for several seconds. Then, with a powerful bound, she fled with her babies into the woods.

Mattie wondered what had frightened them. She turned to shrug at the boy, but his attention was riveted elsewhere. He gasped, and Mattie followed his gaze. What she saw made her jaw go slack.

Death was coming. There was no other description for the grim beast that charged toward them. Another ten strides, and she'd be lucky to sputter out the Lord's Prayer before he devoured them both with those snarling white teeth.

CHAPTER 9

The boy trembled beside her, and before she could wonder at her own sanity, she thrust him behind her, placing her body solidly between the child and their attacker.

"S-stay back! I'm w-warning you!" she cried, painfully aware that stammering did nothing to enforce her threat. "Don't come any closer."

The splayed hand she held in front of her looked pale and useless against the menacing beast, which loomed nearer despite her admonitions, and she suddenly longed to have the butt of Doc Jim's rifle settled against her shoulder.

But it was too late. She couldn't abandon the boy clutching in terror at her skirts. Instead, she clasped the lad's arm with feigned assurance, squeezed her eyes shut, and prayed for a swift end.

He stopped mere inches from her, close enough for his warm breath to ruffle her hair. Lord, she could feel heat and strength and danger emanating from his body. And she could smell him. His scent was complex, as wild as the wood, a blend of sweet smoke and spicy laurel, of fresh trout and tanned leather. She dared not move. She dared not breathe.

As the seconds ticked by, measured by her racing heart, and no attack came, she finally risked peering through her lashes.

She wished she'd kept them closed. Her mouth went instantly dry. The savage towered over her, eclipsing the sun with his dark, shaggy head and leaving her eyes at the level of his formidable, muscular chest. He glared down at her with eyes as black as a raven's wing, eyes so steadfast and deadly in their perusal that his sudden snarl of "Hintsuli!" made her start in alarm.

The boy jerked behind her. Mattie shook in her boots, but refused to budge.

Then the attacker grew even more menacing. A deep breath swelled his chest, and his hands curved into fists the size of roasting hens.

"Hintsuli!" he growled again, narrowing his eyes to angry slits.

The boy whimpered in panic behind her, a string of words Mattie couldn't understand, but the pathetic sound plucked at her heartstrings and broke through her fear. She had no idea what the brute was demanding nor what he intended, but she'd be damned if she'd put up with his brand of bullying. She didn't care that the half-naked savage was twice her size and meaner than a bear. He had no business raging about, frightening little boys and defenseless women half out of their wits.

"N-now, listen, you!" she commanded, garnering his full attention. She swallowed hard. His eyes chilled her like chips of black ice. "You just g-go on and leave the boy alone. He's fine with me." She didn't know what she was promising, but she couldn't bear the thought of leaving the poor child in the hands of the vicious barbarian before her. "Go on," she said with a timid, dismissing brush of her hand. "Shoo."

The man's eyes hardened even more, while Mattie's knees turned to jelly. He slowly perused her face, tracing her hairline, lingering on her trembling lips, resting briefly in the hollow of her throat, where she was sure he could discern the fluttering of her heart. Dear God, she realized, the beast could probably snap the thin column of her throat in one of his great paws without a second thought.

Then, to her relief, the fury drained from his face. His brows still curved downward in irritation, but the cold fire disappeared from his eyes. He straightened and folded his arms across his chest.

The gesture should have eased her worries. After all, standing thus, he couldn't very well engage her in fisticuffs. But the posture made him look even more forbidding. Strands of glossy black hair slashed across his shoulders, allowing taunting glimpses of the considerable girth of his bare arms. They might be idle now, but the pure strength in those arms was glaringly apparent.

"Hintsuli," he said once more, but now his voice was low.

The boy peered around her skirts, and his face couldn't have looked guiltier if he stood beside a broken vase with a pea shooter. Slowly, he ambled forward, his head hanging low on his chest. He glanced balefully up at the stranger, then at her, and patted his chest.

"Hintsuli," he explained.

Mattie frowned. So Hintsuli was the boy's name. The man was summoning him then, not cursing him. He was calling...his son. Of course. She should have guessed. The family resemblance was obvious. The two shared the same dark scowl and flashing eyes, the same coppery skin, the same astonishingly beautiful...

She hauled her gaze away from the Indian. It wouldn't do to stare. The man clearly didn't want his son socializing with a white woman, and no doubt he felt the same way about her himself. Which was fine with her. After all, a person of such a volatile temperament could hardly be enjoyable company. And if Mattie had just for a moment imagined the stunning portrait she could draw of the noble savage, it was only a ridiculous flight of fancy. There were plenty of subjects from which to choose among the miners. Besides, she doubted the man could sit still long enough for a decent portrait.

Father and son were speaking to each other now in their soft, guttural language, the boy pouting, the man biting out his words. She caught that word, Coh-ah-nuya, on Hintsuli's lips more than once, and she noticed that the man actually looked discomfited at the mention of it.

With a scowl, he stooped to the boy and began unbuttoning the calico shirt.

"No," Mattie said, resting her palm for an instant on the back of the man's hand.

He glanced at her fingers, and she pulled away as if she'd been burnt.

"I mean, he may keep it."

The man continued to unfasten the shirt.

She tried again. "It's all right. I don't need it. He can have it." She pulled the collar of the shirt back around Hintsuli's neck. "Take it. Please. Take it."

The man looked up at her, and she wondered how he could still seem so overwhelming, crouching at her feet.

"I..." she said breathlessly, "I don't need it. It belonged to my...my husband."

The man's brows lanced sharply downward. He didn't bother unfastening the rest of the buttons. He tore the front of the shirt, and the remaining buttons popped off like kernels of dried corn over the fire.

Hintsuli wailed, and the man muttered something in hushed anger.

Abruptly, the boy stopped his tears and looked askance into his father's eyes. "*Hudesi*?" he asked.

The man shot her a disparaging glare and nodded. "*Hudesi.*"

The boy then let his father take the shirt from him. The man wadded it into a ball and cast it back toward the door.

Mattie knew she should bite her tongue. It was no concern of hers whether they took the shirt or not. It didn't matter if she never saw the two of them again. Why should she care that Hintsuli's father had looked at her as if she were the devil incarnate?

"You know, this wouldn't have happened," she said, wagging a finger at him, "if you hadn't let your son run around loose like a wild In—" She choked on her words.

The man gave her one last thorough inspection from head to toe that stole the breath from her before he grabbed Hintsuli by the hand and started off across the clearing.

She muttered after him. "And what kind of a mother is your wife to let a child his age gad about unsupervised?"

Mattie hadn't noticed before, paralyzed by fear, but now that she had the leisure to look, she saw that the man was dressed in no more clothing than the boy. As he ambled off, she could see all too clearly the bronzed contours of his back, his narrow hips, his muscular legs. The edge of his loincloth flapped up suddenly, revealing the hollow of one buttock, and her heart leaped into her throat. Sweet Lord, he was magnificent.

"Wait!" she cried before she could stop herself. "Your drawings, Hintsuli!" She scrambled to gather them up from the porch, cursing the blood that rushed to her cheek.

For a long moment, no one moved to close the distance. The man stared at her, still clutching Hintsuli's hand, while the boy looked up at his father for approval. Mattie felt something flow between her and the Indian, some current, some force like lightning that seemed to darken the rest of the world until there were only the two of them, caught in space and time. She heard her heart beating in a rhythm not of its own making. A breeze rustled the man's sleek hair, and then swept her way, as if the wind carried his spirit to her, and she gasped as it enveloped her soul.

But then a hawk wheeled high overhead, splitting the silence with a hungry screech. The spell was broken. The moment was lost.

Sakote released Hintsuli's hand, and his little brother raced to get his "toys." Sakote, of course, didn't dare go near the property, the cabin, the woman again. That was not the wind of The Great Spirit that had brushed by just now. It was the ghost of the *hudesi*, the monster who had lived there, and he'd given Sakote a warning. How else could Sakote explain his sudden weakness when he looked at the white woman and the way his soul felt pulled from his body when she returned his gaze?

His heart shivered as he thought about Hintsuli wrapped in the *hudesi*'s garment. Didn't the woman know that it was dangerous to keep the possessions of such an evil man? The Konkow would have burned all the *hudesi*'s things, forcing his condemned spirit to wander elsewhere.

He watched as Hintsuli took the papers from the white woman. All day he'd searched for his troublesome little brother. He'd driven himself half mad with worry, fearing the boy lost or mauled by a bear or shot by miners. To find him with the woman he'd told him was Coh-ah-nuya, the child-eater, happily whiling away the afternoon, had filled him at first with relief, then with the desire to turn the boy over his knee.

The woman stood not much taller than his little brother as he watched them together on the porch, and she could be no heavier than one of the fawns they'd seen earlier. With her delicate skin, pinkened now by the sun, and the wisps of tawny hair as fine as spider's web circling her face, she looked about as defenseless, too. But she'd tried to protect Hintsuli. Despite her weakness, she'd stood bravely between him and harm. She had a brave heart, a warrior's heart.

Sakote blew out sharply. He had to turn his own heart aside. Hintsuli's life depended on it. The lives of his people depended on it. The Konkow must stay away from the *willa* and their evil ghosts. The woman was dangerous. To Hintsuli. To him. To his tribe.

The woman squeezed Hintsuli's shoulders, and then sent him on his way. As she gave him a wave of farewell, Sakote noticed that the skin of her forearm was as pale as sycamore bark, and he wondered if it felt as smooth.

He grimaced, and then shook his head like a muskrat shaking off water. He mustn't think of such things. He mustn't think of the tiny brown dots that spattered her nose, the dimpled acorn point of her chin, the way her hair glistened gold in the setting sun, how her eyes shone greener than deergrass.

Hintsuli joined him then, and Sakote almost succeeded in walking away without a backward glance. But the woman's lilting voice summoned him again.

"I wish you would let your son keep the shirt!" she called, hefting up the garment. "It'll be cold, come winter."

He didn't mean to reply. It was wiser to leave in silence. But she spoke with such concern. Words fell out of his mouth, unbidden, like a trickling spring from the earth.

"I won't let him go cold," he said. "And he isn't my son. He's my brother."

Then he turned to go.

There was no earthly reason why the Indian's reply should have sent Mattie's heart rocketing skyward. It shouldn't even surprise her that he spoke English. After all, white men had lived here for twenty years or more. She shouldn't care that Hintsuli was his brother and not his son. But somehow, she did. Somehow, that bit of knowledge sent her thoughts wheeling in all sorts of unwelcome directions, wondering how old he was, what he was called, whether he had a squaw of his own.

She would have liked him to linger, to answer some of her questions, to tell her about his life and his world. Lord, she would have liked to just gaze at him a while. But by the time she collected herself, the two savages had vanished into the forest.

Of course, the man's image was penned in India ink on her brain. She'd always had good powers of observation. It was what made her a decent artist. Every bone, every shadow, every eyelash was as vivid to her now as when he stood before her. He lived in her mind's eye. But she feared losing him. Already the light was fading, but perhaps if she hurried...

A half hour later, Mattie rocked back off of hips that had grown numb from sitting on the hard pine porch. Her forehead was beaded with sweat, despite the coolness of the encroaching evening. Her shallow breath barely stirred the air, but her heart hammered as if it sought escape, and she knew that if she looked into a mirror, her eyes would appear haunted and hungry.

At last she let the pencil fall from her fingers, a stubby, dulled instrument that had sacrificed itself to create this—a portrait that rivaled SIREN AND SAILOR. The paper shivered in her hand like a living thing. The lank, sculpted figure seemed to charge from the page, every muscle taut and quivering. Wind appeared to flutter the deerskin slung about his hips and lash his chest with whips of his long hair. Tension curved his mouth downward and carved deep wrinkles in his brow, and his nostrils flared in agitation. But the eyes, they were the window to his spirit. As shiny as polished jet, they stared out at her in accusation—demanding birth, demanding life, demanding release from the page.

The rendering was inspired, and yet it terrified Mattie. It was the portrait of her dream, the one she couldn't see clearly. She knew it was. Yet, trembling here in the falling shadows of twilight, she could hardly remember drawing it. How long had it taken? Where had she started? What had forced her hand to such uncharacteristically bold strokes? She couldn't say. She didn't know. And that shook her to her very core.

"I don't s'pose you'd be willin' to part with that one, would you, Miss?"

Jasper Colton wiggled the twig from one side of his mouth to the other as he scowled at Mattie's latest sketch. It was a drawing of him, thigh-deep in the stream, washing the gold in his pan. His rumpled hat was kicked way back on his head, exposing an unruly lock of lank black hair, and his shirt showed stains of sweat under the arms. Around him, the creek eddied in sparkling play, as if winking at the man's folly, and scrub pines leaned their feathery heads forward to watch.

"My ma'd be right happy to see her son ain't some no-count squatter like his old man." He rubbed his stubble-peppered chin. "How much you want for it?"

Mattie bit back a shout of delight and pretended to contemplate the purchase. She honestly had no idea how much to charge for her work, particularly since everything here seemed to be bought and sold with ephemeral gold dust. She wrinkled her forehead and tapped her lip.

"I could give you half an ounce," he offered.

Half an ounce of gold for a quick sketch? The rendering wasn't her best work. It certainly had none of the fire of the portrait wrenched from her soul last night. Half an ounce? Good heavens, at that rate, she'd be wealthy in a matter of weeks.

Jasper mistook her hesitation for displeasure. He spat the twig from between his teeth and scratched his florid cheek, his eyes never leaving the page. "All right, three-quarters of an ounce."

"Mr. Colton," Mattie protested, "I have no intention of letting you pay—"

"Damn!" he exclaimed, licking his lips like a beggar contemplating a three-course dinner. "If that don't look just like me, spit 'n' image. You drive a hard bargain, ma'am, but I'll give you a full ounce if you let me have that pitcher."

Mattie was stunned. But she wasn't stupid. She nodded mutely, sealing the transaction, and watched in amusement as Jasper spat on his hands, wiped them on his trousers, then took the sketch from her by the corners, treating it as if it were the finest Belgian lace.

"Much obliged, ma'am," he growled, digging in his pocket for a pouch. "This here's a full ounce. If you don't have your own scale, you can check it on Tom's back at the Bar."

She would have shaken his hand, but he seemed preoccupied with his new prize. Mattie dropped the pouch into the bottom of the empty peach tin she used for her pencils and picked her way downstream toward her second subject.

Red Boone was even less hospitable than Jasper. He was a large man, heavy of frame, broad of neck, and dense of skull, and Mattie feared that thickness extended to his wits as well. He gave her mistrustful sidelong glances the entire time she sketched him. When she finished, she set the drawing down carefully and drew her skirts around her to perch on a rock.

Eventually, Red's curiosity got the better of him, and he moseyed his way over to her.

"What's that?" he asked, nodding nonchalantly toward the drawing.

"It's a picture of you," Mattie replied. "I hope you don't mind."

His laugh was a scoff, but his eyes gleamed with interest. She rotated the drawing so he could see it. The grin vanished from his face at once, and his mouth hung open in awe.

"How'd you..."

He studied the sketch with such intensity that she feared he'd brand the paper.

"I ain't never had a pitcher done before," he said in wonder.

"Well, Red," Jasper piped in, sauntering by, "don't get your longhandles in a bunch." He snickered over Mattie's shoulder. "It ain't free."

"You're sellin' this?" Red asked.

The innocence of his question made Mattie want to press the sketch into his hands as a gift. She supposed, however, that his friend Jasper would have something to say about that, having just paid an ounce of gold for his.

"Do you like it?" she asked, delaying the inevitable bout of bargaining.

"'Course he likes it," Jasper interjected, slapping the bear of a man on the back. "Damn! It's his spit 'n' image, spit and image, I tell you. Ain't it, Red?"

The big man nodded.

"Then come on, pard, pony up. Pay her your ounce, and you can take it home, hang it up in your parlor."

He snorted at his own joke while Red dug in his trouser pocket and fished out a Double Eagle.

"Much obliged, ma'am." Red offered her the coin and confiscated the drawing, concealing it against his immense belly as if the sketch were his own private masterpiece.

Mattie couldn't help but hum as she merrily followed the

stream along its winding path through the canyon. She had enough gold now to buy at least half a month's provisions, all from two sketches that had taken her less than an hour, and the day was yet young. There were miners all along the creek, miners who so far seemed only too willing to pay a king's ransom for a little bit of artistry. She might just purchase those chintz curtains sooner than she planned.

Mattie made and sold three more portraits, sketches of Billy and Bobby Cooper and their Granny, before she decided she'd better return home. She had earnings to cache and a lunch she'd left simmering.

Supping on a substantial meal of beans with salt pork, Mattie wondered idly what Hintsuli was eating for lunch. Did his big brother catch fish for him? Or rabbits? Did they eat like squirrels, living on nuts and berries they found? The more she thought about it, the more curious she grew. What did their homes look like? What did they do for entertainment? Who were their gods?

She'd learned two of their words, *utim* and *tem-diyoki*, acorn and deer. But there was so much about the Indians she didn't know, so much about *him*.

The features of Hintsuli's brother crystallized again in her imagination as if he'd been waiting for her. Even in memory, he took her breath away.

What was his name? How many brothers and sisters did he have? What did he look like when he smiled? When he slept? When he bathed?

Even as her cheek flushed with the wicked turn of her thoughts, her fate was sealed. She must know the answers to her questions.

With three pencils, a tiny sharpening knife, and her sketchbook, she set out through the forest at the spot where the pair of Indians had disappeared the night before. She had no idea where she was going, but if a six-year-old boy had found his way to her cabin through the wood, there must be a clearly marked trail back to his home.

"Mati," Sakote whispered to himself, shifting the two freshly slain rabbits slung across his shoulder and climbing from rock to rock along the canyon rise. It was a Konkow word. Acorn-bread. A strange name for a white woman. But Hintsuli insisted that was what the *willa* called herself. "Mati."

The sun was high now, and the day was hot. There was little chance that wildcats or bears would rouse from their midday naps to thieve his kill. Still, he longed to finish his journey, a journey that seemed more and more foolish the farther he walked.

He'd yearned to speak to the elders last night about the white woman, to ask for their counsel at the evening fire. But he couldn't. The incident with the white doctor was his sister's secret to keep. He wouldn't betray her trust. His little brother, however, was not easy to silence. Sakote had had to dangle Hintsuli's precious pictures over the flames before he'd agree to keep quiet.

And now, because of the promise to his sister, Sakote brought food for the *willa* woman so she wouldn't starve to death. It was...what was the word Noa used? Harebrained. The woman would either live or die, according to Wonomi's will. She would either learn the way of The Great Spirit's earth, or she would be conquered by it. Sakote couldn't change the course of her life's river. Yet he longed to guide her along the current.

He wouldn't speak to the woman again. He still regretted revealing his command of English to her. As he'd learned from his sister, once you began talking with a woman, it was often difficult to make her stop. But there was something else. She was a white woman in a camp of white miners. If Sakote were seen near her, on her doorstep, in her house, the *willa* would probably wind a hanging rope around his neck.

No, he decided, he'd quickly drop the rabbits just inside her door and leave.

"Mati," he murmured once more, wondering what the letters looked like in the white man's writing. Perhaps Noa would show him.

He crested the ridge, slipping into the pines that surrounded Mati's house. He avoided the trail as always, choosing instead his own path over thick needles that would hide the marks of his passing. It was something the Konkow had always done, for it disguised one's presence to the enemy. And now that the *willa* arrived like flies on fresh venison, threatening the shrinking world of the tribe, it was a necessity.

The noise from the bushes ahead caught him by surprise. He froze, and then slowly melted back into the bark of a camouflaging oak. He cocked his head, listening for more sounds, and peered through the fork of the oak's branches.

"Damn it all!" she bit out.

It was Mati, struggling out of a patch of deerbrush as her hair snagged in the branches. She bent to examine her skirt. Something had ripped a fist-sized tear in the cloth.

"Oh!" She stamped her foot.

Then she straightened and scanned the forest around her, her gaze crossing blindly over him. She wiped her forehead with the back of her arm and sighed.

"What happened to the trail?" she asked the trees.

Choosing an opening in the manzanita, she marched forward, so close to him that he felt the air of her passing. He couldn't breathe or blink.

Where was the woman going? This passage joined up with a rough trail that traversed the canyon wall in a more conspicuous incline. But there were many offshoots of that trail. If she lost her way...

He had no choice but to follow her and make sure that didn't happen. After all, what good would it do to leave supper at her door if she never found her way home to eat it?

She was a nuisance, he told himself, as unpredictable as a rattlesnake and more trouble than Hintsuli. He should never have made the promise to his sister to watch after her. But his heart still flipped over like a landed trout when he spied her delicate white arms and her hair that shone like sunlight.

He followed her as softly as mist, so that even when he walked only four spear's-lengths behind her, she didn't hear him. Several times she uttered the word—"damn"—that Noa liked to use and a few other words he hadn't heard before. It was clear she didn't know her way, for she crossed the same clearing twice.

Finally, she broke free of the wood and headed toward the high ridge cresting the canyon. Pausing like a triumphant warrior at the top, she began her descent.

It would be more difficult following her here, for few trees grew out of the canyon wall to conceal his passage. It was also treacherous ground. The way was steep and littered with loose earth and pine needles. She maneuvered carefully down the slope, and he watched with growing impatience and worry as she slipped farther and farther from his sight. When the top of her head finally disappeared, he crept out from the trees to pursue her.

Sakote had taken only two steps when he heard pebbles showering down the sheer cliff ahead of him. His heart knifed through his chest, and he sprang forward. The sound grew in volume, first a heavy rain as he raced to the edge of the canyon, then a thunder of rock. The woman shrieked like a wounded eagle. Sakote dropped his hunting pouch and his kill and bolted toward her as fast as he could. It felt as if he staggered through clay.

Just as he closed the distance to the rim, a horrible thud from below ended the scream. The pebbles, their work finished, slowed to a trickle. Sakote's breath caught, and his pulse pounded in his ears as he peered over the edge of the cliff, dreading what he would find.

CHAPTER 10

Stunned, Mattie lay on her back, staring up at the periwinkle sky in wonder. A final insult of gloating pebbles trickled down to rest beside her shoulder. There was no pain—just a strange, still numbness in her body, a heavy hollowness to her breathless chest, and a faint quivering inside that left her as weak as a babe. There was no fear—just her pulse whooshing like a river through her ears.

How silly, she thought, to be lying on the ground like this. She should stand up, dust herself off, gather her things, and push onward. At the very least, she should tug down the skirt that had slipped immodestly high on one thigh. But she was curiously unmotivated.

There was no pain. No fear. No air.

Indeed, she might never have taken another breath.

But the bright sky suddenly plunged into darkness. It seemed as if a great black condor swooped down upon her. The startled gasp she drew through her collapsed chest felt like a sword pulled from a wound, and instantly every bone in her body felt the impact of her fall. She opened her mouth to scream, but coughed on red dust instead.

"Don't move!"

She squinted up at the figure silhouetted against the cloudless expanse. Not a condor. The Indian. Hintsuli's brother. What was *he* doing here? Now she *knew* she should fix her skirts. She stretched her fingers down and tried to sit up on the narrow ledge despite the limpness of her body.

"Don't move!" he insisted, willing her compliance with a stern glare.

He crouched over her, and for one moment she feared he intended her harm. She'd heard the accounts—decent pioneer women abducted, raped, murdered by Indians. And here she lay, as helpless as a kitten, completely at the savage's mercy. She squeezed her eyes shut and waited for the slash of a scalping knife. It was only gentle fingertips that brushed over her forehead, but she flinched from his touch.

"Are you in pain?" he murmured.

Mattie opened her eyes. In one glance, she realized she was mistaken about the Indian. He didn't mean to ravage her. In fact, worry curved his brow. There was genuine, pure concern in his expression.

"Where does it hurt?" he whispered, bending close.

She wanted to reply, but her eyelids suddenly grew unbearably heavy, and her already feeble strength waned. The Indian's voice sounded distant now, pleasant, deep and airy, like the voice of the wind. It made her want to float away.

"Mati!"

Her eyes flew wide. How did he know her name?

"Mati, don't leave me."

It was a strange thing to say. She understood his meaning. He meant don't faint on him. But something in the words he chose, something in the soulful, desperate look he gave her, made her believe he meant precisely what he said.

"I...won't," she promised, startled by the thickness of her own voice.

"Don't move. I'll help you."

Mattie believed him. For no good reason. He was a savage, after all, from a culture whose healing practices likely consisted of rattling bones and the incantations of medicine men. But she believed him. He looked trustworthy. He looked confident. And he looked like the only other human being around for miles.

"Does it hurt?" he asked again.

"No." In truth, now she could feel very little of anything, but her body had begun to shiver as if she were lying in snow.

He stared at her a moment, measuring the truth of her words.

"The pain will come soon," he said.

"I'm fine. I just need to..." She broke off with a gasp as she spied drops of fresh blood smearing his fingertips. "Am I bleeding?" She reached up to explore her forehead herself. A bump the size of a quail's egg rose high on her brow, and when she pulled her fingers away, they were sticky with blood. "Oh!"

She quivered uncontrollably now. Heavens, how badly was she hurt?

"Lie quiet," the Indian told her. "Breathe slow."

She didn't want to lie quiet. She wanted to get up off her back, brush off her skirts, pack up her sketchbook, and be on her way. She didn't want to be...broken.

Only the gentle touch of the man's hands on the crown of her head convinced her to stay. He spread his fingers carefully and methodically over every inch of her scalp, taking the weight of her head in one hand. When he was satisfied she hadn't cracked her skull, he tenderly returned her head to the ground and took hold of her left wrist, turning it over.

The palm was completely raw and glistening. She wished she hadn't looked. She could feel it now, the faint sting of oncoming pain. The underside of her forearm was likewise scraped, and bits of gravel dusted its length. He grasped her shoulder with one hand and slowly lifted her arm, testing the joint, and then repeated the entire process with the right arm. Her drawing hand, thank goodness, hadn't suffered a scratch. In fact, it looked like she'd sledded down the hillside using her left arm as a runner.

One of her boots had come loose in the fall. Crouching between her parted ankles, the Indian tugged off its mate, leaving her stocking-footed. She gasped at his impropriety. Decent men didn't look at—let alone lay a hand on—a lady's limbs. But the sensation of his warm palm cupping her foot, gingerly checking it for injury, left her breathless. His thumbs searched her ankle, then higher along her shin, as if it were the most natural thing in the world. She bit back the cries of outrage she knew she should be making as he touched her where no man had before.

But then his questing fingers grazed her knee, and she sucked in a gasp of pain. Lifting her head, she saw the source of her hurt all too clearly. A ragged, gravel-peppered wound decorated the cap of her knee. And protruding from its center was a wicked inch-long splinter of rock.

Panic whispered in her ear. Her breath came fast and shallow, and her heart raced. She wanted to turn back the clock, to pretend the accident had never happened. Why, oh why had she decided to hike down the canyon?

"I'll make it better," the Indian told her, placing a comforting hand on her forearm. And as absurd as it was, something in his voice eased her. "Breathe like the wind, slow and steady."

She looked into his face, into the calming depths of his eyes—so darkly foreign, but so soothing. She swallowed hard and breathed with him.

But he didn't touch her knee again. Instead, he moved

higher, probing the long bone of her thigh. There was no physical discomfort there, but Mattie closed her eyes against pangs of shame. Though his touch was far from sensual, something in his frank manner aroused her. And yet it was ludicrous, she thought, to feel such stirrings while her lifeblood drained away onto the ground. She winced as his thumb found a nasty bruise on the bone of her hip. He grunted in acknowledgment, then shifted to examine her other limb.

Her right leg seemed to be undamaged, aside from the brands she was sure his fingers left on her flesh, and it was with a curious blend of regret and relief that she finally opened her eyes, thinking he was finished.

He wasn't.

Now he trapped her hips between his moccasined heels, and the hanging edge of his breechcloth flirted with her skirt as he crouched directly over her. A lock of his long, thick hair fell forward over his shoulder and onto her breast like a brazen paintbrush as he slid his fingers gently along her lowest rib.

Two layers of cotton separated their flesh, but she felt the heat of his fingers like a crimping iron as he tested her ribs one by one. She stared at him, scarcely daring to breathe. Twin creases marred his otherwise smooth brow. His hair shone as black and sleek as a raven's wing. His nostrils flared as he worked, and his lips tensed in concentration. His bare face and chest seemed sculpted of caramel clay. She was forced to take a quick gulp of air when he released her diaphragm, and then she caught his fascinating scent—the scent of smoke and deerskin and mountain bay. It made her feel lightheaded.

His thumbs prodded methodically along the outer edges of her rib cage now, deftly sliding over the bones, till she flinched back with a gasp.

He frowned and slipped his fingertips carefully again into the same spot between the ribs. Again she winced.

Then he lifted one fine, coal-black brow and slowly wiggled his fingers. This time, a giggle slipped out of her before she could stop it.

A knowing grin quirked up one corner of his mouth, and Mattie enjoyed a moment of heart-melting delight at the sudden transformation of sullen savage into adorable rogue. Then, absurdly, he began to tickle her, and it was all she could do to think straight.

She was in mid-laugh when he did it. Reached behind his back and pulled the splinter out of her knee. All at once, with no warning. She yelped and bent forward in pain, but he ignored her protests, wadding a fold of her dress over the wound and leaning his weight on it to stop the bleeding.

It hurt. Oh, Lord, it hurt. She could feel every heartbeat throbbing in her knee. How could he have done such a horrible thing—betraying her trust like that?

His smile was gone now. He stared at her with mild interest while he waited for the bleeding to subside. It was unnerving, that stare of his, an unsettling combination of amusement and remorse.

"Why did you do that?" she sulked when at last she could speak.

"You wish I'd left it in?"

She thrust her chin out in defiance.

After a moment, he nodded, pretending to search the ground. "I'll put it back."

"No!"

There was more than a little chiding in his answering smile.

"No," she said more calmly. "I don't mean to appear...ungrateful. It's only that..."

Now he was staring at her lips. It was almost too much to bear.

"Must you...sit on me?" she asked.

"Until the bleeding stops."

The sun blazed down, scorching her skin, leaving her slippery with sweat, but it was nothing compared to the heat emanating from the man hovering over her.

"Is that the way you remove arrows from your brave warriors?" she asked, casting a dubious glance his way. "By tickling them?"

"No." His eyes crinkled in mild amusement. "This is how I take thorns from my little brother."

Effectively insulted, Mattie huffed out an angry breath. She started to cross her arms in defiance, but forgot about her injured elbow and winced when it caught on her dress.

"Don't move, Little Acorn," he said, and the pet name rolled off his lips as easily as if he'd known her all his life.

She felt her skin flush. Indeed, the Indian was becoming too familiar. He took too many liberties, assumed too much. And yet his easy manner was enormously comforting, almost as if they *were* old friends.

"*Akina*," he said, finally easing the pressure from her knee. "It is done."

He moved away from her then, careful of the cliff's edge, and his sudden distance left her feeling awkward.

"Well, then," she said, gingerly working her way up to a sitting position, "thank you. I'll just be on my way. Did you happen to see where I dropped my—"

"Sketchbook?" he asked, sweeping it up from the ground nearby.

"Yes, thank..."

Drawing back his arm like a pitcher for the Knickerbockers, he hurled the sketchbook upwards over the lip of the cliff. Her boots followed. Then he shoved the two recovered pencils between his teeth and bent down toward her. For a moment, she wondered if he intended to toss her up there as well.

Before she could sputter out an objection, the Indian plucked her skirts out of the way, turned his back to her, and hunkered down between her knees.

"Hold on," he said.

Nonplused, she stared at his broad, smooth, perfect back. She had no intention of getting one inch closer to that blatantly masculine body, let alone clinging to him like a baby monkey.

"This way," he mumbled around the pencils.

He planted her arms about his neck and hauled her up from the ground before she could think of a reply. Then he bent forward even further, and hiked her knees up around his waist.

"Hold on," he told her again, blessedly unaware that she was too mortified to speak.

It was completely indecent the way he carried her. She scarcely knew him, and yet her arms encircled him like a lover. She could feel the beat of his heart where her forearm contacted his throat. The bare skin of his sun-warmed back burned against the flesh of her thighs as she clung to him. It felt wrong and forbidden...and sinfully wonderful.

She had to hold on tightly, she discovered. The cliff was steep, and instead of scrabbling along the pebbled passages as she'd done, he chose instead the granite boulders, leaping from rock to rock up the cliff face.

Once, when she felt his foot slip, she panicked, glancing over her shoulder at the long drop below, and tightened her hold. He grunted and she grimaced as her heel found the worst possible place to lodge. But he didn't complain, and in another minute, they lit safe and sound at the top of the cliff.

Sakote knew he was crazy now. He was packing a white

woman on his back, in the clear light of day, atop a cliff visible from the entire valley, a woman whose stray foot had just reminded him he was a man. He might as well braid the hanging rope himself.

He had known it was dangerous to go near the woman, that she'd bring him only trouble. And now he'd interfered with The Great Spirit's plans by changing the woman's destiny.

But as he carried her toward the thick trees—her pale arms wound around his neck, her legs entwined about his hips, her soft breasts pressed against his back—he knew it was too late to change his path.

His heart had stopped when he feared Mati lay broken at the bottom of the canyon. A terrible dizziness had overcome him as he peered over the edge. And when he found her at last, tucked back onto a ledge of rock not far down the slope, within his reach, such hope had entered his spirit that he thought he'd burst with it.

It tore at his insides to see her injured. He'd rather have the wounds himself. Her skin was delicate, finer than a child's, and it looked even paler against the patches of blood marring her body. Her limbs were scraped, and her brow was gashed, but the shard of stone in her knee concerned him the most. He thanked the Creator that she, like Hintsuli, was ticklish, for it was the quickest way to wrench the sliver from her.

But his worries ran deeper than her wounds. They were connected now, the two of them. Her blood stained his fingers, and her trust claimed his soul. He'd altered her fate, and she his. The path ahead was perilous, but now there was no turning from it.

"If you'll put me down, I'll be on my way." The woman's voice was taut, almost frightened, and she shivered like a newly hatched *cheeztahtah*—robin.

Of course, he had no intention of abandoning her in the

middle of the wood. She'd only lose her way again. Besides, she probably didn't know which plants to use on her wounds. He must take her to a safe place where he could tend to her cuts. With his mouth full of the writing sticks, he grunted in reply.

While the woman was still slung across his back, he retrieved her sketchbook and boots and his hunting pouch. As for the kill he'd brought for her, he could see through the brush that Trickster Coyote was already slinking off with it, his teeth grinning around the rabbits. Sakote sighed in disgust.

"Sir."

He paused. Strands of the woman's fine hair tickled his ear.

"Sir, I really must insist..."

Sakote had no time for her insisting. It was hazardous to stay so long in the open. He scrutinized several possible paths traversing the canyon and finally chose one of the deer trails. It wasn't the best way to go. There were few places of concealment along the way, and he would leave footprints. But the trail was fairly level, and it led swiftly to his destination. He started forward.

"Mr. Indian!" The woman yanked the drawing sticks from his mouth, scraping them between his teeth. "Where are you taking me?"

"Not far, but we have to go quickly," he said, nodding. "Along the canyon."

"But where...what's along the canyon?"

"A place, a good place." He could tell she didn't like his answer. But, in the same way he'd taken the splinter from her, sometimes it was best not to know everything.

"But I don't...I don't want to go." She began to loosen her grip on him. "I want to go home."

He dropped her things and let her slide gently down, bracing her when she tottered on her injured leg.

"You weren't going home when I found you."

To his amazement, she didn't reply, but only blinked her eyes many times, soundlessly moving her mouth. It was an expression he'd seen on Hintsuli's face many times when the boy was about to make up a story.

And like his little brother, the woman seemed to need answers for everything. She would probably hammer at him like the woodpecker all the way along the trail if he didn't explain where they were going.

He sighed. "I know a good place to wash your wounds, where the miners don't go to look for gold." He stopped, distracted for a moment by the color of the white woman's eyes, so much like the eyes of the white eagle in his dream. They were all the various greens of the precious serpentine stone that lined the cave in the mountain beyond the village.

"I can wash my own wounds."

"You'll lose more blood if you walk home. The mining camp is distant. The place I'm taking you isn't far." His next words were not his own. He didn't know where they came from. "It's a beautiful place. Your body will find comfort there. Your heart will find peace."

The words slipped like sacred smoke blown by The Great Spirit between his lips. They twisted Sakote's fate. They sealed the white woman's destiny.

CHAPTER 11

Mattie soon discovered the Indian was right. The pain indeed came. And though he carried her with the easy grace of a wildcat, never jarring her, never even allowing a stray branch to scratch her, by the time they entered the shaded copse, Mattie's arm felt on fire, and her knee throbbed like the devil.

The moment she spied the waterfall, however, she forgot all about her discomfort.

It was the most beautiful, idyllic spot she'd ever seen, something she might have sketched in her imagination. A grand tower of churning white water cascaded over black rock, plunging down two stories or more into a deep, dark, round pool. The sound was like thunder, softened only by the babble of the creek and the hiss of the spray obscuring the fall's end. The pool was carved like a great jade bowl, with the middle so black it appeared bottomless, and the surface of the water rocked with gentle, widening rings that glimmered in the sunlight. Bright green mosses studded the vertical rock wall where the mist hovered. A huge boulder of granite intruded into the water, reflecting sunlight onto the undersides of the lush trees encircling the pond.

The moist air soothed Mattie's parched throat at once. Her nose filled with the pleasant scent of wet rock and mud. And, true to the Indian's promise, a sense of calm descended upon her as they climbed down the bank.

He set her down on a small, sun-splashed boulder at the water's edge. It was warm, almost hot in contrast to the damp earth she could feel through her socks. She wanted to take them off, to feel the cool mud on the soles of her feet, to dabble her toes in the bracing water.

As if he read her thoughts, the Indian bent on one knee and began peeling off her white cotton stockings.

"It's lovely," she sighed. "What is this place called?"

He shrugged. "The waterfall."

His hand still cupped her foot, and she realized with a jolt how natural it seemed to let him touch her.

"And what about you, Mr. Indian?" she breathed. "What are you called?"

He quirked up one corner of his mouth and wriggled his fingers beneath her foot, tickling her. "Why do white people need a name for everything?"

She had no answer for him—not that she could have formed syllables anyway. The twinkle in his eye and the curve of his lips—so sensual, so inviting—charmed the words right out of her head.

He tossed her socks aside. "We need to wash your wounds."

She didn't think much about what he'd said until he reached around and began unfastening the buttons at the back of her dress.

"What are you doing?" She seized his wrist. Lord, it was thick and strong.

"These...buttons you call them? They're difficult."

She flushed. "Well, maybe they're supposed to be difficult," she said in a heated rush, "to keep men like you from..." The minute she looked in his eyes, she knew she had misjudged him. He meant no offense, and he certainly intended no seduction.

She glanced down at her dress. Of course, he wouldn't dream of seducing her. She was a mess. Her gown was filthy, torn by the brush, and where he'd used a wad of it to stanch her blood, a giant macabre rose bloomed crimson against the brown. The garment would never be the same. And yet it was the only thing she had to wear back to the cabin.

He withdrew his hands, suddenly uneasy. "Don't you wear the longhandles?"

She blinked. "The long..." When she beheld his solemn face and realized what he meant, she couldn't help but smile. He'd obviously learned his English from the local miners. And he obviously knew nothing about women's clothing. "Yes, Mr. Indian, I have, well, something like the longhandles."

She couldn't very well swim in her dress. The wet linsey-woolsey would weigh her down on the trip home. She'd have to strip down to her cotton chemise, which would dry quickly. It was clear the Indian was one step ahead of her.

"Very well," she said as stoically as possible. "You may assist me with the buttons."

It took him a painfully long time. She supposed he'd had little practice with buttons, and there were at least two dozen down the back of this particular dress. She'd skipped a few of them herself, since she had no maid now and because her diminished size allowed her to slip the thing up over her hips. It wouldn't have been so awful, except that the way he casually crouched beside her, she got a perfect view of his long, tan thigh, and it took every ounce of her will not to reach out and sample its smooth-muscled texture.

Despite his boyish look of triumph when he finished the

task, Mattie blushed keenly at the thought of standing before him in her unmentionables. It was silly, really. After all, he seemed to think nothing of traipsing all over God's earth in scarcely more than a fig leaf.

With as little fuss as possible, and careful of her injuries, she stepped out of the ruined garment.

The sun felt delicious, the breeze decidedly wicked as it riffled the sheer cotton of her embroidered chemise. She shivered as a light gust blew waterfall mist over her.

"Is the water cold?" she asked as he began untying his moccasins.

He shrugged and gave her a dismissive shake of his head. "No."

Resisting the urge to cover herself, and falling short of limbs to fully accomplish the task anyway, Mattie studied her surroundings more thoroughly. A tiny gray lizard sunned itself on the biggest rock while vivid blue damselflies buzzed and nipped at the air. Water striders left tiny circles on the top of the pool, and here and there, she could see the sleek movement of fish beneath the surface.

He nodded toward her knee. "You're bleeding again."

She followed his gaze. Bright red seeped through the white cotton of her chemise. She snatched the fabric up out of the way. Blood trickled lazily down her shin.

"Come," he said, and in one swift movement, he swept her into his arms, cradling her like a babe, and carried her toward the water.

His chest was firm against her, but resilient and warm, like her father's leather wing chair after he'd been sitting in it. But unlike the chair, which smelled of pipe tobacco and macassar oil, the Indian's scent was laced with wood smoke, rawhide, and a potpourri of intoxicating herbs.

The pond deepened sharply, and Mattie gasped as he fearlessly waded forward.

In three steps, he was thigh-deep in the water.

On the fourth, he dropped her in.

"Oh sh-!"

That was all the woman could yell before she went under. Of course, Sakote instantly hauled her up again by the waist and tugged her to shallower ground as gently as he could, despite her floundering like a netted salmon and sputtering words he'd never heard, even from Noa.

Her hair lay flat on her head now, wetted to the color of last year's baskets, and her eyes burned through strands of it like hot coals prodded to life. She shuddered, and he wasn't sure if it was with cold or anger.

"You said it wasn't cold!" she finally managed to spit out.

"It *isn't* cold." He settled her onto a ledge of stone just beneath the water's surface and rucked up the drenched hem of her underdress to inspect her knee. "When the snows come, then it's cold."

He washed water up over her leg.

"Ah!" she cried.

"Be still, Little Acorn."

"But it's freezing!" she complained, shrieking when he splashed another wave over her.

"You scream like my little brother at his bath." He ladled more water over her.

"You make him bathe in th—?" She gasped again as he rinsed the wound. It was almost clean now. "What kind of heartless scoundr—?" She shivered at the next splash and fell silent, but that did not keep her from speaking to him with her eyes. They fired at him like serpentine-tipped arrows.

"Now your arm," he said, ignoring her glares as he'd done Hintsuli's many times. Sometimes children didn't know what was best for them. It seemed the same was true for Mati.

"I am *not* going to put my arm in that icy water," she said, thrusting out her chin like a Yana warrior.

Sakote considered her for a moment. She'd fight him if he tried to force her into the water, and she'd only hurt herself. He rubbed his chin with the back of his hand. Perhaps there was another way.

"What if I give you a prize for enduring this trial?"

That earned her attention at once.

"What kind of prize?"

He shrugged. He'd always offered Hintsuli small things for his concession—an arrow, an extra bite of his acorn bread, an afternoon playing the grass game. What would please a white woman?

"A squirrel for your supper?" he asked.

She wrinkled her nose. Perhaps, he thought sourly, she wouldn't have liked the rabbits he'd killed for her either. He tried to think of the silly trinkets that gave his sister joy.

"A string of clamshell beads?"

She bit her lip, clearly not impressed.

How difficult this woman was. "A grinding rock."

She only stared at him blankly. He was about to make his final offer—that he wouldn't "shake the stuffing out of her," as Noa liked to say—when she came up with her own prize.

"I know!" Her face lit up. "You must let me sketch you."

"Sketchoo?"

"Yes. You must let me make a drawing of you. If I endure this torture without a peep, you must sit quietly for me so I can draw your picture."

How strange her request was. Why should she want to make a picture of him with the writing sticks?

He narrowed his eyes. "You won't make magic with this sketchoo?"

"Magic?" She lifted her brows. "You mean, will I steal your soul?" She smiled. "Of course not. It's only a picture."

He wasn't so sure. He'd seen the pictures Hintsuli had stolen, and he understood why the boy believed the animals were trapped on the page. They were so perfect that they seemed to need only the breath of Wonomi to come to life.

But these were fears of old times. The white man brought many things, tools and toys, that seemed at first to be magic—the spinning top, matches, rifles—but they were no more magic than the caterpillar that turned into the butterfly or the oak that grew from the acorn. They were only unknown to the Konkow.

He nodded his agreement to the terms, and her smile blossomed as bright as a dogwood flower.

Mati was not quite silent while he bathed her, but she fought hard to keep her whimpers sealed behind tightly closed lips. There was little flesh left on the base of her hand, and just for a moment, before he remembered who she was, he felt sorry that she wouldn't be able to grind acorns for many days. In the end, she was braver than Hintsuli would have been, despite the fact that her face was as white as birch bark and her lips pale and shivering.

He pulled her, dripping, from the water, and set her on a flat rock beside the pool. Then his gaze dropped past her face, past her shoulders and lower, and he stopped comparing the woman to his little brother.

He couldn't understand why the white people wore such thin clothing. It offered no protection against the snows of *ko-meni*. Why didn't they wear deerskin? Good white deerskin didn't turn to mist when it became wet.

By The Great Spirit, he could see every part of her body as if she wore such a mist now—the points of her breasts, tautened with cold, the delicate ridges of her ribs, the shallow cave of her navel. And lower, he glimpsed the tousled nest of her woman's curls.

Sakote swallowed hard, as if he swallowed an acorn, shell and all, and he didn't know why. It wasn't as if he'd never seen a naked woman. He'd played pleasure games with many women from the surrounding Konkow villages. They seemed to enjoy his company and his body, and many wished to become his mate. But they were his people. They were Konkow. Never had he looked thus upon a white woman. Never had he imagined that their woman's parts were nestled in gold.

It made him want to take her, here, beside the pond. He wished to lay her back on the sweet grass and lick the droplets from her shoulders, to fondle her breasts through the mist-cloth, to plunge his thickening spear into the golden tangle of her woman's hair and...

"W-w-will you s-s-sit for me now?"

Her words startled Sakote from his vision, and he scowled in self-disgust. What was he thinking? How could he desire to lie with the woman? It was crazy. She was not of his world. She was white. And she was the mate of a bad *kokoni*. She was willful like the bear, stubborn like the coyote, and, like the squirrel, she seemed to chatter on and on. How could he want to lie with her?

And yet he did. He wanted to stretch out beside her, and he wanted to press his lips to hers in that white man's ritual—the kiss—he'd spied between Noa and his sister late one night, the one that had made Towani sigh.

She stared at him now, her bottom lip shivering, and he wondered—did her mouth taste salty like the dried meat the miners always ate? Or bitter like their dark coffee? Was her breath warm with the white man's whiskey? Or sweet with mint?

A tiny frown crossed her face, and he realized he hadn't answered her question. He'd been wasting time with his dreaming. He forced his gaze back to her eyes, his thoughts back to her pain.

"First I must finish with your wounds." His voice was a hoarse whisper, and he hoped his breechcloth hid the proof of his lust.

A patch of milkweed grew in the crevice between two

great slabs of granite. With a whisper of thanks to the plant, he plucked several stems.

"W-w-what is that?"

"It will heal you."

She eyed the plants with mistrust. "B-b-but it…"

"It will heal you."

He dribbled white juice from the plants onto her knee first, and she sucked a quick breath of pain through her teeth.

"It's good," he assured her. "It will stop the bleeding."

He lifted her arm to drip the liquid down its length, trying to ignore her moon-white breast with the pink bud visible through the wet cloth.

For her forehead, he tore one leaf and gently dabbed the edge of it to her cut, holding her head still with his other hand. She winced, but didn't complain.

"You aren't cold anymore?" he asked.

"The pain has distracted me from the cold."

He grunted, amused. She sounded as grumpy as an old grandmother.

"*Akina.*" Finished, he dropped the spent stems into the water. "Now I'll bind your wounds."

He tore the edge of her brown dress quickly, before she could protest, for he knew how women were about their clothing. As he expected, her jaw dropped open and her eyes grew wide.

"What the devil are you—"

"I told you. I have to bind your wounds."

He shouldn't feel guilty. There was no other way. He'd try to tear as little as possible, but he had to use her garment. Perhaps he'd bring her another. Yes, that was it. The white man's clothing was useless for winter. Perhaps he'd bring her a Konkow garment—a soft deerskin cloak or a robe of rabbit fur. How beautiful she'd look all in white, like a winter deer…or the eagle of his dreams.

"Are you a...medicine man?"

"No." He carefully wrapped a strip of the cloth around her knee.

"Then how do you know what you're doing?"

"All the Konkow know this."

"What's a Konkow?"

The white people were so full of questions.

"My people." He tied the ends of the strip to secure it.

"Konkow," she repeated. The word sounded strange from her mouth. "And do you have a family?"

He nodded and began to wrap the second strip between her thumb and finger, around the pad of her hand.

"A mother? Father?" she asked.

"A mother."

"And your father? Is he...alive?"

Sakote drew an uneasy breath in through his nose. He had not spoken of his father in four years, not since Noa had asked him the same question.

She sucked suddenly through her teeth.

He glanced at his handiwork. He'd wound the cloth too tight. He unwrapped it and started over.

The woman spoke softly, sorrowfully. "My mother and father are both dead."

He paused, but didn't meet her eyes. "You mustn't speak of them."

"Why?" She seemed truly bewildered.

"It's dangerous to speak of the dead." His mother had named her second son, the son of Sakote's uncle, after Sakote's father, Hintsuli, so that she wouldn't slip and speak the name of her dead husband.

The white woman became quiet then and very sad, and he almost regretted his words. The air seemed too quiet without her chattering.

He'd wrapped the last coil of the cloth around her arm and

was knotting the ends when she finally broke the silence.

"Do you have a wife?"

He almost tied his thumb into the knot. Why did she want to know if he had a *kulem*? Was she interested in him? No, he decided, it must be his imagination. He finished the knot. "No."

"You don't...want a wife?" Now she was like a chipmunk, poking her nose in the acorn flour where it didn't belong.

He rocked back on his haunches and considered ignoring her question. But it was an interesting one, one he'd left in the shadowy part of his mind for a long time. He liked the women of his tribe, and there were even a few from the neighboring villages he'd considered taking to wife. But starting his own family was always something he'd placed in the seasons to come. He was too busy raising his little brother, seeing that his sister found a mate, protecting the tribe from the dangers of the white men, dangers that the elders, the shaman, and even his wise headman uncle didn't understand.

"I'll have a wife," he conceded, "one day."

She seemed satisfied with his answer. "Will you sit for me now?"

He wasn't sure what she wanted from him, and he felt very foolish as he lowered himself onto the grass beside her so she could make his picture.

"Now sit very still," she said, reaching for her sketchbook and the drawing sticks.

It was easy for him to sit still. He did it all the time when he hunted. The difficult part was having her stare at him as if he were a fawn and she a wolf, hungrily measuring every bite of him with her eyes.

Chapter 12

Mattie's fingers shook as she touched the pencil to the page. That same hunger—the possession—that she'd felt the night before, depicting the Indian from memory, overcame her. He was magnificent, even more glorious in her presence, and it was a daunting task for her to translate that magnificence to paper.

She began with the eyes. They were calm now, steady—twin jewels of polished jet. They caught the light off the sun-washed granite and shone like candles at midnight. The crinkles at the corners spoke of laughter in his life, but the furrow between his finely arched brows told her he was just as wont to brood.

His nose was prominent, not hooked, but with a bold ridge that complemented his proud cheekbones. Her pencil faltered as she imagined how it would feel to have him nuzzling her neck.

His chin was straight, and despite the fact that it was without stubble, like a youth's, his jaw was strong, capable, masculine. His mouth was straight and wide, his lips spare but supple. She liked the way they could curve into a crooked smile. She wished he would smile now. And she wondered, in her most secret heart, what those lips would feel like upon her brow, her cheek, her mouth.

She gave her head a small shake. Where had her concentration gone? Focus was the key to drawing a respectable portrait. She couldn't let herself be distracted.

The cords of the Indian's neck were broad, and she could see the beat of his heart in the hollow of his throat. A tiny nick marred his collarbone, a small scar from some past mishap, and she carefully pencilled it in.

Last, she added his hair. Much of it had come loose from the rawhide tie now, and it hung like shredded silk about his face. High on one side, where the sun struck, it shone in the rainbow colors of a raven's wing. Mattie remembered combing Hintsuli's hair. Did his older brother's feel as soft, as lush?

As a final touch, she lightly shaded the whole face, using her thumb to smudge the pencil strokes, giving his skin a dusky finish. Then she scribbled the title, MR. INDIAN, at the bottom and signed it.

When she flipped the drawing around to show him, he didn't move a muscle, but only stared at the portrait, silent.

"You can move now," she told him.

When he did, it was to lean back skeptically and fold his arms across his chest.

"It doesn't look like me," he groused, though she could tell by his face that the picture did indeed impress him.

"Of course it does. It looks *just* like you."

He gave the work his harshest scrutiny, and one hand went up to touch the scar on his collarbone, but he only grunted.

"Well, if you don't like it," she said, pretending to be miffed, "I'll just keep it myself."

She wasn't prepared for the speed at which he snatched the sketchbook from her hands. He brought the drawing close to his face, scowling all the while.

"I'll take it," he announced, "in payment for saving your life."

She would have liked to think her life was worth a bit more than a sketch. But she supposed it was definitely worth the look of grudging amazement on his face to show him the picture.

"The next time," he told her, "draw the rest of me, not just this...head."

Before she could recover from her shock at his mention of a next time, he rose in one fluid movement to his feet and, taking her under the arms, lifted her till she stood before him.

He was a formidable man, and the fact that her chemise, nearly dry now, constituted no more than a few fragile threads between them made him seem that much more formidable. How easily those strong arms had plucked her from the ledge, carried her through the wood, picked her up from the ground. And how easily they could crush her in their embrace. But instead of inspiring fear, the thought sent a thrill of desire through her. How would it feel to have his arms enclosing her bare shoulders, to feel his hands splayed across her naked back?

The thought burned her cheek and made her eyes grow heavy. Her gaze settled on his lips, parted enough to glimpse the tips of his white teeth. What would he taste like? Bay? Mint? Smoke? She absently ran the tip of her tongue across her own lips.

They had been silent a long time now, and yet he hadn't dropped his gaze from her. His eyes had darkened, if that were possible, turning a deeper shade of black. As Mattie plumbed their depths with her own stare, she sensed danger for the first time. Not dread. Not menace. But a profound, exhilarating power that threatened to insinuate itself into her heart, to seize her soul.

The quick flash of a doe's ear through the trees alerted Sakote, dragging his attention from the white woman. Over Mati's shoulder, two deer boldly advanced toward the water. Sakote stared in mute surprise. For the first time in his life, an animal had crept up on him.

He frowned. What was wrong with him? He was the best hunter in his tribe. He'd made his first kill when he was no older than Hintsuli. And at the *Simi*, the deer dance, he was always given a place of honor. How, then, had the pair of does caught him unawares?

It was the woman. She stole his eyes and ears from him as simply as she'd drawn them on the paper. And she stole his sense from him as well.

For one moment, he'd looked at the woman, truly looked at her, and he'd seen a destiny—afternoons swimming together, nights lying entwined in her arms, seasons of sun and snow and children and laughter. In the blink of an eye, a whole lifetime had seemed not only possible, but certain.

Now he knew it was only deception.

The woman wasn't a shaman. She had no knowledge of even the simplest herbs. But she had power, dangerous power, power to blind and deafen him to the things of the Konkow world. He must break her control over him.

"Come," he said roughly, startling the deer.

Mati turned at the sound of rustling leaves. "Oh, look!" she whispered. How innocent her voice was, like a child's. Her face lit up with delight. "*Tem-diyoki.*"

That wasn't the right word. They weren't fawns. And though it impressed him that she knew something of the Konkow language, it was best that she forget. Without another word, he laced his moccasins tight and prepared to take her home.

"You must return to your camp." And I to my people, he thought.

He saw a brief longing pass over her eyes, the same longing Hintsuli showed just before he begged to play the grass game for just one more finger of sunlight. She was happy here, as he'd known she would be, and she didn't want to leave.

But they both had responsibilities. He had to repair his fishing net and chip a new arrowhead. And she had to pan for her precious *oda*.

He helped her pull the dress over her head. How ugly it was. The brown sack concealed her beauty like the soap root hid the tender white bulb within. Mati sighed when she saw the garment's ragged hem, but said nothing. She pulled on the boots, which seemed too large for her tiny feet, and gathered her sketchbook and drawing sticks.

He knew she couldn't walk all the way to her *hubo*. The knee wound would begin to throb and bleed again, and the fall might have given her injuries she wouldn't feel until tomorrow. It was a grave risk he took, walking to the *willa*'s camp with a white woman in his arms, but he had no choice. Bowing his back, he lifted her to nestle against him.

Her hair was wet against his chest, but he liked the smell of it, fresh and clean like the creek.

"Mr. Indian, I assure you, I can walk on my own." The softness of her voice belied the stiff words.

He ignored her, flicking his head to toss his hair over his shoulder.

And then she touched him, spread her small white fingers across his chest. He felt her imprint like a tattoo.

"You needn't..." She broke off her words as her gaze halted on his mouth.

He stopped breathing.

She took her hand from his chest and lifted it with the

stealth of a wildcat. Her fingertips brushed his lower lip, tracing it with fire, then came to rest lightly on his cheek. Before he could utter a sound, she leaned forward, so close he could feel her breath upon his mouth. Then she closed her eyes and pressed her lips to his.

He couldn't move. He couldn't speak. It was that thing, that rite that made Towani sigh with joy. His lips tingled where Mati touched him, and he felt a bolt of current stab through his body like lightning, straight to that place where desire resided. It was wondrous and powerful and terrifying all at once. He wanted to answer her with his mouth, to breathe her breath, to drink her like manzanita cider.

But she suddenly broke off from him, blushing and shielding her eyes with her lashes, and he was left with the gnawing hunger of the bear awakening from his winter sleep.

He was silent all the way back, but his thoughts chattered on. Over and over they told him he must forget Mati. He must forget her serpentine eyes and her tawny hair and her delicate hands. But most of all, he must forget her soft lips and the way they'd almost sucked his soul from him.

She, too, was quiet, and he couldn't guess her thoughts, but their journey through the woods would be over soon. Then he'd no longer trouble himself with her. *Akina.* It was over. He'd saved the white woman's life. The bad *kokoni* would not return. Now Towani would be safe. The Konkow would be safe.

"Look. Someone's at my—"

It was all Sakote allowed her to say. With one hand, he buried her face against his chest, muffling her voice, and froze, staring at the figure on her doorstep. Mati struggled in his confining embrace until he hissed at her for quiet.

Through the meager veil of pine branches, Sakote studied the visitor at Mati's house. He had curly hair the color of dead wood and skin as red as salmon. The man had no flowers, but his arms were full of tins, and Sakote knew the tins were full of things to eat. More courting. He curled his lip. How easy it was for the white man to bring her food. He didn't have to perform the hunting dance or make his own bow and arrows. He didn't have to pray for the animal's spirit or give thanks to Wonomi. He didn't have to hide in the brush all morning and cut meat all afternoon.

Mati pushed up from his chest with a frustrated shove and a harsh whisper. "What's the matter with you?" She followed his gaze. "You're afraid of him?"

He shot a glare of disdain at her. Afraid? How could he be afraid? The man on her doorstep couldn't even hunt his own food.

And yet, in a sense, she was right. He was terrified of the white man. Of what the *willa* brought to the land of the Konkow. Not just the disease that had killed his father and half of his tribe, but of his relentless hunt for gold and his love of strong drink. And of what he would do to Sakote if he caught him with a white woman.

Mati slid from his embrace like a seed slipping from its hull, leaving him empty and cold. She straightened her skirts, shook her hair back from her shoulders, and looked up at him with eyes as clear as the summer sky.

"Wait here," she breathed. "I'll be back."

He let her go. Even though his heart grew heavier with each step she took away from him. Even though the same light that brightened the man's face when he caught sight of Mati cast a shadow over Sakote's spirit. Even though he knew he wouldn't be waiting when she returned.

Getting rid of Ned Buttram was no easy chore. He'd brought her supplies, after all. Though his motives may have been selfish, Mattie couldn't very well turn him away, especially when he began to go on at length about his dead wife. The self-involved man didn't seem to notice her damp hair, her cracked forehead, her bandaged hand, or her ripped hem, apparently distracted by his own determination to prove his suitability as a suitor.

When he finally got to the crux of his conversation—whether Mattie would allow him to call on her—she was beside herself with anxiety, her thoughts a thousand miles away. Would the Indian still be waiting for her? Would he come inside her cabin? Would he have supper with her? Would he stay the n-...

"That is, if you don't mind, ma'am."

Mattie shook herself from her daydreams. "Mind?"

"If you don't mind me comin' to call." He rolled the brim of his doffed hat in his fingers and pursed his lips, awaiting her reply.

"Um, well, to be perfectly candid, Mr. Buttram," Mattie said uncomfortably, racking her brain for some plausible excuse, "I'm still, well, my husband only recently...er..."

"Well, you say no more, ma'am," he replied, taking her hand and patting the back of it in a fatherly manner. "I can see you're still aggrieved about Doc Jim. Just put it right out of your mind then." He blinked sympathetically and turned to go. Then, glancing at the half dozen tins he left behind, he thought better of his investment. "You prob'ly better bear in mind, though, ma'am, bad weather's not far off. In the gold fields, there ain't much time for nothin', not grievin' or marryin' or gettin' braced for winter."

Guilt washed over Mattie like rain. "Mr. Buttram, I'd like to pay you for the food you've brought."

He snorted. "I won't hear of it, ma'am. It's the least I can do for a purty lady."

Mattie stifled a chuckle. She'd never been called "purty" before, and at the moment, she couldn't deserve the compliment less. "Then let me give you something in return," she offered. "Would you like your portrait sketched?"

He beamed, and after a little hemming and hawing, was convinced to take her up on her offer.

She whipped out her sketchbook, sharpened a pencil, and proceeded to render the fastest, most careless drawing of a person she'd ever done. Ned didn't know the difference. He was, in his own words, as pleased as punch, and she managed to get him out her front door in a matter of minutes.

Mattie was disappointed, but not surprised to discover the Indian had left. The day had grown late. He probably had to return to his village before dark. Still, she wished he'd waited for her. She wanted to look at him once more, to speak with him. She gazed up at the plum-colored sky and wrapped her arms about her. Lord, she wanted to kiss him again.

What madness had driven her to do it the first time she didn't know. Aside from her kin, she'd never kissed a man. And yet it seemed the most natural thing in the world when no one was there to see and his mouth hovered so near. His lips were soft, much softer than his grim countenance would lead one to believe, and his breath was scented with sweet mint.

She wanted to draw portraits of him, to fill a whole book with him. She wanted to sketch him fishing and sleeping, swimming and eating, running and shooting his bow. She wanted to learn his expressions, to capture each emotion, to know every curve and plane and scar of his body intimately.

With a languorous sigh, Mattie sat on the edge of her plank porch and watched for the first star of evening. Where was the Indian now? While she sat alone, wistfully observing the night sky glimmer to life, what was he doing? Licking his fingers at supper? Telling ancient stories to Hintsuli? Smiling over the fire at the faces of his family? Or were they both gazing pensively at the same heavens?

The questions obsessed her. What did he do? How did he subsist? Where was his village? He surely couldn't live in a house much sturdier than hers, and yet the Indians had survived thus for generations. What were his people like? Did his mother sing his little brother to sleep? Had his father taught him to fish? What did they eat for breakfast?

She smiled as the first star winked on. She truly was her father's daughter. Like him, her intellectual curiosity was insatiable. Suddenly, she must know everything about the Indian's tribe, his family, him.

She wrapped her arms around her knees, mindful of her injuries, and let her eyes dance across the lacy silhouettes of the pines against the sky. The Indian dared not come into her world. There was too much fear here. He'd chased Hintsuli from it before, and tonight, he'd remained at the verge of her property, as if a physical barrier separated their domains.

No, she decided, taking one last breath of twilight before she took shelter for the night in her cabin, if she wanted to know more about the enigmatic Indian, she would have to go back to the waterfall, back to his world.

"Your thoughts are not with us tonight, my son."

Sakote's mother gave the acorn mush a stir, sprinkling in bits of wild onion. She was still beautiful, Sakote thought, despite the wrinkles that made tracks across her face and the silver that tipped her hair like the fur of an old grizzly. And as always, she could tell when his mind was not at peace.

"I'm thinking about my sister," he lied. "I wonder if she's safe." He couldn't tell his mother the truth—that he'd become so enchanted by a *willa* that he'd let deer come upon him unawares, that he'd carried the white woman through the forest by the light of day, that he'd forgotten his father's hunting pouch at the waterfall. He couldn't let her know that for one brief moment in time, his heart had betrayed his mind.

"My daughter will find her way," she told him, piercing him with shiny black eyes that could winnow the truth from his words as readily as skin from an acorn. "But I sometimes worry about my son."

"The little one?" Sakote frowned in concern and clenched his arms around his bent knees. Hintsuli was *his* responsibility. At least, Sakote felt that way. If the boy had done something wrong... "Does he offend the old ones? I've tried to teach him the way, but he's young. He's curious, like Raccoon, and there are many new things in the world to—"

His mother interrupted him with a soft chuckle. "He is like his father, full of dreams. But he'll grow and learn. One day his heart will yearn for another, and she will calm his spirit. Then he'll find his place." She rolled the heating rock through the basket of mush with her looped paddle. "But it isn't the little one I speak of."

Sakote lifted his head to meet her eyes.

"I worry about my first son."

He rocked back on his haunches, confused. He scanned the village quickly to make certain no one listened. The elders talked amongst themselves before the *kum*, the sweathouse. The children played with a buckskin ball. The women stirred mush and turned the roasting trout.

He leaned forward to murmur, "Why does my mother worry about her first son?"

She dipped a finger into the warm mush to test its flavor, then continued stirring.

"His heart is divided like a tree struck by lightning. His spirit walks in two worlds."

Sakote rubbed his thumb across his lip. "The Great Spirit will lead him down the true path."

She was silent for a long while. The soft crackle of fire, the

155

murmur of old men's voices, the scuffle of pine needles beneath the feet of shrieking children all receded into the distance. He heard only the slow, rhythmic stirring of the paddle through the mush basket.

"He is like...that other Hintsuli," she finally said, ignoring Sakote's startled intake of breath. It was dangerous to speak of his dead father. He stared at her, stunned silent, until she let the paddle rest against the side of the basket and returned his direct gaze. "He must make his own path."

Sakote thought about her words all through supper. Afterward, while his father's brother told the tale of Turtle and the beginning of the world, he thought about her words. And even when the elders gathered before the fire to discuss the *Kaminehaitsen*, the Feather Dance to come with the next moon, Sakote could think of nothing but what his mother had said.

When he slept that night, he dreamed again of the white, green-eyed eagle and the two eggs, of leaving his home and following the eagle north. But when he awoke, he was no closer to understanding either the dream or the destiny words of his mother.

Hintsuli occupied most of his morning. The boy was excited about the *Kaminehaitsen*, for he would see his brothers of the neighboring villages, some he hadn't seen since the last Feather Dance. He was as pesky as a yellow-jacket, wanting his own *wololoko*, a splendid headband of feathers, so he could impress his Konkow brothers. Of course, Hintsuli was too young to wear a *wololoko*. He wouldn't be stolen by the elders for his *yeponi* ceremony for many years.

But his little brother needed something, some symbol that he wasn't the same boy they'd met last year. Sakote had a long, slender piece of basalt he'd been saving to make a hunting knife. Perhaps he'd give it to Hintsuli.

They worked all morning together. Sakote flaked bits of

rock from the blade to make it sharp but strong, carved the wood handle and sealed them together with hot pitch. Hintsuli cut an old piece of deerskin into a long strip to wrap the handle. By the time it was finished, the boy beamed with pride, and the sun was high and hot on the earth.

As Hintsuli ran haphazardly off through the woods to show his friends his new prize, Sakote yelled after him to be careful.

He'd planned to snare a few squirrels today for the evening stew, but he'd left his hunting pouch at the waterfall. He frowned. He'd hoped to avoid places that would remind him of the white woman. But he had to retrieve it. The deerskin pouch was a gift from his father, and the tools in it— the snares, the knives, the mountain hemp line—would take days to replace.

So with a parcel of dried deer meat and a promise to his mother that he'd bring back some woodpecker feathers for her husband's *wahiete*—his ceremonial crown, Sakote set off for the waterfall.

The pouch was where he'd left it, beside the great boulder. But he couldn't help searching the wet banks of the pool, looking for some sign of the woman who'd come here with him. There was nothing. She'd left behind no scrap of cloth, no scent, not even a footprint.

Of course, that didn't mean her spirit was gone. She lingered here still—in the gurgle of water over the stones, so much like her laughter, in the verdant depths of the pool, like her eyes, and in the heat of the sun upon his shoulder, reminding him of the warmth of her arms around him.

"Damn!" There were no words of anger or frustration in Sakote's language, so he borrowed the curse from the white man.

It didn't matter what the elders said, what the dream tried to tell him, how tempting Mati was. He must follow the old ways, the ways of the Konkow, or they would be lost. The white woman showed him another path, a dangerous path, a path he must not take.

The sun continued to blaze upon his back, and he knew a quick swim in the pond would cool his blood. He took off his moccasins, freed his hair, and loosened the thong around his breechcloth, letting it fall to the ground. Climbing to the crest of the boulder, he took a full breath and dove into the shimmering midst of the pool.

The bracing water sizzled over his skin as he plunged deep through the waves. The chill current swept past his body, swirling his hair like the long underwater moss, washing away his thoughts.

He broke the surface and shook his hair back, then swam for the waterfall. It pounded the rock like a *kilemi*, a log drum, and made a mist that hid the small cave behind the fall. He climbed out onto the slippery ledge and stood up, easing forward into the path of the fall, where it pummeled him with punishing force, driving white spears into his bent back and shoulders. The pounding awakened his body and challenged him. He slowly raised his head, braced his feet, reached toward the sky with outstretched arms, and withstood the heavy fall of water with a triumphant smile.

Unfortunately, the loud thunder of the fall prevented him from hearing that he was no longer alone at the pool.

Mattie's jaw dropped. Her breath caught.

After sketching miners all morning, she'd decided to make a few drawings of the waterfall. She remembered the way there, and though she might have hoped the Indian would return, she didn't really expect him. The fact that he had indeed come back, and in such bold display, couldn't have amazed her more.

What in God's name was he doing? He stood at the foot of

the waterfall, as bare as the day he was born, letting the water beat him within an inch of his life and grinning all the while.

She thought to yell out to him, to reprimand him for such indecent behavior, such outrageous liberties, such flagrant...but then the artist came out in her. She realized that what she beheld was beautiful, that *he* was beautiful. Watching him in all his naked glory was like witnessing the birth of a god.

She perched on a rock wedged between two trees, hoping the lush foliage and her drab plaid dress would conceal her. She found an empty page and set to work sketching.

He couldn't remain there long, she knew, or else he'd be pounded into the rock. She had to work quickly, penciling in the bare bones and trusting the rest to memory.

Sure enough, just as she finished the roughest of renderings, he brought his arms down through the fall like great white wings and dove into the middle of the pool.

His naked body slicing through the water sent a rush of delicious fire through her. Her pencil hovered over the page. It was wrong, what she did, spying on him and sketching him in his altogether without his knowledge. And yet, she thought, patting a cheek grown hot with impropriety, it felt so right.

He bobbed up and flung his hair back, spraying droplets of water across the rippling surface.

Mattie pressed her pencil against her lower lip.

He swam forward, gliding through the waves as smoothly as a trout. Then he wheeled over onto his back and floated on the surface, boldly facing the midday sun like some pagan sacrifice.

Mattie's teeth sank into the pencil.

She could see everything—the naked sprawl of his limbs, the corona of his long ebony hair, the dark patch at the juncture of his thighs, and its manly treasure, set like a jewel on black velvet.

He was Adam. Or Adonis. He was Icarus fallen from the sky. Hera cast into the sea. As innocent as an angel. As darkly beautiful as Lucifer.

Mattie blushed to the tips of her toes. She most definitely should not be witness to this...this...she had no word for his wanton display, but she was sure it was completely indecent. Still she couldn't tear her eyes away. He was utterly, irrefutably perfect. And looking at him left her faint with a mixture of emotions as dizzying as whiskey and as unstable as gunpowder.

She slid the pencil from between her lips, flipped to a new page, and began to draw. Despite her rattled nerves, her hand was steady, for she captured every nuance of shade, every subtle contour, each flash of translucence, as if the water lived and moved upon the paper. And the man... He was so true to life that she half expected the figure to lazily pitch over and swim off the page.

A fern tickled her nose, and she brushed it back, and then leaned forward to put the finishing touches on the portrait—a few more branches dabbling in the waves, a leaf floating by his head. She decided on the title, scribbling it at the bottom beside her signature.

Just in time. The Indian knifed under, a flash of sculpted buttocks and long legs, disappearing beneath the surface and into the emerald depths.

Sakote saw the movement of branches from the corner of his eye, but gave no indication. If it was a deer, he didn't want to frighten it from its drinking place. If it was a bear, his splashing would scare it soon enough. If it was a *willa*, he'd have to be clever. He floated a moment more, letting the waves carry him gently toward the deepest part of the pool, watching for sudden movements through the dark lashes of his eyes. Then he gulped in a great breath and dove to the bottom, where the water was cold and shadowy.

He came up silently on the concealed side of the big granite boulder and eased his way out of the water and around the rock until he could see what hid in the brush.

Mati.

She wore another ugly brown dress with lines of other colors running through it like mistakes, and her hair was captured into a tight knot at the back of her head. She bit at her lower lip and leaned out dangerously far between two dogwood saplings, shielding her eyes with one hand, searching the pool for him.

Sakote didn't know what he felt. Joy. Or anger. Relief. Dread. Or desire.

Worry wrinkled her brow, and she leaned forward even farther, bending the saplings almost to the breaking point.

"Oh, no," she murmured.

Her words were only a breath of a whisper on the breeze, but they carried to his ears like sad music. Mati edged between the two trees and took three slippery steps down the slope. Meanwhile, Sakote moved in the opposite direction, up the rise. While she scanned the water, he crept behind her, stopping when he found the sketchbook on the ground, frowning when he saw the figure floating on the page.

Now he knew what he felt. Fury. He glanced down at his naked body, at his man's pride, shrunken with cold to the size of an acorn, then at its perfect duplicate drawn on the paper. And he felt as if he would explode with rage.

He must have made a sound, some strangled snarl of anger, for Mati turned. And screamed.

CHAPTER 13

Sakote reached for the sketchbook. He was tempted to throw it into the water, but instead used it to shield his man's parts from her view. To his satisfaction, the white woman began stammering and blushing, and when he took a step toward her, she almost tripped backwards into the pool.

"What is this?" he demanded, tearing the page violently from the book and shaking it at her. "You make such pictures to shame me?"

Her chin trembled and she blinked many times, but he was certain she wouldn't cry. No, she was like Hintsuli when he got caught using Sakote's yew bow. She knew what she'd done was wrong. She knew she deserved his anger.

He grunted, and then dropped the sketchbook to give his full attention to the page he'd torn out. With a determined scowl, he placed his fists together at the edge of the paper and began to tear.

"No!"

Her shriek unnerved him almost as much as her dive

toward him. He had torn only a small rip in the paper when she either threw herself or fell to her knees before him.

"Please!" she begged. "Don't ruin it!" Her hands dug desperately at his thighs. "I'll never do it again. I promise. Only don't tear it."

Sakote grimaced. Why did she plead so passionately over a piece of paper? And why did she have to touch him like that? Son of Wonomi! Her woman's touch softened his anger and made him weak. He wondered if she knew the power she wielded, if she knew how close she was to arousing him, how only the thin sheet of her sketch stood between his awakening spear and...

Her lips. They trembled, and her eyes shone like acorn caps full of rain. Now she looked as if she might indeed weep.

His mouth twisted. Troublesome woman! Why did she want the drawing of him so badly? It didn't show him hunting or dancing or making fire. It only showed him floating helplessly on his back like a leaf, twirled by the will of the water. By The Great Spirit, with his male parts shrunken by the cold, he didn't even look like he'd grown to manhood. He wondered what insult she'd scribbled at the bottom.

"What does this say?" He rapped the paper with his knuckle.

"What?" She was startled by his question. "It's...it's a name."

"What name?"

She seemed reluctant to tell him. "Ne-, Neptune."

"That's not my name."

"No."

"Who is this Neptune?"

She didn't answer, and he prepared to tear the page again.

"Wait!" she relented, blushing like poison oak in fall. "Neptune is a god! He's the god of water."

God? It was the last thing Sakote expected. *Fool* maybe.

Drowning Baby. Or *Crazy Mr. Indian Who Calls Himself a Man*. But *God*? He was simultaneously pleased and horrified.

A drop of water eased down his dark thigh and over her pale finger. His will, too, seemed to slip as easily from him. How could he deny the fragile, golden-haired angel who named him god? Especially when she looked up at him with wide green eyes as moist and innocent as a doe's? Those eyes could steal his soul from him, he knew, and when his gaze dropped to her mouth, the memory of her lips, sweet and yielding upon his own, sent a lethal rush of warm blood through his veins. He wanted to taste her again. He wanted to bury his hands in her gold-dusted hair and nuzzle her soft cheek, to press his mouth against hers and feel her breath slip between her lips.

"Why do you call me god?" His voice sounded strange to his ears, like the hoarse whisper of the wind, and like the wind, his words rushed out with a will of their own. "My name is Sakote."

Silence hung between them like fog, and he began to wonder at his own wisdom. Why had he told her his name? A man's name was for kin or close friends, not for *willa* women who would cast it about carelessly.

"Sakote," she murmured.

Like that, he thought, and yet he didn't flinch. His name sounded right on her lips, like the soft rattle of the instrument for which he was named. He wished to hear it again upon her tongue.

An escaped spiral of hair lay upon Mati's cheek. He longed to take away the pins and let all the curls tumble like a waterfall. And that wretched dress...it was like the thorny covering of the gooseberry, concealing all the sweetness. Yet Sakote's heart quickened, remembering the graceful curve of her waist and the small flower buds of her nipples. He was so close to her, in arm's reach. Close enough to see her heart beating in the column of her throat. Close enough to feel the faint breeze of her warm breath upon his river-cold skin. Wonomi help him, he longed to do far more than kiss Mati now. His heart pounded, and his body filled with need.

But he couldn't play courting games with her. It wasn't right. She hadn't asked for his touch. And Sakote wasn't like her *willa* husband, to force himself upon a woman. No, he was Konkow, and this was one of those dangerous ways from which he must turn.

With a grunt of regret, he surrendered the drawing to her unharmed. His only consolation was her startled squeak as he stood newly revealed before her, no longer shrunken with cold, but like a warrior roused for battle. Scowling, he turned and trudged down the embankment to find his breechcloth before that determined warrior could betray him completely.

The Indian was halfway down the slope before Mattie could suck air back into her lungs. Even then, she couldn't breathe properly. His naked backside gleamed tan and taut as he scaled the hill, and the thought of what graced his *front* side, the proud member that had loomed inches away just a moment before, left her jaw lax and her body boneless.

For a time, obsessing over her sketch, she'd almost believed he was a god—distant, perfect, untouchable. But when she'd seen him on the embankment, dripping from the stream, his brow furrowed, his eyes snapping, all flesh and blood and muscle, the truth struck her like a thunderbolt.

He wasn't a god. He was a man. And he was far from untouchable.

In fact, if he'd remained before her one more moment, she feared she might have proven that without a doubt. Wicked thoughts had run through her head and did still, thoughts of running her fingertips along the smooth bands of his stomach, of lapping up the drops of water that trickled down his chest, of hurling herself into his savage embrace to seal her passion with a breathless kiss.

But he'd escaped. Now he donned his breechcloth and tied it up with a decisive jerk of the thong. Mattie struggled to her feet, slipping on the leaves. He paid her no mind, but pulled his moccasins up over his heels. She glanced at the drawing still clutched in her hand. It was beautiful. *He* was beautiful—savage, proud, and pure. And he was fast eluding her.

"Sakote!"

He raised his head, but wouldn't look at her.

If he left, she thought in inexplicable panic, she might never see him again. "Please, Mr. Sakote," she called softly, "allow me to draw you again."

He lifted cool black eyes to her.

"However you want," she added, worrying the edge of the paper between her fingers. "With your horse or...or in your teepee, with your peace pipe, anything."

A small frown crossed his brow.

"Please." She glanced at the drawing again, then placed it diplomatically behind her back. "I don't wish you to leave with anger between us."

After a long while, the Indian finally nodded.

Mattie felt a breath of relief rush out of her. She resisted the urge to clap her hands together in glee.

"Come after the sun rises tomorrow," he told her.

"I won't be late," she promised.

Before she could utter another word, he vanished into the wood.

Mattie studied the sketch of him one last time. It was perfect, except for the small tear at the top of the page. And upon closer inspection, she decided even that was perfect, for beside the tear was the muddy imprint of the man's thumb. Sakote had signed his portrait. She ran her own thumb across the mark like a caress. She could hardly wait till tomorrow.

At sunrise, Sakote took care to make no noise as he combed and tied his hair neatly back with a thong. But when he shouldered his bow and slung his rabbit fur quiver across his back, Hintsuli attacked him with so many questions that he feared the boy would wake the whole village.

"Where are you going?" the boy wanted to know. "What are you hunting? I want to go, too."

"No," Sakote whispered. "Our mother only wishes me to get woodpecker feathers."

Hintsuli knew better. He eyed Sakote's *punda*, the bow and arrows, weapons too large for shooting woodpeckers. Sakote could see the boy preparing to launch a loud, long protest. He held up his hand to halt it.

"All right, little brother," he muttered. "I'll make a trade with you. If you say nothing of my hunt today, I'll take you to the valley tomorrow to visit Towani and Noa."

Hintsuli's eyes lit up. The boy would keep silent.

Sakote managed to leave unnoticed, which was fortunate, since it wasn't even the right season for hunting deer. It would have been difficult to explain to the tribe that he was taking his bow and arrows to have his picture drawn.

At least, that was the reason he gave himself for why he was going to see the white woman again. He wanted a picture, a *decent* picture—Sakote the Hunter with his bow—to show at the *Kaminehaitsen* dance, a drawing to impress the Konkows from the other villages. And perhaps gain him a woman.

That last thought filled his mouth with a bitter taste like unleached acorns. He didn't really want a woman, at least not the women he knew from the neighboring villages. They were sweet and adoring, some of them, and some of them could stir his loins with a look. Many of them were pretty, and most of them were willing. But they didn't speak to his heart.

The truth was his blood warmed only at the thought of

seeing Mati. But why was he so attracted to her? What was it about the white woman that made him feel powerful and alive?

He asked himself those questions as he hiked through the wood, scaling granite walls, crossing deer trails, all the way to the waterfall. His only answer was his heart's leap of joy when he saw that Mati was already there, sketching something at the water's edge.

Squatting by the pool in a beige dress that puffed out around her, she looked like a succulent *yo meningwa*—mushroom. One hand braced the sketchbook while the other covered the page with confident strokes. Her hair was pulled back again into a tight knot at the back of her head, exposing the slim pillar of her neck, as delicate as a doe's. As he came up behind her, he battled the desire to press his lips to the hollow at the back of her neck. Instead, he peered over her shoulder.

"Salamanders," he said.

She gasped and nearly toppled into the water. He made a grab for her elbow to keep her from falling.

"Oh!" she cried, clapping one hand to her throat. "I didn't hear you."

A wave of fragrance wafted off her hair. She smelled good, almost like blackberries, but lighter, warmer.

"Stealth makes a good hunter," he said.

"You must be an excellent hunter then," she said with a smile. She showed him her drawing. "I was just sketching these...what did you call them?"

"Salamanders. It's the white man's word."

"Do they bite?"

He laughed softly. Hintsuli had once asked the same question. "The females are harmless," he told her, just as he had his little brother. Then, with a straight face, he added, "But the males have long, sharp teeth that can bite through deerhide."

168

He took the sketchbook from her, setting it aside, and turned her hand palm up, cupping it slightly. He scooped a small amount of water into her hand, and then reached gently down to capture one of the slippery black creatures. Her mouth grew round in amazement as he lowered his clasped hand atop hers, slowly opening it to let the animal settle onto her palm. For a moment he kept his hand there, forming a dark cave, and he was astounded by how small her hand looked beneath his, small and pale and helpless. Then he slowly lifted his hand to reveal the treasure beneath.

Mati took a closer look. "Oh, aren't you lovely? Such sweet eyes, and look at your delicate little toes."

Sakote shook his head. Why did women always fuss over small creatures?

"And look," she said, showing him, "under her belly, she's as bright as a poppy." She lifted trusting eyes to him. "She's absolutely lovely."

He fought to keep his face solemn as Mati fell neatly into his trap. "She?"

Mati froze. Then her eyes widened, and she opened her mouth in a silent gasp. Sakote grinned and grabbed her wrist before she could fling the poor salamander halfway across the pool in terror.

"You!" she accused when she discovered his jest. The corners of her mouth twitched with amusement. "This isn't a male!"

He shrugged.

Her brow furrowed in wonder. "They don't bite at all, do they?"

His grin widened, and he shook his head.

She lowered the salamander back into the water. "Well, swim along home now, darling," she sang sweetly. Then she turned to Sakote with a mischievous look in her eye and gave him a shove that almost knocked him off his haunches. "Bite through deerhide indeed," she said smugly. "Mr. Sakote, I believe you have a bit of the devil in you."

He chuckled. If she could read his thoughts, she'd know he had more than just a bit of the devil in him. He wanted her to push him again, harder, to lay him out flat on his back. He wanted her to sit astride him with her bare flesh to his. And he wanted her to make that kiss with him again. And again.

Mattie hoped the Indian couldn't read minds. He'd be appalled at the unladylike thoughts whirling through her brain. As if his sly, charming grin and eyes that twinkled like the night sky weren't enough to send her pulse racing, now he'd exposed flashing white teeth and revealed a charismatic laugh that was nothing short of contagious.

She wanted to play, to wrestle with him as if they were a pair of frolicsome puppies. She wanted to spread her hands across the massive chest she'd just shoved, to feel the heat and strength of him, to tickle his ribs until he gave her the gift of laughter again. And as he giggled, she wanted to press her lips to his and catch his delight in her own mouth.

"Are you ready?" he asked.

His words caught her off guard. She stared at him blankly.

"The sketch?" he prompted.

She could feel the color rise in her cheeks, and she gave her head a mental shake. It was time to be professional. "Yes." She gathered up the sketchbook and pencils and tried to focus on finding a good location for the portrait. "I see you've brought your bow. Could you, that is, would you show me how you stand when you shoot it?"

With alarming grace and speed, he whipped an arrow from the quiver, nocked it to his bow and knelt on one knee.

"That's...that's perfect." It was. And so was he. His hair, sleekly caught in back, revealed the swell of his shoulder as he drew back the arrow. His back was straight, a good contrast for the bend of the bow, and the way his legs were positioned exposed the impressive muscle of his flank. She swallowed hard.

"If you could pose just like that in the patch of sunlight on the far bank," she breathed, "then I'll sketch you from this side."

He crossed over the narrow part of the creek opposite the fall and knelt in the grass on the other side. Calling out over the water, she guided him to the angle she wanted, not an exact profile, but faced slightly toward her, enough to capture both his dramatic silhouette and the expression on his face.

"Yes, there. Stay there. I'll tell you when you can move."

He was an impressive model. He didn't move a muscle, though his arm must ache from holding the drawn bow. In fact, he was so still, Mattie worried about him.

"Are you still breathing, Mr. Sakote?" she yelled over the fall.

"You sketch," he called back. "I'll breathe."

She smiled. He was one of her most patient subjects, if not her most eloquent.

In fact, he remained completely still for at least ten minutes as she penciled in each strand of hair, every tendon, the blades of reeds bent beneath his knee. Only then did his eyes begin to shift occasionally, to glance along the bank where she worked, as if gauging how much longer she would take. She looked up for reference less frequently now. The drawing was almost finished. She had only to add a few overhanging branches, a bit of shadow to the rocks.

So when all at once he pivoted toward her, her heart did a quick flip.

Dear God! His arrow was pointed straight at her. She fumbled her pencil, dropping it, and then froze in shock.

His face grew hard as granite, and cold murder crystallized his narrowed black eyes into chips of flint. The corners of his mouth drew down into the same grim curve as the bow, and his arm flexed back an inch more.

Mattie screamed.

The bowstring snapped, and the arrow sped toward her.

CHAPTER 14

Swede rapped his knuckles on the door frame for the third time. "Miss Mattie, are you home?"

He and Zeke had come to tell her that new supplies had arrived in camp by mule. If she wanted to special order anything, she had to do it now. He was also supposed to invite her to the fandango later this evening, a little Saturday night diversion some of the boys had gone whole hog putting together.

Zeke spit a stream of tobacco off the porch. "Maybe she's gone prospectin'," he volunteered.

Swede rocked back his hat and scratched his forehead. "Aw, she's probably off doin' some of them pitchers for the boys. Have you seen the one she made of Jasper?" He chuckled. "Ugly as mud. True to life, but ugly as mud."

"At least she found somethin' to bring in a little chicken feed. Lord knows old Doc couldn't pan shit outta that claim of his."

Swede shook his head. "Well now, Zeke, we both know there ain't a body in Paradise Bar that'd let a purty little thing like Miss Mattie go narry cent. Hell, half the camp's gone a-courtin' the lady."

Zeke spat again, wiping a dribble from his chin with the back of his tobacco-stained sleeve. "She take up with any of 'em?"

Swede crossed his arms over his chest and raised a brow at his partner. "Why? You interested?"

"Me?" he squeaked. "Hell, no." He straightened his coat and gazed off dreamily across the meadow. "You know Granny's kinda sweet on me."

Swede laughed so heartily his arms came unfolded. "Granny? Sweet on you? Shit! She's sweet on you like vinegar's sweet on pickles."

Zeke hooked his thumbs under his suspenders, none the worse for wear for the insult. In fact, there was a twinkle in his eye. "I reckon I'm an acquired taste."

Swede clapped him on the back, and they both had a good laugh over that. But the day was moving on, and the man with the mule wouldn't wait all morning. They had to find Miss Mattie.

Swede squinted into the fried egg sun and scratched at his ear. "You don't reckon the little miss got herself into trouble, do you?"

"What kind o' trouble?"

Swede shrugged. "Any kind o' trouble."

They stared at each other a minute.

Then Zeke cussed. Now that Swede had planted the seed, of course, they were obliged to make sure Mattie was all right. "There goes my payroll for the day."

"We'll check the crick first."

Swede hoped they'd find her fast. The boys would never forgive him if he didn't bring her to the fancy party they'd been slaving over. And he'd never forgive himself if something bad happened to the little lady.

Mattie's scream was swallowed in a bloodcurdling yowl as she fell backward in a tumble of skirts, landing hard on her elbows. The arrow had missed her, but where had it gone? And what had made that sound?

She whipped her head around, and what she saw made her heart lurch. The shaft had lodged in a rotting stump behind her. And snarling in anger top the stump, baring a mouth full of sharp, curved teeth, was the biggest cat she'd ever seen.

Mattie froze, afraid to move a muscle. The beast looked like a lion—nearly as large as a man, with a sleek, muscular body and paws big enough to fill a pie tin. Its teeth were long and pointed, clearly designed for tearing...meat. Dear God, was it going to kill her?

Sakote barked something at the animal, and the cat, flattening its ears, reluctantly hopped down to slink off through the brush. Mattie let out the breath she'd been holding.

A splash alerted her to Sakote's approach. He crossed the stream, concern etching his features. He dropped his bow and hunkered down beside her.

"Are you all right?"

"I...I think so. What *was* that?"

"The miners call it a mountain lion."

She gulped. She'd been right then. She'd almost been its dinner. "If you hadn't... If I'd been... Oh, Sakote." She lunged into his arms, falling into his embrace as naturally as a fearful child burrowing into a mother's skirts. "Thank God. Thank *you*."

"Shh."

With the lion gone and Sakote's heart beating strong and steady against her ear, soothing her, it wasn't long before her thoughts began to drift to the hero who'd come to her rescue. His bare chest was as solid and smooth as a mahogany cabinet, and his sun-kissed flesh felt warm against her cheek.

The scent of spice and rawhide and the stream that clung to him wreathed her head. And when his arms tentatively enfolded her, his hands coming to rest gently at the small of her back and the crown of her head, she closed her eyes to revel in the sensation. It was so forbidden, this embrace, and yet so natural, so protective, so comforting.

Sakote knew he shouldn't touch the white woman. He knew how dangerous the road of desire was. But Mati felt so right tucked against his chest. Her breath tickled him, and her curled fingers felt cool on his skin. He tentatively brushed the curve of her back, the back of her head, and then, with a sigh at his own recklessness, succumbed to pulling her close against him.

When he'd seen the mountain lion edging toward Mati, dwarfing her with its large, muscular body, his heart had dropped to the pit of his stomach. He'd acted on pure impulse, firing the arrow to frighten it away.

Never had he felt such a powerful surge of protectiveness. It didn't matter that the beast had likely not intended to hurt her, that it had only come to the pool for water. The need to keep Mati safe was overwhelming.

She settled into his arms now as easily as he slipped into his moccasins, fitting perfectly into the crook of his shoulder. Her hair felt like soft doeskin beneath his fingers, and her scent...

Sakote breathed deep of the woman, and he realized he didn't want to let her go. The thought was terrifying.

The silence stretched between them like a canyon, growing deeper and harder to cross by the moment, as he stroked her hair and listened to the ragged sound of her breathing.

Finally she tilted her head up to look into his eyes and whispered, "You saved my life...again." She tried to smile, but it quavered on her lips.

Her words pleased him, and her eyes—so green, so grateful, so trusting—took his breath away. But he couldn't take more credit than was his due. He thumbed a stray lock of hair back from her forehead. "You probably frightened him more than he frightened you."

She pushed away slightly, leaving her small fists upon his chest. "He wasn't hunting me?"

"He came to the water to drink." He slid his hand down to rest at the back of her neck, longing to wrap the curls around his finger.

"But you shot at him."

"Only to chase him away."

Mati seemed to consider this for a moment. She caught her lower lip beneath her teeth. He remembered how soft that lip was. "Will he come back?"

Sakote almost didn't hear the question. He could think only of her mouth and how he wanted to make a kiss with her again. His voice cracked. "Eventually."

"Maybe I'll wait till he returns and do a sketch of him."

Sakote raised a brow. He doubted the mountain lion would sit still for a picture. And just because he hadn't been interested in eating the white woman didn't mean he wouldn't be hungry later. Attacks were rare, but they did occur.

"Oh!" Mattie said, pulling out of his embrace. "Your portrait." He began to miss her warmth at once as she reached down to pick up the drawing that had fallen to the ground.

He furrowed his brows over the sketch. It made him look like a capable hunter, worthy of the title of headman. "It's good."

Mattie stared at the portrait. It *was* good. But she could do better. At a distance, his manner was too aloof. The sketch didn't capture the proud jut of his jaw or the sparkle of his eyes. It didn't capture his spirit. He deserved something more intimate, more revealing.

"Don't give it the name of a god," he instructed.

She smiled, taking the drawing from him and locating a pencil. "What shall I call it then? Fierce Konkow Warrior? Hunter of the Great Lion? Sakote the Magnificent?"

"Just Sakote."

She placed the tip of the pencil on the page, keenly aware he watched her every move. "How do you spell that?"

He gave her such a quizzical look that she forgot her nervousness and almost giggled.

"I don't," he said.

It was her turn to be puzzled. "You don't? What do you mean, you don't? Do you mean you can't write?"

"The Konkows don't write words. There's no need. I am called Sakote."

Nonplused, she lowered the drawing to her lap. "But if your people don't write, how do you...remember anything?"

He chuckled, then locked his arms around his knees. It made him look boyish and utterly charming. "Words."

"Words?"

"We...tell stories."

Just the way he said it, with a twinkle in his eyes, Mattie knew Sakote must be a master storyteller. She imagined him sitting by the fire, holding Hintsuli spellbound with tales of adventure. "What kind of stories?" she prodded. "Can you tell me some of them?"

He shrugged and poked a finger at the ground, feigning reluctance. "They wouldn't interest you."

"Oh, but they interest me immensely. Please won't you tell me one?"

He absently drew a line in the dirt. "Maybe later."

He was being intentionally coy. It made her heart flutter. And now she knew how she could achieve the sketch she desired. "Please?" she crooned. "I'll make another portrait of you while you're telling the story."

The corner of his mouth curved up, and she knew she'd convinced him.

"Come into the light," she urged.

The waterfall framed him perfectly, a dark angel against the churning white froth, and his skin glowed like polished bronze in the sunlight. Mattie found the effect he'd had on her before, from across the pool, only intensified at close range. Now she saw the rise and fall of his splendid chest and the flex of his shoulders as he settled cross-legged onto the grass. This close, she glimpsed the subtle curve of his lip and the tiny wrinkles at the corners of his eyes that spoke of a happy life.

This portrait would be special. This was the one she would keep by her bed to look upon, years hence, when Sakote sat around the fire telling stories to his children...and she slept alone in her cabin in the gold camp, when the nights grew cold and her heart lay empty.

Where that ridiculous, melancholy thought came from, she didn't know. After all, her future still lay bright before her, didn't it? Besides, it was absurd to pine over someone she hardly knew.

She picked up her pencil and touched it to the paper. He was staring at her. Why it unnerved her, she didn't know. After all, she'd just spent several moments in the man's arms. But his black eyes seemed to bore into her soul.

She cleared her throat and tried to focus on the page. "Perhaps if you..."

She looked up. Something was wrong with his pose. His hair. It should be down, flowing over his shoulders, a visual echo of the water coursing over the rocks.

She set aside her sketchbook and approached, crouching beside him.

"If you could..."

She lifted her hands to his hair, but her fingers trembled as if she were trying to touch lightning. Mentally scolding herself, she set about briskly untying the thong binding his hair. When it loosened, the strands spilled like ink over her fingers and down his back. She moved before him then and ran both hands through the hair at his temples, bringing his locks forward over his collarbone. His hair felt like China silk, and she brushed her fingers through it several times before she realized he'd stopped breathing.

His eyes had a dark cast now, as if a mist of desire clouded them, and she felt the same mist darken her own vision. His nostrils quivered once, like a hound that has caught an unfamiliar scent, and she sensed momentary fear in him. Her fingers still wove through his hair, white warp against black weft, and she rubbed the gossamer texture between her fingers. She wanted to feel those silken threads across her cheek, against her mouth, upon her breast. Her eyes grew languid with the thought. His skin, vibrant and lush, shone the color of creamed tea. She wondered if he tasted as smooth. Her lips parted of their own accord, and Sakote's eyes lowered at once at their invitation.

She could think no more. All she could do was react. Curling her fingers into his hair, she drew near, letting her eyes flutter closed as longing overwhelmed her. Touch alone guided her mouth to his, and when her lips found their harbor at last, she gave a small whimper of relief.

His breath was sweet as it rushed out of him. She pulled him even closer, wanting to taste more of him, needing to devour all of him. She let her tongue slip between her lips and brush over his, and white-hot fire seared her body.

Suddenly he was answering her, and a thrill of fear sent her heart racing. His mouth consumed her. His tongue danced over her lips and plunged deep between them, ravishing her thoroughly, sending flames of lust flickering along her skin. A low growl sounded in his throat as he trapped her in his embrace, holding her helpless in unyielding arms.

She moaned in sweet anguish as he knelt closer, catching her thighs between his own and pressing his body boldly against hers. There was no mistaking the rigid member brazenly making its presence known against her belly. Mattie gasped softly. Lord, she'd witnessed but a fraction of his vigor before. She had every reason to be terrified. He was strong and commanding, seductive and powerful. But, God help her, she was overwhelmed and hungry for more all at once.

Sakote groaned and felt his groan echo inside Mati's mouth. He no longer controlled his actions. A wicked spirit must possess him to make him do such savage things to the white woman. His arms enclosed her like the eagle guarding its kill, and he fed on her like the great bird of prey, attacking her brutally, savoring the taste of her flesh. He'd never put his tongue inside a woman's mouth before. The sensation was like lightning snaking through his veins, searing his body alive.

But he couldn't stop. Though she whimpered and dug her fingernails into the flesh of his chest, he couldn't silence the storm raging all around him. He crushed his man's-knife against her soft belly, desperate to quiet its relentless longing.

And then the worst happened. He heard a noise.

"*Pinsuani!*" he hissed in the wrong language, jerking back from her and cupping his hand over her mouth to insure her silence.

He could hardly quiet his own ragged breathing, and it seemed like his heart beat as loud as a *kilemi* drum. He knew what the sound was. He'd heard it many times. It was the sound of menace, something far more dangerous than a mountain lion.

He had to run. Now. But how would he explain to Mati?

He pressed a forefinger to his lips in warning and released

her mouth. Her eyes were wide with fear, but she wisely made no outcry. He ran his hand through his hair, and then clasped her by the shoulders. Great Wonomi, she was so beautiful. He could hardly bear to leave her.

"It's...white men," he whispered. "I have to go."

Her brow crumpled in disappointment, and he felt as if a stone fell upon his chest. But there was no time to waste.

He scanned her face, memorizing her features. Then he retrieved his arrow, snatched up his bow, and sprinted up the hill, turning to take one final glance, one final drink of the intoxicating woman kneeling forlornly by the pool.

It was reckless, but he lifted his voice to her, just enough to carry to her ears. "Tomorrow?"

Taking heart at her quick nod, he crossed the stream and melted into the trees just as the two prospectors crowned the top of the rise.

CHAPTER 15

Mattie supposed it was good Sakote had left when he did. If Swede and Zeke had come upon her draped in wanton abandon across an Indian—which she very well might have been in another minute—they would have...well, she didn't know what they would have done, but with the fatherly concern Swede seemed to have for her, he might have stripped out a willow switch and turned her over his knee.

At any rate, given her dishabille and the flustered state of her nerves, she was less than civil when they came traipsing over the rise. Blushing furiously, she stammered in no uncertain terms that this was where she'd chosen to make her ablutions, for heaven's sake, and if they respected her delicate sensibilities as a lady, they ought not to come by unannounced ever again.

The ruse worked. Swede turned berry red, and Zeke nearly dug himself into a hole, kicking abashedly at the leaves. While they explained they'd been worried about her, Mattie gathered her things, careful to conceal her morning's sketches, and followed them back to the camp.

At Paradise Bar, purchasing supplies for the next week took Mattie's mind temporarily off of the morning's indiscretion and the pair of sparkling black eyes that made her heart skip. It also took the bulk of her earnings. She'd used up most of her reserves and eagerly bought all the tinned peaches and oysters the supply man could spare. Looking over the pinch of gold dust that remained in her bag, she realized she'd have to wait till the next mule's arrival to buy the yardage of calico to line her cabin walls. Then, on sudden inspiration, she poured the last of her wealth into the man's palm and took a handful of nails in exchange.

An hour later, Mattie dusted her hands together and perused the interior of her cabin. Her own sketches lined the walls, tacked artistically here and there to make a time line of sorts of her adventures, as well as covering the drafty cracks between the timbers. Argonauts and Panama natives, crusty miners and fresh-faced boys peered at her from the pictures, along with quail and lupines, manzanitas and butterflies. The only sketches she omitted from the gallery were those of Sakote. They were too personal, too revealing to include on the walls. No, those she would keep for her own private viewing.

She skimmed one of them now, the one she'd first drawn from memory in a heated passion. Even the rendering of the man had the power to make her heart beat unsteadily. But as she studied the drawing, she realized it was flawed. The portrait was recognizable as Sakote, but it didn't truly represent the man. In life, his eyes were not as cold as they appeared on the page, and his lips—had she really imagined them so unyielding?

A loud knock at the door startled Mattie from her thoughts, and she quickly stuffed the drawing back inside her portfolio.

It was the Campbells. All four boys, their hats doffed and their manners well in hand, had come to beg her attendance at some festivity the camp planned for the evening. At least, that was what she could glean from their chatter.

"We'd be much obliged if you'd…"

"…it bein' Saturday night an' all."

"…nothin' real fancy, just some of the boys…"

"…a few card games and whatnot to…"

"If you could see your way to join us…"

"…lots of eats and a little dancin' maybe."

"You do know how to dance?"

They waited with eyes agog and hushed breath. Of course she knew how to dance. She was a lady, after all. And how could she refuse the handsome lads?

"I'd be delighted," she told them, and her warm smile ignited a surreptitious nudging match between the siblings.

Only after they left did she pause to wonder how a camp full of men could possibly conduct a proper dance.

Her question was answered as she milled about the party later that evening. Because of the new supplies, Amos had prepared a savory supper—roast beef *and* boiled ham, as well as a rich oyster soup, sourdough biscuits, a velvety peach pie, and Madeira nuts and raisins. Everyone gathered in the blossom of light thrown by the dozen or so oil lanterns hung in the trees. The men cleared an area of the hard-packed dirt and let the first couple take the floor.

Swede bowed to his partner with solemn dignity and extended a meaty hand, the nails of which had been recently scrubbed to near white. His beaver hat and his black coat, though spare in girth and short in the sleeve, made a striking contrast to his freshly washed moon-bright hair, and his newly shaved chin was as round and smooth as a baby's bottom.

He nodded to the musicians. One of the Mexican brothers

strummed the guitar, Tom blew a lilting run on his fife, and Frenchy leaned into his weeping violin. Then, on Frenchy's hushed count of four, they proceeded to play a curious but danceable Mexican ballad interwoven with an Irish jig.

Swede's partner rushed to finish knotting a red kerchief around one arm, and then placed a hand lightly atop the big man's paw.

Without cracking a smile, the couple sashayed off.

Mattie bit back a horrified giggle at the mismated pair, yet no one around her appeared the least bit disturbed by the sight of Swede and Zeke circling around the packed dirt like the handsome swain and the belle of the ball. In fact, before the musicians could finish two more bars, several other "couples" joined in to take a turn about the deck. Nobody seemed to mind whether they wore the hat or the kerchief, as long as someone swung them around the dance floor.

Mattie knew she couldn't avoid the expectant stares of the miners for long. Granny was the only other *real* female in the camp, and by the look of the sour old woman lurching about to the strains of the lively music, she took to dancing like a cat took to water. Sooner or later, Mattie would have to accept the miners' invitations to dance.

She'd avoided looking at the huge cask of brandy that dominated the creaking table, set there by men who had no qualms about leaving it unattended. But now she believed she might need the liquor's fortification. Otherwise, it'd be a long night. Bracing herself, she managed to down four sips of the strong stuff before the song came to an end.

Everyone cheered, and all eyes went to her in askance. Swallowing her dread, she clapped her hands appreciatively.

"That was wonderful, gentlemen. I do believe I'm ready to dance now."

Mattie soon had cause to regret her words. The men didn't give her a moment to catch her breath. As soon as one gent finished up with a miner's minuet, another clasped her hand to beg the subsequent reel. She was passed from man to man like downy thistle on the wind.

The miners were cordial and decent—Swede watched with a stern frown to ensure that no one's hands strayed from her waist—but soon the dancing became sloppy. As the level of the brandy cask lowered, so did the facility of Mattie's partners. Billy Cooper might have fallen had it not been for her support as they keeled a bit too near the band. Red Boone stepped on her foot twice. Jasper Colton, his breath reeking with liquor, declared his sudden affection for her as they swayed over the food table. Even Zeke was drunk, dropping his head on her shoulder for a little snooze, mid-dance, before she jostled him awake and handed him off to Granny.

But the real chaos began when Dash, the oldest Campbell boy, asked her to dance.

"You'll have to forgive me if I sit this one out," Mattie panted, resting a hand on her bosom. "I'm a bit out of breath."

His younger sibling, Ben, smirked and elbowed him aside. "Why would she want to dance with you anyways? You were trompin' all over her the last time."

"What?" Dash gasped, mortified.

"Come along, ma'am," Ben continued with a wink, clasping her elbow. "I'll show you how a gentleman does it."

"No. Truly, sirs," Mattie intervened, removing his fingers from her arm with as much diplomacy as she could. "I'd be delighted to dance with either of you in a moment, but just now, I'm a little fatigued."

Jeremy, the youngest Campbell, had wandered up by now to see what the fuss was about. "You feelin' all right, ma'am?"

"Just a little tired," Mattie replied.

"You hear that?" Ben poked a finger at Dash's chest. "She wouldn't be tired if you hadn't plum wore her out."

"Me?" Dash shoved his sibling. "You were the one doin' all them fancy-dancy..."

Harley, the fourth brother, stepped between them. "What's all this about now?"

Dash pushed him aside. "She don't need you comin' to her rescue, little brother."

"Now wait a damn minute. Who the hell are you to..."

Dash's eyes grew wide, and he snagged the front of his brother's shirt in his fist. "What was that? What did you say? And in front of a lady?"

"Well, now, ma'am, I apologize," Harley said, tipping his hat, "and to show you just how contrite I am, I'd like to offer you my arm for the next dance."

"The hell you will!" Dash hollered.

"I'll be! Dash cussed!" Jeremy cried with glee. "Dash cussed!"

Jeremy hit the ground, followed shortly by Harley, both of them shoved there by their oldest brother.

"Dreadful sorry about that, ma'am," Dash tried to apologize, wiping his hands on his trousers. "The boys've got a wild nature, and—"

"Oh, yeah," Harley complained, scrambling to his feet again. "I got a wild nature, but you're the one's been pinin' away over the lady like a moonstruck cow."

Dash blushed ferociously. "I never—"

"Ah, criminy, you have, too," Jeremy piped in, getting up. "All of us have." He slugged Harley on the shoulder. "I even heard *you* composin' a ditty to the lady."

"What!" Harley bellowed. "Why, you good-for-nothin'..." He seized his accuser by the back of the collar, spun him around, and planted a swift boot to the seat of Jeremy's pants.

After that, Mattie lost track of who insulted whom and what fist contacted whose face. But the mayhem grew as fast as a wildfire, igniting every miner, Campbell or not, close enough to catch a stray fist. While she cowered behind the food table in mounting horror, the dancing deteriorated into a brawl.

The musicians seemed well-prepared for the eventuality. Their music fizzled to a halt, and they carefully stashed their instruments just inside one of the lean-tos. Then, to Mattie's dismay, they eagerly returned to join the fracas themselves.

Jasper Colton was the first casualty. He had imbibed generously from the cask of brandy, so the punch Ben threw to his chin pushed him over the edge of oblivion. Red Boone, drinking two cups to Jasper's one, soon followed when one of the Mexicans slammed into him, ramming him headfirst into a pine tree. Billy and Bobby Cooper fought their own private battle until Granny beaned them both over the head with one of Amos's giant iron skillets, while Zeke, too drunk to stand, cheered her on. Even Tom took a hefty swig of brandy, rolled up his sleeves, and rubbed his hands together, ready to go to work on anyone who looked at him cross-eyed. Frenchy, hardly a fighter, but unwilling to be left out, delighted in crowning unsuspecting victims with what remained of supper, and at least half a dozen miners battled with beans slopping down over their faces.

For Mattie, it was a nightmare of swearing, spitting, and smashing. Blood and sweat spattered the ground at every sickening thud of a fist, and grunts of pain filled the air. But worst of all, despite all the shocking violence, in a sense, the men actually seemed to be enjoying themselves.

It was Swede who eventually came to her rescue, and even he proved a dubious hero at best, swaying from the effects of overindulgence and cheerfully booting several brawlers back into the fray. But he was alert enough to see that Mattie was mortified, and sober enough to see her home.

How long the melee ensued, Mattie didn't know. She tucked herself into bed and covered her ears against the offensive din. It was still going on when she dropped off to sleep.

Towani looked well when Sakote and Hintsuli arrived at dawn to Noa's little rock-and-plank cabin nestled in the Valley of the Squaw Men. Sakote had never seen his sister so happy. Noa swung the little boy around in greeting, his grin a great crescent moon in his face. It was clear by the blush on Towani's cheek and the brightness of her eyes that there was great affection between his sister and his good friend, that perhaps they'd at last shared a bed.

The thought made him remember his own unrequited desire, and he chased the hope away before it could manifest in an unfitting manner.

"My brothers!" Towani squealed, running to greet them. "Welcome to our *hubo*."

Noa's house was the same, but not the same. Sakote saw Towani's touch everywhere—baskets and a grinding stone by the fireplace, a bunch of lupines in a cup on the table, her rabbit fur blanket tossed across the bed. Even Noa wore a pendant of shells Towani had made for him. And his sister was changed as well. She wore the long cloth skirts of a *willa*, and he recognized the blue shirt buttoned over her chest as Noa's.

The first thing Towani wanted to know, whispering to Sakote while Noa entertained Hintsuli with a deck of playing cards, was how the white woman fared.

"I had a dream," she murmured, picking at the buttons of her shirt. "I dreamed that the white woman had no food for winter."

He took her gently by the shoulders. "She has gold to buy food," he assured her. He didn't add that the miners provided food for Mati as if she were some old and respected shaman.

"Still my heart is uneasy," she told him. "If something should happen to the woman..."

"Nothing will happen to her."

She bit her bottom lip and coiled a lock of his hair around her finger. "If I could only be sure..."

Sakote sighed. His sister could always pester him into doing things he didn't wish to do. He tugged on the point of her chin. "All right, pesky mosquito. I'll make sure she has food for the winter."

Her eyes lit up. "Thank you," she breathed, and then she did something she'd never done before. She stood on the tips of her toes and kissed his cheek. He frowned. It was a curious custom, this kissing, and he wasn't sure he liked it coming from his sister.

Noa served biscuits, and they gathered near the fire. Sakote and Hintsuli sat on the dirt floor while Noa and Towani occupied the two split-oak stools. Sakote told them all the village news, which was little, and about the *Kaminehaitsen*, the Feather Dance, to come.

"My brother helped me to make a knife!" Hintsuli added, drawing the blade dramatically from its sheath.

"Ah!" Noa exclaimed. "That's a fine blade. Are you going to show that off to your friends?"

Hintsuli nodded enthusiastically, then put the precious knife away. "But the best thing is the pictures I got from the white woman."

Sakote's glance of condemnation shot toward Hintsuli like an arrow, but too late. The boy tugged several crumpled and folded pages from the back of his breechcloth. Noa and Towani looked on curiously.

"The white woman?" his sister asked.

"The white woman that used to be a *kokoni*," Hintsuli answered, smoothing the papers on the floor.

Towani paled.

191

"Hintsuli!" Sakote scowled. "She was never a *kokoni*. She's a white woman. That's all."

"Then how does she draw the magic pictures?"

"Those are some fine drawings," Noa said, turning his head to study the sketches. "Where did you say you got them?"

"Mati gave them to me," Hintsuli said.

"Mati?" Towani asked.

"Mati is the name of the white woman," Sakote explained, annoyed at Hintsuli and his loose tongue. "She makes pictures of the white men. That's how she gets gold."

"These are very good." Noa examined them closely.

Hintsuli plucked one from the bottom of the stack. "This one is me," he proclaimed proudly.

"So it is!" Noa said, holding it up at arm's length. "It looks just like you. Are you going to take this to the Feather Dance?"

Hintsuli nodded.

Towani was leafing through the sketches when she stopped, and a curious look came over her face. "And who is *this?*" Her eyes gleamed with mischief as she reversed the page.

Sakote clenched his jaw. Hanging from Towani's delicate fingers was the portrait of him with his bow.

He snatched it as fast as lightning, slamming it protectively against his chest, but not before Noa got a good look at it. Sakote was stunned. How had his little brother found the sketch?

"Well," Noa said, clearing his throat after an uncomfortably long silence. "I'd say that's a picture a man can be proud of."

Sakote didn't feel proud. He felt foolish. He fired a glare at Hintsuli that would have scorched wood, and the boy's eyes grew round as river rocks. As soon as he got Hintsuli alone, he vowed, he'd have a few choice words for him. His only consolation was relief that he'd let Mati keep the sketch of him naked.

"I...pulled the white woman from a ledge where she'd fallen." His explanation sounded lame, and his cheeks burned with humiliation. "She made the picture to repay me."

Noa and Towani exchanged a glance of amused conspiracy, which only added fuel to the fire of Sakote's shame. But instead of entangling himself further into their trap with weak words, he fought them with silence.

Hintsuli must have known Sakote was angry with him, for when Sakote rose to leave at midday, the boy made every excuse, even to the point of letting his eyes brim with tears, to stay with Noa and Towani. Finally, they relented, and Sakote was only too happy to make the journey home without his troublemaking little brother. Besides, watching his friend and his sister—the way she rested her hand with affection on Noa's sleeve, the way he tenderly brushed the hair back from Towani's eyes, the secret, loving gazes between them—made him long for the white woman who stirred his heart.

When Mattie awoke after the dance, it was so quiet she morbidly wondered if the miners had all killed each other. She performed quick ablutions and put on her best dress. It was Sunday, after all, the day of contrition, and Mattie suspected several miners had a wealth of confessions to make.

She was right. When she arrived at the makeshift church, most of the men looked as if they'd been dragged from their beds, unshaved, unwashed, bruised and miserable, still sporting last night's brandy-, sweat-, and blood-stained shirts. Only Tom Cooligan, thumping on his Bible at the fore of the ragtag congregation, had a cheery face for her. He may have been the only one who'd avoided getting bald-faced drunk, but Mattie was sure it wasn't from lack of trying. Nonetheless, Tom managed to deliver a ringing sermon that had the miners grimacing in pain and covering their ears. By the time he was finished with his scolding, Mattie thought she'd never seen such a remorseful bunch of wretches in her life.

It took them most of the day to do penance, what with Amos baking Mattie a special peach tart and the Mexicans singing her a ballad of apology that must have had two dozen verses. The Campbell boys, their handsome faces now swollen masses of plum-colored bruises, delivered their regrets one by one. Zeke punctuated his apology with several spits of tobacco, and Granny muttered something under her breath that Mattie would have sworn included the phrase, "better git used to it." Frenchy presented her with a nosegay of wildflowers and the recitation of a romantic poem which he performed in both French and English. The Cooper brothers couldn't remember much of what happened, but, egged on by their Ma, no doubt, they were more than willing to volunteer their strong backs and capable hands to do any odd jobs she needed done in penitence for whatever it was that had occurred last night.

Most contrite, of course, was Swede. He came to her cabin in the afternoon. As Mattie opened the door, she tried to hide her disappointment. She'd just combed her hair and pinned a few of Frenchy's flowers onto her bodice, preparing to meet Sakote at the waterfall. Now she'd have to delay the trip.

Swede crushed the brim of his doffed hat between his hands.

"May I come in, Miss Mattie?" he murmured.

"Of course." She swept her skirts aside and indicated the stool at the table.

The way he sank down upon it, she could tell he intended to take his time. She heaved a silent sigh and put on a brave face.

"Seems like I failed you, ma'am," he began, and from there on, despite her reassurances, he seemed to sink further and further into despondence.

By sunset she'd heard his whole life story. She learned that he had a wife and six little girls, each one not more than a year apart from the next, family he hadn't seen in two years. He'd been a poor sharecropper, and it had been his dream to come to California for a half-year at the most, long enough to strike it rich and return a wealthy man. But fate hadn't seen it that way. Instead, he was stuck at Paradise Bar, too proud to go home penniless, but too practical to hold much hope of riches.

Mattie, he said, reminded him of sweeter times back home, times when he was a decent husband with a good wife, and he was appalled at his behavior the previous night. What kind of father could he be, anyway, if he fell prey to demon liquor and forgot all his manners?

Mattie gave him all the bolstering she could, but by the time he finally pushed up from the stool and got ready to leave, her flowers lay wilted upon her breast, and the bottled candle on the table burned low. She'd missed Sakote.

Swede apologized, saying he didn't know why he'd burdened her with all his troubles. But Mattie knew why. She was a woman, and he was far away from his wife. The poor man needed a sympathetic feminine ear. Inwardly scolding herself for thinking about Sakote while Swede poured his heart out to her, she gave him a big bear hug. He sniffled once, then cleared his throat, jammed his hat down over his brows, and bid her good evening.

Sakote watched from the bushes outside Mati's cabin as the two shadows came together on the white cloth covering the window. Mati and...some man. His heart sank like a rock in a deep pond. He couldn't stop staring at the flickering silhouette. His body was suddenly weary, as if he'd run a very long way. Finally, he tore his eyes away and turned to walk home through the black night on feet made of stone.

He'd waited for her at the waterfall. While the sun crossed

the sky and skimmed the tops of the trees to the west, he'd waited for Mati. The sky turned to the color of poppies, then redbud, then coyote mint, and still he'd waited.

Then he'd begun to worry. What if something had happened to her? What if she'd fallen off another cliff? Or lost her way? Or crossed the mountain lion's path? His pulse racing, he'd charged recklessly along the path to her cabin, listening for sounds of distress over the fearful beating of his own heart.

And even when he saw her cabin, saw the cheery flicker of candlelight and heard the murmur of voices coming from within, he worried that perhaps a bad *willa*, an evil white man like her dead husband, might hold her captive.

But the shadows on the cloth had told him the truth. The man had taken Mati in his arms, and she'd returned the embrace. She hadn't come to Sakote at the waterfall because she preferred the company of another.

His chest ached deep inside, and though he tried to blame it on the long foolish run he'd made searching for the white woman, he knew the pain came from his heart, broken into shards like splintered obsidian.

CHAPTER 16

It was the following Friday when the miners decided something had to be done.

Swede ran a hand over the back of his neck and murmured, "Are you sure she's tucked in for the night?" He didn't like meeting this way, in secret, in the shadows. It was like they were a bunch of Paradise Bar vigilantes getting ready to string someone up.

"Her candles were all blowed out," Jeremy reported.

Swede gave one final glance in the direction of Mattie's cabin before he began. "Fellas, you know I don't cotton much to this kind of sneakin' around. Miss Mattie's a decent woman. She wouldn't think too kindly on us spreadin' tales."

"Well now," Tom Cooligan said, perching his hat toward the back of his head, "that's all well and good, but it's for the lady's sake we're meetin'."

Swede might not approve of their methods, but he agreed they had to take action. For five days now, Mattie had moped around her cabin like a kicked hound. Jasper and Red never saw her come to work her claim. Nobody got their picture drawn. Her gentlemen callers, and there'd been at least a dozen, had all been served a portion of the same polite disinterest. Something was troubling Mattie, and since she was the camp's resident darling, he supposed maybe the men's cloak-and-dagger goings-on could be forgiven.

"Maybe the lass is feelin' poorly," Tom volunteered.

"I tell you," Frenchy insisted, wagging his finger under Tom's nose, "her heart is broken."

Tom crossed his arms over his chest. "And what makes ye so sure o' that?"

Frenchy shrugged. "I am French. I know these things."

The rest of the miners nodded sagely.

"All right then," Swede said, looking real hard at the faces of the men gathered around the fire. "Which one of you did it? Which one of you broke her heart?"

They all looked about as comfortable as nuns in a whorehouse. Finally, Dash Campbell spoke up. "Mighta been me."

His brother Ben promptly smacked him with a hat, which couldn't have felt too good on that yellow bruise Dash still had from last Saturday's brawl.

"Aw, she never even looked twice at you," Ben said. "I was the one she had eyes for."

"You're both idjits," Bobby Cooper told him. "Me and my brother, why, we been up to her place three times now."

"Yeah," Harley jeered, "like pesky 'skeeters she can't get rid of."

"Oh yeah?"

"Yeah!"

The boys looked raring to start another round of the fight they never finished on Saturday. Swede sighed. He never thought having a lady in camp could cause so much grief. He stepped between them, clamping a hand on each boy's shoulder before they could inflict damage.

"Hold on now. Don't get your feathers all fluffed up."

Granny raised a hand.

"What is it, Gran?" Swede asked.

"It's prob'ly Zeke who broke her heart," she mumbled, spitting on the ground.

Zeke glanced around quickly, like he'd just woken up. "Me?" he squeaked.

"Yeah, well..." Granny kicked the dust around with the toe of her boot. "What lady *wouldn't* be sweet on him?"

Swede could have knocked Zeke over with a feather after that.

"No, no, no," Frenchy fussed, fluttering his hands in the air. "Perhaps it is not even one of us."

"Then just who in the hell would it be?" Harley challenged.

"Boys, boys," Swede scolded.

Red scratched at his chest. Then his eyes grew round. "Hey!" he said in sudden enlightenment. "Maybe Frenchy's right. Maybe she's got a sweetheart back home."

Swede sighed with exaggerated patience. Sometimes Red could be thick as molasses. "Red, she came here to marry up with Doc. I don't think she's got a sweetheart back home."

The men were quiet a while, stewing over the possibilities.

Then Dash started nodding thoughtfully. "Hey, maybe she's, you know, expectin' a visit from the stork. That always left our Ma kinda down in the mouth."

Swede felt the hackles rise on his back, just like a grizzly's. He didn't want to think Miss Mattie might have gotten herself with child out of wedlock. Why, it was vulgar for Dash to even mention it. On the other hand, the boy could be right. Maybe she was going to have a baby. Maybe that was why she'd hightailed it out of New York and headed out West to marry up with a man she didn't even know. It sure made sense.

He cracked his knuckles and came to a decision. "All right, here's what we're gonna do. Maybe Dash is right. Maybe some bounder left Miss Mattie with a babe in her belly. Now that don't mean she ain't just as much a lady as before. But she's gonna need her a man, and right quick. So what we—"

"I'll do it!" Harley's hand shot up in the air.

"The hell you will!" Bobby fired off.

Swede shook his head. "Look, boys. Nobody's gonna bully their way into the job, you hear me?"

Tom tugged thoughtfully on his mustache. "What do ye say we make a wee wager then? A few rounds o' faro or monte, with winner takin' the lass."

Most of the men actually thought that was a good idea. Swede was disgusted. "Are you out of your damn minds? You can't wager on a woman."

"Pah! You Yankees!" Frenchy spat. "You cannot win a woman's body without first winning her heart."

That gave the boys food for thought.

"Frenchy's right," Swede told them. "So if you're gonna try to win the little lady's heart, I think we need some rules so's we don't have a free-for-all. This ain't no claim-stakin', after all."

"I say only one Campbell a day gets to visit her," Billy Cooper stated.

The Campbell boys set up a loud protest at that.

"No one should get to visit her more than a quarter hour at a time," Jasper advised.

"Ye should take turns," Tom agreed, "like gentlemen."

"And not a word about her…condition," Frenchy insisted.

When the rules were pretty well established, the group broke up to hit the hay and dream about all the courting they planned to do. Swede stayed awake a mite longer. The feeling that he'd just set a bunch of wild bulls loose in Miss Mattie's flowerbed weighed heavy on his mind.

Sakote didn't know if Mati ever returned to the waterfall. He didn't go. It was painful enough for him to wait outside Mati's cabin in the brush, night after night, until the last of her suitors left so he could leave his gift of food on her doorstep. If only he hadn't promised such a thing to his sister, his wounded heart might find peace. Then he could follow his path and leave Mati to hers.

He glared at the loaf of acorn bread, wrapped in wild grape leaves and tied with hemp. His mother had pressed it into his hands without question, as if she knew where he went every evening and what he did. What would she say now, he wondered, if she could see her brave son crouching in the dark like a field mouse, waiting for the loud miner inside Mati's cabin to grow weary of his own bragging and go home.

At last the door opened, and a blanket of light spilled out from the cabin. As always, Sakote's eyes hunted the white woman's face, looking for signs of weakness or sorrow or remorse. And as always, Mati hid her feelings behind the quiet smile she wore for all her suitors. Every night he told himself that he'd washed his hands of her heart's blood, that she was no longer a part of him. And every night, his heart betrayed that belief, beating wildly when he caught sight of her.

She was beautiful tonight. Her hair shone in the moonlight like the white man's gold, and the faint wind blew long strands of it loose across her breast. Her hand, perched lightly on the frame of the door, looked like a pale blossom of dogwood. She said something to the man on the porch, and though Sakote couldn't hear the words clearly, her murmur made soft music on the air.

Sakote bit the inside of his cheek and forced his eyes away. His heart already throbbed with pain. It would break if he saw Mati make a kiss with the man.

Finally the man tipped his hat and stomped off the porch, carelessly crushing the grass on his way back to camp. Several moments later, Sakote eased forward with his gift, making his way silently toward the cabin.

Candles still lit the inside of the house, and Sakote could clearly see the outline of Mati crossing the room to do some woman's task. One day, she'd do such tasks for her own husband. If, he thought sourly, she could ever choose from among all the miners.

He bent to leave the gift of food, knowing she'd find it, as she had the others. Then, for a moment, he stood brazenly framed by the door, so close that his breath moved the cloth covering it. Mati wouldn't be able to see him. The candlelight blinded her to the shadows outside. But he willed her to feel his presence, to know that he, Sakote, the Konkow warrior, stood outside her *hubo*.

It didn't work. She didn't come to the door. And when he turned to go, his spirit defeated, he didn't even care that he stumbled like a fawn on its first walk as he stepped off the pine planks.

Mattie strained her ears. Something *was* out there. She'd felt it a moment ago, some presence loitering outside the cabin. The impression had been strong enough to freeze her in her tracks. And yet, despite the fact that she lived in the wilderness where any manner of beast might lurk beyond the door, she felt no fear.

What she felt instead was a tiny tingle of hope.

Every day for the past week, she'd gone to the waterfall, praying she'd find him—the Indian who stared back at her from sketches tucked under her pillow. Yet all she ever saw of him were the gifts of food he left on her doorstep each night—smoked venison, dried salmon, roasted pine nuts.

Why did he torture her like this? There was a connection between them, a mysterious, compelling magnetism as powerful as gravity, a force that made her forget all else but the desire to see him, touch him, kiss him. Surely he could feel it, too.

It was Sakote who lingered beyond the door. She knew it. His presence filled the pregnant air like the heavy scent of rain before a storm.

But he didn't knock. He never knocked. Night after night, he left his packages on the porch without a word. And as always, he crept away in silence.

For four nights, she'd prayed for that knock. It never came. And for four nights, she'd wept herself to sleep. Well, by God, tonight, she was done with tears. Come hell or high water, she'd make him speak to her, even if she had to follow him all the way home. If he wouldn't face her in her world, she'd confront him in his.

Her heart raced, recognizing how foolhardy her intentions were. She had no idea, after all, where her recklessness would lead her and what beasts stalked the woods tonight. But she paid no mind to the warnings in her head. Before her prey could escape into the forest, she rashly swirled her cloak over her shoulders and grabbed the rifle from the wall, checking to make sure it was loaded.

After she blew out the candles and slipped the door open, it took her eyes a moment to adjust to the moonlight. Sure enough, she found the familiar bundled offering on the porch. He *had* been here.

Across the clearing, the brush rustled. Sakote. He was escaping already. She had to hurry. Easing the door closed behind her, she crept rapidly toward the path. When she reached the cover of the trees, she listened for his footfalls. The manzanita rattled further ahead, and she scurried to catch up.

By night, he traveled quickly, using less stealth than by daylight. She could hear the muffled scuff of his moccasins in the leaves and the soft slap of branches against his body.

She followed for what seemed like miles, over rugged rock and between low-slung limbs, guided only by the meager spots of moonlight dotting the forest floor and the increasingly fainter sound of his steps. Her chest ached, the rifle was heavy, and it was nearly impossible to quiet her gasping breath. But she couldn't give up, not now. She was so far from her home that she couldn't possibly find her way back.

So she hurtled forward, desperate to catch him. She turned a deaf ear to the tiny skittering of unknown creatures. She ignored the spiked branches that clawed out to slow her progress. She focused only on the stepping stones of pale light, until they dwindled and she lost sight of the moon and the stars entirely beneath a thick canopy of trees. Then the suffocating, black walls of night closed in like a deep well above her. She strained to hear anything, any sound at all even remotely human, but the silence turned as profound as the night.

She'd lost him.

She'd lost her way.

And she was alone.

Her racing heart beat faster. What would she do? She had no idea where she was. As far as she knew, she might be standing at the mouth of a bear cave or at the edge of another steep precipice or beneath the hungry gaze of that mountain lion. What had she been thinking?

She didn't dare move now. She could barely see in the dark, forcing her to rely on sound, which was nearly impossible with the blood rushing through her brain. Her palms grew sweaty around the cold barrel and oily stock of the rifle, and she suddenly wished she'd brought extra ammunition.

Quivering in her boots, she began to concoct all sorts of dire scenarios—her body, broken at the bottom of a ravine, mauled by a bear, eaten by wolves, buzzards pecking at her grisly remains.

She thought she heard a sound then, a faint shivering of leaves. She stiffened. Something was in the brush to her left. A bear? A wolf? The mountain lion? The brush rattled again, ever so slightly, and Mattie froze, afraid to move, afraid to breathe. Her heart pummeled against her ribs as she slowly, carefully cocked the hammer of the rifle back and raised the weapon. Her finger trembled on the trigger as she silently counted to three.

The attack came before she could fire. Or breathe. Or scream. Her arm was knocked sideways, and suddenly she was pinned from behind in a bone-crushing embrace. Her fingers tightened reflexively, and the rifle went off.

The report shattered the quiet of the forest and echoed across the canyon. The smell of gunpowder stung Mattie's nose as she clung to the useless weapon for dear life, struggling to free herself from the savage grip.

Fear tasted like iron in her mouth. She was about to die. Something had caught her. Something big and strong and snarling. It was going to kill her. And there was nothing she could do.

CHAPTER 17

Swede's rifle was cocked and ready before his feet even hit the floor. He charged out of his cabin while the gunshot still echoed along the ridge. His neighbors, too, bolted out of their shacks as fast as a pack of loosed hounds.

"What in blazes?" Billy yelped, buttoning up the back of his long-johns.

Frenchy juggled his Bowie knife in shaking hands. "*Sacre Dieu!*"

Zeke spat on the ground, then nodded at Swede. "Which direction you figure?"

Swede squinted into the moonlight. "Hard to tell. Down the canyon somewheres."

Tom tugged at his ubiquitous derby. Swede wondered if he slept in the damn thing. "Is there anyone missing?"

They all looked around. Swede did a quick count of heads. All the miners were accounted for, everyone except...

"Miss Mattie," he whispered. Something ugly fluttered in his stomach. If anything had happened to Miss Mattie...

"You think she..." Granny began.

Tom made the sign of the cross. "Sweet Mary."

Dash fought his way forward through his brothers. "Not Miss Mattie."

"*Impossible!* What do you think could have..." Frenchy gasped as he pricked his finger on the knife.

Swede didn't even *want* to think.

The men clammed up, but it was obvious what was going through their heads. Without another word, they scrambled into their britches, lit a couple of lanterns, and followed Swede to Mattie's cabin.

Zeke was the first to notice the package. He poked at it with his rifle, scowling at the crude rope tied around the wrapped leaves.

"It's Injun," he decided.

His palms sweaty, Swede raised a fist to bang lightly on the door. "Miss Mattie? Miss Mattie, are you there?"

No answer. Maybe she hadn't heard him. He knocked harder. "Miss Mattie?"

"She ain't there."

"Shut up, Harley." Dash cuffed his brother.

"Maybe she's gettin' decent," Granny volunteered.

"Miss Mattie!" This time Swede banged good and hard on the wall.

But no one answered. Afraid of what he would find, Swede took a big gulp of courage and slowly pushed the door open. The men passed a lantern forward, and he peered into the dark room.

He wasn't sure if he was relieved or worried that Mattie wasn't inside. He'd half expected to find her slumped in a pool of blood, shot by her own rifle in some terrible accident. But no, her cabin looked to be in order. The candles were blown out. Clean dinner dishes sat on the shelf. Even her sketching paper and pencils were stacked neatly at the foot of her bed.

But if she wasn't here, where was she?

Zeke scratched at his beard. "Maybe she just stepped out to, you know, pee."

Maybe. But Swede didn't think so, for two reasons.

One, that package on the porch didn't just drop out of the sky—it meant something.

And two, Mattie's rifle was missing.

Sakote's ears still rang from the explosion. He wrenched the gun from Mati's hands before she could fire it again and hurt someone. With a growl, he seized her shoulder and wheeled her around to face him.

"Are you crazy?" he demanded.

"Sakote?" With a little cry, she flung herself into his arms, laying her cheek against his chest. "Oh, Sakote, thank God it's you!"

He frowned. He wished he'd never told her his name. It sounded soft on her tongue, soft and helpless, like her body. But no, he wouldn't be tempted by her woman's ways. He wouldn't be fooled by the *willa*'s trickery. He set her purposefully away from him.

"Why are you following me?" he snapped, though in truth it felt like the frightened yip of a cornered coyote. His hand shook as he raked the hair back from his forehead. The gunfire had shocked him terribly, but not as much as the knowledge that he'd been tracked by a white woman nearly all the way back to the village, and he hadn't noticed. How could he have been so careless? "And why did you fire your rifle? You could have killed someone! What if I had been my little brother?"

Mati crossed her arms defensively. "What if you'd been a bear come to eat me?"

"Bears don't eat crazy white women."

Her voice grew suddenly quiet. "Is that what you think of me? That I'm a crazy white woman?"

Sakote clenched his fists. No. That wasn't what he thought. But fear and worry twisted his words into crooked spears that he threw at her.

She lowered her head. "I'm sorry," she whispered, and he heard the hurt in her voice. "I thought we were..." A soft sob caught the rest of her words as she turned away.

Sakote's heart sank. Not tears. Anything but tears. He wished to be angry with Mati. He wished to scold her for her recklessness. He wished to punish her for breaking his heart. But already she softened his warrior's spirit. She stifled a sniffle, and the sound melted his rage.

With a great sigh of defeat, he propped the rifle against a tree and reached out for her. He clasped the back of her head, and ignoring her weak protest, gathered her into his embrace, holding her close to him, against his foolish heart.

A pang of protective longing streaked through him as her ragged breath warmed his chest. Instinctively, he stroked the back of her head. Her hair slipped between his fingers, finer than his own, and it waved beneath his touch like the surface of the creek. He'd forgotten how perfectly she fit against him, how right she felt in his arms. And she smelled good, like sweet spice and pine smoke. He could hold her forever.

But Mati wished to talk.

"Why didn't you visit me?" she whispered against his chest, absently twining a strand of his hair around her fingertip. "I went to the waterfall every day. I thought we were...friends."

"Friends?" Sakote did not fully understand the language of the white man, but to him, a friend was Noa or one of his Konkow brothers. What he felt for Mati was far beyond friendship.

Mati withdrew her hand. "I'm sorry. I thought you..."

"We are...friends," he told her.

"But you never came to me."

"You were busy," he said pointedly.

"I missed you," she breathed.

Sakote tried to remind himself that she'd let other men hold her like this. She probably had made kisses with the miners, maybe even mated with them. He wasn't special to her. He told himself these things, but he didn't listen to his own words. When she leaned toward him, her mouth parting as if to drink from him, he heard only the beating of his heart.

Her lips were gentle on his, and he closed his eyes with the wonder of her tender touch. Her sigh caressed his cheek as she tipped her head, deepening the kiss. His pulse leaped wildly out of control, but he coiled his fingers tenderly in her hair, holding her head still so he could taste each corner of her mouth.

She purred like the wildcat, deep in her throat, and the sound seemed to call an animal forth in him, for he hauled her to him then, crushing her softness against his hard chest, opening her mouth with his tongue to seek the succulent fruit within.

Her hands moved over his shoulders and across his chest, sculpting his muscles like they were made of clay. Then she broke from the kiss to devour the rest of him, nipping at his jaw, nuzzling his throat, gasping with desire as she tasted his flesh so wantonly that it made him tremble.

His loins ached, and he pressed her hips against his need, longing beyond thought and beyond reason to join with her, this woman who drove him to the edge of madness.

"Ah, Sakote," she whispered breathlessly against his ear. The sound seemed like the wind of destiny.

He reached down with one desperate arm and gathered her skirt aside, letting his fingers glide up along the fawn-soft skin of her thigh. By the son of Wonomi, he wanted the white woman. He wanted his man's-knife inside her and her legs wrapped around his bare back.

Mattie wanted...Lord, she didn't know what she wanted. Him. More of him. All of him. He left her with a ravenous hunger impossible to quench, though she fed on his delicious flesh with lips and teeth and tongue till she could scarcely breathe. Her hands explored his body with blind need, memorizing each curve and swell. She turned her ear to his wide, warm chest, reveling in the strong, rapid beat of his heart against her cheek. She quivered as his callused fingertips grazed her thigh. And she gasped as he pressed his hips boldly to hers, branding her with his iron-hard desire.

Floating in a sleepy haze of rich sensations, Mattie made no protest as he pulled her into a faint patch of moonlight, his hand slipping higher up her leg, over the hollow of her hip, along the edge of her linen drawers, inside the fabric. She moaned and arched closer.

But something stopped him. Just as his fingers began to tangle gently in her woman's curls, he blew out a long, sharp breath and pulled away, leaving her cold. Stunned, she mewed in complaint and lifted heavy-lidded eyes to his face.

Whatever battle waged there was hard-fought. Sakote's brow darkened with deep furrows, and he wouldn't meet her eyes, despite the vulnerability of his parted mouth and the winded heaving of his chest.

"No," he said gruffly. "No." He took a full step backward, clenching his fists as if he fought for control. "We must go."

"But—"

"Come!" he barked, grabbing her rifle and setting off, expecting her to follow.

Sakote thought he'd rather be shot by Yana arrows than endure this torture. His body wanted Mati. His man's-knife ached with need.

But nothing had changed. He and Mati were from two

different worlds. And if they didn't take care, if they let their passions cloud their thoughts, those worlds might collide. There wasn't much time. He'd hesitated too long already.

Everyone had heard the gunshot. The young braves in the village would come soon to investigate. Then the miners would come. And in the dark and confusion, their fear would create misunderstanding. Someone would get hurt.

No, for the sake of his people, Mati and he must not be found together.

He couldn't abandon her. She wasn't safe here. And if she tried to return home, she'd lose her way in the dark. He helplessly shook his head. Though it was a great risk, he had to take Mati back to her cabin.

"Come," he said more gently when she didn't budge. "I'll take you home."

Bewildered, she turned to him with welling eyes, but he had to ignore her. If a hunter let himself be distracted by every wide and innocent gaze, he would starve. But that watery gaze swiftly turned to ice, and with a glare of accusation and a furious snap of her skirts, Mati strode off ahead of him.

He quickly caught her and took the lead, glancing back from time to time to make sure he didn't travel too quickly for her, but he didn't want to look at her face. Like his sister, Mati wore her thoughts in her eyes, and he was ashamed at what he knew he'd see there, ashamed of the pain and rage he'd caused.

But he could change nothing. Mati didn't understand. She couldn't. She was a white woman. She'd never had to protect her people, never felt fear for her family, never worried about food or shelter or cold or sickness. She didnt realize that the peace between the Konkows and the miners was like a thread of spider's web, easily destroyed by the wave of a hand.

As they crept through the trees, Sakote listened carefully.

He heard no white men in the forest, which troubled him greatly. He could always hear the *willa* as they clumsily made their way through the leaves. He should hear them now, unless...unless they lay in wait.

When he finally emerged into the clearing, it was too late. He was right. A crowd of miners stood guard outside Mati's cabin, teeth bared, eyes glowing fiercely in the moonlight. A dozen weapons instantly swung about to murder him.

Mattie didn't notice them at first. In fact, she collided with Sakote's back when he halted suddenly. She was surprised she didn't break on impact, for between hurt and anger, she felt as brittle as bone china.

"Hold it right there, Injun!"

She peered around Sakote's massive arm, the one clutching her gun, and gasped. Standing before them, brandishing rifles, revolvers, knives, and pickaxes, were the residents of Paradise Bar. Swede, holding aloft a flickering lantern, stood at the fore.

Dash spoke. "If you hurt one hair on Miss Mattie's head, Digger, I swear..."

Frenchy finished the oath. "I will carve your red carcass up like a Christmas goose!"

"Put down the gun, son," Zeke said, spitting a wad of tobacco onto the ground.

Mattie blinked. "What is this about? Mr. Jenkins? Mr. Swede?"

Much to her consternation, the men ignored her.

"Lay down the rifle nice and slow," Swede repeated, cocking his weapon.

Sakote made no move to surrender the weapon. Mattie's heart flipped over. Did the miners mean to shoot the both of them?

"For heaven's sake," she pleaded with Sakote, tugging on his arm, "put the gun down."

He refused, growling some word at her in his own language. Her jostling only made the miners more nervous.

"Back away, Miss Mattie," Tom advised.

She'd had enough of the men's inanity. "And just what do you intend to do then?"

"Shoot the bastard!" Harley cried, and his brothers joined in with enthusiasm.

"You'll do no such thing!" Mattie protested. "Can't you see—"

"Go on and put the gun down now," Swede said softly to Sakote, "so's the lady don't get hurt."

Mattie looked up at Sakote, his black hair gleaming in the moonlight, his eyes like polished beads of jet. His breath slowed somewhat, but there was an anxious sheen of sweat above his lip.

She stroked the sleek muscle of his upper arm. "It's all right, Sakote. They won't hurt you. They're my friends."

He turned to her, and she thought she'd never seen such sad and wise eyes as his. He warred with some great decision as he searched her eyes. Then he sighed, dropping his shoulders in surrender.

The rifle had barely thudded on the ground when the miners rushed forward to haul Mattie out of harm's way. Before she could cry out in dismay, four of them wrenched Sakote face-down to the ground. A dozen guns aimed at his naked back, pinning him there.

"No!" she screeched.

Red kicked him once in the ribs, and Sakote grunted in pain, spurring the Cooper boys to throw in a couple of hard punches.

"Stop it!" she shrieked, battling against Tom and Frenchy, who tried to restrain her. "What are you doing?"

"Don't ye worry, Miss," Tom said. "The boys'll make this Digger so black and blue he won't be able to move for a week, never mind tryin' to abscond with our womenfolk."

"Abscond..." Mattie gasped. Was that what they thought? "He didn't..."

But the mob wouldn't listen to her. They'd already made up their collective mind. They formed a circle around Sakote and began pummeling him with fists and the butts of their rifles as if he were a rabid dog they had to kill.

With a cry of horror, Mattie finally tore herself from Frenchy's grasp and broke through the maddened crowd. Before another cruel blow could land on Sakote, she threw herself atop him, shielding him with her own body.

"Don't you touch him!" she screamed. "Don't you dare touch him!"

The ugly pack still brandished fists and weapons, their monstrous leers and rolling eyes made garish by the lurching light of the oil lamps. Mattie scarcely recognized them. Good Lord, would they strike her down, too?

"Aw, Miss Mattie," Zeke said sheepishly, "maybe you should get back to your cabin. I s'pose frontier justice ain't what you're used to."

"Justice?" she demanded. "For what? Why are you beating him? He's done nothing wrong!"

"Nothin' wrong?" Harley spat. "You call an Injun stealin' our women nothin' wrong?"

"He did not steal me," she insisted breathlessly. "And I am *not* your woman."

"Aw, come on, ma'am," Jasper whined. The bloodthirsty gleam in his eyes was almost too much to bear. "Just stand back so's we can give the savage his due."

Mattie felt sick. If she hadn't thrown herself over him, Sakote would have been beaten to a bloody pulp by now. The men she'd befriended, dined with, trusted, still stood by like a pack of wolves eager for the kill. And beneath her, Sakote lay still, silent despite the brutal battering he'd already endured. Who, she wondered, were the savages now?

"Go away," she told them, her voice low with misery and betrayal. "This man has done nothing to warrant your hatred. He's been only kind and decent toward me. He didn't steal me. I followed him. He only meant to return me safe to my home."

The men, dubious, stared and shifted uncomfortably on their feet.

"He didn't nab you from your cabin?" Zeke asked, scratching his head.

"No."

"He didn't steal you away to make you a white slave?" Jeremy wondered.

"Of course not."

"He did not," Frenchy inquired, delicately clearing his throat, "compromise you?"

Mattie blushed at that. She *longed* to be compromised by Sakote. But she lifted her chin and answered him. "No."

The men looked almost disappointed.

"I thought you were good men, decent men," she told them, swallowing hard, her eyes wet with furious tears. "I thought you cared about me. I thought you were my friends."

With that, she gathered her skirts and her dignity and bent to attend to Sakote. She touched his back lightly, and he recoiled. There were no marks as yet, but she was sure there'd be bruises tomorrow.

"Oh, Sakote, my poor, dear Sakote."

Sakote brushed her hand aside with a grimace and hauled himself painfully up to his haunches. He was a warrior. The last thing he needed was a woman fussing over him like a sickly babe. Especially in front of the white men.

He'd known what they would do. He'd been prepared for their violence. In fact, before he'd dropped his weapon, he'd intended taking on the whole company of miners—until that man spoke of Mati's safety. Then he realized he couldn't let his pride endanger her. No matter what they did to him, he couldn't let her get hurt. So he surrendered the rifle. He let them beat him. And he showed his courage in the Konkow way, by his silence.

But now, Mati tried to steal that courage from him.

He wouldn't allow it. Clenching his teeth against the pain, he slowly stood and faced the *willa*, creasing his forehead in a mask of anger meant to intimidate enemies. Even Mati gasped at his stern expression. He eyed the miners one by one, as if marking them for death. Some of them sullenly held his gaze. Most of them looked away. When he was satisfied that his pride, the pride of a Konkow warrior, had been restored, he turned to leave.

"Sakote!" Mati cried.

Curse the woman, he thought, hesitating in his tracks. Now the whole *willa* camp knew his sacred name. He frowned and strode away.

"Wait," she begged.

He continued walking.

"Please, Sakote, wait."

"You'd best do what the little lady says, Injun, unless you want a bullet in your back." Sakote froze. It was that big man, the one with the pale yellow hair, the one who wanted to make certain Mati was unhurt. Now the man looked as full of shame as a boy caught in the women's *hubo*. "I don't cotton much to savages," he said, "what with their poachin' and scalpin' and whatnot, but it's plain as day you've turned Miss Mattie's head for some reason."

The other miners put up such a protest at that, Sakote wondered if they might beat the big man now, too.

"Quit your bellyachin', boys. Like I said, it's as plain as day," he told them, then spoke again to Sakote. "Now I'm real sorry me and the boys roughed you up, and, well, bein' Miss Mattie put herself in harm's way to keep you safe, I'd say you owe her at least a word or two."

That he understood. Mati *had* shown bravery. Though it shamed a warrior to have a woman beg for his life, Mati's courage somehow made him feel proud. And the man was right. He shouldn't let that go unanswered.

But the white men knew his name now. They'd felt his body crumple beneath their kicks. He was vulnerable. That made his people vulnerable. And above all, he must protect the Konkow.

He must end it now—his contact with the white world, his contact with Mati—no matter how painful. And he must end it quickly.

Scowling to hide his broken spirit, he turned to her. "You have shown much bravery," he said. "I give you thanks." Then he made a crossing motion with his arms, the formal gesture of dismissal. "But now it's finished between us. *Akina*."

Mati gasped, and the anguish that flickered in her eyes felt worse to him than all the pummeling he'd endured. He knew he would carry the scars from her stricken look for a very long time. All the weight of the world bowed his shoulders as he turned toward home, toward the place where, for better or worse, he belonged.

CHAPTER 18

Swede frowned and ran a hand over his stubbled cheek as the Injun vanished into the trees. He guessed he and the boys had really done it this time. Miss Mattie's face reminded him of the time his little girls' runt lamb had refused to nurse, and up and died. They'd looked at him with just such hurt, like it was his fault. There'd been nothing he could say to fix things then, and there was nothing he could say now.

Aw, hell, he thought, it was probably best this way. Even the Injun knew it. Mattie's heart might be broken now, but things would only get worse if she took up with a savage. That was no kind of life for a well-bred white woman. The sooner she accepted that, the better.

None of the men spoke up to offer their condolences or apologies, but then Swede's throat, too, was clogged with shame. The wind kicked up in the pines, sawing a sorrowful tune to fill the silence. But it wasn't loud enough to cover the sob that sneaked out of Miss Mattie as she walked, her head held high, past them and into her cabin.

It was a sound Swede couldn't get out of his head. Not the next morning, when the man from Marysville brought a letter from home. Not the following day, when Red unearthed a gold nugget near as big as a gambling die. Not even that night, when Tom cracked open a good bottle of whiskey to celebrate and poured everyone a dram. Miss Mattie holed up in her cabin, and without their pretty ray of sunshine, the whole camp took on the air of a funeral.

Then, as if the incident with the Injun wasn't sorry enough, on Sunday afternoon, the worst trouble any of them had ever faced rode into Paradise Bar.

Nine men, himself included, had stayed behind in the camp—Frenchy, Bobby, Tom, Zeke, and the Campbell brood. Everyone else chose to try their luck in the creek instead of risking it all on the game of chance Tom dealt across the makeshift card table.

By noon, the Campbells had lost interest in the gambling. They set up a row of tins along an oak branch and took turns blasting them to smithereens with a rifle. Every few minutes, the loud bang would jolt Frenchy awake, which was the only thing keeping him in the poker game.

Swede mopped his brow with the back of his sleeve. He hoped the others couldn't tell it was his bad hand and not the late afternoon heat that made him sweat. But then, he'd never been good at bluffing, especially when he was this drunk.

"Aw, shucks! I fold." Bobby slammed his cards down. He tipped back his stool and downed a slug of whiskey, burping loudly.

"Ye play like a damn milkmaid," Tom complained, mocking the boy. "I fold, I fold."

Bobby banged his fist on the table, toppling Tom's stack of Double Eagles.

"Damn you, Tom!" the boy hollered, his eyes glazed with liquor. "You take that back!"

Tom's face began to redden. "I'll take it back when ye pick up your cards and start playin' like a man."

"And just what would a limey leprychaun know about that, huh?" Bobby challenged, jutting out his chin.

"What did ye call me?"

Dash fired off a rifle round, censoring Bobby's reply.

Swede rolled his eyes. Zeke shrugged. Frenchy was no help. His drunken gaze roamed lazily from man to man, like he was watching children tossing a ball back and forth at a snail's pace.

Swede let out his breath in a heavy sigh. Ever since the night they'd beat up that Digger Injun, everyone seemed to have grown a temper as nasty as a mule and a kick just as bad. And Mattie had only made things worse, pining away all alone in her cabin, depriving the men of her company. Lord, who would've thought a ruffled skirt and a pair of big, wide, innocent eyes could cause such a stir? It made him wonder how they'd gotten along before she came. Hell, most of the boys stayed as drunk as skunks just to keep from lamenting over Miss Mathilda Hardwicke. Himself included.

But mostly he drank out of shame.

Miss Mattie had put them in their place, all right. That poor savage didn't deserve what Paradise Bar had dished out. It was just all too easy to assume he meant her harm. But Swede knew, from the looks of him, that the man had sacrificed himself to keep Mattie safe. And damned if the Injun didn't know well enough to end things before they got out of hand. Swede had to hand it to him—the Digger had a head on his shoulders and his own brand of honor. It was no wonder Miss Mattie had taken a shine to him.

He took another swallow of his tin cup of whiskey while his fellow players exchanged insults and compared their lineage, their faces growing more purple by the minute. Finally, he whacked the back of Bobby's head before the lad could have a conniption fit.

"Come on, boys," he said, his tongue thick, "just get on with the game."

Bobby crossed his arms over his chest and pouted. Tom bristled, but resumed scrutinizing his hand. Zeke silently folded. Frenchy, however, had fallen asleep where he sat. His head lolled backward, his mouth hung open, and his cards splayed loosely in his hand.

Tom made no bones about examining Frenchy's cards. He clucked his tongue. "He's only got two pair, and low numbers at that. Swede, ye haven't got piss, have ye?"

Swede scowled, humiliated yet again. He threw in his hand, and Tom scooped the pot toward his growing stash with a chuckle.

"Care for another round?" Tom licked his thumb, ready to deal.

"Not for me," Zeke said, spitting tobacco on the ground.

Frenchy snorted in his sleep.

Bobby got up sullenly from his spot, clearly finished.

Swede wiped a hand across his blurry eyes. "I'm all done in." He was about to see if he could push himself up from the table without staggering sideways when he heard the distant bray of a mule. The weekly deliveries weren't due, so it could mean only one thing. A stranger was coming to Paradise Bar.

Henry Harrison, "Ace" to those who presumed to challenge him to cards, had never worked so hard to maintain his legendary poker face as when he first glimpsed Paradise Bar. He'd heard about the gold camps. Indeed, he'd always intended to try his luck with the pick and pan. But the lure of one-eyed jacks and his own easy brand of mining had kept him in decent clothes, good whiskey, and San Francisco. Until recently.

His fortune had turned nasty, spurred on by a sore loser who had flapping jaws and friends in high places. The charge was tampering with the deck, and not even the offer of a sizable donation to the city could keep the law off his tail. So he'd sent the meddling gossiper to an early grave with the help of Mr. Deringer, as he had countless others who'd dared to cross him. Only this time, it had turned him into a wanted man.

Fortunately, Lady Luck had always been his mistress, and it wasn't long before she dealt him a wild deuce. It seemed his older brother had, the letter poetically informed him, "passed out of this world and on to the next." Needless to say, he decided it was time to pay his respects to dearly departed, gold-fevered Dr. James Harrison, who'd conveniently settled in a remote mining camp in the middle of nowhere.

He hardly remembered James. If it wasn't for the boastful letters he got from him every couple of months, the man could have dropped off the face of the earth for all Henry knew. Truth to tell, they'd never spent much time together anyway, what with the eight years between them. But blood was blood, and if you couldn't turn to kin in times of hardship, what good were they?

Still, clinging for dear life to the back of a pesky mule all the way up the canyon, he'd had second thoughts. He was plainly out of his element. In the wilderness, every flicker of light, every rustle in the bushes had him as spooked as a new bride. It was no wonder he'd shot that Injun kid at the last switchback, what with the boy sneaking up on him like that. And now that Paradise Bar proper sprawled in all its dilapidated glory before him, only the possibility of inheritance and the memory of the gallows awaiting him in San Francisco kept him from hightailing it all the way back to the Bay.

So he pasted on a counterfeit smile, pretending he held four kings when it sure looked like a pair of threes. He tipped his hat as, one by one, the miners took notice of him.

"Evening," he said, remembering to color his friendliness with a touch of melancholy.

To his trained eye, the residents appeared to be soused, and some of them gambled at cards, a combination that spelled easy winnings. He licked his lips. His fingers itched to deal a hand of poker.

But penny ante poker wasn't why he'd come. He'd had to get out of San Francisco, true, but he also needed to bankroll his escape, and for that he needed big money. He intended to change his name and buy his own small, discreet gambling establishment in Sacramento, comfortably close to the sweet smell of gold dust, far enough from San Francisco to lay low. And James had obliged him by giving up the ghost, leaving behind what he'd constantly bragged was enough riches to keep a man in "whiskey, wine, women, and whiskey" for life.

"Hello," he said politely when a giant of a man with haystraw hair lumbered forward.

"Howdy." The man sized him up, his drunken eyes slowly perusing him from beaver hat to polished boot. "You're new to these parts."

"That I am, sir." He dismounted as gracefully as he could, considering his legs still quivered from the harrowing ride. Then he doffed his hat and extended his hand. "My name's Henry, Henry Harrison. I'm...James's brother."

The big man's eyes narrowed, and he whistled a quick breath in through pursed lips.

A skinny old man with a threadbare beard hobbled up alongside him. "You mean Doc Jim?"

Suddenly the miners were all ears. They shuffled forward, staring at him as if he were a particularly intriguing bug.

"Yes, I suppose that's what he go-...went by," he told them.

"Ye got my letter then, did ye?" A dapper Irishman in a derby came forward and took his elbow.

"Yes. Yes, I did."

"'Tis a shame, 'tis." The man doffed his hat, holding it over his heart for a respectable period of time, then tapped it back onto his head. "Come along then, lad, and we'll drink a wee dram in his honor."

Henry usually avoided liquor in unfamiliar company. It slowed his wits and distorted his judgment, banes of the gambler. But he didn't intend to gamble this afternoon. There'd be time to fleece the miners later, and from the looks of things, it'd be as easy as stealing peppermint drops from a child. Sure, he'd drink with the gang. Why not? He was a decent, companionable fellow, just like them, wasn't he? Besides, he was just a mite shaky still from shooting that Injun kid.

By the time he'd choked down half a cup of their noxious whiskey, he knew the Irishman's entire ancestry, and his head was buzzing like a horsefly.

"So how did it happen?" he asked. After all, it wouldn't do to appear indifferent, even if he and James had never been closer than apples dropped at opposite ends of the orchard.

They told him James had died peacefully, in his sleep. If he knew his brother, it was more likely a drunken stupor.

"Did he leave anything behind?" *Like a trunk full of gold?* he wondered, remembering to withdraw a handkerchief from his pocket to dab at his eyes. "Any memento I could send to our dear mother? A piece of clothing? A journal? His medical bag?"

"Well, shit, er, shoot," the big blond man said. "You see, your brother was fixin' to marry himself up with a young lady from back east. Wouldn't you know it, she arrived the day after he kicked the bucket."

The skinny prospector elbowed the man in the ribs.

"That is," the giant amended, "after he passed on."

The Frenchman, who'd awakened only moments ago, chimed in, "She had not a friend in the world. We could not leave her out in the cold."

"We gave her Doc's things and put her up in his cabin over yonder," a strapping lad added, pointing to a path that led off toward the woods.

"It was the least we could do, seein' as how she was a widder and all."

Henry nodded in agreement, but his thoughts spun away quicker than a wheel of fortune. A woman? What the hell business could James have with a woman? And what was a woman doing in a gold camp anyway?

Spending James's fortune. That's what she was doing. Why else would a woman take up with his drunkard brother?

"Would you or the lady have any objections," he humbly offered, "if I took a gander at a few of his personal effects just one last time before I go?"

The big blond man hesitated, scratching the back of his head. "Well, to tell you the truth, the lady's been feelin' kinda poorly of late."

"She ain't gonna want to see nobody anytime soon," said a strapping lad cradling a rifle against his side.

"That's right," the skinny old man added. "She's...in mournin'."

The rest of them nodded in agreement, and Henry had to fight to keep his temper in check. He saw the looks they exchanged. They were hiding something, these miners, and he intended to find out what it was. He hadn't come almost two hundred miles just to smile, shrug, and walk away. No woman was going to stand between Henry Harrison and his hard-won inheritance.

He hung his head with as much meekness as he could muster, and said, "I understand." Then he pretended to be suddenly inspired. "Do you think she might take comfort in meeting kin?"

The miners exchanged doubtful glances, and Henry longed to scream in frustration.

"She don't want to see nobody," brooded the boy with the gun. "Not after what we done."

The rest of the men seemed upset by the boy's vague confession. Henry decided he wouldn't take the bait, at least not yet. "What they'd done" could come later. For now, he just wanted to get his hands on that stash.

"But perhaps if I spoke with her…"

"I told you, Mister," the boy warned, "she don't want to see nobody." He could see now that the lad's eyes were bloodshot. Lord, he was drunk as a sailor. And he had a gun.

"Come on, Dash." Another boy nudged his shoulder, but he angrily wrenched away. "He don't know nothin' about that."

The skinny miner scratched his chin. "Maybe if you were to stick around for a few days—"

"She don't need no one stickin' around." The boy's words came loud and slurred and belligerent as he shifted his grip on the rifle. Henry could almost smell the hankering for violence on the kid.

But what the hell. It didn't matter. Things were rapidly slipping past the point of negotiation anyway. Henry didn't have time to "stick around." And he was fast tiring of minding his manners. Maybe it was time to take a firm stance.

"Now look here," he said, drawing himself up to his full height, "James was my brother. This…woman apparently didn't even meet him. I believe I have the right to—"

"What're you sayin'?" the kid challenged, his fingers dancing a frenzied two-step on the stock of the gun. "What're you sayin', Mister?"

"Jeeze, Dash!" His companion tugged on his arm.

Henry narrowed his eyes. It was clear the kid was looking for any excuse for a fight. He was that drunk. Hell, he wondered if the boy's gun was loaded.

"Look, son," he said reasonably, "where I come from, a man doesn't let himself be led around by the nose, and certainly not by some Jezebel in dungarees." He'd seen the kind of woman that answered the call of the gold fields, and they weren't a pretty sight.

"You!" The boy's voice broke. "You take that back!" He batted away his friend and lifted the rifle to his shoulder. "You take that back or I swear I'll shoot you dead!"

He'd never be sure if it was the click of the gun being cocked or the blaze of fire in the boy's eyes that set him off, but Henry's instincts took over. As fast as a rattler striking, he slipped the golden pistol from his vest and slugged a smoking hole in the boy's chest.

The smell of gunpowder filled Henry's nose like a potent drug. Shit! There was no turning back now. The boy hit the dirt, and Henry took that instant to punch the kid's sidekick into oblivion with the butt of the pistol. Then, discarding the empty weapon, he snagged the boy's rifle from his death grip and turned on the rest of them. There wasn't time to aim. He sent a blast from the rifle toward one of them. Before the sound finished echoing down the canyon, he whipped the Deringer from his boot and fired it off, too. Then he swung the rifle butt-first in a wide arc, clipping a couple of heads with the heavy stock. He dropped the Deringer. The round from his last pistol, the one at his hip, cracked the air like thunder. With no time to reload, he gave up the gun and let his Bowie knife do the rest of the damage.

By the time the gun smoke cleared, not one of the nine men remained standing.

Henry swore and kicked at the ground. Now he'd done it. Made a stupid mistake. If he'd only been a little more patient, a little less edgy, he might have walked away from the camp without more blood staining his hands. But now, if he didn't find the loot and get the hell out of Paradise Bar, he'd find himself wanted all up and down California.

He cussed once more at his fool temper and gathered up

his guns. He had one more stop to make, and this time, he wanted to be ready. He plucked a bullet from his vest pocket and packed it into the golden pistol. He didn't intend to use it, at least not right away. After all, he had to find out where the gold was stashed. And he'd never shot a woman. But then, the way the bodies were piling up, what difference would one more make?

CHAPTER 19

Despite the constant barrage of gunfire all day, Mattie flinched when she heard the knock at her door. It certainly wasn't *him*, she sternly reminded herself, vexed at the way her heart raced hopefully. *He* wasn't coming back. He'd made that perfectly clear. Not that she could blame him. Sakote was lucky he could walk, considering the beating the miners had given him.

No, it had to be one of the men from Paradise Bar. And that didn't exactly give her heart ease either.

It wasn't that she was afraid of them exactly. After all, they'd bent over backwards, Swede in particular, to let her know how sorry they were that things had gotten out of hand. They'd only been trying to protect her.

She understood all that. But that night had irrevocably awakened her to the violence of which the miners were capable. A wall had risen between them, and she had to bear in mind that while the men of Paradise Bar might mean her no harm, they were still as dangerous as loaded guns.

The knock came again, a little louder. Wiping her hands on

her apron and eyeing the rifle hanging on the wall, she moved tenuously forward to open the door.

"Howdy, ma'am," the stranger said, his gaze floating over her in brief but obvious surprise. He removed his hat.

"Hello."

He wasn't unattractive. He was tall, neither fat nor thin, and in the young prime of his life. His clothes, though dusty and rumpled, were well-tailored and stylish, and his boots looked finely crafted. His brown beard and hair were neatly trimmed, his features balanced, if nondescript. His brown eyes were dull and unremarkable. In fact, the only remarkable thing about them were that, at the moment, they displayed absolutely no discernible expression at all. It was a rather bland face, one she'd have difficulty sketching.

"May I help you?" she said, peering briefly past his shoulder to ascertain that he was alone.

He glanced meekly down at his hat. "I'm Henry Harrison, ma'am, the brother to your late, er, husband."

"Oh." His words took a moment to register. "Oh!" She bit her lip, unsure what to say, then backed away as gracefully as she could. "Won't you come in?"

"Much obliged."

She showed him to a stool, and then crossed to the stove. "May I pour you coffee?"

"No thanks, ma'am. I just..." He broke off, and to Mattie's dismay, seemed to bite back tears.

"Are you...all right?" she ventured.

He nodded, but his mouth formed a taut line. "It's just...such a shock is all. Here I come looking for my dear brother, and..." A sob escaped him, and he ducked his head.

Mattie felt wretched. It had never occurred to her that James Harrison might have family that needed to be notified of his death.

"Awful sorry, ma'am. I didn't mean to bring you more grief."

"No, that's all right," she hastened to tell him. "I never really had the chance to meet your brother. We had only corresponded by post."

He tugged a handkerchief out of his inside pocket and blew his nose soundly. "I just wish..." he said, blinking hard, "I just wish I'd been able to tell him goodbye."

Mattie wrung her hands, growing more and more miserable by the minute, while he snorted into his handkerchief.

"Is that..." he finally asked, nodding to Doc Jim's black bag, "Is that his valise?"

"Why, yes," she replied, eager to distract him from his weeping. "Would you...would you like to have it?"

He looked aghast. "Oh, no, I couldn't. I just couldn't. He meant for you to share his worldly goods, and—"

"I have no use for a doctor's bag," she assured him, fetching it from the foot of her bed. "I doubt it has much value...to anyone else anyway. I'm certain he would want you to have it."

"Our mother will be so grateful," he managed before his brow crumpled yet again.

Mattie felt sorry for all the unkind things she'd thought about Mr. Harrison when he'd come to the door. He was certainly not unremarkable, and his eyes were far from unfeeling, moistened now by tears of honest grief. No, he was a gentleman, unlike the men with which she'd been acquainted of late. Henry Harrison wouldn't beat a man senseless as the miners had, nor would he, like Sakote, abandon a woman who had shared her heart with him. He was...decent.

"I'm terribly sorry for your loss," she told him, laying a hand on his forearm. "If there's anything I can do—"

"No. I've troubled you far too much already." He cast a glance around the room. "Just being here, amongst his things, has brought me peace."

Mattie felt a lump grow in her throat. How long had it been since she'd heard such a sentiment? It sounded like poetry. Here was a man she could talk to, a man who felt deeply, a man concerned with more than just gold dust, cheap whiskey, and high stakes poker.

"Would you," she said on a whim, "care to join me for supper? I haven't anything fancy, but there's sourdough rising, beans on the stove, and a tin of peaches on the shelf."

"Well, ma'am, I wouldn't want to be any trouble."

"It's no trouble at all," she decided, whirling away from him to stir the beans bubbling over the fire. After several days bemoaning the convoluted ethics and twisted logic of men, Mr. Harrison was beginning to restore her faith in the gender, and she wasn't quite ready to let him go.

While she readied supper, she asked him casual questions about his background, where he'd grown up, what his family was like, what he did for a living. His answers were vague, and he seemed uneasy. He came from St. Louis, Missouri. His family was nice. He worked in shipping or transport or some such field. But he didn't elaborate. He seemed far more interested in the contents of Doc Jim's bag, opening each of the little vials to peer within.

"Did my brother leave...anything else of personal value?" he asked.

"Personal value?" She poked at the fire and added another log. "You mean a watch or a locket or the like?"

"Anything. Anything at all."

She scratched her nose. She wished she had an answer. It seemed to mean a lot to him. But Doc Jim had left very little behind.

"I don't remember seeing anything like that, just his bag.

He was," she paused, reluctant to talk of macabre things, "buried in a suit, but I don't recall any jewelry. All he left in the cabin were his clothing, a pair of boots, and his mining tools."

Mr. Harrison smoothed his mustache with one hand. "Do you suppose I could take a look at those?" He nodded toward the miner's kit.

"Certainly. Help yourself."

She liberally patted her hands with flour and took a hollowed-out tin down from the shelf, using it to cut the spongy sourdough into rounds.

When he finished perusing the tools, Mattie's drawings caught his eye.

"These aren't Jim's, are they?"

"No. They're mine."

"They're very good."

"Thank you." She couldn't help her flush of pride as he carefully examined each sketch.

"How do you find time to draw such pretty pictures, what with a claim to work?"

"Actually, I don't work the claim much." She dusted off her hands and tucked the biscuits into the bottom of her Dutch oven. "Some of the miners pay me for the portraits I make of them. I've been able to get along fine on that."

"Well, surely James left you something to live on?"

She tucked her lip under her teeth. She didn't wish to disillusion the young man about his brother, but it didn't seem to her that James had set aside a single penny. "It's my understanding that his claim ran dry a while back, and I suppose most of his doctoring was done for barter."

Henry nodded. "I see." He rubbed thoughtfully at his beard. "Barter, you say?"

Something flickered in his eyes then, alarming her—a spark of dark amusement, a wink of evil—but then it vanished, and he only stared at her with that baleful gaze.

She nodded, blushing under his unwavering scrutiny. "I, I suppose."

"You suppose?" He pursed his mouth and blew out a long sigh. His eyes flattened. "So he left you nothing."

"I'm sure he didn't mean to—"

"My gold-mining doctor brother left you nothing?" This time the sardonic edge to his voice sent a frisson of misgiving along her spine. He whispered, "You expect me to believe that?"

Mattie opened her mouth to speak, but could form no reply.

His abrupt bark of laughter cracked the air like thunder out of season.

She recoiled in surprise.

"You expect me to believe that!" He cackled as if she'd just told him the most uproarious joke. "He left you nothing!" he crowed. Then he suddenly sobered and slammed his fist on the table, startling the breath from her.

Mattie was completely unprepared for his sudden flare of temper, uncertain toward whom it was directed. She dropped the Dutch oven with a bang onto the woodstove.

"Nothing at all!" he snapped. "No coin? No note? Not even a store of gold?" The man was fast growing livid, his face purpling, the veins in his neck protruding like tree roots.

Shock froze Mattie to the spot.

His voice dripped with sarcastic venom. "How could he do that? How could that son of a bitch leave his wife-to-be with nothing?"

Mattie blinked. She was moving her mouth, but no sound came out.

"I'll tell you how!" His mask of ire evolved into a terrifying leer. "He didn't!" He paced back and forth in the small space, his boots making ominous thumps on the floor. "You're hiding something from me, Missy," he said, wagging a finger at her. "You're not telling me everything. I know full well what kind of riches my brother pulled out of the ground up here. Now are you gonna try to tell me he left nothing, *nothing* behind?"

The bitter taste of fear crawled onto Mattie's tongue, and she cast a nervous glance at the rifle on the wall. He followed her gaze.

"Oh, it won't come to that," he assured her, every trace of guilelessness completely eradicated from his face. "Because you're gonna tell me where it's hidden, aren't you?"

Mattie swallowed hard. The man was clearly insane. She could see that now. And as dangerous as a mad bull. How could she have thought him a gentleman? How could she have trusted him so readily?

"*Aren't* you?" he snarled, pulling a pistol from inside his coat and training it on her.

The gun was made of polished gold, and for a split second she thought it was a toy. But then he cocked it, and her heart vaulted into her throat. "But I don't...there isn't..." Would anyone hear her if she screamed? Lord, she didn't dare try, not with that gun pointed at her.

"Don't waste your breath, little Missy. Now I haven't got all day. I want that stash, and I want it now."

Mattie tried mentally cataloguing all the nearby objects that might be used as weapons. A spoon. A pencil. Her biscuit cutter. Tins on the shelf. It seemed hopeless. Perhaps she'd try reasoning with him once more.

"Mr. Harrison, believe me," she said, her voice quavering, "he left nothing behind that I know of. Now if you would kindly put down your g—"

With a growl of rage, he swept his arm across the table, spilling the tin of wilted wildflowers across the floor.

Mattie's heart banged like a sledgehammer against her

ribs, and her mouth went dry. She had to do something, *do* something!

"Answer me, Missy." He advanced, and she backed away till her hip struck the shelf behind her. "I don't have to kill you outright, you know," he warned. "I could just cripple you a little."

Holding her breath, Mattie sunk her hand surreptitiously into the flour sack. He took a step forward. She bit her lip. The barrel of the gun looked enormous. He grinned and took another step. Then in one brash movement, she tossed a fistful of flour into his eyes and dove out of harm's way.

Henry howled in rage and clawed at his face, momentarily blinded. But he didn't drop the gun. And there wasn't time to get her rifle.

Casting desperately about, she lunged for the woodstove. She hauled the bubbling pot from the fire and flung its contents toward him, gasping as the hot cast iron seared her bare hands. He jerked in pain as scalding beans splattered his face and oozed down his suit. It only delayed him an instant, but it was long enough for Mattie to snatch a pencil from the floor and lurch forward beneath the weaving pistol.

She didn't aim. She just plunged the pencil forward, wincing as it sank into yielding flesh.

His scream was hideous. She shuddered. Had she killed him?

She didn't want to look. But her eyes were drawn inexorably toward him.

The pencil protruded obscenely from his belly, buried at most a few inches. There was no blood, not yet. And though he wailed in agony, the injury could not have been more than superficial. As she feared, in the next instant he yanked the instrument free with a yelp, pressing a fistful of shirt against the wound to stop the impending flow.

And then the shiny golden butt of his raised gun dove toward her, slamming into her temple.

She must have lay unconscious for a few minutes, long enough for him to rip linen from the bed to bind his wound, but not long enough for his temper to cool.

He yanked her up to her knees and pressed the barrel of his pistol against her forehead.

"I should just shoot you!" he raged, and for one terrifying moment, she glimpsed the madness in his eyes and felt the tremor of his indecision.

When he at last lowered the gun, it was only to slap her across the face. Hard enough to make her eyes water.

"Are you gonna tell me where that stash is, or do I have to beat the Holy Jesus out of you?"

"I don't" she gasped, "know."

He backhanded her, and his ring scratched painfully across her cheek. "Oh, I think you do."

Her heart fluttered like a panicked dove flapping its wings against a cage. "Believe me...if I had it..."

He held nothing back this time, plowing his fist full force into her chin and knocking her backwards onto the floor. Stars exploded across her vision, bright white, then dimming, dimming...

His boot jabbed hard between her ribs, turning her vision red, and she moaned, only half-conscious.

"Now let's try again," he said with mock patience, jerking her up by the arm.

Tears flowed down her cheeks, but she couldn't think or form the answer he wanted, even when he shook her hard enough to rattle her bones.

"All right!" he yelled, shoving her back down to the floor. "You want to play rough?" With the toe of his boot, he levered open the door of the woodstove. Inside was a split log, untouched by fire on one end, aflame on the other. He snatched it from the stove. "Everything you own is in this cabin, isn't it? All your worldly goods?"

She cringed from the heat, too stunned to answer.

"You tell me where it's hidden, or I'll burn up everything, starting with these pictures here."

"No!" That woke her up. Whatever he did to her, however hard he beat her, it couldn't possibly hurt her more than...

He grinned, edging the burning brand close to a drawing of the steamship.

"No!" Her drawings were her memories, her friends, her journey, her life. She had nothing else. She had to prevent him, but she didn't know the magic words to make him stop.

He let the paper catch fire, and it was as if she were back in her uncle's house again, watching her beautiful masterpiece melt into oblision.

"No!" she screamed, clawing at his arm. But he pulled away, and, one by one, he lit the pages. The edges of her sketches smoked and curled. Monkeys and quail and pines and deer alike flared, then turned to ash and drifted in gray flakes to the floor. She tried to tear them from the wall herself before he could reach them, but he knocked her across the cabin with the back of his arm, swinging the lit brand perilously close to her hair.

A cough tore at her throat. The pitch of the wall planks had caught fire and was smoking now, thickening fast.

"Where's the gold?" he growled. "I'll burn this whole house if I have to! Melted gold's as good as any!"

He sneered and ignited the mattress. Flames leaped up from the ticking at once. In a flash of daring, Mattie managed to pull one drawing out from under the pillow, crumpling it into the pocket of her apron. Then she scrambled out of the way, inhaling a noxious lungful of smoke, and crept toward the door.

He lost his patience then and, throwing down the brand and his gun, snatched handfuls of her bodice and wrenched her to her feet.

"Where the hell is the stash!" he cried, shaking her so violently she feared her head might rock from her neck.

In a last defiant gesture, she spat in his face, and he lost the rein on his control. By the fourth punch, she could no longer feel pain. She couldn't breathe in the smothering haze.

She vaguely sensed him dragging her out the front door and felt the sweet cool rush of fresh air as they emerged.

Behind her, the cabin crackled and hissed. Paper and wood and cloth and tin flared and melted in turn, and a gray cloud slowly curdled the twilight sky.

CHAPTER 20

Sakote broke through the cedars and looked up at the violet sky, where Wonomi had lit the first few star fires. He felt it again—that sensation of wrongness, the hunter's instinct that something dangerous was nearby.

He shouldn't be here, so close to the gold camp. His body still ached from the fists and boots of the white man and the injuries he'd concealed from the tribe.

He'd said it was finished, *akina*. That night he'd severed the bond between the Konkows and the whites. He'd shown the miners with his words and his actions that he would come no more. Yet here he stood, like a kicked wolf pup returning for more kicking, at the boundary of the *willa's* world.

All because of Mati.

He'd tried to banish her from his thoughts. He knew he shouldn't worry about her. The miners would take care of her, especially that big yellow-haired man. He saw in the man's eyes that he would protect Mati with his life.

But Sakote hadn't slept well in days. He'd lain awake beneath a moon as white as milkwood sap, remembering the way her eyes glowed like new grass and the sprinkle of freckles that crossed her cheek like stars, imagining the softness of her hair and the dizzying sensation of her blackberry-sweet lips pressed to his. He missed her laughter. He missed her scolding. He missed the fiery passion that darkened her gaze when she made her sketches.

And last night, when sleep finally came to him, he dreamed of Mati. She was the white eagle, flying above as always with her two eggs. But this time, her wing feathers fluttered and then bent, twisted by some unseen force. Wounded, she careened wildly through the sky. One of the eggs slipped from her grasp, and she screeched in despair as it broke upon the ground. And then she followed it, plummeting arrow-quick, her wings useless, her talons clawing the empty air, toward the earth, toward Sakote.

He awoke suddenly as if emerging from the *kum*, the lodge—his body beaded with sweat, his skin shivering. All day, he couldn't purge the disturbing image from his mind. Finally, when he snapped at Hintsuli for asking him too many questions, his mother took him aside.

With her gentle voice and her calm manner, she prodded his troubles from him. And he told her everything. About his dream. About his encounter with the white men. And about Mati.

When he was finished, his mother sagely shook her head.

"My son's path cannot be more clear," she said. "His heart knows the way." She grasped his hand solidly in her own. "He is meant to be with the white woman."

He would have answered her, but she held up her palm for silence.

"The world of the Konkow is changing," she told him. "My daughter lives in the valley with a settler. My youngest son plays with the toys of the white man. Perhaps this woman of my older son will bring peace between the whites and the Konkows."

Sakote wondered if there could ever be peace between their peoples.

"A man must follow the will of The Creator," she said. "He cannot ignore the messages of Wonomi, who speaks in dreams. If the white eagle is in danger, he must go to her."

Sakote nodded. In truth, his mother's words relieved him. He felt like a hunter who'd traveled many miles to finally unload a heavy deer from his shoulders. He must go to Mati. His heart knew it. His mother knew it. And Wonomi told him so.

And so Sakote, his spirits light, had left just before the sun slept, stopping to pluck a bright bunch of poppies that he knew would give Mati pleasure.

But now, as the shadows of the evening began to paint the trees, he was troubled by that sense of danger. He slowed his pace. Something wasn't right. The air was too still, and the forest animals were restless. He hadn't yet come to Mati's clearing when he recognized the smell of smoke.

It wasn't the smoke of a cookfire. The scent was too strong, too heavy. It smelled like a brush fire or like the ritual fires of Weda, where baskets and clothing were burned in honor of the dead. But it wasn't the season for lightning. And it wasn't the time of Weda. The smoke seemed to come from the north, toward...

Mati's cabin!

The flowers fell from his fingers.

He raced forward through the slapping branches, throwing care to the wind. Quail and chipmunks scattered from his path. His heart beat against his ribs, matching his headlong stride as he crashed through the manzanita. All the while, he prayed to Wonomi to keep Mati from harm. At last, he burst through the trees.

And froze.

His worst fears were confirmed. Before him, Mati's cabin blazed with flame to rival the towering fires of Weda. Thick white smoke churned into the sky. The air shimmered with intense heat, like images in a spirit vision. Sakote's gut tightened.

Mati. Mati might still be inside.

Unaware he was even speaking, he began to plead with Wonomi. "Please don't let the white woman be in her *hubo*," he murmured. "Please let her be safe."

He lurched forward till he reached the cabin. A wave of searing air struck his face as snowy ashes settled in his hair.

He died a hundred deaths searching for her. Flames licked dangerously close to his flesh as he squinted through the fiery portal that was once her window. Smoke billowed around him as he frantically circled the blazing structure. He bellowed her name, but the sound was lost in the roar of the fire.

And then he spied hope. At the far reaches of the haze, past the jointed corner of blackening logs, flapped the hem of Mati's brown dress. A booted foot appeared, then a pair of fine white hands, and finally Mati's disheveled but unmistakable mane of tawny hair. She stumbled forward, and a knot of grateful tears strangled Sakote as he fought his way toward her.

She wasn't alone. A man dragged her farther from the fire. The pair of them looked as if they'd met up with an angry bear. The man wheezed and stumbled through the smoke, clutching a bloody rag against his stomach. Mati's skirt was torn, her hair had come loose from her braid, and her face was pale and streaked with blood. But she was alive.

The man had saved Mati's life. He'd delivered her from harm. Sakote felt a twinge of shame that he hadn't been there to rescue her, but his heart was too full of relief for regret. Closing his eyes briefly, he sent up a thankful prayer to Wonomi.

When he looked up again, he thought his eyes deceived him. He watched in horror as the man suddenly yanked a fistful of Mati's hair and threw her to the ground. Shock took Sakote's breath away. Disbelief paralyzed him.

Whatever the white man was, he wasn't her rescuer. The brute kicked once, hard, at her still body. Pure fury raged through Sakote's veins as he sprang forward. Before the man could rear his foot back to deliver a second blow, Sakote pounced on him like a yowling wildcat.

The man grunted beneath his attack. Sakote wrapped a vicious fist in the man's hair and ripped a hank from his head, ignoring his scream of agony.

The man's elbow jabbed backward, catching Sakote in the stomach. He doubled over, and the man's boot stomped hard on the arch of his foot.

The pain scattered stars across Sakote's eyes, but he shook them free like a wolf shaking off water. The man's fist barreled toward his face, but Sakote caught it, twisting the monster's arm savagely behind his back till it cracked.

And still the man fought. Spittle flew from his mouth. He cursed and wheeled on Sakote, one arm hanging useless at his side, the other swinging wildly. Then he swept his stiff boot beneath Sakote's foot, knocking him backward onto the earth with a thud.

The man would have stepped on Sakote then, broken his ribs and squashed him like a beetle. But Sakote seized his raised foot and wrenched it sideways, throwing the man over.

And then the spirit of the vengeful grizzly came upon him. Relentlessly, he punched the brute, caving the man's abdomen, crunching the bones of his nose and jaw. Sakote loosed his wrath like a bee-crazed bear until sweat dripped from his forehead and blood slicked his fists.

Only when the blinding red haze gradually dissolved did Sakote come back to himself. He looked down at his victim.

Had that bloody mess been a man? Had *he* wrought such damage? He looked at his culpable hands, swollen and dripping with the man's lifeblood. He hadn't known he was capable of such violence.

And yet he would do it again.

The man had hurt Mati.

Mati! He staggered forward. She lay so quiet, so still.

"Mati." Her name rasped against his throat like frozen wind. He hunkered down beside her, cradling her limp head against his arm. "Oh Mati, don't go from me." His chest tightened with pain. He brushed the hair back from her forehead and pressed his bloody fingers to her temple, feeling for a pulse. Thank Wonomi, her heart was still beating. But she didn't waken.

He began to pray aloud, closing his eyes, lifting his head to the sky, rocking back and forth with the rhythm of his words. He placed his palms upon her, summoning The Great Spirit's restorative power, even though it was his mother who was the healer of the tribe. He asked forgiveness for the man he'd killed and promised that he would take care of the white eagle.

Mati coughed then, and tears trickled from the corners of her eyes. She licked her swollen lips to speak.

"Sakote." She tried to smile at him, but it seemed too painful. Then her gaze drifted over to the burning cabin. "My...my sketches," she murmured forlornly, pulling some tattered piece of paper from her pocket. "He burned them—all my beautiful sketches."

The page was wrinkled, but he recognized the man in the picture. It was him. She'd saved it from the fire. He swallowed down the lump in his throat and tucked the paper back into her pocket.

Sakote didn't know why, but more than her injuries, her despair wounded his heart. Partly because he felt to blame. If only he'd stayed with her, watched over her...

He cast a quick glance toward the miner's village, and anger flared in him like the first spark of fire. The miners—why hadn't they protected Mati from this *hudesi*? Where was the big man with the yellow hair?

Before caution could stop him, he gathered Mati tenderly in his arms, wincing as she moaned in pain. Carrying her, he made his way brazenly to the settlement of the gold camp, determined to confront the *willa* with what they'd done to Mati.

What he found stole the breath from him in a loud hiss. The camp looked like the grisly aftermath of a Yana battle, a bloody massacre. Before him, the bodies of the miners—the man with the round hat, the young boy from Mati's porch, the yellow-haired giant—lay bleeding and broken, scattered like dead leaves. The stranger that had hurt Mati must have slaughtered them before continuing on to her cabin. Sakote tried to turn away from the ghastly sight so Mati wouldn't see, but she clutched at his arm, peering over his shoulder.

Her heartsick sob caught at his heart, and suddenly he wasn't sorry at all that he'd killed the *hudesi.*

His voice sounded like empty wind against the terrible silence of death. "There's a healer in my village. I'll take you there."

But Mati had already drifted off.

Mattie had no idea where she was or how long she'd been asleep. It would help if she could open her eyes, but right now it was too much of an effort. Nothing seemed familiar. The textures, the smells, the sounds, even the sensations within her own body were foreign, strange, almost as if she'd been born into another being, into another life.

Perhaps she had.

The last things she recalled were the stench of smoke, the

agony of watching her sketches burn, and that horrible man driving his fist toward her face.

No, that wasn't all. She recollected snatches of other things, too—the miners lying dead in Paradise Bar, patches of moonlight as she was carried through the woods, murmurs in another language, strange pungent aromas, and Sakote...

Sakote. He had come for her. She remembered that much.

But where was he now?

Only one eye would open properly. The other seemed to be pasted shut. She peered about her as best she could.

She lay in a dwelling of some sort, like a cave or the inside of a tree. Sunlight sneaked in through gaps of limbs here and there and poured like a stream through the one low opening at her feet. But it hurt to look at the bright beam, so she turned her head aside.

Sakote must have brought her here. It smelled like him. Crisp cedar and sweet reeds, wood smoke and tanned leather scented the air, along with several odors she didn't recognize—oily, herbal, bitter substances.

Her tongue ventured as slowly as a snail from its shell to wet her swollen, cracked lips, and she squinted toward the perimeter of the hut in search of something, anything, to drink.

Mounds of pine needles covered the floor, and a collection of baskets woven with angular designs squatted in the corner. Assorted animal skins and red-feathered bands, strings of white beads and strips of leather hung from branches along one side of the curved wall, and crouching at the foot of the wall was what appeared to be a giant stone mortar and pestle.

But it was what lay propped against the mortar that made her heart race and brought mist to her eyes. It was her drawing of Sakote, wrinkled and soot-stained, but intact.

Wincing as she craned her stiff neck upwards, she strained to see farther and almost choked on surprise. Sitting cross-legged, as quiet as death, was Hintsuli, staring back at her with doleful black eyes.

She gasped.

The boy's brows knitted suddenly in worry, and he murmured something in his own tongue.

"You frightened me," she tried to explain, though she was certain her voice—as rough as a rasp filing glass—offered little comfort.

Now that she was wholly awake, Mattie felt the full impact of what she'd endured. Her jaw ached, and, peeping through the tiniest slit of her right eyelid, she could tell her cheek was puffed up like bread dough. Her head throbbed, and her hands stung from the burns that had left red welts in her already injured palms. She shifted on her makeshift bed, grimacing as her bruised ribs protested.

"Where am I?" she asked vaguely, knowing Hintsuli couldn't understand her.

But though he didn't say a word, his expression was perfectly eloquent. Pity. He felt sorry for her. Heavens, she *must* look a sight then. Her hair was probably matted, and her dress...

Good heavens!

With a squeak, she burrowed deeper into the nest of furs. Where was her dress? She took a quick peek beneath the covers, mortified to discover that not only her dress, but every stitch of her clothing, was missing.

"Hintsuli!" Sakote's voice, an angry hiss, came from the low doorway at the foot of the hut.

Hintsuli didn't answer. His eyes widened, but he set his lips in a stubborn pout.

"Hintsuli!" This time the whisper was more irate.

When the boy didn't respond, Sakote's large shape darkened the entrance, and Mattie tugged the furs up protectively over her head.

Through the blankets, Mattie heard Sakote growl something, and the boy chattered back. Then there was a long silence.

Slowly, steadily, the furs were pulled from her grip until her face lay exposed.

"You're awake."

She wasn't sure if Sakote was rejoicing in the fact or accusing her, but she didn't care. It relieved her to see him again.

He frowned. "Did my brother wake you?"

"No," she croaked.

He glared dubiously at Hintsuli, and the boy crossed his arms in smug defiance.

"Where am I?" she asked.

"You need to drink," he observed. Then he barked some command to Hintsuli, who scrambled outside to obey.

"Where is the pain?" he asked, kneeling beside her with such tender concern that it made her eyes tear.

She considered his question for a minute, and then brought one arm from beneath the covers, holding up her little finger. "This," she told him. "This is the only part that doesn't hurt."

To her amazement, his scowl slowly melted into a sympathetic grin. And if it hadn't hurt so much, she would have mirrored that precious smile.

"My brother is bringing willow bark tea to take away the pain," he promised.

She nodded. "Thank you."

She stared at him for far too long, she knew, but she'd forgotten how pleasant he was to look upon. His bruises had healed, and his hair, pulled back now from his face, revealed his strong jaw and prominent cheekbones. His mouth, grim at first, curved into an easy smile, softening the lustrous black of his eyes.

And he didn't look away.

"I thought you'd left me," he murmured.

His words made her heart flutter.

"I thought I had, too," she whispered.

Her gaze settled on his parted mouth. How inviting it was. In the filtered light, the tips of his teeth shone against his swarthy skin. If only her lips weren't so bruised...

He seemed to read her thoughts. He glanced once at her mouth, then, with a crooked smile, lifted her hand carefully to his lips. Very tenderly, he placed a single kiss on her little finger. His touch was intimate, more intimate by far than the kisses to the hand she'd endured from the simpering suitors at Uncle Ambrose's parties.

She blushed, or at least she supposed she did. It may not have been discernible beneath the swollen mass of blue bruises on her face.

"I must look like a monster," she said, lowering her gaze.

"No," he told her, lifting her chin with the tip of his finger. "You are beautiful always. Your spirit is beautiful."

His words, so simple, so heartfelt, melted her bones. For a long while, she couldn't speak.

"You," she said finally, her voice cracking, "you undressed me?"

He gave her a sly grin. "No."

"No?" She blinked. "Then who..?"

"My mother. She's been caring for you."

"Your mother?" Mattie tried to sit up, but it hurt too much. "Your mother is here? Are we in your village?"

"Yes."

All at once, she felt panic. "I can't stay here. I don't belong here. I have to go back to my..."

What? Her cabin? It had burned to the ground. Along with all her possessions. She had no food. She had no clothing. No tools, no dishes, no candles, no pencils, no paper... And her friends? They were dead. Frenchy and Dash, Zeke and Swede, poor Swede...

She couldn't bear to think of it, but Sakote didn't give her time to wallow in misery.

"My mother is a good healer," he said, carefully brushing a lock of hair from her brow. "She'll make you well. Then you can worry about going back."

"But how long will that take?" she asked anxiously. "And where will I live in the meantime? I have no money. How will I eat? What will I wear?"

He pressed two fingers against her lips to silence her. "You're full of questions. I'll grow old answering them."

His touch soothed her fears. In fact, a moment more, and she might have slipped her tongue out to sample his warm fingertips as they brushed her open mouth. But someone was coming through the passageway.

Sakote's mother. It had to be. The woman possessed the same golden skin, strong cheekbones, and dark eyes wrinkled at the corners by crow's feet of happiness. She wasn't happy now, however. Lugging a clay cup and a basket of twigs and leaves, she made her way past Sakote, muttering all the while.

Sakote made a brief response, to which the woman answered with a shooing motion of her hand.

"No!" Mattie begged him. "Don't go, please."

Sakote crossed his arms in a perfect imitation of his little brother and made some rebellious comment to his mother.

The woman grumbled under her breath, but let him stay, pointing to the farthest corner of the hut, where she insisted he remain. Then she offered Mattie the cup.

The cool drink had a slightly bitter flavor, but she didn't care. She supposed this was the willow bark tea. The moisture soothed her parched throat. She finished it before the woman could even set down her basket and kneel beside her.

Once she was settled, the woman began to examine Mattie

so thoroughly that Mattie wondered if she should have asked Sakote to leave after all. She was gentle, but her fingers poked and prodded at every inch of her patient till Mattie was sure she was as red as an apple from head to toe. Apparently, nothing was broken, despite the dull ache of her ribs.

When the woman was satisfied, she plucked a small black oak gall from the satchel at her waist and ground it to a fine powder in her stone mortar. Then she drew a bunch of freshly cut, dripping milkweed stems from her basket and proceeded to squeeze the sticky white juice over the powder, mixing it to a thin paste. This she painted with her fingertips over Mattie's scrapes, murmuring soft syllables that sounded almost like a song.

Mattie hoped the woman knew what she was doing. Her concoction was disturbingly reminiscent of a witch's potion. But a quick glance at Sakote was all the reassurance she needed. After all, if he could dwell in the wilderness, hunting and climbing and doing all the dangerous things growing boys dared, and survive under the doctoring of his mother, she supposed it was good enough care for her.

Mattie sucked a quick breath between her teeth. The sap stung where her skin was broken. Sakote's mother blew gently on those places as she smeared them with the juice.

The woman's ministrations recalled a bittersweet time when Mattie was a little girl, when her own mother sat her upon her lap and cooed to her over a scraped knee. This woman, of course, looked nothing like her mother. Her complexion was as dark as the polished floors of Hardwicke House. Fine wrinkles crisscrossed her weathered face. Her hair, long and loose about her shoulders, hung like gray-streaked curtains, and her eyes were as black as a raven's. Most peculiar were the three black stripes painted from her bottom lip to her chin and two more extending from the corners of her mouth across her cheeks.

Mattie suddenly wished she could sketch the woman. She would draw her kneeling as she was now, surrounded by those intricately patterned baskets filled with bouquets of herbs and ferns and wildflowers. Perhaps she would even draw Hintsuli at her side, his arms wrapped fondly about her neck. If only...

If only she had her sketchbook.

All at once, she keenly felt their loss. When she got back on her feet, she would work hard to replace all she'd lost. But food would come first, and shelter, and clothing. A luxury like pencils and paper...

A tear squeezed from her swollen eye. She knew it was selfish of her. After all, she was lucky to be alive. Still, she'd lost so much—her parents, her home, her friends, all her worldly possessions. She couldn't bear to add to that list her dreams.

The woman's finely arched brows came together in a frown, and she said something to Sakote. He nodded and came near.

"My mother says she can heal your body, but not your spirit. She says you've wandered from your path, but you'll find it again."

Mattie swallowed hard and tried to smile. "Tell your mother I'm grateful for her help."

Sakote relayed the message, and the woman's eyes creased at the corners as she answered.

Sakote chuckled. "She says you may not be so grateful when you are well enough to grind acorns and tan deerhide and gather grasshoppers."

Mattie had no idea what that meant, but the warm humor in the woman's face melted the last of her anxiety. She snuggled against the fur blanket, whose twisted strips of rabbit skin made it miraculously soft on both sides, and watched in silence as the healer finished her work. By the time the woman gathered her tools in her basket and ducked back out of the hut, Mattie had drifted off to sleep again.

Sakote grunted when his mother told him to let the girl rest. He didn't intend to disturb Mati, but he wasn't yet ready to leave. He wanted to be with her. He wanted to watch the rabbit fur blanket rise and fall with her breath, to see the flare of her nostrils and the flutter of her eyes as she walked in the world of dreams. But mostly he wanted to look at the future, a thing that was hidden to him.

His mind traveled there of its own will, seeing visions it shouldn't, planning destiny as if a man were free to carve out his own path along Wonomi's earth.

He saw Mati dressed in white deerskin, her hair loose over her shoulder, kneeling at the grinding rock beside his mother, laughing, her belly big with child. He saw her bouncing their handsome son on her crossed knees as she sang a Konkow cradle song to send him to sleep. He saw her running across the meadow with their beautiful daughter, her basket full of acorns, her face flushed with joy, lupine blossoms tucked behind her ear. He saw her sitting across the fire, surrounded by grandchildren, her hair streaked with gray, her face crinkled from years of happiness, her eyes still shining bright with love.

Then he frowned. It was useless, this dreaming. She was here now, yes, and it felt right for her to be here. But Mati couldn't live forever with the Konkows. The miners from Paradise Bar had reminded him that a white woman in the company of an Indian was assumed to be stolen.

She wouldn't want to live here anyway. Why should she? Her world was so much more...civilized. She was accustomed to houses with wooden floors, dresses made of cloth, food that came in tins. When she was healed, she'd go back to her world, and there was nothing he could do to change that.

Yet it didn't stop him from imagining her falling asleep in

his arms every night. It didn't stop him from dreaming of waking up beside her every morning. It didn't stop him from yearning to make children and share grandchildren with her.

The breath left him on a soft sigh. Damn, he thought, if Wonomi didn't intend for the two of them to share a destiny, why did he keep putting the white woman on Sakote's path?

He touched Mati's hair, and then rose to go, turning to look at her one last time.

He must go to the *kum* now, scrape the sweat from his body with a deer bone and chant the words of the cleansing ceremony. He'd taken a life today, and it was necessary to wash the blood from his spirit as well as his hands.

But he knew his mind would wander from the chant.

The white woman was hopelessly tangled within his spirit, and, like a young stag, his heart foolishly bounded across the meadow with no thought for what might lie ahead.

CHAPTER 21

Mattie had no idea what she was eating. All she knew was that her stomach had growled all morning, and finally a young girl had brought her food. The fact that the girl was naked on top except for a long string of white beads made Mattie edgy enough to gobble down the mealy bread without question. The tea she offered was deliciously sweet, almost like apple cider.

The second girl possessed wide eyes that couldn't conceal her curiosity as she timidly handed Mattie her garments. Mattie's brown dress and accompanying underclothes had apparently been washed and then dried over a fire, for the bloodstains were faded, but the skirts reeked of smoke. At least they covered her more modestly than what these ladies wore. Their reed skirts reached no farther than their knees. Graciously, she accepted the clothing, shuffling awkwardly into it beneath the rabbit furs and the wondering stares of the two girls.

Once she was decent, the girls entertained themselves with her ablutions, examining the tucking and buttons on her dress, smearing an oily salve on her cracked lips, and chattering away as they smoothed her hair with a dark-quilled brush.

Just about the time Mattie had begun to fret about finding a convenience of some sort, the girls seemed to understand her distress. One girl took her hand, and they motioned her to come out of the hut.

Blinking back the bright morning light, Mattie was astonished by the appearance of the village. There were no teepees of the sort she'd always seen in pencil sketches, only a half dozen more of the conical stick and mud huts and a larger domed structure covered with cedar bark, hidden away under the pines. Baskets of all shapes, sizes, and designs huddled outside the houses, and here and there stood wooden racks of fish drying in the sun. A red-tailed hawk sat tethered to a perch beside one of the huts, and three animal hides lay stretched and pegged to the ground nearby.

The rest of the villagers, dressed no more modestly than her two companions, stopped what they were doing and stared unabashedly at her, as if they'd never seen a white woman before. A lopsided leather ball rolled unpursued into the grass as a pack of boys no older than Hintsuli halted their game. A pair of toothless old men with woven caps stopped their argument to frown at her. A bevy of old women looked up from patting dough into cakes over the fire, and three youths with tiny red feathers protruding from holes in their nostrils crossed their arms and raised their chins in challenge. Several young women with black chin stripes shifted baskets of seeds on their hips, their mouths forming oh's of surprise, but Mattie's pair of escorts haughtily ushered her out of their way, no doubt jealously guarding their elevated status as her personal companions.

She was given as much privacy as the woods could afford, after which the girls returned her to the village. As a result of their friendly curiosity—the little boys encircled her, chattering like chipmunks, the older women clucked over her injuries, and the young women reverently fondled her dress, one of them actually running a brazen hand across her bosom—Mattie felt as out of place as a nun at a debutante ball.

It was clear from the scowls of the old men that though she might be a source of intrigue and amusement at the moment, she was also an unwelcome threat, like a darling baby mouse in a sack of grain.

Mattie was accustomed to disapproval. After all, she'd seen it in the faces of every Hardwicke who'd foolishly offered to take her in. But they'd at least been kin. Here, she was truly a misfit. The Konkow clothing was strange. Their food was strange. No one spoke her language. Even the kind woman who'd tended to her needed a translator. The only one who could understand her was...

"Sakote," she said to the girls. "Sakote?"

They looked at her in surprise, and then pointed to the large domed structure. But when she started toward the building, they tugged her back, admonishing her with frantic waving hands. She glared at the thin stream of smoke rising from the middle of the bark-covered hut. It must be forbidden to her, she guessed, like the silly gentlemen's clubs in New York where women weren't allowed.

She sighed. Her head ached, and her body hurt, and she knew that no matter how long it took her to heal, she would never understand these savages, any more than she understood her priggish family back East. Sometimes she felt like Cain, shuffling from place to place, shunned by all, cursed and alone in the world. Sometimes it seemed Mathilda Hardwicke didn't belong anywhere.

Days passed, and the moon grew fat as Sakote watched the

bruises fade from Mati's face and saw her hands heal over with new white flesh. He even coaxed her from the *hubo* to come to the evening fire a few times, though she was never allowed to sit within the circle. The elders still looked upon her with hostile mistrust, and the old women with worry, though Mati ate the food of the Konkow, drank manzanita tea, and even learned enough of his language to speak brokenly with the two girls entrusted with her care.

But his mother was right. Though her body healed readily enough, her spirit was wounded. And nothing—not the bunch of lupines he brought her, not the cloak of deerskin he gifted her with, not even the clutch of newly hatched quail he showed her in a patch of buckbrush—could bring the smile back to her eyes.

In the end, it was his little brother who did that.

The boy had been poking around where he didn't belong, as usual. He'd returned to the white man's village, hiding himself in the bushes.

According to Hintsuli, not all the miners were dead. A man riding on a *lyktakymsy* had arrived, carrying a pack full of toys, and the miners had talked with him. The man had given them gifts from the big pack—colorful tins of food, red cloth, a shiny knife, a black cooking pot. But there was one gift that turned down the corners of the men's mouths. They talked about it for a long time, and then the man with the funny round hat and the bandaged head decided he would put it in his *hubo*.

Hintsuli waited until the miners left for the creek, and then he crept into that man's house and found what he was looking for.

If Hintsuli had stolen it out of greed, Sakote would have punished the boy by making him stay in his *hubo* for the entire ceremony of Kaminehaitsen. But Hintsuli's motives, if not pure, had been kind.

When the boy gave Mati the new sketchbook, along with pieces of charcoal from the fire to draw with, and when Sakote saw the shine of joy return to Mati's eyes, he wanted to pick his little brother up and swing him around as he had when the boy could barely walk.

After that, Mati came out of the *hubo* more often. Her drawings of the tame hawk they kept for feathers and the young squirrel that crept into the village each morning fascinated the old women. The boys loved her sketches of them playing the hand game with bones and kicking their buckskin ball. And the young women loitered nearby when Mati had her sketchbook, hoping to have their faces captured on her pages. The elders, however, didn't approve. They had never seen this kind of magic before, and anything that was new earned their disfavor.

They wouldn't forbid Mati from drawing. Sakote's mother made sure of that, for she saw how it healed Mati's soul. But they grumbled whenever she sat by the evening fire, her fingers smeared black, moving the piece of charcoal across the paper, and when they thought Sakote couldn't hear them, they spoke about the bad luck the white woman would bring to the tribe.

Mattie stared dejectedly at the twisted tangle of reeds perched on her lap like a long-abandoned magpie's nest. Knowing the difference between the rye, which was round, and the sedge, which was angular, didn't mean she could weave them successfully into a basket. Gaping holes slipped open faster than she could close them, and every few moments, the long, stiff reeds springing out from the center poked her.

Beside her, Sakote's mother worked, weaving the splayed reeds as deftly as a lady's maid arranging curls. Stripes of willow and redbud ran through her intricately patterned basket, and the coils were so compact that not even water could penetrate the weave.

A sedge reed jabbed Mattie's cheek, and she sighed in surrender, letting the basket slide apart as seemed its wont. Sakote's mother chuckled, but it was a warm laugh without a trace of scorn, and Mattie grinned sheepishly.

She'd conquered a few of the Konkow skills. Hintsuli and Sakote had taught her some of the language, and she knew how to grind manzanita berries for cider. Though she clung steadfastly to her more civilized attire, she became accustomed to the sight of the bare-breasted women around her, and she even wore a string of abalone shell beads made by her two honorary "sisters." On one morning, Sakote's mother had taken her to gather bracken fern and miner's lettuce for supper. In the afternoon, she learned to dig up camas and beargrass bulbs for cooking in a nest of hot rocks. She practiced making bread from acorn meal and flower seeds, and she learned to do without utensils as the Indians did, making a spoon of three fingers to eat acorn mush. Hintsuli even allowed her to participate in the sacred ritual of casting his lost baby tooth toward the setting sun.

But basket weaving, the Konkow woman's most important skill, she couldn't master. And it made her even more aware of how alien she must seem to them. If Mattie couldn't fit in with her own kin in New York, who shared a bond of blood, if she couldn't fit in at a gold camp, where she at least spoke the same language, how much less did she belong here, where her words, her customs, even her appearance were so totally foreign?

She sighed softly, but Sakote's mother seemed not to notice, distracted by the twinkle of sunlight off black obsidian from across the camp. She followed the woman's gaze. Sakote, crouched in the shade of a yellow pine, labored with as much natural dexterity as his mother, assembling a fishing spear, gluing the barbed stone point to the wooden stick with pitch, then wrapping it around and around with fiber.

She glanced at Sakote's mother. Now the woman was looking at her with a curious expression, almost as if she could read her thoughts. Then she returned to watching her son as he knotted off the tie and cut it with his teeth. She called him over, and they exchanged words.

"My mother says you should only make baskets when you are contented," he said, "or they will remain as empty as your heart." He hunkered down beside her, picked up her poor excuse for weaving, and flashed her a wicked smile. "She thinks I should show you how to hunt for yellow-jacket eggs instead today."

The way he looked—his bound hair glossy in the sunlight, the shadows dancing upon the bronze muscle of his shoulders, charm lighting up his eyes—she couldn't stay gloomy for long. The sun shone bright, the world was fresh and young, and when he winked at her like that, she thought she'd gladly follow him anywhere, hunting for yellow-jacket eggs or fire-breathing dragons.

She nodded a shy farewell to his mother. Sakote wriggled a slow-burning log from the fire and took her by the hand.

Mattie felt like a truant child as they left the village, wading through the young meadow grass strewn with wildflowers, watching the black swifts race against the sky, listening to the lazy drone of bumblebees. The sun beamed wonderfully warm upon her face, and it seemed impossible that it was the same sun that blazed down upon the busy streets of New York.

As they hopped from boulder to boulder, she wished she'd relinquished her stiff boots in favor of the more supple Konkow moccasins. Sakote insisted on climbing mountain faces instead of circling on the path like the miners did. He'd told her once it was to hide from enemies, and it only occurred to her much later that the enemies he spoke of were white men.

They stopped in a sun-splashed clearing. A tiny spring meandered through the thick grass, and the air was alive with red dragonflies and blue damsels.

Sakote handed her the burning brand and plucked a puff of down from a nearby milkweed plant.

"We must feed and trap the first yellow-jacket," he told her.

"They eat...that fluff?"

He smiled and shook his head. "They eat blood."

Before she could continue her line of questioning, Sakote unsheathed his stone knife and pressed the point of it to his thumb. Blood welled forth almost at once, and Mattie gasped, almost dropping the log.

But Sakote only chuckled. "It's a small offering for what we'll take from the yellow-jacket."

Mattie didn't think he should take the loss of his blood so lightly. No matter how he smiled, that cut must have hurt.

He squeezed a drop of blood onto the milkweed down. Then, popping his thumb in his mouth to stop the bleeding, he carefully placed the trap a few feet away, beside the trickling water.

"Let me see that," she said.

"What?" he mumbled around his thumb.

"Your thumb."

He showed it to her. She sucked her breath between her teeth as blood seeped again from the tiny cut.

"It's nothing." He shrugged, taking the brand from her.

"It is *not* nothing."

He stuck the thumb back in his mouth.

"Don't do that! What if there's infection? What if it—"

"Shh!" he said, jerking his thumb out and pointing toward the spring.

Already a wasp hovered near the trap, its striped hindquarters pulsing. It neared and retreated, neared and retreated. Then it settled slowly down upon the bloody puff, its antennae twitching as it sampled the fare. It apparently decided this was too great a feast to eat all at once, so it collected the feather-light prize and rose into the air.

Sakote exploded from his crouch, yanking Mattie after him.

"Come!" he cried. "We must follow him!"

He must have lost his mind, Mattie thought. Why else would a grown man leap and gallop and dodge and weave across a meadow after an insect? Yet she went mad right alongside him, for she never let go of his hand. Giggles like bubbly champagne spilled out of her as they dashed crazily through the grass after the yellow-jacket, which took a route more circuitous than a courting swain driving his sweetheart home. By the time it arrived at its nest, Mattie had laughed and run so hard she could scarcely breathe.

Sakote's chest heaved, too, and his eyes shone with a hunter's triumph as he spotted the papery abode clinging to the underside of a pine limb. He murmured a string of words in his own language. She didn't need to ask what he said. She'd learned that the Konkows thanked and blessed whatever they took from nature, be it rock or plant or animal.

"Now what?" she asked, laughter still rippling under her breath.

"Now we find a dead pine branch with needles."

Whatever he planned, it certainly seemed an elaborate scheme just for a few yellow-jacket eggs. She wondered what was so special about them anyway.

He found what he was looking for and lit the needles with the brand. Smoke curled off the tips, and Sakote blew on the ends to insure they would continue burning. Then he slowly waved the smoking branch around the wasp nest. Mattie cringed. Surely the smoke aggravated the yellow-jackets with their angry buzzing and their twitching tails.

But to her surprise, they seemed to calm. A few of them dropped off of the nest, and the movements of the rest slowed. Sakote handed her the brand and the smoky branch and used the flat edge of his knife to brush the remaining wasps off the nest. Then he carefully cut the nest from the tree and tucked it into the satchel he wore at his waist.

"What do you do with them?"

"The yellow-jacket eggs?"

She nodded.

"Eat them."

She wrinkled her nose. It sounded like another food to add to her list of Konkow delicacies she'd rather not try.

Still, she had to admire their resourcefulness. Never would she have suspected one could survive like this, living not from a cook's daily excursions to the local shops, nor even out of the tins a delivery mule could pack to the mining camp, but off of the gifts of the land. It pleased her. And while some of the suppers she'd shared with the tribe qualified for that list—acorn bread was stiff and gritty and slightly bitter, and acorn mush was downright bland—there was nothing quite so tasty as fresh-caught salmon and wild mint tea, roasted hazelnuts and sweet manzanita cider.

"You'll try them," Sakote told her, his voice half-teasing, half-warning. She supposed he hadn't gone through all those antics to have her turn up her nose at the fruits of his labor.

"All right, I'll try them." Then she reconsidered. "You *do* cook them, don't you?"

"Yes. They're my friend Noa's favorite."

She'd heard of Noa before, mostly from Hintsuli, once from Sakote. She knew only that he was from Hawaii, that he had toys, and that he was married to Sakote's sister.

"He says they taste like your sweetcorn," he said.

He said it just like that, sweetcorn, as if it were one word. She smiled. The way he spoke could be so charming, like the way he said Mah-tee. It wasn't the Konkow way to use proper names. They referred to each other as brother, mother, friend. But sometimes she ignored Sakote until he was forced to call for her by name, because she liked the way Mah-tee rolled off of his tongue.

"Have you ever tasted corn?" she asked.

He grinned and shook his head, and Mattie suddenly experienced a profound longing for this savage who seemed to be half-boy, half-man. She wanted to introduce him to the pleasures of her world—oyster soup, mince pie, and tinned peaches—as he had shown her his. "You would love corn. It's warm and sweet."

He smiled again, and Mattie saw the devil enter his eye, the sly twinkle that meant he was up to mischief. "It couldn't be as warm and sweet as the kiss you make for me."

He stared directly at her as he said it, unashamed, forthright, apparently unaware of the intimacy of his words. Mattie's cheeks grew hot. In New York, her Aunt Emily would have expected her to put the knave in his place. Men didn't speak so blatantly about such things.

He was staring at her mouth now, and the smoky charcoal of his eyes made the blood surge in her veins. The corner of his lip curved up, and her own lips parted in response. Then he tipped his head and bent toward her. Goodness, he was making a kiss for her now. She let her eyes flutter closed and waited breathlessly.

Chapter 22

The kiss never came.

Sakote leaped back with a loud yelp and a string of Konkow words Mattie couldn't decipher. He smacked his hand across his naked thigh and began leaping about as if the devil had a hold of his soul.

"Come!" He snatched the now extinguished pine branch from her, casting it to the ground, and relieved her of the brand as well. Then he seized her hand, and they were off and running again. Mattie figured out what all the fuss was about when she glanced behind to see a cloud of angry wasps coming straight for them. While she and Sakote were speculating on that kiss, the effects of the smoke had evidently worn off, and now the yellow-jackets were hot for revenge.

Mattie could barely keep up, and Sakote had to hook an arm around her waist to swing her up over one difficult pile of rocks. They rushed through the cedars and scrub oak at a hectic pace, skipping along a shallow stream, but the wasps swarmed after just as quickly, and Mattie wondered how they'd ever outdistance the vermin.

She was just about ready to surrender. Surely the wasps' stings couldn't be as painful as the knife-ache cramping her side from running.

But Sakote yelled, "Jump!"

And before she could even take a breath, they went plunging, hand in hand, over the crest of Sakote's waterfall and into the deep pool below.

She hit the water with a smack. Her dress whipped instantly over her head as she sank beneath the frigid waves. She scrabbled at her skirts, trying to claw them away from her face, but they clung stubbornly, pulling her down with their weight.

She'd almost run out of breath when a strong arm wrapped around her, tugging her dress from her face and hauling her up to the surface.

She drew in a large gasp of air and shivered, half from the cold, half in fear. Through the soaking strands of her hair, she could see Sakote, his hair gleaming wetly, his teeth shining, his eyes bright with victory.

"Safe," he proclaimed.

Mattie gripped his broad shoulders, too afraid of drowning in her waterlogged garments to let go. He seemed to have no trouble supporting the both of them, even though the bottom of the pool lay far below, and she marveled at the strength in his body. She supposed it was from swimming so much. The muscles of his shoulders bunched as he made wide ripples through the water with his arms.

Safe, he'd said, and yet she didn't feel safe at all, not with the way his eyes glistened and his arms flexed and his sumptuous mouth hovered only inches away. He was so near she could count the drops of water rolling down his chiseled cheek and whiff the faint scent of mint tea on his breath. Safe? On the contrary, she felt completely vulnerable.

"You weren't stung?" His ebony brows curved upward in

the most endearing way when he asked her a question. She wanted to reach up and touch one of them.

She shook her head. Then her eyes settled on his mouth again—his wide, wet, sensual mouth that slowly, languorously curved up into a delicious smile.

"You still want me to make the kiss with you," he accused.

She blinked, startled. Were her thoughts painted on her forehead? Sakote certainly didn't waste his breath on coy flattery. No one would ever accuse him of mincing words. But somehow his manner was oddly refreshing, and she saw by his easy grin, there was no need for her to reply.

The world slowed as he inclined his head toward her. The water lapped gently at her skin, and the damselflies made lazy circles through the air. His breath felt warm upon her mouth, but as he pressed his lips to hers, she could taste the chill creek upon him. Their kiss was sweet, tender, innocent, and Mattie got the fleeting notion that perhaps Sakote had never kissed anyone before her.

That impression didn't last long, or else he learned quickly. He captured her head in one hand, holding her still to slant his mouth across hers, deepening the kiss. Her lips softened beneath his, opening for him, and the shock of his warm tongue upon her cool flesh made her gasp with pleasure. His breath quickened upon her cheek as he feasted hungrily upon her.

A moan rasped across her throat, and he gentled his touch, nipping at his leisure, savoring each joining of their lips. Every fiber of her being centered on the fire they made with their mouths, and it wasn't until icy water gurgled into her nose that she realized they were sinking.

He jerked, too, apparently as startled as she. Then he laughed lightly. It was a seductive sound, intimate, and it flowed over her like warm honey.

"We should climb out. I'd be happy to drown here in your

arms," he murmured, "but my mother would mourn the loss of her favorite white woman."

Mattie swallowed hard. She didn't know what to say. She knew she must be troublesome to Sakote's people, and yet, with a few words, Sakote made her feel so treasured.

He half-turned in the water, giving her his back, and looped her arms around his neck.

"Hold on."

Then he swam for shore, his muscular back twisting beneath her with powerful strokes, his legs kicking up a froth behind them.

Her garments as heavy as a wet carpet, Mattie attempted to climb from the pool. Sakote gave her his arm, but his drenched moccasins afforded little purchase on the slippery stone.

"This dress, it's dangerous," he told her when he finally managed to pluck her from the water.

Mattie had to laugh at that. Dresses with plunging necklines and bare shoulders were dangerous. Her high-buttoned, prim, proper, practical frock was nothing but, well, frumpy. And at this moment, it was a bother. It would take hours to dry, but, thanks to Doc Jim's brother, she owned no other garment.

Without a word, Sakote began unfastening the buttons at the back of her bodice, which were even more challenging when they were wet. She felt she should stop him, but there really was no other way. She certainly couldn't manage them herself. And she had to get out of the dress to dry it.

After several long, silent minutes with little progress, Sakote finally spit out a phrase that sent Mattie into gales of laughter.

It wasn't that she hadn't heard and said "damn it" of late herself. It just sounded so comical coming from this noble savage. But before her laughter could die, she heard a rip, and the back of her dress fell forward in a spontaneous curtsey, revealing her chemise.

"What did you..?" she demanded.

He showed her his knife. "Later I'll make laces for the dress," he explained. "Laces are better."

"Laces are not better," she argued. Although they might be more convenient, buttons were the hallmark of a civilized society. She certainly couldn't walk around with rawhide laces running through her gown.

He didn't bother to counter her. He knew he was right, and she'd learned he had the patience to wait days if necessary for her to admit the truth. With an exasperated sigh, she wiggled the dress down over her chemise and stepped from the pile of drenched fabric. Her irritation didn't last long, especially when he beguiled her by sweeping the dress up and flinging it over a sunlit bush like some cavalier gentleman of old.

"Climb onto the rock, and I'll take off your shoes."

His gaze skimmed her body as he spoke, and she suddenly felt naked despite her chemise. Still, she resisted the strong urge to cross her arms over her breasts. She knew her dip in the pool had reduced the linen to little more than a diaphanous mist covering her body. But she supposed Sakote was accustomed to seeing women's breasts. Even his mother, with her sagging and wrinkled bosom, seemed to think nothing of roaming the camp without her deerskin cloak. And Mattie had to admit, it gave her a giddy, sensual freedom to flaunt society's morals, feeling the warm breeze shiver across the cool, clinging fabric.

Using Sakote's arm to steady her, Mattie took a step toward the rock.

"Wait!" he warned.

Mattie peered down. A salamander wriggled across the wet stones at her feet. "Don't worry. I won't step on it."

"You must hold one hand behind your back."

Mattie frowned. What did he mean?

"If you step over a salamander," he confided, "you must hold one hand behind you, or you'll be cursed with back pains."

She glanced sharply at him, and she could tell at once that he only half believed what he said. It was a Konkow superstition then, like throwing salt over your shoulder.

She obliged him in exaggerated fashion, taking a giant step over the little creature and perching atop the granite boulder.

Sakote removed his own moccasins and hung them upside down on the maroon branches of a manzanita. Then he reached for her foot.

Her damp shoe squeaked as he tugged the laces apart and seesawed it from her foot. She wiggled her toes while he removed the second and placed the shoes alongside his on the bush. How small they looked beside the big moccasins, and how uncomfortable.

He guessed her thoughts. "Your toes are unhappy. When we return to the village, I'll make moccasins to make your feet smile."

They were smiling now, she thought. He'd cupped one of them in his hand and he began to massage it, spreading her toes and running the wide pad of his thumb along the arch till she groaned in ecstasy. By the time he finished the other foot, she sagged on her elbows atop the rock, her eyes closed in pleasure, her head nodding back in the brindled sunlight, content as a well-scratched hound.

He was so quiet, she almost didn't notice when he stretched out beside her on the boulder. She opened one eye to peek at him. He had such a noble profile, with his high cheekbones, his arched nose, and those deep-set eyes, now lidded as he basked sleepily in the sun. A half-smile touched his lips, and she wondered what amusing thoughts crept through his mind. He *was* Neptune, with his hair splayed across the rock and his skin adorned with crystal gems of dew. Now and then a silvery drop would roll off one of his splendid muscles to disappear into the black and white pattern of the granite or to join the tiny pool formed by the hollow of his navel.

Mattie bit her lip. She wanted to touch him. Her cheeks flamed as her thoughts flew on against her will. She longed to lick the droplets from his chest. She imagined the taste—the metallic tang of the water, the clean evergreen flavor of his skin. She wanted to nuzzle his wet hair, to feel the strands like watered silk upon her cheek. And she longed to follow the contours of his body with her palm, gliding over his wide chest, across the smooth plane of his belly, around the hipbones protruding above the edge of his low-slung loincloth.

If it was possible, her blush blushed then, for in the sopping state of his meager garment, his hipbones weren't the only thing protruding. With an internal squeak of panic, Mattie slammed her eyes shut and lay back on the rock, knocking the back of her head on the hard granite. She tried to lay quiet, but her mind raced a mile a minute, and it was a long while before the sun lulled her out of her stiff posture into a light doze.

The sun had risen a full fist higher when she awakened to the skittering of something between Sakote and her, something that halted beside her shoulder. Out of the corner of her eye, she spied a gray lizard pushing up and down on its front limbs. She would have gasped and leaped to her feet, but Sakote's hand snapped out like lightning, capturing the tiny dragon.

"Ah, Sister Lizard, have you come to visit the white woman?"

He braced up on one elbow and peered at the reptile, whose head peeked out from between his thumb and first finger. Mattie sat up cautiously, edging out of harm's way. She wondered how long Sakote had been awake, how long he'd been watching her.

"I think you've frightened her," he murmured.

"How could I frighten her? I was sleeping," Mattie said defensively.

He smiled. "I was speaking to the lizard."

Mattie opened her mouth, then clapped it shut. She crossed her arms over her chest. "I'm not frightened."

He swung his hand toward her. "Do you wish to hold her then?"

"No!" she answered all too swiftly, earning a toothsome grin from Sakote.

"It's all right, little sister," he soothed, stroking the head of the lizard, which now wriggled in his hand. "She means you no harm."

Mattie shuddered. She hoped Sakote wasn't like the naughty schoolboys who liked to drop frogs onto girls' laps.

He sat up, cross-legged, on the boulder. "I'll tell you a story," he said, "to ease your heart."

She glanced up at those wickedly innocent brows. "All right, but I'm not sure..."

He chuckled softly.

"Don't tell me," she said. "You were talking to the lizard."

He grinned. "Sister Lizard likes my stories."

She rolled her eyes, but settled herself, cross-legged like he was, on the rock, so that they sat almost knee to knee. She liked the Konkow stories, too. By the campfire, Sakote had translated for her, and she'd learned about the creation of the world by Wonomi and Turtle, who'd dug up the clay of the earth. She'd heard the legend of the first man, Kuksu, and his woman, the morning star, who was made of red earth and water. And she knew the way Oleli, Coyote, had introduced death to the Konkow. They were tales she would never forget.

"This is the story of how Oleli stole fire."

Mattie's lips twitched. Sakote truly *was* speaking to the lizard, frowning intently down at the thing nestled in his hand.

"Oleli, in his travels to Histum Yani, the mountain of Wonomi's sweat lodge, discovered there a people who had fire. They cooked with this fire, and kept warm by it, and the fire lit up the darkness of the night. Now Oleli knew how the Konkow, the people of the valley, suffered in the time of *komeni*, how they feared the cold and death of winter, so he told the Konkow he would bring the fire to them."

Sakote's low voice was musical and breathy, like a wind blowing through the glade, part of nature, and Mattie sighed as his words wafted across her ears.

"Oleli waited until the Fire People were sleeping, and he stole a part of the flame. But the Fire People woke and chased Oleli to the bottom of the mountain. One of them reached for Oleli's tail, and burned it. Today you can see that the tip of Coyote's tail is still white."

Sakote glanced up to see what Mattie thought of this, and she gave him a dubious smile. Then he turned the lizard over in his hand so its pale belly lay exposed. As he spoke, he began to stroke the creature with his fingertip.

"At the bottom of the mountain, Oleli flung the fire away from him. But the other animals had come to help, and so Squirrel caught the flame and carried it on her back, fleeing from the Fire People by leaping through the trees. After a while, the flame burned her back, too, so that her tail curled up. And so it has been ever since."

All the while he told the tale, he kept stroking the lizard, which lay blissfully on its back.

"Squirrel then threw the flame to Chipmunk, but Chipmunk was too frightened to run. The Fire People reached out for him and clawed at his back just before he could escape. And to this day you can see Chipmunk's stripes from their claws."

Mattie felt hypnotized herself, watching Sakote work his magic on the lizard. Before, the reptile had twitched and wiggled in his hand, but now it lay docile, as if it were perfectly natural to bask in the palm of a man's hand.

"Chipmunk tossed the flame to Frog, but the Fire People grabbed Frog by the tail. With a great leap, Frog tore himself free, but he left his tail behind. And so it is that Frog has no tail."

Mattie watched Sakote's finger, stroking so lightly, so carefully along the belly of the little creature, and she suddenly yearned to feel that touch upon her own skin. Her eyes grew strangely heavy, and she squirmed at the disquieting bent of her thoughts.

"Finally, Frog cast the flame onto Wood, and Wood swallowed it. But no matter how they tried, how much they sang and shouted and struck it, Wood would not give the flame back to the Fire People. And so the Fire People returned to Histum Yani."

She wasn't listening to the story anymore. All she could think about was the brush of Sakote's fingers and how she wanted them upon her lips, on her cheek, caressing her throat, and, God help her, slipping lower.

"Now Oleli knew how to get the flame out, and so he returned to the Konkows and showed them how to do it—by rubbing two sticks of Wood together. And that is how Oleli stole fire. *Akina*."

Mattie blinked as if coming out of a dream. *Akina*. That meant the story was done. Sakote had stopped petting the lizard, and it lay quiet in his hand now.

"Sister Lizard likes my touch," he murmured.

Mattie's tongue felt brandy-thick. Sister Lizard wasn't the only one, she thought. Mattie stared at the beautiful savage, at the fall of his silken hair about his shoulders, the golden angles of his face, the soft sparkle of his eyes, and felt a rush of undeniable desire.

He held her gaze for a moment, amusement smoldering into something else, something dangerous and unpredictable, before he looked away. He carefully set the lizard upon a small rock, then returned his attention to Mattie.

"Did you like the story?" he breathed.

She nodded, but she was too full of longing to smile.

He leaned forward, his knee touching hers, to tuck a strand of hair behind her ear, and she shivered at the intimate gesture. He left his palm upon her cheek and gently but willfully commanded her gaze.

"You wish you were Sister Lizard," he whispered.

Mattie's face flushed, and she gulped.

His thumb traced her trembling lips. "Don't be afraid."

She wasn't afraid. At least not of him. She was more frightened by her own feelings. She felt as if she was about to render the most wondrous portrait, and she didn't know where to begin.

Sakote wanted to make a kiss with Mati. Her mouth was as warm and sweet as the honey of *kawkati*, summer, and he thought he'd never fill his hunger for that taste. But Mati was afraid, quaking under his palm even more than the lizard. He must be patient.

"Your skin is smooth and pale like the white deer," he told her, brushing his knuckles over her cheek, letting the soothing music of his voice work its enchantment. "And your hair, it catches the colors of the sun." He rubbed a strand of it between his fingers, and then he circled the rim of her ear with the tip of his finger. Her eyelids flagged, and her soft sigh sent an unexpected bolt of desire through him. He raked both hands through her hair, capturing the damp tresses, smoothing her forehead with his thumbs, watching the fluttering of her nose and the parting of her lips. By Wonomi, he wanted to make a kiss with her. Now.

His breath came heavy in his chest. Mati's eyes drifted close, and he pulled her closer, inclining toward her until he felt her breath upon his mouth. This kiss was warm with sun and as sense-stealing as the white man's whiskey. Sakote felt the world slide and tilt as he closed his eyes to savor the nectar of her lips.

Her small hands touched the hollow of his throat, where his heart beat strong, and then he felt her fingers curl upon his chest as their tongues mingled. She half-moaned, half-sighed into his mouth, and low in his belly, he tightened like the sinew of a bow.

Without releasing her lips, he rocked forward and, cradling her head, lay her back along the boulder. He rested on one elbow, freeing his other hand to work its magic on her. He trailed the back of his fingers down her throat, between her breasts, over her belly, soothing her with the same motions he'd used on the lizard. Her clothing was thinner than a moth's wing, and he could clearly see the sinuous contours of her body. It was driving him mad, this patience. His man's-knife stood stiff and ready. It didn't understand the hunter's vigil.

But again and again he moved his hand over her, sometimes the tips of his fingers, sometimes the flat of his palm, each time slipping lower and lower, nearer the source of her woman's pleasure until she arced with longing toward his touch. Then he tugged loose the ties of her underdress and parted the sheer white petals until her fair flesh gleamed in the bright sunlight. She made small motions of protest, but when he grazed the bare skin of her bosom with his fingertips, she stilled in surrender.

By Wonomi, she was softer than the finest doeskin. Her nipples were small and pink, like manzanita blossoms. He wanted to make a kiss there, too.

He let his hand trace her quivering belly until it nestled at the top of her woman's curls, and listened while her breath grew sharper, swifter. Then he bent to nuzzle her throat, placing kisses upon the pulsing line to her heart as she gasped softly near his ear.

Again, he stroked her with his palm, this time close to the crest of her breast, and he made a trail of kisses along the bone of her shoulder. She shivered as his hair brushed across her, and he smiled wickedly, sweeping his head intentionally, lazily, back and forth across her torso, lashing her slowly with his hair until her nipples hardened to delicate points.

He groaned at the sight. His heart pounded against the basket of his chest till it hurt. His belly knotted. His loins ached. He could endure no more.

He bent to close his lips around a delicious nipple, sighing at its sweetness. Mati flung her arms wildly about his neck, arching into the palm of the hand that cupped her below. He sought to pleasure her, parting her delicate flower to fondle the bud within.

Mati gasped, a sound of wonder and dismay all at once, and Sakote was surprised by both. He froze. Did she not know this pleasure? Surely the young men of her world had shown her...

But Mati was a white woman. Perhaps, as Noa had told him, it was true that the whites didn't play pleasure games.

His doubt quickly vanished as Mati strove against him, her face alight with joy and yearning. His smile of triumph became a grimace of pain as his loins swelled with need. But he made the dance of pleasure for her, moving his practiced fingers nimbly over the petals of her womanhood, like the gentle rain upon a spring flower.

He watched her face with half-lidded eyes, delighting in her ecstasy, breathing with her, tensing with her, until his own lust was almost too much to bear. And then she stiffened, gasping, her fingers clawing at his arms, and he watched her soar over the precipice of desire like the eagle taking flight over a canyon. Her face glowed with rapture. Sakote had never seen anything so beautiful.

And after the shudders racked her body, he held her close, never wanting to let her go, and whispered Konkow words of comfort against her ear.

CHAPTER 23

Mattie felt like her bones had melted into the rock, fused like limp lichen to the granite. Only her soul still spiraled lazily overhead, reluctant to return to the earthly shell that had cast it free a moment ago.

Gradually, Sakote's strange whispered words enticed her home. She heard again the soft whine of dragonflies, felt the rough rock beneath her and the alternating wash of parching sun and delicate mist from the waterfall. She drew a ragged breath through her parted teeth.

What had he done to her? She felt broken asunder, yet recreated even more whole. The sun laved her naked skin in places it had never touched before, and yet she felt no shame, only its cleansing warmth. She smiled the smile of unlocked secrets, of freedom.

Sakote growled playfully in her ear, and she lifted her languid gaze to meet his. But even as she reveled in her own contentment, she saw yearning in his smoldering eyes, an unrequited fire.

He'd done this to her—sent her aloft on a cloud of ecstasy,

let her glimpse the realm of angels. Now she longed to do the same for him, to bring him pleasure, if she could figure out how.

She lifted a tentative finger to his lips. His nostrils flared once as she slowly traced his mouth. He liked her kisses. She knew that much. She ran her tongue over her lip. Already his taste—sweet, musky, warm—was imprinted on her memory.

She eased forward until their lips met. He clung to her, delving deeply into the recesses of her mouth. His breathing was harsh and desperate, like a carriage horse run hard.

She devoured him with her hands, snagging his damp, coal-black locks, riding the wild pulse in his throat, spanning his broad shoulder, gliding across the shallow planes of his chest. And then her hand strayed lower, brushing timidly over the strained hide of his breechcloth.

The breath seemed to scrape across his teeth as he gasped. In pain? She searched his eyes, but they were squeezed shut.

A sudden pang of indecision struck her. Perhaps she'd done the wrong thing. Perhaps she'd offended him, or worse, injured him.

"I'm..." she whispered. "I'm sorry if I hurt you,"

The last thing she expected was Sakote's rueful chuckle. "It's..." He sighed on a growl. "A good pain."

He took her hand, pressing it firmly against him then, against that part of him that swelled even as her palm made contact, and closed his eyes in self-imposed anguish.

His voice was strained. "A very good pain."

The blood rushed to Mattie's face. She'd done this to him, this...improper thing. She knew she should withdraw, yet her hand continued to brazenly rest where it shouldn't. It was so immoral, so unladylike, so...fascinating. And like a naughty child, halfway down the street with a stolen sweet, she'd gone too far to turn back.

Before she could think twice, the words spilled out of her in a heated rush. "And how do I relieve this pain?"

His groan seemed less agony, more pleasure this time, and he measured her with a long and dangerous stare that almost made her regret her words. Almost.

Then he turned her hand over, carefully twining her fingers in his own. His nostrils flared, his eyes burned dark, and suddenly she felt swept away in their depths.

With his free hand, he unfastened the knot of his breechcloth and folded back the deerskin, revealing...everything.

He was more magnificent than Mattie remembered, and the sight of him did queer, wonderful things to her insides. If she could only capture that male essence on paper, she thought, with her pencil and...

Sakote caught her wrist. Now was evidently not the time to ask him to sit for a portrait. And if he kept looking at her like that, all smoldering and heathen and hungry, she wouldn't be able to keep her hands from shaking anyway.

He closed his eyes and lay back, and while she watched with tattered breath, he guided her hand where he wanted it. His skin was like velvet where she clasped her fingers about him, and for a moment he held her hand there, letting her experience the warm throbbing of his blood. Then he led her, sliding her palm in a slow dance that drew the breath from him in frayed gasps. She could feel the strength in him, yet also a tenderness she'd never imagined a man could possess. As she held him literally in the palm of her hand, a heady sense of power overcame her, for she knew she'd become the instrument of his salvation.

Steadily he guided her with clenched fingers, his brow furrowed in a longing so intensely bittersweet that it caught at her very soul.

Suddenly she wanted him, wanted to touch every part of his body, every fiber of his being, wanted to hear his every thought, know his every feeling.

284

As if he read her mind, he murmured something to her in his tongue and wrapped his arms around her, pulling her closer, against his heart, giving her full rein to take him where she willed.

Instinct and nature showed her the way. As his thrusts became gradually more deliberate, she answered them in kind. When the heaving of his chest grew more rapid, she matched the rhythm of his breath. And when his gasps of anticipation echoed around her and he clasped her tighter, she cleaved to him in breathless wonder. At last, his brow creased in ecstasy, and his body flexed like a powerful lunging animal as he groaned in release, hugging her again and again, shivering off the last of his need like a wolf shaking off frost.

His eyes were still closed when he collapsed, spent, upon his back. His nostrils quivered, and his chest still rose and fell rapidly. But his limbs and his long black hair draped over the boulder as if he were no longer a man, but part of the rock itself.

Moments later, as Mattie propped herself up on her forearm to gaze down at him in awe, she bit her lip. How she wished she had her sketchbook now, to depict Sakote in all his naked bliss. With his golden skin, his sculpted contours, his sparkling eyes, his flashing teeth, no one could more perfectly represent unconstrained art...pure emotion...unadulterated nature.

His lips curved into a broad, lazy smile, and he murmured, "Ah, Little Acorn, are you sure you have not done this before?"

She gasped at the idea and gave his shoulder a soft chiding punch. When he opened one eye and frowned in puzzlement, she realized he'd meant no insult.

She tried to explain. "Of course I haven't done this before. In my world, proper ladies don't just..." Proper ladies. Now Mattie sounded like her priggish aunt. "One must guard one's repu-..." How rigid it all seemed. "To do...this...without the benefit of wedlock..."

"Wed-lock?"

The way he said the word made her laugh. Sakote sometimes had a way of making English sound absurd and unnatural. Perhaps it was.

"Where I come from," she said, rolling onto her back and gazing up dreamily into the leafy bower overhead, "it's considered...uncivilized...to act upon our desires. Instead, we keep them leashed, hidden away."

He pushed up on one elbow and frowned down at her. "And this is civilized?"

She nodded. It truly *was* silly when you said it aloud.

He broke off the stem of a foxtail, rolling it thoughtfully between his fingers. "So if you have a desire to eat?"

"You pretend you're not hungry at all."

His scowl deepened. He brushed the furry tip of the weed lightly under her nose. "What if you have an itch that needs to be scratched?"

She twitched beneath his teasing touch. "You keep a stiff upper lip."

He tossed the stem aside and let the tip of his finger take over, caressing her mouth with infinite patience, making his tortuous way down her throat, between her breasts, and lower. She held her breath as he smoothed over the gathered skirt at her waist, then delved farther, deeper, sinking into the aching space between her thighs.

She moaned as her body responded, rising to meet the lovely pressure of his hand.

"And if you wish to feel pleasure?" he murmured.

"You...deny it."

His soft chuckle was as rich and delicious as cream. "I think I do not wish to be civilized."

She smiled on a sigh. "Nor do I," she whispered, throwing her arms about his neck and crushing her breasts against his chest.

The shadows of the leaves moved gradually from one end of the boulder to the other as Sakote initiated her into his savage, delectable, uncivilized ways. Mattie had never felt more precious, more alive, more part of the world around her as she let him explore every secret of her body and learned every mystery of his.

When he was done with her, she had not an ounce of strength left. Every inch of her bare skin tingled from his arousing, soothing, invigorating touch. And she felt as if the last drop of civilization had been wrung from her like water from a wet rag.

This was paradise, she thought—a place with no responsibility, no guilt, no shame.

"I wish I could stay here forever." But the cool breeze soon reminded her that the day was growing late, and she was forced to wrap her chemise about her. She sat up, fussing with the ties, trying to restore herself to some semblance of order. "But I suppose I can't just do whatever my heart desires."

He sat up beside her, wrapping his arms around his knees. "Why not?"

"Well, because...because..." She twisted her mouth, unable to come up with a reasonable answer. "What about you? Do you always do whatever your heart desires?"

After careful consideration, he replied, "Always."

"Even if it's...immoral?"

"Immoral?"

"Improper, indecent."

He scowled at her. "I don't know these words."

She let her hands fall to her lap and stared at him. He really *didn't* know those words, and something about that was terribly endearing. "Surely you have things that are forbidden?"

"Ah." He nodded. "It's forbidden to eat the wolf. It's forbidden for men to enter the woman's *hubo*. It's forbidden to speak the names of those who have gone to the other world."

"And this?" Against her will, her gaze slipped to his loins, and she blushed.

He looked at her as if she were crazy. "Why would this be forbidden?"

All she could think was, how odd. A man couldn't utter a dead person's name, but it was perfectly admissible to make wild, passionate love in the middle of the woods.

She shook her head in amusement as she smoothed down her skirts. But then an ugly thought occurred to her.

If this wasn't forbidden—if exchanging intimate caresses in the forest was completely acceptable—then this probably wasn't the first time he'd done it. In fact, Mattie was probably just one of *many* women he'd pleasured. She was nobody special. She was just another of his conquests.

She knew she shouldn't be hurt. It was simply how he'd been raised. But she suddenly felt humiliated, and she turned away in silence, unable to explain the hollow pain in her chest.

"This is forbidden in your world?" he asked cautiously.

Her chin quivering, she tried to give him a casual reply. "No, it's not forbidden...between a husband and wife."

"Ah. Then you don't play the pleasure games until you have the marriage?"

Games? Was that all this was to him? A game? It was as if an anvil fell on her heart, and she fought to hold back the tears. Still, a tiny mortified sob escaped her as she tried to climb to her feet.

He caught her by the arm before she could escape. "I've made you cry."

"I'm not..." But it was no use to deny it. The tears were thick in her voice.

"If you don't wish to do this, Mati," he said under his breath, "then we won't."

"Fine. After all, I'm sure you have plenty of other women to play pleasure games with." The words snapped out of her like a spring from an old pocketwatch, and even the wise voice of regret couldn't push them back in.

He rubbed his thumb along her arm and screwed up his forehead, baffled. "I didn't mean to hurt you, Little Acorn. It's just the Konkow way."

Mattie's heart sank further into the pit of her stomach, and her throat tightened with tears. The Konkow way. Society's dictates. What was the difference? She'd given him the gift of her passion, but it wasn't special to him at all.

Suddenly she was reminded of a story her father had told her once, about a tribe of natives he'd encountered in the tropics. He'd given the chief a valuable strand of pearls as a token of friendship, which the chief had politely accepted as if it were a rare treasure. But the next day, her father had seen the pearls adorning the wrist of a little girl with a dozen such bracelets.

So it must be with Sakote. Her passion, her body, her virtue—the most precious things she possessed—meant nothing to a man who had willing women at his beck and call.

Her eyes filled with hot tears, blurring the dogwood blossoms and the chartreuse ferns and the sun-sparkled creek into a messy palette of watercolors. She was hurt and embarrassed. And though she knew in her heart Sakote had done nothing to deserve her anger, she wanted to hurt him back.

Salvaging the shreds of her dignity, she flung her hair over her shoulder and tried to control the wavering in her voice. "If it's the Konkow way, then perhaps I should try to learn. Whom do you think I should play the pleasure games with next—Domem or Bercha?"

Sakote scowled with displeasure, and she knew she'd hit her mark.

They didn't speak all the way back to the village.

CHAPTER 24

Sakote frowned into the flames of the night fire. Mati's distant laughter—made for another man—was as annoying as the taunting jabber of the blue jay.

Why had Mati mentioned his tribal brothers, Bercha and Domem? Was she interested in them? Had they spoken to her? How had she learned their names? His scowl deepened. He didn't like this turn in the path.

Earlier today, when he and Mati had played the pleasure games, they'd been caught up in the joy of their bodies. He'd been convinced she cared for his spirit as well. But now he wondered if he was wrong, if it wasn't so. Perhaps it was only that she'd never played the pleasure games before. Perhaps he wasn't sacred to her at all.

He sighed. He could never understand the mind of a woman. Their ways were a mystery to him. He could hardly figure out his sister, who was Konkow. How would he ever untangle the twisted thoughts of this *willa*?

Sakote narrowed his eyes at Bercha, who sat across the fire. The youth's handsome face glowed in the orange flame.

He was two leaf-falls younger than Sakote. He was strong. His shoulders were as broad as the oldest cedar in the woods, and he could shoot an arrow all the way across the clearing. But he was not as good a hunter as Sakote. *He'd* never been honored by dancing in the rafters at the *simi,* deer ceremony. Besides, Bercha was in love with another. Sakote was certain of it. So why would Mati want to play the pleasure games with him?

He shifted on his haunches, looking past the circle of faces until he found Mati's, shining white like the *poko,* the moon. Laughter brightened her eyes as Domem told the tale of mean-spirited Skunk, who'd caused acorns to stink so that women would have to work hard to make them edible. Domem told the story in the Konkow tongue, but his wrinkled nose and crossed eyes were easy enough to understand.

Domem had always been a good storyteller. Perhaps that was why Mati liked him. But he was never serious. He entertained the children, but the elders didn't respect his counsel. They said Domem had his mind in the mist, that he was always dreaming of fish, never catching them. Why would Mati want to play the pleasure games with someone so childlike?

No, he decided, pressing his lips together. She shouldn't play the pleasure games with Bercha *or* Domem. His mind made up, he rose from the fireside and beckoned her with a motion of his hand and a questioning lift of his brows.

Outside her *hubo*, it took him a long while to gather his thoughts, especially when the moon painted her hair in glowing waves and the touch of her sun-warmed skin was still fresh in his memory.

"I've been thinking," he told her.

"Indeed?" It was only one word—a fairly meaningless word—but Mati made it sound as cool and distant as the stars.

He wished Mati could speak his tongue. Konkow was so much simpler, more direct. English seemed like the language of Henno, Trickster Coyote, who might whip around at any time and bite him.

"On this matter of the pleasure games."

"Ah."

"I've decided that if it isn't the way of your people, *akina*, you shouldn't play the pleasure games."

"I see." He didn't like the look on her face. It reminded him of Towani's expression when she was about to spin a web of words to trap him. "But I don't agree. If I'm to dwell among the Konkows, then I should learn the ways of *your* people." She looked past his shoulder toward the fire, where the children continued to giggle at Domem's silly antics. "I think Domem might be willing to..."

He grabbed her by the shoulders, harder than he meant to. "Domem..." Then, confused by his own roughness, he loosened his grip. "Domem is...foolish and simple."

"Hmm," she said, thoughtfully scratching her cheek. "And Bercha? He's as handsome as the devil, I must say, and—"

Sakote let out a growl of exasperation. He shoved a hand back through his hair. How could he make her see?

He sighed and gazed down at her. Mati's eyes shone like pebbles at the bottom of the creek. Starlight glazed her hair to the color of sun-dried grass and poured like acorn milk over her shoulders and across her breasts, places he knew now, places that made his fingers tingle to recall.

He knew the truth, deep in his heart. He couldn't bear to think of anyone else touching her. Now. Or ever.

Still, he was reluctant to tell her. If he confessed his love, he had to be willing to make a promise of commitment to her. And once he made that commitment, he'd be left with two choices. He would either have to defy the elders, who'd say Mati was bad luck, or he'd have to leave the village.

It was too soon to make such a difficult choice. It was customary for a serious Konkow suitor to spend weeks in courting—speaking with his intended's father, bringing gifts to her family, playing the pleasure games with her, bringing her a deer to prove his ability to provide for her.

He'd known Mati such a short time. Yet he'd already chosen her. His dreams had shown him the way long before the white woman had even come. They belonged together, Sakote and the white eagle.

He took a steadying breath and commanded her gaze with his own. "I don't wish you to play the pleasure games with anyone else."

The cold glare in her eyes shivered like icicles melting in the sun, but mistrust lingered there. "Really? While you continue to consort with Haikati and Yalalu and...and..."

"No." He frowned. What was she speaking about? He'd never played the pleasure games with Haikati. Haikati's heart belonged to another. And Yalalu was his uncle's daughter. Most of his encounters had been with girls of other Konkow tribes. And they all faded in his memory when he thought of coaxing Mati's beautiful flower to blossom and remembered the touch of her smooth white hand upon him. "I don't wish to play the pleasure games with anyone else. My heart is with you. My spirit is with you."

Despite Mattie's best intentions to remain aloof, Sakote's words made her heart flutter.

All evening, he'd seethed with blatant jealousy. Every time she glanced at Bercha, Sakote curled his lip in disgust. While the rest of the tribe laughed at Domem's story, Sakote furrowed his brows. True, his jealousy had soothed her damaged vanity, if not her bruised feelings. But this...this was unexpected.

She looked into his eyes—darkly beautiful as they mirrored the black expanse of the heavens above—and she saw the truth. His heart *was* with her. He didn't know the sugared phrases gentlemen used while courting. He offered none of the empty flattery and poetic comparisons that wearied a woman's ear. But his simple words and his steadfast gaze were far more eloquent than anything she'd ever heard in a parlor.

Her heart went all soft. "You're sure?"

He lifted a brow in question. "Have I not said so?"

She almost smiled at that—it never occurred to Sakote to lie—but instead, she let her gaze drop to his mouth. Ever since this afternoon, when they'd indulged in things that made her blush to remember, she could think of nothing else but touching him again. Her body felt drawn to him, like iron to a magnet. And this close, where she could see the soft glow of the moon in his eyes and inhale the sensual aroma of his skin, that tug was almost irresistible.

"I don't want to...be...with anyone else either," she admitted, her voice a wisp of sound.

Relief relaxed his features. He tipped her chin up and smoothed the worry from her brow, then framed her face gently in one hand. She held her breath.

His hair swept like a curtain across her cheek as he bent to kiss her. He tasted of mountain balm tea and the sweet corn flavor of yellow-jacket eggs, but mostly he tasted of Sakote, that wonderful, indescribable ambrosia she'd grown to crave. She drank deep, weaving her fingers through his silky locks, slipping her hands under the edge of his buckskin cloak to trace the surging swell of his chest.

She longed to toss the cloak off of his shoulders, to tear the breechcloth from him, to see and touch and taste all that she remembered from the waterfall. Her own clothing felt like a tight cocoon from which she might emerge a glorious butterfly. But not here, not in the village, not in plain sight. Children still laughed around the evening fire. Young women flashed coy glances at young men across the flames. And though Sakote's great body shielded her from their view, she knew the elders cast disparaging looks in her direction.

She held him close when he ended the kiss and whispered against his mouth before she had the sense to stay silent. "Stay with me tonight. Please."

He stiffened, and for an instant she feared she'd been too aggressive. But then he clasped her head to his chest, near his rapid-beating heart.

"Are you inviting me to...stay in your *hubo*?" he murmured against her hair.

"Yes."

Sakote felt as if his heart would swell and burst. Mati wanted him. She accepted him. And at this moment, nothing else mattered.

He wouldn't think about tomorrow. Tomorrow always brought a new sun that lit up a new path. For now he thought only about tonight, a night blossoming with promise, a night he'd remember all of his days. He thought of the sacred stream they'd cross together tonight, he and Mati.

He grasped her hand and let her lead him into her *hubo*.

It was dark except for a few slashes of starlight along the ground left by gaps in the roof. Sakote would have preferred firelight. He wanted to see Mati, to look into her shining eyes as he pleasured her, to see her lips blush from his kiss, to watch her face as her body finally exploded like stars over a waterfall.

But there would be time for that later. Tonight they'd travel in darkness. Tonight was only the first step of the journey.

He navigated by touch, kneeling, then swinging his cloak over the reed mat and mound of pine needles that made Mati's bed, softening the nest. Mati's skirts rustled as she knelt before him. He could no longer hear the storyteller's muffled voice, only the rasping breath of their two hungering souls.

"It's dark. I can't..." Mati whispered.

Her hands stumbled across his chest, and he caught them, anchoring them against his ribs.

"See me with your heart," he murmured.

She sighed, and he ran his thumbs gently over her eyelids to close them. Closing his own eyes and trusting his instincts, he reached out for her lush tresses, her soft cheek, her delicate jaw. She began to caress him as well, gliding along the muscles of his bare chest. Her hands felt so small upon his body, and yet he could feel their magic all the way down to the place where his man's-knife awoke.

He widened her jaw with his thumb and covered her open mouth with his, imagining the breath of his spirit flying from him and into her. He moved his lips in a gentle feast, tipping his tongue to hers, so wet and warm that he couldn't help but compare this blossom to her tempting woman's-flower. The thought wrenched a groan from him, and she answered by twining her arms about his neck.

He loosened the laces he'd made for her at the back of her dress, and the garment slipped from her as easily as the sigh slipped from her lips. The filmy gown beneath, sheer as a butterfly's wing, threatened to tear in his eager fingers, and he wondered if he had the patience to take care with the thing...and with her.

His hand found its way along the pulsing vessel of her throat, and then stole lower, wrinkling the frail fabric that made a poor guardian of her bosom. Her breast curved perfectly into his hand, as if it were made for him. As he swept his palm over the insubstantial garment, she moaned, and her nipple rose to meet his touch.

His blood raged now, making *whit-tum-tumi*, thunder, in his ears. His mouth hungered for her. His man's-knife demanded sheathing.

But he wouldn't be led by his desires. He was a warrior. He

was strong. He was a good hunter, because he possessed both strength and patience, and he must use those now.

Very slowly, so she wouldn't be frightened, Sakote tugged loose the ties of her underdress, and then pressed Mati back upon the fur-covered reeds. And though the air was chill, he burned as he opened her chemise with his teeth and lowered his head to suckle at her breast.

Mattie felt as if a bolt of lightning coursed through her body. She arced to meet his mouth as the sweet current struck and echoed on and on. Soon, like a jealous twin, her concealed breast longed for his touch, and after a while he rewarded its yearning flesh as well.

She entwined her hands through his hair—his glorious, long hair—wishing she could keep him there forever. But he quenched his thirst and kissed his way up to her face, holding her head in his two hands to plunder her mouth deeply with his ravenous tongue.

Breathless, she clung to him as the world spun around her. She ached for him now, low in her belly, ached for the relief she knew he could bring.

He ended the kiss, and then nuzzled her cheek until he found the lobe of her ear. His hot breath sent a shiver along her neck.

"I want to taste you," he murmured. She gasped as his hand slid gently between her legs. "Here."

"Oh," she cried, unable to speak. Such a thing was indecent, unthinkable, impossible, and yet...her body arched against the pad of his palm with a hunger so sharp it frightened her.

He took her silence to mean assent, lowering himself toward the center of her lust, and she bit her lip in a torment of anticipation.

The chemise slid with maddening sloth over her skin as he drew it back from her. For a long moment, all she could feel was the moist heat of his taunting breath along her thighs. Then he kissed her...there...and she gasped with a spasm of excruciating pleasure. A hot river of desire burst from the spot and rushed through her veins, leaving her skin tingling with fire. She flung the back of her hand across her mouth, afraid her cries of sweet agony might pierce the night as he bathed her most secret places.

She should make him stop. What he did was primitive and wicked and sinful. And yet she found no words to belay his heathen assault, no strength to fight his thrilling seduction. She knew the cliff he led her toward, and all the dragging of her heels made no difference. Once there, she knew she'd leap willingly from that precipice.

Her body belonged to Sakote. Every inch of her skin prickled with desire for him, as if she were somehow attuned to him—could respond only to his touch and could only be slaked at his bidding. It panicked her, this sensation of entrapment, and yet she trusted him completely. He knew what he was doing. He would be gentle with her. After all, he was experienced in the ways of love.

Sakote prayed for Wonomi's guidance, for he'd never taken a woman before in this way. Mati's feminine scent made him feel as if he were drunk on the white man's whiskey. But the blood surged in his loins now. He must join with Mati soon, before his man's-knife wearied of the hunt and grew reckless.

Leaving one hand to comfort her, Sakote moved up her body, kissing her belly, where one day their child would grow, and the place between her breasts, where her precious heart beat. Beneath the deerskin, his man's-knife dragged across her thigh as he crept higher, at last capturing her gasping mouth in his own.

When he turned aside, it was only to quickly unfasten the rawhide lace of his breechcloth. Finally free, his man's-knife fell heavily upon her hip, and he groaned at the warmth of her flesh on his. He panted against her cheek, unable to think of the English words to speak to her. He knew he should turn her on her belly. It was the way of mating, the way of Coyote and Lizard and Mountain Lion. But he wanted her like this. He wanted to press his heart to hers, to feel her breath, to swallow her cries in his mouth.

In ragged gasps, he began to say the words of love that would bless their joining.

Mattie couldn't understand a word Sakote said. She could scarcely hear anything over the mad rushing in her ears and the moans coming from some primal place deep inside her. But she could feel him, hard and warm and wet, between her thighs. And the ache within her womb became a hollow yearning.

He nudged at her tentatively, cautiously, but her body would have none of his timid advances. With a wild gasp, she arched up carelessly, enveloping him all at once. His fierce groan drowned out her sharp cry of pain, but did nothing to ease the horrifying burn that suffused her woman's parts, and she stiffened in fear.

For a long while, he only held her, his breath labored and shuddery against her neck, and as if by magic, the pain inside her dwindled to a dull throb. Then he began to move, languidly drawing out of her, then returning, until she became aware of every magnificent inch of him. A haze of sensual wonder made her forget the pain and beckoned her to greater delights. Her body danced on its own, answering a rhythm it seemed to know, withdrawing, and then thrusting up to meet him again and again. She thrashed across the rushes, wanting, needing...something.

She drew her legs up around him, clasping him in a closer embrace, digging her heels into the sleek, flexing muscle of his buttocks. He shivered, growling deep in his throat. She burrowed her head against his chest, bathing her face in his sweat, smothering herself in his essence.

His growls became more and more urgent, his movements more deliberate, driving her to a reckless frenzy of passion. In one moment, she writhed in delicious anguish. In the next, the breath caught in her lungs, and time suddenly hung like a pocketwatch suspended from a chain.

Then they sailed free together, soaring breathlessly like they had over the waterfall, until they plunged earthward and their hot bodies sizzled into the cool, calming waters of repletion.

Sakote was afraid to move. Never had he felt such ecstasy. Mati had shattered him like obsidian beneath the blow of the adz. He dared not shift for fear of crumbling to pieces. And yet, he'd never felt more whole.

The pleasure games were satisfying, but they were nothing like this...this exchange of souls. He felt as one with Mati, as if they shared not only their bodies, but their spirits as well.

Even here in the dark, he'd never seen his path with such clarity. With Mati, he'd touched the face of The Creator. He knew now the power of a god. He knew what Wonomi intended, why his mother called him He Who Lives in Two Worlds. The Great Spirit wished him to join their two peoples—the Konkows and the whites—by joining with Mati, by making children with her.

He cupped her face in his hands—Mati, his beloved, his *kulem*—and for the first time in his life, he felt at peace. Happiness filled his heart and dampened his eyes.

"My heart is with you, Mati," he breathed again, but this time, the words had true power. Mati *was* the woman of his heart.

CHAPTER 25

For Mattie, the days passed in idyllic bliss. The meadow grew knee-high with deergrass and foxtails. Refreshing spring showers coaxed orange poppies to spring up like bright jewels set in the emerald grass. Often she'd grab her sketchbook and wander off to the woods or down to the stream or toward the rise overlooking the canyon. It was impossible to capture everything on paper, but Mattie returned each day with at least a dozen sketches.

The Konkows grew accustomed to her habits. They no longer tagged along to spy on her when she left the village to sketch, which was fortunate. Otherwise, they would have learned every intimate detail about her couplings with Sakote. They'd had so many of them, in every possible setting, from the cradling crook of an ancient oak to the bracing cold of the creek bed, that it was a wonder they hadn't been caught. It made her cheeks flame to recall their last encounter, high on a canyon ledge by the light of the rising sun.

Mattie had never felt closer to the earth, to nature, to truth than when she lay naked with Sakote in the wild of the wood and the warmth of the sun. It was this emotion the Pre-Raphaelite artists spoke of, she was sure—the clarity of the soul, born of the pure expression of nature in its unadorned glory. Nothing was more dramatic, more moving, more beautiful.

If she lived here forever, Mattie knew she could never capture all the splendor around her. With the vast sky for a canvas, Sakote's Creator was a far more inspired artist than she could ever hope to be. On one morning, thunderheads curled on the horizon like the heavy beards of grumbling old men. On another, the heavens burned so clear and pure and blue that it made Mattie's eyes water to look at them.

And even on days when the canopy was only a wash of gray and nature turned a cold shoulder, Mattie always found nurturing warmth in Sakote's arms. He brought her a comfort and security she'd never known, even as a child, when her parents might be gone for months at a time. And he brought nourishment, not only to her body, but to her hungering soul as well. His embrace made her forget the past. His kiss blinded her to the future.

In fact, her sense of time centered only around the coming Kaminehaitsen, for which the tribe busily prepared.

Today, the first day of the festivities, Mattie was caught up in the excitement. The spring air shimmered with life—darting yellow-jackets, flickering butterflies, swooping blue jays, and a fine mist of pine pollen that settled over everything like fairy dust.

She waded with her two Konkow sisters through the lush, flower-bedecked grass, toward the cedar grove, wearing the comfortable moccasins Sakote had made for her. They went to pick wild mint to brew into tea. Some of the other tribes had already arrived, and Mattie learned that just as in the Hardwicke household, guests expected to be greeted with refreshments.

Of course, the strange white woman had instantly become a topic of much conversation. The adolescents of the other tribes whispered conspiratorially behind their hands, mothers shooed their children away, and the elders frowned mistrustfully at her.

But, accustomed to disapproval, Mattie was undaunted. In fact, she decided to court their affections. It was her intent to serve the mint tea to the headmen of the other tribes herself. After all, pouring tea was a sign of hospitality in her civilized culture. Surely it was thus for the Konkows as well.

They were almost to the mint patch when her sisters stopped suddenly. Mattie heard voices, angry voices, coming from the forest. They spoke in the Konkow tongue, and the two girls listened with deepening scowls. But as they turned to retreat, hauling Mattie with them, she recognized Sakote's voice.

She didn't mean to eavesdrop. Surely it was a wicked thing, even in Konkow society, and her sisters seemed determined to drag her away. But she waved them off, and using the light, silent step Sakote had taught her, she drew closer until she could make out the shapes of several Konkow men among the trees.

Behind her, her sisters gestured frantically for her to come away, but curiosity got the better of her, so she ignored the girls until they gave up and marched home on their own.

She couldn't understand the men's words, but their sharp gestures and harsh, guttural syllables made it clear that they were engaged in some heated debate. One of the visiting Konkows, a headman by the looks of him, scowled and crossed his arms over his chest. Three of the elders with him did likewise. Sakote shook his head in refusal, and one of the younger men chattered at him, waving an accusing finger at his face. Sakote ran his hand through his hair in exasperation and spoke quietly to the others.

Mattie leaned against the pine trunk beside her. Even when colored with anger, the Konkow language was musical and engaging. It started deep in the chest and came out like the whisper of the wind. She could listen to Sakote speak his native tongue all day long. But it saddened her to see him so distraught. She wondered what troubled him.

As she watched, a beetle crawled down the tree trunk and across her hand, and she snatched back her arm to shake it off, stepping onto a pine twig with a distinct snap. All at once, a dozen pairs of angry male eyes pinned her to the spot. She swallowed hard, blushing furiously. Even Sakote looked vexed with her.

The chattering young Konkow resumed his prattle, smugly stabbing his finger toward her this time. Sakote barked something at the man over his shoulder, which instantly shut him up. Then he stared at Mattie with a tortured expression she couldn't decipher.

Suddenly, she realized they'd been talking about *her*. Embarrassed, she turned away, wishing she could disappear or erase time and undo whatever it was she'd done.

Disappointment. That was what she'd seen in Sakote's face. It surprised her that she hadn't recognized it at once. After all, she'd lived under that curse most of her life. But coming from him, it dealt her a crushing blow. Unable to face him, she walked stiffly off, determined to remain stoic under the men's scrutiny.

She'd gone barely a dozen paces from the tree when he caught her shoulder. She tried to break free, but he held on, wheeling her gently into the wall of his chest. He asked no questions and offered no explanation. He simply enveloped her in his arms, holding her to his heart and stroking her hair until she sank against him and surprised herself by weeping.

Sakote felt her tears on his chest as if they were his own,

and yet he didn't know how to stop them. For days, he'd soared as free as the eagle. He'd thought of nothing but Mati—the welcome of her smile, the smell of her skin, the comfort of her body. He'd deceived himself with dreams of their many moons to come, the children they would have and the peaceful winter of their lives together. But this day, that soaring eagle of his heart, so newly borne to the winds, now bore a bloody arrow in its breast.

Sakote had been a fool. The wise men of the other tribes, who left now in disgust, would agree. Living in two worlds was not a blessing. It was a curse.

"Why do they hate me?" Mati's sobs tore at his heart.

"They don't hate you," he said fiercely. "They're only...afraid."

"Of me?" Her eyes brimmed with tears.

"Of your kind, of the *willa*."

"But why?"

He swallowed hard. She truly didn't understand. She knew only that their people were different. She'd never seen how those differences could fill a man with hate, could drive a man to kill.

He'd seen it, from the time the first whites brought death in the form of a sickness that had slaughtered half of his people. Since then, his sister had been raped, a pack of drunken miners had strung up three Konkow elders, and even the white man's pigs had gorged on the acorns the Konkows needed to survive the winter. And not long ago, according to the elders, a neighboring headman's young son had been shot and killed by a *willa*.

The settlers created havoc. And yet, many of them, like his friend Noa and the kind yellow-haired man Mati called Swede, bore no blind hatred for the Konkows. They, like Mati, simply didn't understand the ruin they brought.

How could he explain all that to her?

The Konkow elders had made it clear they didn't trust Mati. But he couldn't tell her that.

Mati gazed up through her tears, her eyes as bright as serpentine rocks in a stream, and Sakote knew at once he would never give her up, no matter how he displeased the elders. She was his *kulem* now. Whatever happened, he would stay by her side.

He'd never defied the elders before. But though he feared for his people and feared what mayhem the white men might bring to the village, he loved Mati even more.

"I won't let you go," he vowed. "You're mine, *kulem*, and I won't give you back to the whites."

Sakote's words, whispered against Mattie's hair, brought fresh tears to her eyes. She loved him fiercely, passionately, and she couldn't bear to cause him such anguish among his own people.

Somehow she'd fix things. She'd learn to speak his language. She'd learn to like the taste of grasshoppers. She would even learn to weave a basket. She'd do whatever it took to belong to his world.

Comforted by renewed determination, she sniffed back the dregs of her sorrow and wiped away her tears.

"You shouldn't cry," he teased, tucking a curl behind her ear. "My little brother will think I've beaten you, and then he'll tell our mother, and she'll beat *me*."

His silly words coaxed a smile from her. Dear Sakote, he always knew just what to say. She looked into his dark eyes, twinkling now like the first stars of evening, and felt suddenly overwhelmed. He knew her so intimately now, not only every inch of her body—which he'd touched and kissed and bathed and worshipped till she no longer remembered what modesty felt like—but also her heart.

Yet, as close as they'd become, she felt as if she'd hardly scratched the surface of his soul. His life might be simple, but he was as complex as the shifting color of his eyes and as deep as the waterfall's pool. She wondered how long it would take to know Sakote, truly know him. She doubted anyone could ever learn him completely. But she prayed she'd get the chance.

She straightened his abalone shell beads and stood on tiptoe to brush a soft kiss upon his lips. "I'll make them like me," she promised him, trying not to think about all the times she'd murmured those words in the past.

"*Kulem*, how could they not?" Sakote took her head between his hands then and kissed her so thoroughly that when he was done, her heart hammered like a woodpecker, her knees turned to custard, and her only coherent thought was that for a novice, he certainly had mastered the art of kissing quickly. She moaned in protest when he pulled away, and he chuckled at her wanton complaint. They both knew that Kaminehaitsen was upon them, strangers filled the woods, and this was neither the time nor the place for lovemaking.

Sakote left to greet the arriving guests, and Mattie remained behind to pick wild mint from the cedar grove. When she returned, she dismissed the curious stares of her sisters and set about making tea, dropping a hot stone into the tightly woven basket of water to heat it, as she'd seen Sakote's mother do.

Meanwhile, more and more guests arrived, and, despite the racks of dried salmon, the burden baskets of acorn meal, and the dozens of camas bulbs she'd helped to dig up, Mattie wondered if there'd be enough food to last the several days of the celebration.

Certainly there was enough tea. Those few who actually accepted the drink Mattie offered did so with great reluctance. She supposed they feared the nefarious white woman might have slipped poison into it. Nonetheless, she tried to remain as gracious as possible under their scrutiny, mimicking her Hardwicke cousins' unflappable grace.

It was sunset by the time the last tribe padded into the village. A huge fire was lit, and gradually everyone gathered around it, chattering and laughing, elbowing each other, talking behind their hands, squirming to get comfortable. Mattie smiled. Their celebration bore a striking resemblance to the affairs Uncle Ambrose hosted. She supposed their purpose was no different. It was called Kaminehaitsen, the Feather Dance, but it may as well have been dubbed the Hardwicke Winter Ball. It was an occasion for friends to exchange news, young swains to court, and old ladies to gossip.

Sakote's mother directed the serving of supper—roasted trout, yellow-jacket eggs, and bread made with acorn meal and flower seeds. Sakote sat beside her so he could serve as translator while the visiting Konkows finished their meals and began a series of formal speeches.

As the stars glimmered overhead, putting the crystal chandeliers of Hardwicke House to shame, the best storytellers of each village related the news of their tribe. If Sakote's translations were to be trusted, the tales seemed to be more fable than fact, but everyone listened with hushed interest and nods of accord to what were surely grossly exaggerated accounts of bravery and cunning.

One man claimed to have battled a pack of *yeleyena*, wolves, and come away without a scratch. Another recalled his flight in the talons of a sacred eagle. A third had spoken to Henyakano, Old Man Coyote, and tricked him into revealing where a herd of fat deer grazed.

She could see by Sakote's bemused expression that he, too, doubted the verity of the stories. But stretching the truth was apparently a Konkow custom of the highest order, and Domem, the storyteller of the village, carried on that tradition with just as much bluster as his brothers.

As soon as he began, Mattie froze, her cup of mint tea halfway to her lips. Everyone had turned to stare at her.

Sakote translated in a murmur. "Domem will tell the tale of the white woman's bravery." He clearly approved of the idea.

Mattie felt ill. She wasn't brave. She couldn't even enter her *hubo* without checking for stray rodents first. What possible story could Domem tell? Or invent?

He began by making a swirling gesture with his fists, and Mattie recognized the movement instantly.

"The white woman," Sakote translated, "once lived in the village of the men who winnow gold rocks from the water."

Mattie, trembling, set her tea on the ground before her for fear she might spill it. Ever since that horrifying spectacle she'd caused at her Uncle Ambrose's party, she hated being the center of attention.

"She came over many mountains to be the woman of the healer there," Sakote whispered. "But when she arrived at the gold camp, her man had already traveled to the other world."

Mattie swallowed uncomfortably. The way Domem described the rugged journey, it sounded almost poetic.

"The white woman was filled with sorrow," Sakote told her.

Domem mimicked a woman wailing, and Mattie had to bite her lip to keep from laughing. Heavens, she hadn't wept that loud when her own parents died. She certainly wouldn't make such a fuss over a husband she'd never met.

"And so when the brother of her husband came to the village, she welcomed him."

Mattie stiffened. She didn't want to hear about Henry, didn't want to relive that horrible incident.

"But the man was a bad man, an evil spirit."

Domem raised his arms over his head and grimaced, frightening some of the children into giggles. But Mattie could no longer enjoy the story.

The storyteller growled, baring his teeth, and began swinging his arms about violently, chopping and hacking. Mattie didn't need to be told what event he portrayed.

Sakote spoke through clenched teeth. "The evil spirit attacked the men of the village. He tore them into pieces with his sharp teeth and claws, stabbed them with his knife and shot them with his golden gun."

Mattie could hardly breathe. The Konkows around her seemed entranced by the story, but she felt sick, as if the cool, crisp night was airless.

"But when he came to the house of the white woman, she did not know all this, and she invited him in."

Mattie felt dizzy, remembering, but not so dizzy she didn't notice some of the tribesmen muttering amongst themselves as if they argued.

A headman with cropped hair raised his hand suddenly to stop the story, which drew gasps from the villagers and a look of shock from Domem. It was undoubtedly a breach of etiquette to interrupt a storyteller. The headman asked Domem something which Sakote didn't translate. Domem replied. Then the headman raised himself to his full proud height and issued a proclamation that made the village fall utterly silent.

Sakote jumped up, startling Mattie, and began arguing with the man. She sat, bewildered, while two younger men joined the debate against Sakote, poking fingers in her direction. Finally, Sakote's mother placed a comforting hand upon Mattie's forearm, but worry clouded the Konkow woman's face. Mattie knew she'd done something terrible again.

She wished she could understand what they were shouting. Sakote seemed very upset, and the Konkows of his village muttered nervously amongst themselves, glancing fearfully in her direction from time to time.

"*Akina!*" Sakote spat the word at the larger of the two men. Apparently their argument was at an end. The man grunted back, and everyone returned to their place by the fire. But Sakote wouldn't look at her, and his brow was deeply lined with brooding. He mumbled something to his mother, and she motioned for Mattie to follow her.

Mattie was only too happy to oblige when the woman led her away to her *hubo*. The peaceful ambience of the evening had been destroyed, and somehow she was to blame. Disapproval from a society whose language she couldn't comprehend was even worse than the cutting remarks she'd overheard in her uncle's parlor about "that wayward Hardwicke girl."

But she didn't intend to give up or run away—not this time. The tribes' approval was important to Sakote, and she'd do everything in her power to assure that approval.

She nestled into the rabbit fur blankets and fell asleep to the faint sound of singing around the distant fire.

Chapter 26

In the middle of the night, Mattie was startled awake by a strange Indian girl holding a makeshift pine torch. The beautiful young woman bore the black chin stripes of the Konkows, and her face was framed by sleek curtains of ebony hair, but her skirt was made of blue calico, and she wore a red flannel shirt. She stared curiously at Mattie, and Mattie sat up, self-consciously brushing back her own sleep-tousled tresses.

Trailing after the Konkow woman was a man who was dark-skinned, but not an Indian, and who looked as uncomfortable in her *hubo* as a hunting dog invited into the parlor. He wore a woodpecker feather in his miner's hat and a Konkow soapstone pendant around his neck. The man shifted from haunch to haunch, doffing and fidgeting with his hat, then replacing it, clearly full of something to say and unsure how to begin.

The woman had no such problem.

"I am the brother of Sakote," she said proudly in English, sitting cross-legged on the ground before Mattie.

"Sister," the man corrected, "sister of Sakote." He nodded

to Mattie. "Hello, ma'am. Sorry for the intrusion. I'm—"

"Noa?" Mattie guessed. She supposed she should be more cordial. Aunt Emily would have scolded her for her lack of manners. But she was too drowsy for hospitality. Besides, they hadn't even knocked.

"Yes, ma'am, I'm Noa."

"Mathilda Hardwicke." She didn't bother to extend her hand.

"Yes, ma'am, I know." He touched his hat in a vague greeting. The whites of his round eyes gleamed, and his jaw worked as if he were chewing the words up before he spit them out. "Now, ma'am, I know it isn't my business. But Sakote's a friend of mine and a brother, and I'm very..."

He clamped his lips together, as if he might actually start to weep. Towani, Sakote's sister, rested a calming hand on his arm. He cleared his throat, then swept off his hat and whacked it against his thigh. "The fact is, we're very worried about him."

Towani nodded in agreement, though Mattie suspected she only understood half of what Noa said.

"I just spoke with him," Noa said. "You know he's in the *kum?*"

That didn't surprise her. Sakote went to the sweat lodge when he was troubled to receive guidance from The Great Spirit.

"Well, he's preparing to fight those brothers tomorrow, ma'am."

"What brothers?"

"The brothers of the boy Henry shot."

Mattie shook her head. Perhaps she wasn't fully awake. "Henry? What boy?"

"Didn't you know, ma'am? Henry Harrison shot the son of the headman from Nemsewi."

Mattie frowned. She remembered hearing that a Konkow

boy had been shot recently by a white man, but she hadn't realized… "How do they know it was Henry?"

"A little girl witnessed the killing. She said the boy was shot by a man with a golden gun."

She nodded. No wonder the headman had been disturbed by Domem's story. "But why are the brothers angry with Sakote? Don't they know he's the one who *killed* Henry?"

Noa sighed. Towani poked at his arm to urge him on.

"The Konkows have a word for it," he told her. "*Hudesi*."

"*Hudesi*," Towani repeated.

"You see, Henry Harrison shot and killed that Konkow boy. But his brother, Doc Jim, the man who was supposed to be your husband?" Noa stared past her, momentarily lost in his thoughts. "He was a bad man, a *hudesi*, too. He…he forced a…" His mouth twisted as he choked on the words. "He raped a Konkow woman."

Mattie clapped her hand to her mouth. She didn't know what to say. What kind of monsters had the Harrison brothers been?

"Then it was a blessing that he died before I…" She gasped, catching Noa's gaze. If James Harrison had raped a Konkow woman, perhaps his death hadn't been an accident. "How *did* Dr. Harrison die?"

Towani frowned and yanked on Noa's sleeve, angry at being excluded from the conversation. She demanded an explanation. Noa said a few words to her in Konkow, enough to appease her curiosity.

Then Towani straightened and said haughtily, "I kill *hudesi*. I kill."

Mattie's eyes widened at the bitter words.

She couldn't decipher the heated argument that followed between Noa and Towani, but it didn't matter. She solved the puzzle easily enough. Towani had been the one raped by Mattie's husband-to-be.

The thought sickened her. Towani seemed so young, so innocent. How could anyone... Then she glanced at Towani, whose proud chin and stubborn pout at the moment reminded her of Hintsuli. Perhaps she wasn't as young and innocent as she appeared. After all, she'd managed to get rid of Doc Jim on her own. If there was one thing the Konkows believed in, it was an eye for an eye.

She bit her lip. She wondered if Sakote knew. He must, she thought. That was why he'd warned Hintsuli away from Doc Jim's house that first day and why he hadn't trusted Mattie.

But wasn't that the end of it now? Mattie was confused. "The Harrisons are dead. So the headman of Nemsewi and his sons, what more do they want?" she asked, halting the argument between Noa and Towani.

Noa ran a nervous hand over his stubbled cheek. "Like I said, the Harrison brothers are *hudesi*. At least, that's what the Konkows call them. They're so full of evil they aren't even welcome in the spirit world. For the Konkows, it isn't good enough just to *kill* a *hudesi*. You have to make sure its spirit doesn't come back."

"And how do you do that?"

He chose his words carefully and watched her closely, to make sure she understood. "The Konkows believe you have to get rid of...of whatever might hold the *hudesi* here."

Some strong emotion seized her heart in a frigid fist. Her chest, suddenly empty, seemed to cave in on itself. All at once, the problem was so obvious. She understood perfectly. There was no need for Noa to say more. "Me."

Rejection. She should be accustomed to it. But it hurt, truly hurt, worse than any of the rejections she'd gotten from any of her family.

"I'm awful sorry, ma'am."

"Sorry, ma'am," Towani aped.

Somehow, Mattie managed to straighten her shoulders.

Somehow, she held back a reservoir of tears. Her voice sounded far calmer than she felt. "No. It's not your fault. I'm...I'm so sorry about your wife, Mr. Noa. I had no idea. I truly never even met James Harrison."

"Oh, no, ma'am, I don't blame you for that," Noa was quick to say. "To my way of thinking, you shouldn't be made to suffer for—"

"And please don't worry on my account." She had to spit it all out quickly, before her emotions got the better of her. "I suppose I always knew this day would come—"

"But, ma'am—"

"And I'm fully prepared to leave."

"Ma'am—"

"I never truly belonged here anyway." The edges of her rueful smile quavered. She hoped they didn't notice. "Now if you'll excuse me, I'll begin packing. I'll go back to Paradise Bar in the morning."

Towani looked to Noa to explain what Mattie said. He didn't bother.

"Ma'am, I don't think you quite understand," he said, staring at her as if she were dim-witted, rubbing his hand thoughtfully back and forth across his chin, not sure how to go about talking to her.

Mattie wished they'd leave, now, before the fragile vessel of her composure shattered into a hundred pathetic pieces. "Or I could just leave now," she rattled on. "I don't have that much to pack anyway, and if I'm gone before—"

"Ma'am," he said, this time reaching out to take her fingers.

She glanced down at his hand, so warm and comforting around hers, and his sympathy was almost her undoing. A sob blocked the rest of her words.

Was it so much to ask, she wondered, just to belong somewhere? Even Noa and Towani had conquered the differences between their worlds. The love they bore one another shone in their eyes. Why couldn't she and Sakote have what the two of *them* shared?

Towani's scowl deepened as she tried to decipher the meaning of Noa's intimate gesture, and for a moment she reminded Mattie painfully of Sakote.

"He won't let you leave, you know," Noa said.

Mattie's head hurt, and her throat ached from holding back tears. She tried to pull away. He wouldn't let her go.

With both she and Towani glaring pointedly at his fingers, he wisely chose to release her. But he clearly intended to speak his mind, even if he had to dispense with good manners to do it.

"He won't let you go, Miss Mattie. It'll be a fight to the death. It's a matter of honor. He's going to fight those boys, come hell or high water."

"Hell or high water," Towani added for emphasis.

"I don't know what you're talking about, Mr. Noa." She pressed two fingers to her throbbing temple. "I told you, I'll return to Paradise Bar of my own free will. There's no need for any fighting."

"Well, ma'am, pardon me, but he sure as hell isn't going to give up his wife."

Mattie jerked, startled for a moment by his words. Then her lips moved into a brittle, bitter smile. "I'm afraid you don't understand. I'm...not his wife."

"Wife," Towani repeated, latching onto one English word she knew well.

"Now just a minute, ma'am."

Mattie was almost out of self-control. She lowered her gaze, thoroughly embarrassed. "I'm..a fallen woman already, Mr. Noa," she muttered. "Must you kick me when I'm down?"

He nervously licked his lips, then spoke in a whisper. "I don't mean to be sticking my nose where it doesn't belong, but I just talked to Sakote, and I think there's something you don't..." He ran his palm nervously over his cheek. "Sakote and you...have you...I mean, are you...you know..."

Mattie's jaw went slack, and she blushed to the roots of her hair, but she couldn't steel herself to make even a cutting reply. She supposed that her red face was answer enough, and that utter humiliation was no less than a fallen woman deserved.

"Because the Konkows," he continued, "they do things different, you see. If you're living under the same roof, why, that's as good as being married. To Sakote's way of thinking, you're his *kulem*, his wife."

"*Kulem*," Towani chimed in.

That was what Sakote called her. She'd never asked him what it meant. The Konkows went by so many nicknames that it never occurred to her to question him about the one he'd chosen for her.

"His wife?" She swayed, and Noa caught her forearm. "He's my husband?" Dear God—how was it possible to feel so wonderful and so terrible all at once? Sakote thought they were married! For one wonderful moment, her spirit soared with the news. Despite their differences, despite the disapproval of the elders, Sakote loved her, enough to pledge himself to her alone, enough to call her *kulem* before his tribe. It made the breath flutter in her breast.

And yet it changed nothing. The Konkows still wanted her gone. Nothing Sakote said would alter that. Wife or not, she couldn't bear to drive a wedge between him and his people. Nor would she allow him to risk his life for her.

"How do I...unmarry him?"

Deep sorrow dimmed Noa's big cocoa-colored eyes, and Mattie perceived instantly what a good friend he was to Sakote. "Why, that would break his heart, ma'am."

Mattie's lip quivered, and tears stung high in her nose. She didn't want to do this, cry in front of this stranger, but the dam of her emotions trembled dangerously now behind a flood of grief. "Then what do I do?"

"You'll do nothing." Sakote's familiar voice drifted into the *hubo* as he filled the entrance.

Mattie gasped. How much had he heard?

Noa scowled. "Shit, Sakote! Don't you knock?"

Sakote scowled back. "I come to my own *hubo,* and here I find my *kulem*, my brother, and my sister, talking in whispers, and you ask me if I knock?"

"Now, it's not like that at all," Noa argued, clearly startled by Sakote's silent arrival. "We were only—"

"Take my sister," Sakote said. "Go to her *hubo.* I have much to discuss with my *kulem*."

Mattie's heart caught. *Kulem.* He called her his *kulem*.

Noa tipped his hat to her. "You know where to find me, ma'am."

Sakote growled low in his throat, and the visitors left in haste.

"My brother and sister," he said when they were gone, "they trouble your sleep."

"No. They wished to meet me," she lied. "To meet the woman you call...*kulem*."

"And they couldn't wait for morning?"

It had been a bad lie. She tried one closer to the truth. "I wanted to know where you were, what you were doing."

"And my brother told you?"

"He said you were in the *kum*, preparing for a challenge tomorrow."

Sakote nodded.

She reached out toward him, resting her palm against the flat of his thigh. Lord, he was still warm from the sweathouse, and he smelled of sweet pine smoke. She would never forget his scent. "I don't want you to fight, Sakote."

"I know, *kulem*."

"Please withdraw the challenge."

"You know I cannot."

Of course, she knew. "No," she said stubbornly, wiping at the tears that foolishly slipped from the corners of her eyes. "I won't let you take up arms against your brothers."

"It's not for you to say."

"I won't let you risk your life simply because I'm...I'm an unwelcome guest."

He grabbed her by the shoulders. "And I won't be told who will or will not be my *kulem*," he countered ferociously. "You're mine, Mati. You're flesh of my flesh and blood of my blood. The Great Spirit has told me so. I won't let them take you from me."

Mattie's throat swelled into a suffocating knot of anguish, and hot tears welled in her eyes. Until now she hadn't realized how much she loved, truly loved Sakote.

His words were rash. He spoke them in the heat of strong emotion, like the vows Hintsuli took to never take another bath. But surely he, too, saw the hopelessness of their plight.

It would be easier for him, she thought. He had his tribe, his family. He belonged to this world of nature and animal spirits and Wonomi, his Creator, as if he were a part of the wilderness itself. In the excitement of the Kaminehaitsen, he would forget all about Mattie Hardwicke. Eventually Sakote would find a woman, a nice Konkow woman, to take to wife. She'd bear his children, lots of them, with silky black hair and sparkling black eyes, children to whom he might one day tell the tale of the white woman he'd taught to hunt yellow-jackets.

A sob lodged in her throat, and she tried not to think of the way his arms felt around her, pretended not to memorize the scent of his body. How could she leave him—this man who tripped her heart with the sparkle of his smile, who stole her soul with the wink of an eye? He made her feel so carefree, so beautiful, so precious.

She would never love again. It was as simple as that. She had given Sakote everything—her heart, her virtue, her soul. She had nothing left to give another man. She'd return to the only home she could afford, a lean-to in a mining camp, and live among her own people. Her own people. She could hardly call what was left of the ragtag bunch at Paradise Bar her own people. Yet, she supposed if she fit anywhere, it was with a group of misfits. There, she'd live out her days, shriveling into a crusty old maid with a bitter tongue and a sketchbook filled with memories of better days.

"I'm going to leave you," she told him, her voice cracking.

"No," he insisted, his eyes smoldering like black coals. "I will win the challenge."

His reckless declaration wrenched at Mattie's heart. Sakote had told her about Konkow challenges. They were violent, bloody, fought with basalt knives. The thought of Sakote's body, slashed by razor-sharp stone, chilled her. Never could she allow such savagery on her behalf.

"I don't want you to win the challenge. I want to go back," she said, though the words came out harder than a stubborn tooth.

"No!" he fired at her. The word was fierce, his eyes fiercer. Iron fingers gripped her shoulders.

Part of her wanted to stay, the part that threatened to crumble into a thousand pieces if she had to think about life without Sakote. But she couldn't. Already she caused strife between Sakote and his people. Already she brought danger to the Konkows. He would grow to hate her if she stayed.

No, she had to end it now. Quickly. For him. For his people. For her sanity.

"I have to go back. I *want* to go back," she said, nearly gagging on the lie. She lowered her eyes, unable to bear the pain in Sakote's face.

Surprise loosened his grip. "You don't wish to live here?" His voice sounded like dead wood, hollow, empty.

The brittle laugh she forced to her lips clanged in her own ears and echoed bitterly in her soul. "Here? Among savages?" She felt his hurt in the way his fingers tightened on her shoulders. Yet it was what she must do—hurt him. "I'll admit, it's been fascinating, these last weeks, seeing how your people live in these little huts and eat roots and berries. But surely you didn't think I meant to *live* in your village?" she continued, her voice too bright, too cruel. God, she hated herself, hated what she was doing to him.

His eyes smoldered dark gray now, resolute and dangerous. "You will stay, *kulem*," he said, softly this time, but unyielding, uncompromising. "*Akina*." He extinguished the torch in the dirt and crawled between the layers of rabbit fur. "You will stay."

Mattie chewed on her knuckles to stifle her weeping and climbed in beside him, but dared not torture herself by touching him. She waited until she heard his deep, even breathing, then stole silently from his side.

She took only one memento with her, and when Noa saw it, his eyes went as dark and sweet as molasses. He tossed a deerskin cloak over her and, bidding farewell to Towani, helped Mattie find her way in the night back to Paradise Bar.

CHAPTER 27

Fourteen days later, Zeke was still talking about it.

"You could've knocked me over with a feather when Miss Mattie sashayed into camp," he said, wincing as Tom, the closest thing Paradise Bar had to a doctor these days, poked at the puckered pink flesh of his healing gut wound. "She sure did go pale as a frog's underbelly when she first laid eyes on us."

Tom rocked the hat back on his bandaged head. "Well, what do ye expect, with all the lass has been through? First that Harrison devil terrorizin' the camp and then bein' kidnapped by the Injuns. 'Tis a wonder she can hold her hands steady enough ta tie her own bonnet."

Swede, almost as good as new except for the extra navel Harrison had carved him, scratched gingerly at his stitches. As a point of fact, Mattie *didn't* tie her own bonnet. Actually, she didn't wear a bonnet at all. She'd taken to pulling her hair back into a long tail like the Injuns and wearing moccasins. And even though Granny had offered to make some bone buttons for her, she'd refused, preferring to keep the rawhide laces on her dress. But Swede was afraid dressing like a primitive wasn't the only thing she'd picked up on her visit with the savages, which was why he'd called the meeting this morning.

Tom was partly right. Mattie had been to hell and back over the past several weeks. The miners had been worried sick about her. At first, they thought she'd died in the fire. Hell, they'd even given her a proper funeral, or what little they could manage in their state of affliction, and put up a cross right beside the ones for Dash and Bobby. It wasn't till Amos went to visit his friend Noa in the valley that they learned the truth. Mattie was living with the Injuns. And right then and there, the boys decided to hit the warpath, to pay the Diggers a visit and get back what was rightfully theirs.

It never got that far. Later that evening, right after the men returned from panning and took down the cross that read "Miss Mathilda Hardwicke, The Sweetheart of Paradise Bar," the formerly deceased, a little weathered, but pretty as you please, waltzed into camp with Noa.

Of course, she was overjoyed to see him and the boys alive and sad to hear tell of Dash and Bobby. She was laughing one moment and weeping the next. Swede had grinned and told her it'd take more than buckshot and a Bowie knife to do him in. But there had been a tear in his eye when he said it, because for a while there, nobody had been sure he'd recover from the nasty gash in his belly that had drained him almost dry of blood.

They moved Miss Mattie into Bobby's cabin right away and gave her provisions to fatten up her scrawny bones. But though she seemed glad enough to see the miners, the light in her eyes never made it much above the flicker of a short-wicked candle.

Of course, they'd been doled their share of misery, too,

thanks to Doc Jim's brother. Hell, they'd buried a couple of good men, and it was only by a pure miracle that young Ben Cooper was still breathing. That bullet had come damn close to his heart. The rest of the boys were pretty cut up, too. Harley had lost a couple of fingers, and Jeremy had come within inches of getting himself gelded.

The door to Tom's cabin swung open with a leathery creak, letting in a blinding flood of sunlight along with the miners who'd come to hear what Swede had to say.

"Howdy, Doc." Jeremy leaned on his homemade cane as he limped in. He'd taken to calling Tom "Doc" on account of him sewing up his family heirlooms so nice and neat.

Harley waggled his fingers in greeting, all three of them.

"How is the patient, eh?" If Zeke didn't know better, he'd swear Frenchy had positioned himself just right for that rakish knife scar he now sported proudly just under his cheekbone.

"Good as new," Tom declared, lifting Zeke's shirt up so the whole world could take a gander.

"Damnation!" Zeke groused. "I ain't on exhibition!"

Close to two dozen miners milled in, crowding into the tiny room which was really only fit for three. Still, being the biggest cabin in Paradise Bar, it was the most fitting place to convene.

They all agreed something had to be done. Mattie wasn't well, hadn't been for days now. And it wasn't just the trauma she'd been through. Swede was afraid it might be some disease she'd contracted from the Injuns.

She wasn't eating. Even when Amos made her a mince pie, she took a few bites and pushed it aside. When Tom brought her Hangtown stew made with his last tin of oysters, she turned a singular shade of green and puked her little heart out on the front porch. The next day, she fainted in the middle of the road and would have hit the dirt if Frenchy hadn't been there to catch her.

"Did ye take her breakfast?" Tom asked Amos.

"Made her my best sourdough rolls and peach puddin'. Didn't touch a thing."

"She's still feelin' poorly?" Tom asked Ben, whose turn it was to keep a secret watch on her.

"All mornin' long, every half-hour or so, she come runnin' out of the house to retch into the bushes."

"If she keeps this up, she's like to die," Jeremy announced, and Ben whacked his brother for stating the obvious.

Jasper scratched his stubbled chin. "Maybe we ought to get ourselves a doc, a real doc, to take a look at her."

"Pah! It is her heart, I tell you," Frenchy insisted, as he'd been insisting for days. "She is in love. She cannot bear the thought of—"

"Oh, for Pete's sake!" Granny elbowed her way to the front of the crowd, shaking her head. "Don't you fools know nothin'? The dang filly's a-breedin'!"

Silence hit so sudden and complete you could have heard the crack of dawn. Swede thought the boys looked the way deer did at night when you came upon them unawares with a lamp—all stiff and fascinated and confused.

Finally Tom whispered, "Do ye think?"

"Of course!" Granny answered, irritated at the ignorance of menfolk. "I'd say, by the look of things, the timin' and whatnot, it was some Injun planted his papoose in her."

Everyone gasped, but Swede knew just who that Injun was.

"The savage!" Frenchy hissed in outrage.

The cussing flew loose and long and loud then, so loud that Swede could hardly make himself heard.

"Calm down, boys! Calm down!" He finally resorted to

grabbing Jeremy's cane and banging it on the floor to get their attention. "All this whoopin' and hollerin' ain't gonna fix nothin'. We gotta take action. Seems to me it's high time we scared up a man for Miss Mattie."

Sakote watched the trout circle again and tried to focus his thoughts. The fish's dull gold scales caught only a small shimmer of sunlight. It swam against the current, hovering for a moment in the swirling water. Sakote drew the spear slowly back, waiting, waiting. Then he hurled it forward. It hit the stream with a sloppy splash, and the fish swam away, unperturbed.

Behind him, Hintsuli giggled. Sakote managed a rueful smile for his little brother, but the expression didn't come easily to his face. A man shouldn't hunt or fish when his heart was troubled, and Wonomi was showing him the folly of this. He'd fished all afternoon with Hintsuli, who sprang from rock to rock, talking to salamanders, making pictures in the mud with a stick, laughing at Sakote every time he missed another fish with his spear, and still he had no catch.

It was amusing for Hintsuli to see his big brother, whom the headman had praised as the village's greatest hunter at the Kaminehaitsen, fail so completely. But the boy didn't understand how unhappiness weakened a man's arm, how grief made his aim unsteady. He also couldn't envision the cold times that would come at the end of *se-meni*, autumn. He'd never seen what happened to a people when there weren't enough fish harvested from the stream, not enough deer hunted, when the oak trees slept and the snows of *ko-meni* came, killing the plants that kept the bellies of the Konkows full.

Sakote had been such a boy once, before the sickness stole his people, before the white man stole his food. He'd grown out of his innocence, and he'd thought there was nothing left for the *willa* to steal. He was wrong. One of them had stolen his heart.

He hauled the fishing spear back in by its fiber line, letting his gaze drift along the sun-flecked ridges of the water, remembering the pain of Mati's betrayal and the brave mask he'd worn at the Kaminehaitsen.

A vision had come to him in the dream world on the night that he decided to challenge the headman's sons. The white eagle with two eggs had flown over him, but this time she didn't come to his hand. Instead, she flew away until she was a speck in the sky. And though he understood the vision, he didn't understand how to change it. By the time he awoke on the morning of the challenge, the eagle had fled. Mati was gone.

His heart had cracked like an obsidian point into many pieces, so many he feared it couldn't be repaired. He'd snapped and snarled at Noa like the wolf at an enemy, but his harsh words mended nothing. And so, for the sake of his people and his pride, like the strong warrior he was, he bound his heart up again with sinew and didn't speak of its weakness.

The next day, the first day of the Kaminehaitsen, Sakote danced with the long feather ropes to the beat of the *kilemi*. He sang songs to the music of the *yalulu*, flute, and he rattled the *shokote* with his Konkow brothers. Since Mati was no longer in the village, no mention was made of the Nemsewis' challenge, and the tribes made peace.

Sakote played the hand game with the men from Tatampanta. He even stood patiently while his mother's husband presented him to three giggling Nemsawa girls of marrying age. But on the ending day of the celebration, when the elders made the ritual marks of acorn paste on the entrances of the *hubos*, Sakote turned his face away in anguish, for painted on his *hubo* was the symbol of an eagle with two eggs.

After Mati left, the elders would not speak of her, and so, to the rest of the village, she didn't exist.

Hintsuli was too busy chattering about the initiation rites of *yeponi* his Konkow brothers had boasted of to notice her absence. Only his mother knew of Sakote's pain, and though she looked upon him with the sad and wise eyes of the owl, out of respect she didn't speak of Mati.

But for Sakote, Mati lived in his heart. She'd left her sketches, all save the one of him, and though he knew he'd be wise to bury or burn them, he couldn't bear to part with the memories they stirred in his soul.

He looked at them often—the baby quail trailing after their mother, the eagle tethered outside his uncle's *hubo*, Hintsuli sharpening his stone knife, the flowers growing beside the stream. But his favorite was the drawing of the waterfall. In it, Sakote crouched by the far edge of the pool, and his face looked back at him in ripples made by the cascading water. A hawk soared overhead, and its twin flew across the surface of the pool. The picture was filled with life and light, and it reminded him of the joy and peace he had found there with his *kulem*, his Mati.

But in the village of the Konkows, the sun rose each morning, and the stars traveled across the night sky. The world didn't stop just because Sakote no longer felt a part of it. Life continued, even though it seemed like his soul had already deserted him, that his spirit wandered the bright belt of stars, trying to find the left fork, the path to Heaven Valley.

A trout jumped, and Sakote shook himself from his thoughts. He'd been staring blindly at the undulating stream for so long that he'd forgotten where he was. When he looked up at the far bank, sudden cold fear plunged like a knife into his heart.

He turned to Hintsuli, shouting, "Run!"

The boy squeaked once in panic, then scrambled down from his rocky perch and shot up the hill as fast as a rabbit.

When Sakote turned back, his breath froze in his throat, and the skin prickled at the base of his neck. He narrowed his eyes, not wanting to believe what he saw.

On the far side of the stream stood a group of *kokoni*, ghosts of the gold camp's dead men, and at the fore was the big one with the yellow hair.

They were as bright and vivid as if they were alive, dressed in fine burial clothing. When they waved and shouted at him, they seemed as substantial as the trees or the rocks or the trout in the stream.

But that couldn't be. He'd seen their blood. He'd seen their broken bodies. They were dead. What did their ghosts want with him?

The *kokoni* began crossing the rocks over the creek, and Sakote flexed his fingers around his fishing spear, even though he knew earthly weapons were useless against spirits.

Running was an option. He thought about it for one panicked heartbeat. But deep inside, he knew The Great Spirit was testing him. And though he felt as if his soul had left him, he still lived in this world. As long as he did, the *kokoni* couldn't harm him. So he stood fast...

Until they came close enough to touch, close enough to smell. Then the big, yellow-haired man grabbed his arm in one solid fist and pointed a gun at his head. And Sakote knew then they were no *kokoni*.

Hintsuli was panting so hard when he ran up to his mother in a scramble of rocks that she could barely understand his jabbering. But the moment she heard the words "Sakote" and "*willa*," she knew the time of confrontation had come.

She'd foreseen it, just as she'd foreseen the coming of the white eagle who would steal her first son's heart. Now it was time for the worlds of the Konkow and the white man to come together.

She dried Hintsuli's tears with her thumbs, rocking him as she had when he was a baby.

It was like making a basket, she thought, weaving the two worlds together. If your heart was pure and happy, the sedge and the redbud would make a fine vessel to hold all the bounty of the seasons to come. But if your spirit was troubled, if there was hate in your soul...

After a moment, she nudged Hintsuli up off her lap. He was, after all, too big a boy to cry at his mother's knee. She would speak to her husband now about Sakote, and he would speak to the elders. But before she did, she would go to the woman's *hubo* and ask for Wonomi's guidance. She would ask The Great Spirit to grant them wisdom and patience, both the Konkow and the *willa*.

Mattie wiped a sweaty palm across her damp forehead and sagged back down onto the lumpy straw mattress of her new abode. So far she'd kept down a few bites of the stale soda biscuits Amos had left her, but she didn't dare try anything else. She cupped her head in her hands and waited for the nausea to pass.

She wondered if the miners suspected. Of course, she'd known from the first sign of sickness what ailed her. She'd seen a maid at Hardwicke House go through the same misery. Uncle Ambrose had eventually let the maid go because she didn't have a proper husband.

Here, she supposed it made no difference. After all, in California, half the men were criminals of some kind, and most of the women were soiled doves. The miners were hardly qualified to turn their noses up at her, even if she informed them she had no plans to marry.

How could she marry? Her heart belonged to only one man. She knew that now. As long as she lived, she'd never feel the things she'd felt for Sakote with anyone else. She'd never love another. She'd never wed another. Even if it meant her child would grow up fatherless.

She didn't plan to tell Sakote. Ever. It would serve no purpose. There was talk among the Konkows that Sakote might one day be the headman of his people. The last thing he needed was the added burden of a child, especially the half-breed kin to a *hudesi*.

Still, all she could think about between bouts of nausea and moments of melancholy was how she carried in her womb a piece of her beloved savage. The baby would have his hair or his eyes or his beautiful amber skin, and it would be as if Sakote were with her...always.

The scuffle of boots on the porch interrupted her thoughts. Someone knocked.

"Just a moment." She brushed her hair back from her face, took a few shallow breaths, and rose on shaky legs to open the sagging door.

Her mouth dropped open. A dozen miners stood on the porch. To a man, they were scrubbed clean, dressed in their Sunday best, as groomed and grim as undertakers. Even Granny Cooper wore a mauve muslin skirt over her miner's boots. Zeke stood at the fore. His beard was trimmed into a neat point, and he carried his droopy hat formally upon his arm.

"Now, Miss Mattie, before you get all weepy on us," he said, "me and the boys want you to know we ain't gonna take no for an answer." Before she could ask him what she might say no to, he produced from behind his back a garment fashioned out of pale blue satin. "Granny's been savin' this in a trunk for her boys."

Mattie raised a brow. It hardly looked like something fit for a boy.

"She said you could wear it for the weddin' on account of the two of you bein' friends and ladies and all."

And then Mattie realized. For days now, Zeke and Granny had been formally courting. They must have decided, in the slapdash manner of the Wild West, to tie the knot today. And knowing Mattie's dearth of proper attire, they were loaning her a gown for the occasion. She was touched.

And she was happy for them, truly she was. But when she thought about the two of them joining hands and hearts in sweet wedded bliss, it made her remember her own unhappy plight. The smile she gave them was shaky, and she caught her lower lip in her teeth, biting back the well of tears that wanted to pour out.

"She don't like it," Granny muttered.

"No, it's lovely." Mattie blinked back the moisture from her eyes, cursing the condition that brought weeping on so readily and bruised her emotions as easily as an apple.

She took the garment graciously and held it up. The style was probably forty years out of date. It was a formal gown, straight and slim, with a low-dipping neckline, ribbon at the high waist, short puffed sleeves, and bows around the hem. It was hardly suitable attire for a gold camp and terribly out of fashion.

"I'd be honored to wear it," she said.

"You go on now and change," Zeke told her. "We'll wait for you."

The gown was too long, and one or the other of the shoulders kept slipping. Mattie managed to cinch the ribbon tightly enough under her bosom to keep the thing on, but there was little she could do about the hem trailing on the ground. She wished she'd had time to pin her hair up properly, but she could already hear impatient boots on the porch, so she smoothed the stray curls as best she could, and opened the door.

"Well, now," Zeke said, nodding in approval, "you look mighty fine, Miss Mattie, purty as a bluebell." He offered her his elbow.

She tucked her hand into the crook of his arm, grateful at least that her stomach had decided to grant her a respite as he escorted her along the main avenue of Paradise Bar.

The rest of the men were gathered in the copse of trees they'd used for a church that first Sunday after Mattie had arrived. Rows of benches and stools split the congregation neatly in half. A stranger in a black suit with a preacher's collar stood behind the makeshift pulpit, thumbing through a Bible. When she arrived, the miners set up a commotion, coming to their feet and doffing their hats. She straightened her spine a little more, wishing now that she'd taken the time to pin up those loose strands of her hair.

Zeke led her down the aisle, right up to the preacher, but then he left her standing there and seated himself in the front row. Mattie frowned. The preacher smiled broadly at her out of a face so shiny it looked like it had been scrubbed clean of sin.

"Dearly beloved," he began, "we're gathered here today to join these two in the holy bonds of matrimony..."

Mattie blinked. There must be some mistake. Heavens, the groom was sitting down, and the bride was nowhere to be...

Her eyes grew wide. Suddenly everything fell into place. Zeke and Granny weren't tying the knot. It was *her* wedding. The men must have discovered her delicate condition, and one of them had offered to make her a decent woman.

She swayed on her feet.

Who? Who had volunteered? Not Zeke. His heart belonged to Granny. Swede already had a wife and children. Frenchy stood with the congregation to the right of her. Beside him, Tom gave her a wink.

She was just about to announce in no uncertain terms that she had no intention of being forced into marriage when she heard a ruckus from the very back of the crowd, and then the ominous click of a gun being cocked. Whispers spiraled forward like an ocean wave. Her stomach flipped over once as she slowly turned to see the groom.

He was stunning in black. Or perhaps it was the way his teeth flashed fiercely in contrast as he fought off the four men restraining him, the way his ebony hair tumbled like a waterfall over his shoulders into the matching pool of the black coat. The white shirt, too tight to button all the way to the neck, looked like snow against his dark skin. They hadn't managed to get him into boots, so his feet stuck out bare beneath the hem of the black trousers.

Sakote was furious. That was clear. But there was something undeniably alluring about all that savagery contained in the confines of gentlemen's clothing. For a moment, Mattie's heart leaped, and she forgot he was here against his will.

That fact was made very plain to her in the next moment as Swede raised the cocked pistol to Sakote's jaw.

CHAPTER 28

Sakote sucked air in hard through his nose and stiffened. The barrel of the pistol felt cold under his chin. Soon death would leave him cold all over.

He didn't understand these whites. Why did they hold a gun to him? What had he done? Why did they dress him in their clothing when they only meant to kill him?

He wasn't afraid of death. He felt half dead already. But he feared for his people. Hintsuli had apparently alerted the tribe of his abduction, for even now, unbeknownst to the white men, Konkow warriors surrounded the camp, hiding in the bushes where the *willa* couldn't see them. If the miners shot Sakote, they would start a bloody war.

The white men hauled him forward toward a shady copse of trees where the miners gathered for some strange death ritual. At first, he struggled against them, but when they dragged him between the back row of seats, he froze.

There at the end of the path stood his *kulem*, Mati, even more beautiful than his merciful memory recalled.

"No," she said with her mouth, though no sound came out.

"Now, Miss Mattie," the big yellow-haired man said, "there's no call for panic. I'm sure the Injun'll do the right thing, won't you?"

Sakote didn't understand.

"He doesn't understand," Mati said. The blue dress made her look like a delicate lupine, and his heart ached when he noticed she still wore the moccasins he'd made for her.

"Beggin' your pardon, Miss Mattie," the big man said quietly, his skin reddening, "but if he understands how to put a papoose in your belly, he ought to understand well enough what he's got to do about it."

Sakote was confused. It was a strange word, "papoose."

Mati walked slowly to him. Sakote held his breath. He could feel her magic, her power, even though she didn't touch him, even though she didn't even look at him, but instead approached the yellow-haired man beside him, placing her hand on his chest. Her scent stirred his nostrils. She smelled like the meadow, young and sweet.

"He doesn't understand, Mr. Swede. He thinks we're already married, that I'm his *kulem*, his wife."

"No," Sakote countered, gazing past her. That much he understood. Mati had left him, which meant they weren't married anymore. "Not anymore."

"Now, look, boy, I'm warnin' you," the big man said. "Either you do the honorable thing, or I'll have to plug you full of lead."

He raised the pistol to Sakote's temple, and at once, twelve Konkow warriors stepped out to surround the white men, legs braced wide, bows drawn.

"Holy shit!" This came from the man with the big book.

Sakote didn't know what to do. He couldn't let his brothers shoot the white men. It would only bring more *willa* to seek revenge upon his people. But neither could he force Mati to be his *kulem* if she didn't want him.

"Sakote, please!" Mati cried. "Tell them to put their bows away! Don't let your people kill them!"

Mati's words tore at his heart. She cared more about the miners than she did the Konkows. He translated the message to his Konkow brothers, but they didn't lower their bows.

"Mr. Swede! You can't force him to do this," Mati said. "You can't. I left him of my own free will."

The big man frowned. "But I thought, we all thought..."

"*Mademoiselle*, you are not in love with the savage?"

"Oh, for the love o' Saint Peter..."

"I am," Mati said. "That is, I was, but..."

"And that's his papoose you're carryin', ain't it?" Swede asked.

Sakote clamped his jaw closed. What was this "papoose" they kept speaking of?

Mati hung her head. "Yes, but I don't...I can't..."

"Look, ma'am," the big man muttered nervously, "we can't stand around jawin' all day, not with all these Injuns breathin' down our necks."

Sakote shared the man's anxiety and impatience.

"I'm thinkin' maybe you need to have a little powwow, just the two of you," the man whispered, glancing at Sakote. Sakote could see the glow of sweat beneath the man's nose.

"My warriors won't lower their bows until you put away your guns," Sakote said.

The big man licked his lips, and then nodded. "Nice and easy now. We don't want nobody to get hurt."

The white men slowly lowered their guns and released him. They backed away to leave him alone with Mati. Sakote called out to his brothers to disarm. This time they complied.

When the miners were out of hearing, he asked her, "What do they want from me?"

"They want you to marry me."

He only stared at her for a moment, unable to comprehend her words. "They want... But why?"

"They..." She bit her lip. "They're afraid I'll be lonely without you."

Sakote frowned. Mati was hiding something. She wasn't good at deception. When they played the hand game together, he always knew which hand held the marked bone, for she couldn't keep the secret from her eyes.

Sakote, however, could hide his emotions. Mati had no idea how her closeness tortured him now, how the sound of her voice made his heart quicken, how the scent of her made his man's-knife swell with longing. "And what do *you* want?" he asked her, pretending he didn't care how she answered.

"I...nothing, Sakote. Nothing."

She crushed him with her words. He flattened his eyes against the pain, and his words tasted as bitter as willow bark tea. "Tell your people to find you another husband, a white man to keep you company, so you won't have to live among savages."

Her eyes filled like a spring swollen with winter rain. "But I don't want to marry anyone else." Her lips trembled. "I'll never love...anyone else."

Sakote blew out a long breath, utterly perplexed. Noa had often told him that a woman had wit and wiles to confound even Henno, Trickster Coyote. Sakote saw this now. He looked to the sky, hoping Wonomi would counsel him. He didn't. "But you said you didn't want to be my *kulem*." Maybe, Sakote thought, he could unravel the truth from Mati the same way he untangled his fishing line, a bit at a time.

Her face crumpled like a dying flower, and it took all his willpower not to gather her to him and let her wilt against his chest.

"I can't, Sakote."

What did she mean? She'd been his *kulem* once. She'd

invited him to sleep with her in her *hubo*. They'd lived as husband and wife. And they'd made love—sweet, spirit-bonding love...

"I can't do that to you," she said.

Sakote tried to understand. Mati could shatter his heart and torment his soul by leaving him in the middle of the night, but she couldn't mend his wounds and return joy to his spirit by agreeing to be his *kulem* again. Noa was right. Women were a riddle impossible to solve.

"Why?"

Mattie knew there were a dozen sound reasons she couldn't marry Sakote. But at the moment, gazing into his midnight black eyes, catching his scent of smoke and mint and deerskin, remembering the warmth of his body shielding her from the evening air while they made love beneath the pines, she couldn't think of a single one.

She hadn't realized how much she'd missed him. The sketch she'd nailed to her cabin wall to wake up to every morning, the one memento she'd taken from the village, the drawing of Sakote on that first day, she now realized looked nothing like the real Sakote. He was no longer the angry young savage she'd drawn. No, he was far more complicated. It was as if she'd rendered only the surface of a pool then, and now she knew what lay beneath.

"Why, Mati?"

"Because..." She owed him the truth. She swallowed hard. "Because I don't belong with your people, Sakote. I've seen how they look at me. I'm kin to a killer, a...what do you call it?"

"*Hudesi.*"

"You see? I can't even speak your language properly. I can't leach acorns or tan deerhide or even weave a basket. I'm just a useless white woman who brings menace to the tribe and steals the Konkow's best hunter from them."

"I would have fought for you," he said quietly.

"I couldn't let you." She raised her hand. She wanted to touch him, to take his hand, to stroke his cheek, but she didn't dare or she'd dissolve into tears. "Don't you see, Sakote? I can't take you away from your village, from your people. You belong there. You belong to them. And I don't."

Sakote was silent a long while. He looked past her toward his warriors, and then let his breath out in a soft sigh. "I don't belong to the Konkows. I belong to The Great Spirit. You belong to The Great Spirit. It is he who has chosen this path for us, this path between two worlds."

His words hung in the air between them. How simple they were. It was one of the things Mattie particularly liked about him. And yet, though he spoke plainly, there was a wealth of meaning in what he said.

Was it true? she wondered, her heart racing at the idea. All her life, she'd tried to belong. But what did that mean? For her, it had meant a lifetime of following someone else's customs and rules and wishes. But that wasn't what her parents had taught her, and it wasn't what Sakote affirmed now.

Maybe he was right. Maybe she didn't need to belong. Maybe she, too, belonged to The Great Spirit, the one who'd made her who she was. Maybe that was what her parents had meant by being true to herself.

The possibility left her lightheaded. She staggered, and Sakote caught her arm. Instantly, bows and rifles were leveled at their heads.

"It's all right," Mattie gasped, clutching to him while the dizziness passed. "I'm all right."

When the bystanders had lowered their weapons again, she looked into his eyes, her beloved Sakote's scowling eyes, and her heart filled with hope.

"Where would we live?" she murmured.

His countenance softened at once, and she saw again the man who'd carried her into the stream and told her stories of Oleli and taught her to hunt yellow-jackets.

"We will live on the land, wherever the path leads," he told her. "Wonomi will guide us."

Mattie compressed her lips, trying not to cry. "Oh, Sakote, I've missed you so much."

"My heart, too, has been empty."

Unmindful of the witnesses around them and unable to refrain from touching him any longer, she placed her hand along the crisp edge of his white shirt where it lay unbuttoned, resting her fingers over the place his heart resided. Before she could have second thoughts, before she could reason her way out of the decision, she had to ask him a question.

"Sakote," she blurted out, "will you marry me?"

One side of his mouth slowly curved up into a beguiling smile as his gaze moved first languidly over her form and then down at his own ill-fitting formal attire. "Yes, *kulem*, I will marry you."

With a laugh of delight, she threw herself so hard at Sakote that she almost knocked the breath from him. But he didn't seem to mind. He hugged her to him, and his deep chuckle resonated in the ear she pressed to his chest.

A great whoop rang out from both factions of observers, the miners and the warriors, and when the men of Paradise Bar dignified their response with polite applause, the Konkows followed suit.

Mattie giggled and pressed a swift kiss to Sakote's cheek. Then she looped her arm through his and tugged him toward the makeshift church.

It was an interesting ceremony, with miners in their Sunday best on one side and half-naked Konkows on the other. Sakote recited the vows with great solemnity and pride, and it was all Mattie could do, gazing up at his incredibly handsome face, his tawny skin and snowy teeth, his obsidian-dark eyes filled with adoration, not to stammer over her own words.

He seemed particularly pleased with the custom of sharing a kiss once they were declared man and wife. As she dissolved into his embrace, the Konkows started up a chant, doubtless a victory song, which was almost drowned out by the gleeful hollering of the miners. Then Sakote grinned, and Mattie knew at last she was exactly where she belonged.

Sakote licked his fingers, sticky with juice. His *kulem* was right. He loved peach pie. And so did his Konkow brothers, who enthusiastically scooped up bits of the sweet fruit and crunchy crust that the miners offered them.

He was not, however, comfortable in the white man's clothing. The coat restricted his bow arm, and the buttons on the shirt seemed ready to burst, especially as he filled himself up on the miners' wedding feast. He felt like a lizard, in need of a new skin. In fact, the only reason he continued to wear the garments was because Mati, perched on his lap, kept looking at him with desire in her eyes, running her palm across the weave of the coat and slipping her fingers between the buttons to touch the skin of his chest.

He swallowed another bite of pie, trying to distract himself from the other hunger raging through his body. How long, he wondered, did a wedding feast continue? He glanced at the sky. The sun was still well above the hills. Would the miners notice if the honored guests stole off into the woods?

Beside him, Mati gasped. "Hintsuli!" she cried happily, jumping up from his knee.

Out of the forest, they emerged—his little brother, his

mother, his sister and Noa, and the women of the village. Sakote rose to greet them.

The yellow-haired man—Swede, Mati called him—scratched his head. "Well, I'll be damned."

As always, Hintsuli, cautious as Bear charging into the stream, raced toward Mati, giggling and falling into her embrace, merrily burrowing his face in her skirts. Beyond Hintsuli, Sakote's mother walked sedately in her finest deerskin cloak.

All around him, the miners stood like rabbits frozen in the stare of a wolf. He lifted one corner of his mouth into a smile. Surely they'd seen Konkow women before. Perhaps it was only that they'd never seen so many in one place, or maybe it was that other thing Noa talked about—the way the Konkow women didn't cover their breasts—that disturbed them.

"My son's spirit is at peace?" said his mother by way of greeting.

Sakote smiled. "They've made Mati my *kulem* again in the white way."

His mother studied the faces of the miners. "These are good *willa*?" she asked.

"They are good *willa*."

The other white woman of Paradise Bar, Granny, trudged up behind him, grumbling like an old she-bear. "Don't you boys got any manners at all?" She nudged him aside and stretched her hand out toward Sakote's mother. "How-de-do, ma'am. My name's Beatrice Elizabeth Cooper, but most folks call me Granny."

Sakote told his mother to give the woman her hand. Her eyes went wide as Granny pumped her arm vigorously up and down, but when the white woman finally let go, there was a twinkle in her gaze to match the stars.

"Come on, boys," Granny brayed. "Introduce yourselves."

His mother learned the hand-shaking ritual quickly, and

some of the braver women of the village joined in as well. And though they couldn't decipher the words of the miners, they understood well their hospitality when the white men offered them boiled ham with beans, oyster soup, and what was left of the peach pie.

The Konkows had brought no food to contribute, but a few of the women gave strings of clamshells and feather ear ornaments to the miners.

The Konkow warriors, swiftly learning the custom Noa called toasting, grew more and more companionable, and soon they started up a hand game. The man named Frenchy took a keen interest in the game, though he lost much to the warriors, gambling away a brown glass bottle, six matches, and a small nugget of gold.

When the sun went to sleep, the miners built a huge fire. The man with the small black hat, Tom, began to make a song, blowing into a strange *yalalu* made of metal. Another miner joined him, making music upon a wooden box fitted with strings like a hunting bow. The sound was wondrous, and soon the people of his village started dancing and spinning before the fire. Noa and Towani joined their arms and began the skipping, turning dance of the whites, and before long, the white men and the Konkows danced together until they were breathless.

Because no celebration was complete without storytelling, Domem began to tell a Konkow tale. Sakote translated for the miners. He told the story of the foolish Konkow woman who abandoned her baby to chase after a butterfly. The butterfly turned into a man who led her to a valley filled with butterflies, and she became dazzled chasing them. The man abandoned her there, and she was lost forever in the valley.

Not to be outdone, Tom stood up and told a story filled with magical creatures—tiny bearded men with pots of gold and great lizards that breathed fire. Hintsuli had never sat so quietly for so long.

Sakote stifled a yawn, and his mother, sitting across the dwindling fire, smiled at him. She leaned over and spoke to her husband. The headman nodded, then rose to speak.

Sakote translated his message of thanks and peace to the white men. Then the Konkows left Paradise Bar as silently as they had come.

When Sakote carried her across the threshold of the cabin, as the miners had told him was the custom, Mattie blushed. It wasn't from the thought of being carried in such a fashion in front of the men. It wasn't even because of the bed that waited in conspicuous invitation. But as soon as he nudged the door open, Mattie remembered the sketch staring blatantly down from the wall.

Sakote grunted as he spied it by the light of her flickering oil lamp. Then he kicked the door closed behind them, shutting out the prying eyes of the miners.

"Who is this fierce warrior that hangs over the bed to frighten my *kulem*?"

She smacked him lightly on the chest. "You know it's you, Sakote."

His half-smile told her that indeed he knew, and that he was pleased, *too* pleased that it was hanging in such a place of honor.

He set her down, took the lamp, and moved to take a closer look. Then he frowned. "This face is hard and angry."

"It was the first I saw of you. I drew it from memory." She came up beside him and ran a finger playfully along his arm. "And as I recall, you *were* hard and angry. I suppose you thought the wild and wicked white woman might hurt your helpless little brother."

Mischief glimmered in his eyes. "Wild and wicked? No. You were frightened. And willful."

She smirked and crossed her arms. "Frightened? I wasn't frightened in the least," she lied.

"No? You *should* have been." He answered her with such a smoldering gaze that it made her knees wobble.

Her reply came out a hoarse whisper. "And I've never been willful in my life."

"Never?" His eyes never leaving hers, he placed the lamp upon the table. The shadows of the room danced and then settled. Without a word, he began to slowly strip off his clothes. A self-assured smile played upon his lips as he moved languorously, like a cat, clearly relishing the idea of seducing her in this way, one garment at a time. He managed to tug the coat down over his shoulders and past his elbows, but once he reached his forearms, the sleeves inverted and bunched around his wrists, trapping him. He scowled.

Mattie's lips quivered as she tried valiantly not to giggle. Sakote's eyes narrowed, and his chest rose and fell with an impatient sigh as he struggled against the cloth bonds to no avail.

Finally, Mattie took mercy upon him. She worked the coat back up over his shoulders and helped him slide out one sleeve at a time. When he would have ripped open the shirt, sending buttons flying everywhere, Mattie intervened, unfastening the garment with greedy fingers.

One glance at Sakote's pleased face told her he had no intention of letting her stop. With quivering hands, she gingerly unbuttoned his trousers and slid them down over his lean hips. She gasped at his blatant display of arousal, and his answering chuckle came from deep in his chest.

"See what you've done," he purred, "willful woman."

Mattie didn't feel willful at all. She felt as weak as a lamb.

How Sakote managed to undress her in turn without tearing the gown, she didn't know, for the way he stared at her, his eyes molten with desire, made her limbs go as limp as boiled cabbage. Soon she stood before him, naked, unashamed, filled with longing.

He touched her first with only his eyes, like an artist preparing to paint her.

"You're beautiful," he murmured, "like the aloalo blossom."

Her cheeks warmed with pleasure, but then the corner of her mouth drifted up in a smile to mimic Sakote's. "And what's an aloalo blossom?"

A guilty twinkle lit up his gaze. "Noa says it's the most beautiful flower in Hawaii. He says it's..." He screwed up his forehead to think. "Dang purty."

Mattie fought back a grin. "Dang purty?"

He nodded. Then he reached out a hand to brush her hair back from her neck, and all thoughts of levity left her. His fingers felt warm and sure upon her skin, and she closed her eyes to savor the sensation.

His hand slipped around the back of her neck, and with gentle pressure, he pulled her closer. His other arm crossed over her back and completed the embrace. She groaned with the ecstasy of flesh against flesh as her cheek brushed the hollow of his shoulder, her breasts pillowed against his chest, and she felt the blunt desire of his man's-knife against her belly.

His lips found her forehead, and his warm breath misted her face as he trailed kisses along the line of her hair. The pads of his fingers branded her, moving languidly over her body, first as lightly as a breeze, then with the strength of a river current.

She opened her mouth, and he came to her, teasing her with delicate flicks of his tongue, drawing her lips between his own, then enveloping her in a kiss so deep, so complete that she wound up draped around his neck like one of those monkeys she'd seen clinging to the trees of Panama.

She moaned. Her breasts tingled with yearning, and the

throbbing between her legs intensified to an aching need. His body was so hot, so sleek, so strong. His long hair fell upon her face and softly lashed her bosom as she drank and drank of his kisses, insatiable.

She would have sunk to the floor, made love to him on the rough planks of the cabin at once, but he wrapped his arms about her and lifted her to the bed.

"Tonight I'm the husband of the white woman," he explained, his voice rough with lust. "Tonight we will join here."

She opened her eyes to slits and gazed at him as he loomed over her on the bed. The lantern's glow lit up his face, accentuating the wide set of his cheekbones, the proud arch of his nose, the lush lashes that swept his cheek as he tossed his head back and closed his eyes in brief prayer to his Creator. Ah, God, he was handsome. A wave of joy washed over her as she thought about the child she carried within her, the babe who would bear its father's beautiful features.

And then her tender thoughts fled as he lowered himself to her, leaving her breathless. The weight of his body pressed her gently but firmly into the mattress, and the heat of him sent a roar like fire through her head. His hands cupped her face as he opened her mouth to entwine his tongue with hers, and she sank urgent fingers into the supple muscle of his back. His hair tumbled forward, blotting out the light of the flame until he flung it aside to whisper in her ear. This time he didn't speak to her in his native tongue. This time she understood every word.

"Don't leave me again, Mati, my beautiful wife," he murmured. "It makes my heart sad. Don't leave me."

His words, so simple, so forthright, touched her deeply. She answered him around a sudden thickening in her throat. "Never."

He bathed her face with kisses then, until the knot of her emotions dissolved into giggles of delight.

When his kisses slowed and moved lower, beneath her chin, in the hollow of her throat, across her bosom, she sighed and arched toward him. He chuckled low, kissing his way around her breasts, laving her lavishly with the soft underside of his tongue, then finally took her nipple into his mouth.

Restless, she writhed beneath his onslaught, shivering as the back of his knuckles skated along her ribs on their stealthy path toward the burgeoning desire centered between her legs. His fingers tangled in her curls, brushed the sensitive skin of her inner thigh, dipped into the dampening crevices of her womanhood. To her mortification, she longed to shove her hips up against him, to press that part of her into his palm, his thigh, any piece of him.

He kissed his way across the spot between her ribs where her heart throbbed, dipping into her navel, then along the ticklish recesses of her hips. But when he moved even lower, she sucked in her breath and made fists of her hands. Surely he didn't intend...not by the full light of the lamp...

He grazed the skin of her thigh with his teeth, and she smothered a cry. His breath was warm upon her. His lips were soft. And his tongue...

She bolted up with the intensity of his touch, shocked and amazed and so full of that single incredible sensation that she grew blind and deaf to all else as his tongue danced over her flesh. If she screamed, she never heard it. If her expression revealed her untempered passions, she never realized it. There was only Sakote and her and a whirlwind of fire spiraling out of control.

Then, for one wonderful, terrible moment, she couldn't breathe. And didn't care. Her fingers snarled in Sakote's hair, her mouth gaped open, and her eyes flew wide in astonishment. Like an eagle, higher and higher she seemed to rise on a wild wind of desire until she rose so high that her feathers ruffled in the thin air and she dove, shuddering, toward the earth.

"Sakote!" she cried as her body bucked violently from the bed.

But he rode her down, staying with her, guiding her, comforting her until the spasms subsided and she settled gently upon the mattress again.

She wanted to avert her eyes. She was ashamed of her unconstraint, of what he might have seen. But he wouldn't let her turn away. His eyes full of earnest wonder, he captured her head between loving hands, demanding her gaze, and blessed her with a single absolving kiss.

Sakote licked his lips. He liked the taste of Mati in his mouth. And he liked the feel of her in his arms, especially when her spirit left her for that dangerous moment to soar among the clouds. It filled him with pride, for it meant she trusted him. And it filled him with desire as well.

His man's-knife poked at her already, rude and impatient. But she didn't appear to mind. And even that warmed his heart.

"Oh, Sakote," she breathed, and his name had power upon her lips. "I want you."

He saw her swallow and knew it had been hard for her to say. Maybe it wasn't the white way to speak of such things. But she was changing, growing closer to the way of the Konkow, to the way Wonomi had made her.

"I want you, too, Mati."

Then, watching her eyes smolder as he did so, he eased his man's-knife slowly into her. Sweat trickled down his cheek as he forced his body to forbear. But when he at last joined completely with Mati, her gaze of pure passion drove him to abandon patience.

He mated with her gently at first, but soon the movement became a dance of their spirits' making. The ropes of the bed squeaked as they thrust together with more force. Mati moaned beneath him, firing his blood, and the growl of the bear came from his own throat in answer.

His man's-knife swelled, and he squeezed his eyes shut, overcome with lust. Sweat dripped from his brow, and the cords of his arms tensed like the sinew of his bow as he held his body to keep from crushing Mati. All at once, the world stilled, and Sakote felt as though he floated on the smoke of the dream pipe. He saw a vision, as clear as the water of the creek. Mati sat before an evening fire, laughing, with a baby in her arms.

Just as suddenly, the vision splintered. With a great roar, he plunged into Mati, shuddering as desire crashed over him like the cascades of the waterfall, draining him of all strength, all will.

When he rolled to Mati's side, she curled up around him, as content as a well-fed squirrel. But he still shook. Not only from what they'd done, but from what he'd seen.

"Mati," he whispered, "what did the big man mean when he said I put a...a papoose in your belly?"

She told him.

He was sure that in his village, a world away, they could hear his great whoop of joy.

CHAPTER 29

Hintsuli didn't understand all the excitement. Mati wasn't the first woman to make a baby. Even the animals could do it. But watching the anxious white men outside Mati's cabin from his hiding place in the manzanita, it looked like they waited for the creation of Onkoito, the son of Wonomi himself.

Sakote was inside the cabin with her. She hadn't wanted to have the baby outside like the rest of the Konkows did. And instead of having an old woman assist her, she was aided by the healer of the mining camp, the white man with the hat. How strange their ways were, he thought.

A branch poked him as he shifted on his haunches, and he grunted. Since *ko-meni*, winter, had stripped the leaves from the bushes, it wasn't as easy to hide in the woods. But the miners were too distracted to notice him, doing their strange ritual dance before the cabin—marching back and forth, puffing on pipes, and pulling out the toys Noa called pocketwatches. Even the man who came on the *lyktakymsy*, riding-dog, the man who brought the supplies from far away, stayed to see what would happen.

Hintsuli wondered if the man would notice if he sneaked over to that *lyktakymsy* and looked in his pack. Sometimes the man brought toys. He came more often now, and Mati always gave him bundles of her sketches. She said the man sold them to the whites who lived far away. She said the pictures of Hintsuli had traveled across the sea on a ship. He'd tried to brag of it to his friends from Nemsewi, but they hadn't understood.

He spent more time with them now, his big Konkow brothers from the other village, Win-uti and Omi. They didn't speak any more about their little brother, the one Mati's husband-to-be had killed, and they no longer wished to fight Sakote. Hintsuli liked them. They spoke to him as a man. Win-uti had shown him how to smoke the dream pipe, and Omi let him shoot a rabbit with his *punda*, bow. Not like Sakote, who ruffled his hair like he was still a little boy.

Hintsuli squinted his eyes and picked a curl of bark from the manzanita trunk. Sakote had no time for him now anyway. He was too busy talking to the elders about something the whites called a treaty, too busy with his woman and the important baby everyone was so excited about. He'd even forgotten about Hintsuli's upcoming rites of *yeponi*.

The *lyktakymsy* stamped its back hoof, and Hintsuli counted in his mind how many steps it would take to get to the animal. He was almost ready to steal forward when the cabin door burst open.

He couldn't understand the excited words of the man with the hat who carried a bundle in his arms. But the white men suddenly crowed like warriors successful in the hunt, tossing their hats into the air and slapping each other on the back. Hintsuli scowled in disgust. The miners hadn't done anything. Why did they make the cry of victory?

Besides, their shouting frightened the baby. It began to

whimper. And then Hintsuli noticed a strange thing. There were *two* voices. He parted the branches to peer closer. It couldn't be. He'd never seen such a thing. But it was so. The man held *two* bundles. Mati had made two babies.

Sakote stepped from the cabin then, and the expression on his face made Hintsuli freeze on the spot. The miners, too, fell silent, until the only sound was the thin crying of the two babies. Hintsuli felt his heart thump against his ribs. His older brother looked pale, as white as the men around him, not like Sakote at all, but like the *kokoni* of Sakote. There was no happiness in his face like the healer had, only an expression Hintsuli didn't understand—anger or sadness or fear. But whatever it was, it made Hintsuli's heart beat faster in dread. What if Sakote saw him and was angry with him for coming to the *willa* camp?

He was afraid. He didn't like to see his brother looking that way.

Breathing rapidly, he waited until Sakote hung his head and turned away. Then Hintsuli tore off, racing through the woods toward Nemsewi, to Win-uti and Omi, who would have time to listen to his story about the two babies and who never got angry with him.

Mattie bit back tears as she tucked the two babies into the double-sized cradle Swede had made for them. It was only fatigue, she told herself, buttoning up her dress. After all, it had been just five days since she'd given birth. A milky film of moonlight filtered in through the linen curtain, just enough to make out the dark heads of her beautiful sons, sleeping now that their bellies were full.

Sakote had gone home to his village. He'd said it was tradition. A new Konkow mother was supposed to be left undisturbed by her husband for several days after childbirth.

But Mattie missed him terribly, especially late at night like this, when the floor felt cold upon her bare feet and even the moon's light was eerie.

Too restless to sleep, she lit a candle and pulled out her sketchbook. Carefully scooting the cradle to take advantage of the candle's glow, she began to pencil in with a delicate hand the features of her slumbering twins.

They had no names. Though Sakote had bent to her will regarding the delivery of their children, he stood firmer when it came to naming them. Of course, Mattie intended to change his mind. She refused to have her little boys running around nameless for two or three years.

Still, she thought, penciling in the feather-fine dark hair atop baby number one's sweet head, she'd agree to anything if Sakote would only return to her.

It wasn't just his physical distance that left her melancholy. It was his emotional distance as well. Something had happened when the babies were born. Sakote had been with her, holding her hand, giving her strength, praying to his god. But after she'd delivered the twins, he'd grown silent, solemn. He'd *left* her. At the time, she'd thought it might be some Konkow custom of respect.

But even when he returned to her side, touching her flushed cheek, brushing the damp hair back from her forehead, his smile of joy was tinged with something else, something almost tragic.

And now she couldn't even ask him about it. The point of her pencil broke as she scrawled her name at the bottom of the drawing, and she sighed. She supposed some of her frustration was caused by what Tom Cooligan liked to refer to as feminine humors. Her breasts were sore from suckling, she was exhausted from wakeful nights, and her composure seemed to slip along the surface of her emotions like a graceless skater on thin ice.

One of the babies stretched in his sleep, and Mattie smiled as his tiny fist poked at his brother's chin, making the boy's lip pout. How could she be unhappy, she decided, when such a miracle slumbered before her? They were her sons, hers and Sakote's, beautiful and whole and healthy, and they were going to grow into strong warriors as handsome as their father.

She glanced one last time at the sketch before setting it aside, then blew out the candle and burrowed under the blankets of her bed. Sakote might not be with her now, but he *would* return. And then they'd have years and years together to grow into a real family, she and Sakote and their sons.

Mattie sensed something was wrong the moment she awoke. The sunlight etched patterns of branches across the curtain, and her breasts felt heavy and full. She frowned. The twins had never let her sleep past dawn before. She was usually awakened by their lusty cries several hours before the sun peeped over the horizon.

Sitting up drowsily on her elbows, she peered into the cradle.

The babies were gone.

The breath froze in her lungs, and she blinked her eyes, disbelieving. A scream built in the back of her throat.

There was a reason, she told herself, trying to calm down, willing her heart to stop its panicked pounding. Surely there was a good reason. Sakote had come and taken them. Or Tom. Or Swede. Whichever man it was, she'd beat him soundly for putting such a scare into her. Still, a frisson of doubt shivered up her spine.

Quaking with fright, she shoved her arms into the men's coat she'd ordered from Marysville for the winter and exploded out the front door of her cabin. The sun blinded her for a moment.

"Why, Miss Mattie, whatever's wrong?"

Swede's pick was slung over his shoulder, and beside him, Tom, Zeke, and the Campbell boys, their gold pans hung from their belts, were on their way to the creek.

The sharp throbbing of her heart returned with a vengeance, dizzying her, and through the rapid plumes of fog her breath made in the chill air, she saw Sakote was finally returning to her, emerging through the trees. But his arms, too, were empty.

Sudden pain stung her nipples. A slow gasp of agony grated against her throat. When she finally found the strength to speak, her voice sounded as hollow as the north wind.

"Where are my babies?"

Sakote hadn't known such anger existed, but the rage of the bear filled him now. His blood burned with the fire of vengeance, his eyes sparked like shards of obsidian, and his arms trembled with the need to kill.

If it weren't for Mati, who quivered like the last leaf on a winter branch, he would have torn the path to Nemsewi with his bare hands. That was how furious he was.

He was sure the babies were there. While he was in the village, his mother had told him that Hintsuli had befriended the sons of the headman, Win-uti and Omi, the sons who had challenged Sakote at the Kaminehaitsen. Why had his little brother made peace with them? Did he believe they'd forget their grudge so soon? No doubt they'd been using Hintsuli to spy on Mati.

Sakote's mouth grew bitter, and he spit into the dirt. It was *his* fault. He should have watched Hintsuli closer. He'd been so preoccupied with the negotiations for peace between the Konkows and the whites, and so busy with his child to come, that he'd forgotten about his little brother.

He was startled from his thoughts by the sound of bullets being loaded into rifle chambers all around him. The miners gathered, their faces grim.

"We're comin' with you," Zeke said.

"No," he told them. "I know where to find my sons. They're in Konkow territory. They're with...my brothers. You stay here. Protect Mati."

"I'm going with you," Mati said.

He shook his head. He suspected Mati would collapse if she took three steps. "No. This is my battle. I'm to blame. I will find them."

"You're not to blame," she insisted, clutching at his arm.

"I left you alone."

"They stole my babies from me while I slept beside them." Shadows darkened her eyes. "No one could have prevented..."

"I could have."

It would haunt him for the rest of his life if he didn't find them, if the headman's sons had already...

He clenched his teeth. He couldn't think of it.

"Why would they take my babies?" Mattie's voice was so small, so helpless, so innocent. It hurt his heart to hear it.

"To anger me," he lied.

He knew why they'd taken his sons. It was the same reason he'd left her in Paradise Bar and gone home to spend every day in the *kum*, praying to Wonomi for guidance. It was the reason his spirit had been filled with dread when he beheld his newborns.

They were twins.

Twins were bad luck.

It was Konkow custom to kill them at birth, along with their mother.

He wouldn't tell Mati. He would never tell her. He should have taken her away long ago, when he'd first had the vision. He'd always seen *two* eggs in the white eagle's talons. He should have known all along. He should have fled with her before she gave birth.

And now, because of a foolish, archaic superstition, he was in a race, like the footraces run between the tribes at the celebration of Hesi, only this one wasn't for glory or honor, but to decide if his sons would live or die.

Slipping past the watchman, identifiable by his single magpie feather, Sakote strode brazenly into Nemsewi and surprised the villagers.

"Where are my sons!" he snarled, drawing his knife. The thunder of his voice scattered the women making acorn mush and drew the attention of the warriors standing by the fire, among them Win-uti and Omi, the headman's sons.

"You shouldn't have come." So spoke Win-uti, the one who had challenged him at the Kaminehaitsen, the one Hintsuli had unwisely befriended.

It was difficult for Sakote to hold his knife still and his gaze steady as he studied the man's crafty grimace for some sign of guilt. Were his sons safe, or had this bloodthirsty savage already killed them? Sakote tensed his jaw. He would know soon. For now, he must show no weakness.

"Where are my sons?" His fingers tightened on the knife.

"Your children bring bad luck to our people," Omi sneered, advancing on him, "just as your white *kulem* brings bad luck." Sakote wondered how Hintsuli could have admired such a rattlesnake.

"What have you done with them?" he demanded.

Omi snorted. "Maybe they're already—"

The younger man never finished his answer, which was probably a good thing, for Sakote would have swiftly ended Omi's life if he'd told him his sons were dead. But his words were interrupted by twin cries from a nearby *hubo*, the unmistakable wailing of hungry babies.

"Give them to me," Sakote said, empowered by the sound of his children, grinding the words between his teeth like acorns between rocks.

"My father was never paid for the murder of my brother by the whites," Win-uti argued, tossing his hair over one shoulder. "Your white sons shall pay the blood price."

"Not while I live," he swore, shrugging the deerskin cloak from his shoulders. "You challenged me before. Now I'll accept that challenge."

He spat into his palms to secure his grip on the knife. Win-uti smiled grimly and made ready to fight.

Sakote flexed his knees and, while the other warriors formed a ring around the pair, began to circle his opponent slowly.

Win-uti leered at him, his eyes wild and wide, and took a few fast jabs. Sakote ducked out of the way, but his reflexes were not as they'd once been. It was the custom of a man whose *kulem* was with child to refrain from the hunt for the moons of her pregnancy, and so Sakote's movements were unpracticed. He felt sluggish, like Brother Bear waking from his *ko-meni* slumber.

He swung his knife around, but sliced only air. Then Win-uti's blade arced toward him, gashing him high on the chest. The shallow cut stung like fire.

Win-uti hissed in victory, his eyes gleaming. He stabbed forward twice more while his Konkow brothers cheered him on, but this time Sakote was able to block his attack. His knife caught Win-uti's forearm, nicking it, but the warrior was too filled with blood thirst to notice.

Like an eagle hopping around its kill, Win-uti swooped sideways, flapping his arms. He dove in for another strike, and Sakote gasped as the blade gouged his side.

Win-uti crowed with glee, but then he became too

confident. He raised the bloody knife in victory, and Sakote thrust forward, slashing the man's belly with his blade. Win-uti doubled over with a gasp, then immediately shook off the blow, too proud to admit his injury.

Win-uti whirled, swinging low and missing, and anger darkened his eyes. Sakote lunged forward again, and his blade caught the thong of the soapstone charm about Win-uti's neck. He sliced through it, and it sailed out of the ring into the dust.

Win-uti's eyes blazed with rage now, and he hacked recklessly. Sakote dodged all of the slashes but one. That one bit deep into his thigh, through flesh and muscle, and he sucked a sharp breath of pain through his teeth. His leg crumpled beneath him, and for a moment, the day around him dimmed as if evening shadows rushed to cover the earth. He dropped to one knee, losing his grip on the knife. Through a muffled haze of agony, he heard the warriors' voices, howling, cheering, rejoicing in his defeat.

And then he heard another sound piercing through their gloating cries. His sons. Wailing. Summoning their father. Calling to his heart.

Their voices echoed through his spirit, filling him with pride and love, giving him strength. How could he have left them? How could he have questioned their fate? These were his children, his sons. They were as much a part of him as his own heart.

Clenching his teeth against the torment of his wound, he wrapped his fist around the knife once more and willfully rose to his feet. His muscles seemed to scream, and sweat dripped from his forehead, but his sons' cries fortified him. He swayed dizzily as the world swam in cobwebs around him, and then shook his head to clear his vision.

Win-uti laughed then, and the sound ignited Sakote's rage faster than lightning triggered a brush fire. He shot forward with his blade, sinking it deep into Win-uti's shoulder, then bowled the astonished warrior over into the dust. The man hit the dirt with a heavy thud, losing his knife. Sakote pulled his own blade free and prepared to finish the warrior.

He held Win-uti down by the throat and raised his knife high. Then he hesitated. Time seemed to slow as it did when he smoked the dream pipe. The dust rose around them, blown crazily by their huffing breath. Shadows crept in at the corners of Sakote's vision, and he watched his own sweat drip down onto Win-uti's chest. The brave warrior didn't struggle, but stared steadily into Sakote's eyes, ready for death. Then Wonomi spoke to Sakote in a vision.

Sakote saw the Konkows scattered like seeds. He saw strangers driving them from their land and stealing their food. He saw the people of Nemsewi hiding and hunted, growing sick and starving, until they were no more.

The vision melted away, and Sakote looked down with new eyes upon the warrior whose life he held in his hands. Win-uti wasn't a bad man. He was a fine Konkow, a fierce fighter, a brave warrior. What he'd done, he'd done with a pure heart and for the good of his people. Win-uti followed the old ways. He meant to keep the rites of the Konkows, to prevent the whites from bringing bad luck upon his village.

But Win-uti didn't understand. It was too late. The world of the Konkows was changing. The *willa* had already come with their food in tins and their riding-dogs and their rifles. And if the Konkows didn't change with their world, they would be swept away by the wind of the whites. They would be no more.

Sakote heard the cries of his sons again—so innocent, so unaware of the turmoil into which they were born. And in that moment, he made his decision.

He lowered the knife and loosened his hold. "Brave brother, I let you go. I will take my sons and my *kulem*, and I'll leave this place. I will return no more. You have my word. *Akina*."

Mattie kissed each of her sons' brows before she passed them off to their father, who'd finished packing up their meager supplies. She wanted to bid a proper farewell to the miners of Paradise Bar. It was hard to believe she was actually leaving, even harder to trust that the four of them would survive a journey on foot at the tail end of winter with so few provisions.

But she put her faith in Sakote. After all, he'd brought her babies back to her. She'd been half-crazed with worry the day they went missing. Then Sakote had limped into camp, bloody and battered, but victorious, a bawling baby in each arm, and she knew at that moment she'd follow him anywhere.

Anywhere happened to be north. He'd seen it in a vision, he'd said, which was good enough for Mattie. After he'd explained that the twins would always be in danger if they stayed among the Konkows, she was only too willing to leave.

Except that it was so hard to say goodbye.

"I was leavin' after spring anyways," Tom Cooligan said with a sniff, "goin' ta Sacramento ta open a real barbershop, since no one here seems ta care whether he's shaved proper or not."

"Are you sure you don't want to be a doctor?" Mattie asked.

His vest swelled at that, and he gave her a wink. "Ye take care o' these wee ones now, or I'll know about it." He bussed her on the brow.

Zeke and Granny, as inseparable lately as peas in a pod, decided to let her in on a secret that, with Granny's abrasive voice, wasn't secret for long. "Zeke's gonna make me a proper missus," she whispered, "soon as we get Billy hitched up with some young filly."

A smile of congratulations was about all Mattie could muster.

Frenchy kissed her on both cheeks. "Such a romantic life you will lead, *cherie*. Do not forget your old *amis*, eh? And if you happen to find yourself in San Francisco, stop by my gambling establishment. I am calling it *Le Paradis d'Or*, The Golden Paradise."

The Campbell boys shuffled forward awkwardly before one of them finally broke the ice and gave her a swift kiss on the cheek. Not to be outdone, the others followed suit.

"Are you leaving as well?" she asked them.

"We're gonna mosey on down to Mr. Neal's place, find us some work where there's real money," Harley volunteered.

The rest of the camp muttered quick and uncomfortable goodbyes, some of them embarrassed by their own sentimentality, others in a rush to get on with their panning.

Swede was the last to amble up while the others left to give him privacy. He wouldn't look at her at first, taking off his hat, staring at his boots, running the brim through his fingers.

"Oh, Swede, I'll miss you so," she whispered, surprised at the catch in her voice.

He pursed his lips, fighting for control. "Now, Miss Mattie, I'm countin' on you to take care of them two boys."

"I will." Her chin started trembling.

"'Cause little ones, you know, they take an awful lot o' takin' care of, and..." He broke off suddenly, and when Mattie reached for his arm, a tearful snort escaped him.

Mattie's heart went out to him, and she caught him in a great bear hug.

"Ah, shoot, Miss Mattie," he said, wiping at his eyes.

Out of the corner of her eye, Mattie looked at the deerskin pouch Sakote had made for her, sitting beside the packs of provisions, and a sudden spontaneous inspiration hit her. She pulled away from the big man.

"How much money would you need?" she asked eagerly.

He frowned.

"How much money would you need to get home?" she clarified.

"Oh, Miss Mattie," he said, shaking his head, "there ain't enough gold left in that creek to get a man by mule to Marysville."

Undaunted, she swept up her pouch, grabbed his hand, and set the gold-filled bag in his oversized palm.

"I want you to go home," she said, and now he looked directly at her in disbelief. "I want you to go home to your girls."

"But that wouldn't be..."

"Right? It's not right for them to be without their father," she told him. "I don't need the money. Sakote is always reminding me that the Konkows have lived for generations without the white man's gold. And it would make me so happy to give it to you."

Swede blubbered so much over her gift that after several minutes of carrying on, Zeke finally smacked him on the back out of irritation and told him to pipe down, that he was probably scaring the Injuns and the wildlife alike.

Their farewell at the village was more subdued. There were no tears, no regrets. According to the elders, leaving the village had always been part of Sakote's path.

A contrite Hintsuli gave his brother one final embrace before he scampered off to play with friends. Noa stiffly shook Sakote's hand, murmuring Konkow words Mattie didn't understand. Towani peered curiously at Mattie's babies while she rubbed her own belly, swollen with child. And Sakote's mother, though she wouldn't touch the twins out of superstition, nevertheless shared a secret smile with Mattie as the boys gurgled in their sleep.

And then Mattie, Sakote, and the babies were heading

north, along an untraveled path, down an unfamiliar road, toward an unknown destiny. Sakote had promised her the earth would provide, and she believed him. His people had lived on the land long before the miners came.

He'd also promised her a home. He couldn't say where or when, but he swore he'd find a place they could raise their sons in peace, a place they could belong.

As far as Mattie was concerned, home wasn't a place. It was wherever Sakote and her children were. No matter where destiny led them, as long as Sakote remained beside her on the path, she was right where she belonged.

Epilogue

Sakote spit out some ridiculous, impossible to pronounce word as he wrapped sinew around the basalt knife he was crafting.

"What?" Mattie asked, lacing the second boy onto his willow and deerskin cradleboard. She slid it gently across the packed earth floor, closer to his drowsing brother and the warmth of the stone firepit, where the flames danced cheerily, casting merry shadows onto the cedar plank ceiling. "You'd give our sons names I can't even pronounce?"

Sakote scowled, but it was a good-natured frown. Now that they'd found a peaceable place to settle, he was far too content to stay angry about anything for long.

She sat back on the low redwood stool and smiled as she put the finishing touches on the sketch of her sons. Then she set the drawing aside and stared into the fire, pretending to consider Sakote's atrocious suggestions and letting her thoughts drift over the events of the past several weeks.

They'd traveled north for almost two hundred miles, much farther than Mattie had ever dreamed, but Sakote had been true to his word. Taking only his bow, his fire drill, and his stone knife, he'd managed to sustain all of them in relative comfort.

He'd cleverly made a fishing line from milkweed fiber and slivers of bone. He'd shot several rabbits to roast in the ground, though he wouldn't let her make blankets for the babies from the skins, claiming that rabbit fur blinded infants. They'd snacked on hazelnuts and wild currants, and he'd shown her how to spot squirrel caches in the snow by the telltale pine-nut shells. She'd eaten things she'd never dreamed were edible, things like the fungus on oaks, the soft inner bark of fir trees, and the sugary powdered sap of the pine.

When the weather grew fierce, they'd hidden in caves or made their own huts out of the furry limbs of young evergreens.

But despite their grand adventure, Mattie was very happy to have secure walls about her now and a hearth to warm her toes by. She couldn't pronounce what this village was called any more than she could pronounce the names Sakote had just spoken, but the native people that had welcomed them, the Hupa, were easy to understand. They were civilized and friendly. Their houses, with their sunken floors and haphazard angles, though clearly of tribal design, were equipped with solid cedar plank walls and gravel porches, and they lined a boulevard of sorts that made up the village of more than two dozen homes.

Best of all, the Hupa didn't seem to mind that she was white or that Sakote was Konkow. They were an easygoing people with abundant game and land, who had little need for formal government since they had so few conflicts. They admired Mattie's artistic hand, and once they discovered Sakote's great talent for hunting, they embraced him as a brother.

"Tell me the first name again," she said with a sigh.

He repeated it. It was truly awful.

"And the other?"

Equally bad. It sounded as if he were choking.

"What do they mean?" she asked, exasperated, knowing it was the Konkow custom to name children for some event that happened shortly after their birth.

Though his eyes were fastened on the knife he made, Mattie thought there might have been the hint of a smile playing about his lips as he answered her. "Snoring-Duck and Pees-in-the-Water."

Mattie's brows lifted, and her mouth made a perfect O. Then, whether Sakote was serious or not, she couldn't help but burst out in peals of laughter.

Sakote ceased his work, raised his head proudly, and furrowed his brow sternly at her. "They are worthy names. They are the names of my ancestors."

Mattie didn't bother stifling her giggles. Sakote grunted and went back to his work.

"I'll make a bargain with you," she decided, reaching forward to rest her palm on his bare thigh. "You said you didn't want to name them for another couple of years. I'll name them now, and if you decide to change their names later, you may."

One corner of his mouth lifted. "Even if you can't pronounce them?"

She returned his smile. "I'll learn."

His eyes sparkling softly, he lifted her hand to kiss her fingertips.

Of course, he was teasing all along. She could see it now in the curve of his mouth. He had no intention of changing their names. Which was just as well, since she'd already chosen them anyway. They were a compromise—good English names with a touch of Konkow tradition, certainly better than Snoring-Duck or Pees-in-the-Water.

Mattie glanced over at their two as yet unchristened sons, snuggled quietly in their cozy nests in a rare moment of concurrent slumber.

She'd tell Sakote their names later, she decided, letting the backs of her fingers trail ticklishly along his muscular thigh. She'd tell him while he lay beneath her, warm between her thighs, while the sheen of lovemaking still misted his skin and the glow of satisfaction darkened his eyes.

"You wish to make a kiss with me?" he breathed, his eyes smoky and a sultry smile on his lips.

"Oh, yes."

CHASE WOLF AND DREW HAWK.

In the drawing, the twins slept with their dark downy heads turned toward each other, snug in the cradleboards their father had made for them. Above them, mingled with smoke from the fire burning on the hearth, were the mystical clouds of their dreams. In one boy's cloud, Sakote waved his arms wildly, shooing away a hungry wolf. In the second cloud, Mattie sketched a hawk soaring overhead. The mist of the twins' visions intertwined with the figures of their parents, and where they met, they formed a perfect circle, eternal and unbroken, like the sacred circle of their love.

AKINA

THANK YOU FOR
READING MY BOOK!

Did you enjoy it? If so, I hope you'll post a review to let others know! There's no greater gift you can give an author than spreading your love of her books.

It's truly a pleasure and a privilege to be able to share my stories with you. Knowing that my words have made you laugh, sigh, or touched a secret place in your heart is what keeps the wind beneath my wings. I hope you enjoyed our brief journey together, and may ALL of your adventures have happy endings!

If you'd like to keep in touch, feel free to sign up for my monthly e-newsletter at www.glynnis.net, and you'll be the first to find out about my new releases, special discounts, prizes, promotions, and more!

If you want to keep up with my daily escapades:
Friend me at facebook.com/GlynnisCampbell
Like my Page at bit.ly/GlynnisCampbellFBPage
Follow me at twitter.com/GlynnisCampbell
And if you're a super fan, join facebook.com/GCReadersClan

AUTHOR'S NOTE

The California Legends series is a love letter to my home town of Paradise, California, where I was once honored to reign as the Gold Nugget Queen in the town's celebration of its Gold Rush roots.

Excerpt from

Native Wolf

California Legends Book 2

SPRING 1875
PARADISE, CALIFORNIA

Chase Wolf lifted his eyes to the grand mansion shining in the moonlight, and the corners of his mouth turned down.

Natives had built this princely manor for a white man who'd probably never soiled his hands on the Great Spirit's earth. While revered Konkow headmen and gifted shamans like his grandmother blistered their palms and bent their backs to serve the rancher, Parker and his family lived like spoiled children, untouched by harsh winds or scorching sun or the indignity of hard labor. He wondered how Parker would fare as a slave, sweating and toiling for the profit of another.

Then a dark inspiration took hold. His lips slowly curved into a grim smile.

The march to Nome Cult.

He would force Parker to endure the march, as his people had. He'd prod the rancher across a hundred miles of rugged land, without water, without food, without shelter, until there was nothing left of him. An eye for an eye, a tooth for a tooth, as his white mother's Bible preached. That was how his grandmother would be avenged. That was how her spirit would find peace.

Resolve—and liquor—made him bold. He silently climbed the steps and circled the porch until he found a window left open to capture the night breeze. He brushed aside the sheer curtain. Moonlight spilled over the sill and into the darkened house like pale acorn soup.

A sudden swell of vertigo tipped him off-balance as he climbed through the window. He made a grab for the curtain, tearing the frail fabric. Luckily, he had enough presence of mind to silence an angry curse, and his feet finally found purchase on the polished wood floor.

He swayed, then straightened, swallowing hard as he perused the sumptuous furnishings of the parlor in the moonlight, feeling as out of place as a trout in a tree.

A pair of sofas so plump they looked pregnant squatted on stubby legs carved with figures of leaves. Four rush-seat chairs stenciled with twining flowers sat against one wall. Delicate tables perched here and there on legs no thicker than a fawn's. A massive marble fireplace with an iron grate dominated the room, and an ornate clock ticked softly on the mantel. A huge chandelier hung from the ceiling like a giant crystal spider, and a dense, patterned carpet stretched in an oval pool over the floor. Sweeping down one side of the room was a mahogany staircase, and the walls were adorned with paper printed in pale vertical stripes.

His gaze settled on the enormous gilt-framed oil portrait hung above the mantel.

Letting the torn curtain fall closed, Chase ventured into the room to take a closer look. The title at the bottom read, SAMUEL AND CLAIRE PARKER. Hatred began to boil his blood as he let his eyes slide up to study the face of his enemy, the evil rancher who'd enslaved his grandmother.

Samuel Parker was a portly old man with a stern, wrinkled face, a balding head, dark eyes, and a trailing gray mustache that made him look even sterner. He was easy to hate. Chase's lip curled as he savored the thought of dragging the villain from his bed.

Then his gaze lit on Claire Parker. A wave of lightheadedness washed over him. It was only the whiskey, he told himself, yet he couldn't take his eyes off of the face in the painting. The woman was half her husband's age, as innocent and fair as Parker was darkly corrupt. She had long fair hair, partially swept up into a knot. Her features were delicate, and her eyes were serene and sweet. He'd never seen anyone so beautiful.

After a good minute of gawking, he finally squeezed his eyes shut against the image. The woman's looks didn't matter. Her heart was doubtless as evil as her husband's.

A flicker suddenly danced across the landing above, and Chase faded back into the wallpaper. The glow of a candle lit the top steps, making shadows flutter about the walls. And then, at the top of the stairs, the portrait of the woman appeared to come to life.

Claire Parker.

The flame illuminated her face, giving her creamy skin an ethereal glow. Her long hair had been cut since the painting. Short, blunt strands now caressed her chin. But the blonde locks shone in the candlelight like the halos of the angels in his mother's Bible. She wore a white lace-trimmed camisole, an ankle-length petticoat...and nothing else. Timidly she descended the steps in bare feet.

He stood frozen while the woman, unaware he lurked in the shadows, crept slowly closer. He didn't dare breathe as she brushed past him.

She hesitated, close enough for him to tell the portrait didn't do her justice. Claire Parker was breathtaking. Yet there were dark hollows beneath her eyes that painted her face in shades of unspeakable sorrow. His heart softened briefly, and he wondered what horrible tragedy haunted her.

Then, just as quickly, he remembered who she was, what she was, and the reason he'd come. He couldn't let a pretty face distract him from his vengeance.

But how was he going to steal past the lady to get to her husband? He couldn't afford to wait for her to go back to bed. The longer he remained in the house, the greater his chances were of getting caught.

Hell. He had to do something. And soon.

Instinct took over. It must have been instinct. Or the whiskey. Because if he'd thought about what he was doing for one minute, he never would have taken that first step.

Sliding his knife silently from its sheath, he slipped out of the shadows and came up behind her. Before she could wheel around in surprise, he clamped a hand over Claire Parker's mouth and set the sharp blade against her slim throat.

It happened in a heartbeat.

For one brief moment, Claire, hearing the soft sound from downstairs and sensing a shadowy presence in the room below, had foolishly believed it might be the spirit of her beloved Yoema. Hope filling her heart, she'd crept down the stairs.

But in an instant, those hopes were dashed. A huge hand closed over her mouth, choking off her gasp of shock. And a sharp edge of cold steel pressed against her neck.

She dropped the candle, extinguishing its light. Her heart jammed up against her ribs, fluttering like a singed moth. Air whistled through her flared nostrils. Her fingers splayed ineffectually as the blade threatened her with a menacing chill. Her throat clogged with panic, and she stared ahead with blind terror, sure the knife would end her gulping any moment.

She felt utterly helpless, not at all like the heroes of the dime novels she kept under her bed. She had no revolver. She had no Bowie knife. And she had no idea what her attacker intended.

For a long, drawn-out moment, the man did nothing, which was almost worse than killing her outright, for it gave her time to think, to dread.

Who was he? What did he want? Was he going to hurt her? Kidnap her? Murder her? The panicked whimper born in her throat was cut short by his tightening grip. Who *was* he?

The pungent smell of strong whiskey and wood smoke rose off of him, stinging her nose. The palm crushing her mouth tasted faintly of blood. His fingers, pressed into her cheek, were rough and callused. One thick-muscled arm, slung heavily across her bosom, trapped her. Where he secured her against his broad chest, he was as hard as a tree trunk.

She didn't dare resist, scarcely dared to breathe while the knife rested so close to her madly pulsing vein. If only she hadn't left her scissors in her bedroom...

The man moved his arm to struggle awkwardly with something behind her. She squeezed her eyes tight, praying he wasn't unfastening his trousers.

Then, for one moment, the cool blade disappeared from her throat. She stiffened like a clock spring, poised to bolt free. His hand fell away, and she sucked in a great gulp of air to scream.

But he was too quick for her. He jammed a wad of dusty cloth into her open mouth. She fought to keep from gagging, wincing as he knotted it tightly at the back of her head. Then he brandished the shiny silver blade in front of her eyes, flashing a silent threat in the moonlight.

This time, instead of cowering in fright, she let his gesture fuel her courage. Mustering her strength and calling to mind all the Buckskin Bill adventures she'd read, she swung her clasped hands across his forearm and brought her heel down hard on the top of his foot.

His forearm didn't budge, and she felt the bone-jarring impact of her bare heel upon his stiff boot all the way up her leg. She winced in pain. If only she'd had her Sunday church heels on, she despaired, she might have heard much more out of him than just an annoyed grunt.

Instead of thwarting him, her struggles seemed to increase his determination. He hugged her closer against him, so close she could feel his hot whiskey breath riffling her hair. He raised the knife in his huge fist till it glinted with menace before her. Then he began dragging her backward across the room.

In desperation, she tried to wrench out of his iron grasp, twisting enough to catch a glimpse of his shadowed face before he jerked her back against him.

What she'd seen surprised her. Even in the dim light, she could tell he was a native. His eyes, narrowed with intent, were as dark as the night, and his short, unkempt hair shone like ebony silk. His features were strongly sculpted and handsome, from the bold arch of his nose and his square jaw to the lean cords of his neck and his strong brow. And though she couldn't imagine why, he looked somehow familiar.

Why would an Indian attack her? The Indians who worked her father's ranch were as docile as sheep. Still, there had been tales of scalpings years ago, perpetrated by savages who'd learned such violence from vicious white settlers. Dear God, did he mean to take her scalp?

Suddenly she could draw no air into her lungs, and a hysterical thought kept circling her brain—she'd surely cheated the man of his prize if he meant to scalp her, for only moments ago, she'd cut her hair short in mourning.

Stunned and breathless, she hardly resisted as he

continued to lug her toward the open window. But when he climbed out and began to haul her over the sill, pushing her head down with one massive hand so she wouldn't bang it on the sashes, she awoke from her stupor.

Dear Lord, the man was abducting her!

They were halfway out of the house when panic made her fight in earnest. She grabbed hold of the window, refusing to let go. Kicking at the wall for all she was worth, she twisted and flailed against him until he hissed a guttural word at her, probably an epithet in his native tongue.

In a matter of seconds, of course, his strength won out. He unlatched her hands with a sweep of his arm and pulled her out onto the porch into the stark night.

Maybe she could still make noise, she thought in desperation. Her screams might not be heard through the gag, but if she stomped on the planks and made a huge fuss, surely her father or one of the ranch hands would come to investigate.

The man must have read her thoughts. Before she could make a single sound, he picked her up, tucked her between his arm and his hip like a sack of feed, and stole off the porch with the silent step that was a hallmark of the local Indians.

Suspended as she was, with her arms trapped against her sides, she couldn't do much more than squirm against him, which didn't hamper him in the least.

She peered between the blunt strands of her newly cropped hair. Though he weaved a bit, he seemed to be heading for the stables.

A slender slice of moonlight spilled in when he eased the door open, but the horses were unperturbed by the presence of an intruder. Hoping to startle them into a frenzy of neighing, Claire thrashed wildly in her captor's grip. He grunted and squeezed her tightly about the waist, cutting off her struggles and her air. Then he took a coil of rope from a nail in the wall and started forward.

He quickly found what he wanted—Thunder, her father's five-year-old prize stallion. He unlatched the gate and, stroking the horse's chest, nudged Thunder out of the stall. With one hand and his teeth, he managed to fashion a loop to slip over the horse's head.

She expected he'd make a break for it. He'd swing up bareback and throw her across his lap, slap Thunder's flank, let out a war whoop, and race into the night. As soon as he did, of course, a posse of her father's men would mount up and ride after him like the devil. They'd put a bullet in the villain before the moon rose even halfway across the sky.

But he did no such thing. He led Thunder out of the stable as stealthily as he'd come in. To her amazement, the normally headstrong stallion followed willingly, as if the two of them were partners in crime.

Still clamped firmly under the brute's huge arm and against his lean hip, Claire tried to calm her racing heart and make sense of things. Surely this couldn't be happening. Surely a stranger couldn't march up to the front door of the formidable Parker house in the middle of the night, snatch her from her own parlor, and make off with her by the light of the full moon.

Yet no one had heard him come. No one had roused when he left. It would be morning before anyone missed Claire. And, heaven help her, she'd left a note saying she was running away. Her father probably wouldn't come after her at all.

What were the man's intentions?

Obviously, he didn't mean to kill her. She'd be dead already if that were the case. Maybe he meant to hold her for ransom. Samuel Parker's prosperity was well known. This savage wouldn't be the first scoundrel to go after her father's wealth.

But he was by far the boldest.

They'd left the drive now, gone out the gate, onto the main

road. The land on the other side was wild, uncultivated and overgrown, and the Indian led Thunder straight into the weeds. Tall grasses brushed the horse's flanks and whipped at Claire's petticoat as she sagged in the man's grip.

Once they'd descended the rolling hill, out of sight of the Parker house, he stopped to remove the noose from Thunder's neck. Seizing the opportunity, Claire thrust out with her feet, kicking one of the beast's hocks, hoping to spook the horse into galloping back to the ranch.

But the Indian calmed the animal with a few murmurs and a pat to Thunder's flank, turning on Claire with a withering glare, as if she'd kicked the horse just for spite.

He righted her then, planting her atop the weed-choked ground. Before she could catch her balance, he dropped the noose about her, cinching it tightly around her waist.

When he casually swept up the hem of her petticoat, exposing her knees, Claire's eyes widened, and her heart skittered along her ribs. Perhaps she'd been mistaken about the man's intent after all.

But, drawing his knife, he slashed a long strip from the hem and let the garment fall. Then he put away the blade and seized one of her hands.

Instinctively she pulled away, but was caught fast in his great fist. He looped the cloth around her wrist, pulled it behind her, and crossed it over the other hand, knotting the cotton strips together.

Satisfied with his handiwork, he stepped back, his thumbs hooked insolently into the waistband of his trousers. She stared at him, wondering how intoxicated he must be to take pride in subduing a woman her size.

He must have read her mind. A scowl darkened his features, and for a moment, Claire thought she detected a hint of shame marring his drunken arrogance. Then he growled and turned his back on her, destroying all notions of civility.

In a movement surprisingly fluid for such a large man, he swung up atop Thunder. Coiling the loose end of the rope around his fist, he nudged the horse forward. The rope pulled taut, and Claire was forced to follow.

Caught off guard, she staggered and almost fell. What kind of abduction was this? Surely the man would want to flee as swiftly as possible to avoid capture. Why wasn't he sweeping her up and tearing off across the countryside?

He rode slowly, but keeping up was difficult. Claire was no longer accustomed to walking barefoot. Her father had cured her of that uncivilized habit years ago. The ground was rocky and uneven. Every few steps, she winced as star thistles bristled against her ankles and sharp pebbles poked her heels. Burrs caught in what was left of her lace hem, and her petticoat grew sodden with its harvest of dew.

She twisted her ankle on a stone and nearly went down again. The pain as she hobbled forward made her eyes water, but she didn't dare stop. She feared if she hesitated, he'd ride on anyway, dragging her through the thistles.

But despite her best efforts to be stoic, her eyes filled, and the stars and the moon and the ground blurred before her. A trickle wound its way down her cheek and was swallowed up by the cotton binding her mouth.

It wasn't the pain that triggered her crying. And it wasn't fear, not really. It was grief.

From the day that Yoema fell ill, Samuel Parker had insisted that Claire hide her sorrow. After all, no one knew the truth about Yoema's relationship to Claire. They assumed the native woman was a servant, no more. So for the sake of propriety and obedience to her father, Claire had kept a stiff upper lip and denied herself the catharsis of tears. When Yoema died, there had been no funeral, and Claire was expected to carry on as if nothing had happened.

But now she was removed from the eyes of society,

stripped of everything that had kept her sailing on a shaky but even keel. Her emotions felt as raw as the soles of her feet. And her father wasn't around to witness her weeping, to be disappointed in her. So all the pain she'd bottled up inside, all the bittersweet memories she'd repressed, all the tears she'd been unable to shed, gushed forth in a torrent so powerful that before long, her chest heaved with wrenching sobs and the gag grew wet with her weeping.

She no longer cared about the stones cutting her feet, no longer wondered about her captor. All she could think about was the woman who'd cared for her since she was a little motherless girl, who'd taught her the names of the animals, who'd held her when she was sad and lonely, who'd told her stories and sang her songs, and whose voice was now silent. Forever.

This time, when Claire tripped on the edge of a rock, she landed hard on her knees. She expected to be dragged through the weeds, and frankly she didn't care if he hauled her that way for ten miles. Now that the egg of her sorrow had been cracked, she realized that nothing could hurt her as much as the loss of the woman she'd called Mother.

The moment she struck the dirt, however, her captor halted, turning to see what delayed her.

Overcome with woe, she sank forward over her knees and buried her head. She didn't care if he watched her. He was nobody. She didn't have to keep a brave face for him like she did for her father. Her breath came in loud, wheezing gasps, filtered by the smothering cloth. Her throat ached with an agony of grief, and the sobs that racked her body felt as if they tore her soul asunder. Overwhelmed by heartache, she didn't notice that the Indian had dismounted and now loomed over her.

His fingers suddenly grazed the top of her head, startling her, and she almost choked on her tears as she glanced up at him. Though his face swam in her watery vision, he seemed shaken.

Of course he was shaken. Men never understood women's weeping. But she didn't care. She stared up at the frowning savage, openly defiant, tears streaming down her cheeks, silently daring him to ridicule her.

His scowl deepened, and he jutted out his chin. His mouth worked as if he were trying to decide whether to swallow or spit. Then, with a whispered expletive, he released her. Winding one arm around her waist, he hauled her to her feet and nodded sharply as if to tell her there would be no more falling down.

She wiped her wet cheek on her shoulder, staring coldly at him, but he refused to meet her eyes. He wrapped his end of the rope one more time around his hand, turned away, and remounted. His back expanded and released once with a deep breath before he clucked to the horse, urging it forward one step.

Claire stood her ground, refusing to move. Her grief was turning rapidly to anger. What kind of a brute abducted a woman by night, force her barefoot across rock-riddled hills, and ignored her tears of distress? In her novels, even the hero's worst nemesis possessed some shred of common decency. Damn his coal-black eyes! If he wanted her to move from this spot, he'd just have to drag her.

When he turned to peer at her, the corners of his mouth were drawn down. He tugged once more on the rope.

Raising her chin, she took a step backward.

His eyes widened. He tugged again, pulling her forward a step.

Incensed, she marshaled her strength and hauled back on the rope as hard as she could.

To her satisfaction, she managed to alter his look of annoyance to one of surprise, though for all her efforts, he didn't budge more than a few inches.

His amazement was short-lived. He simply let up on the rope, and she sank with a plop onto her bottom. Before she could scramble upright, he slipped from Thunder, stalking toward her, muttering under his breath all the way.

Leaning forward, he upended her, slinging her over one ox-like shoulder. The air whooshed out of her, and she closed her eyes against the dizzying sensation of her precarious perch. Then he tossed her sidesaddle across the horse and swiftly mounted up behind her.

Flinging a possessive arm around her waist, he nudged Thunder forward, mumbling what sounded suspiciously like "damn fool Indian," and rode stonily into the deepening night.

At first she sat upright, stiff, unwilling to even think about letting her body come into contact with his. But as they rode on, mile after mile, her strength flagged. The sleep that had evaded her for days finally caught up with her, lulling her muscles into complacency and urging her eyes closed.

She stirred once along the gently rocking ride, fluttering her eyes open long enough to note that the sky had taken on the purple cast of the far side of midnight. Then she settled back in surrender against the stranger's chest. Her grief spent, she found curious comfort in dozing against the warm cotton shirt, safe from sorrow, safe from memories, safe from judgment.

Hours later, the sound of soft snoring woke her. Claire opened her eyes to a morning filled with apricot-colored light. Before her, the rolling hills lay silvered with dew and dotted with dark oaks, and the rising sun stretched fingers of gold across the emerald knolls. For one brief moment, she forgot where she was and simply enjoyed the glorious view.

Then the man—who was pressed far too intimately against her—snorted awake, and she remembered everything. Her captor had apparently slept for some time, for the horse had stopped to graze upon a patch of clover, and it looked like they were miles from anywhere.

"Shit!"

Claire flinched. So the savage did speak English...or at least knew one useful word. He shifted on Thunder's back, and she realized, much to her chagrin, that unless the man wore a Colt down his trousers, her hands, bound behind her, had just brushed the most private part of his anatomy. She curled her fingers in horror, relieved when he finally dismounted.

The stallion neighed, and then returned to chomping at the sweet grass. Her captor circled into her view, hitching up his trousers and scrubbing the sleep from his eyes. Then he lowered his hands from his face, and Claire saw him by the light of day for the first time.

He was truly massive, larger than any man she'd ever seen, broad of shoulder and chest. The muscles of his arms strained the blue flannel of his shirt, and his hands looked big enough to hide a whole poker deck.

But it wasn't his size that made her throat go suddenly dry.

The man was devilishly handsome. She could see now that he wasn't a full-blooded native. His short black hair had a slight curl to it, and his chin was dark with stubble. His skin was as golden as wild honey, and his teeth were snowy white where his lips parted. Deep, brooding eyes, shadowed by fatigue, shone like marbles of obsidian as he scrutinized her. And again, something about him looked curiously familiar.

"Ah, hell."

She blinked, impressed by his command of English, if not his vocabulary.

But the third word she pretended she didn't hear. He turned his back to her and kicked hard at the dirt, raking his hair back with both hands.

She wondered why he was upset. He had no reason to

blacken the air with his cussing. *He* wasn't the one trussed up like a steer for branding. *He* wasn't the one stolen from a snug home and dragged across the hills half the night in his unmentionables. *His* throat wasn't as dry as gunpowder, and his legs weren't bloody with thistle scratches.

He spun back around, glaring at her as if she were somehow to blame. She tried to glare back at him. But Thunder chose that inopportune moment to amble forward, stretching his neck down for a choice bunch of clover. Claire's eyes widened as she began to slide inexorably, helplessly from her perch toward the hard-packed earth.

The instant Chase saw the panic in those big, beautiful green eyes, he instinctively lunged forward and caught the woman before she could slide off. Unfortunately, his efforts trapped her awkwardly between the horse's shoulder and his own chest. Her eyes widened even more, and he cursed, realizing that with her hands tied behind her, she could lend him no assistance whatsoever.

She slipped down his body, inch by delicious inch. Her soft breasts were crushed against his hard ribs, and her flimsy petticoat rode halfway up her legs before he could disentangle himself from her. At last he managed to get her feet on the ground.

Now if he could only regain his *own* balance.

What the hell had he been thinking last night, stealing a white woman? Whatever was in that whiskey, it must have robbed him of his last bit of sense, making him believe he had a hunger for vengeance and the stomach for violence.

Chase wasn't a killer. Or a kidnapper. Hell, he wouldn't go out of his way to step on a spider. Cruelty didn't come naturally to him.

Neither did embracing a beautiful woman. Women didn't come close to Chase much. His size usually scared them off. And if that didn't do it, his scowl would.

Not this one. The lady might be a tiny thing, as pale as a flower, as delicate as a fawn. But there was strength in her spirit, fire in her heart. Damn, even in his sleep, his body had gotten riled up over her.

A moment passed before Chase realized his arms were still wrapped around the woman. Outrage sparked in her eyes, and he released her like a white-hot poker.

She probably figured he meant to ravage her. He was sure white men did such things. But Chase would no sooner take a woman against her will than he'd brand an animal.

He stepped away, shaken, but managed to keep enough wits about him to gather the end of the rope in his fist so she wouldn't run off and get herself into worse trouble. Then he sank down onto the trunk of a fallen tree to consider his predicament.

Shit! Why hadn't he listened to Drew? Chase had had more whiskey than sense last night. And today, unlike the sweet flavor of revenge he'd imagined, the reality of holding a helpless woman captive left a bitter taste in his mouth.

He rubbed the back of his neck, glancing sideways at his hostage, who looked like some beautiful snow-white angel dropped out of heaven into the dirt. What the hell had he done?

A half-breed couldn't kidnap a white woman, particularly the wife of a rich rancher, and not expect half the population to come after him with guns blazing.

Worse, the horse he'd borrowed was a fine-looking animal, probably breeding stock. Hell, Parker might mourn the loss of his stallion more than his wife. Chase didn't know what they did to a man who took another man's woman, but they hanged you for horse thieving.

He scratched uneasily at his throat.

Vengeance had seemed like such a good idea last night. Now it felt like the biggest mistake of his life.

ABOUT THE AUTHOR

I'm a *USA Today* bestselling author of swashbuckling action-adventure historical romances, mostly set in Scotland, with over a dozen award-winning books published in six languages.

But before my role as a medieval matchmaker, I sang in *The Pinups,* an all-girl band on CBS Records, and provided voices for the MTV animated series *The Maxx,* Blizzard's *Diablo* and *Starcraft* video games, and *Star Wars* audiobooks.

I'm the wife of a rock star (if you want to know which one, contact me) and the mother of two young adults. I do my best writing on cruise ships, in Scottish castles, on my husband's tour bus, and at home in my sunny southern California garden.

I love transporting readers to a place where the bold heroes have endearing flaws, the women are stronger than they look, the land is lush and untamed, and chivalry is alive and well!

I'm always delighted to hear from my readers, so please feel free to email me at glynnis@glynnis.net. And if you're a super-fan who would like to join my inner circle, sign up at http://www.facebook.com/GCReadersClan, where you'll get glimpses behind the scenes, sneak peeks of works-in-progress, and extra special surprises.